THE MACKINNON'S

BOOK TWO

RAVEN

TREASA KLÖTH

MAGICK
MOON INK ®

The MacKinnon's Raven
Copyright © 2017 by Treasa Klöth.
For information contact:
http:// www.MagickMoonInk.com
Book and Cover design by Magick Moon Publishing
Logo art by: Ken Cole Jr.
ISBN: 0-9989563-4-1
First Edition: August 2017 10 9 8 7 6 5 4 3 2 1

For: my Mom, who taught me that magick is everywhere in life, you just need to believe in it. Thanks Mom, for always believing in me and encouraging me to follow my dreams. For my best friend/sister Mindy, who nearly broke my computer getting, so, angry with Duncan as she read this story, be patient, one day you'll find your own highlander. I love both of you... T...

To all the people who are helping me to succeed in following my dreams. Thank you! I could not do this without all of you! You are each amazing!

To my readers,

Thank you to each person who buys or reads this book! I hope that you enjoy the adventure! Please, visit my website @ www.treasakloth.com Leave me a review and let me know if you enjoyed the story!

Once more please forgive me for taking some liberties with history and with the MacKinnon Clan and their history, as well as their holdings, as this is a work of fiction and I had to change somethings to make it work for the story.

Prologue

The highland mist surrounded them, as Ian MacKinnon and his brother Duncan, separated to surround the MacLeod men that lay sleeping in their encampment on MacKinnon land. Ian had received word of the attack planned against his clan. As Chieftain of his people, he would see to their safety and welfare. He would drive the enemy from their doorstep.

With a smile, Duncan MacKinnon took fifteen men with him to the right. Ian's younger cousin Aidan MacKinnon, from the border lands, broke off to the left leading another group, and let Ian and his men take the center position to raid the MacLeod base.

On the edge of the MacLeod's camp, Ian asked the Gods to protect his men. Then he gave the signal for the warriors to enter the area where their enemy lay sleeping.

Duncan felt the hum of battle singing through his veins as he made his way into the MacLeod encampment. Taking the dagger, from his boot, he slit the first man's throat. He made it through four MacLeod men, before the alarm was raised. The MacKinnon men shouted their battle cry, "*Cumnich Bas Alpin!*", meaning 'Remember the death of Alpin!', one of the first great kings of Scotland and their direct ancestor.

Claymore in hand, Duncan sliced his way into the middle of the fray. The clash of metal was all around him. Cries of rage and death filled the air. His skills with a blade were some of the best in the highlands. He was after all, a highland warrior from the top of his war braids in his hair to the depths of his soul. Duncan wore the MacKinnon tartan with honor.

He dispatched one MacLeod only to turn and engage another. This one was well skilled with a blade, he thought. Duncan relished the fight and countered the moves of his opponent. As the man swung his claymore toward Duncan's head, he blocked with his own sword, and Duncan thrust his dagger into the man's stomach.

Pulling his dagger from the man's stomach, he turned to engage yet another MacLeod, meeting him in a bloody clash of swords. This one was young, no more than a score of years, at best. He was but barely a man and probably not yet married, or had wee bairns of his own. It was no doubt that this was one of his first battles and he would not live to see the rise of the sun.

At more than a score and ten summers, Duncan had lived a full happy life. It wasn't until this last year that he had even thought of finding a woman and making her his, or considered the possibility of wee bairns of his own. He was a warrior with a warrior's heart and a love for battle. However, since he had returned from the border lands and his cousin Lachlan MacKinnon's home there, his mind had turned to settling down with a woman and family of his own.

He parried and thrust with the lad hoping to wound the boy and put him out of the battle, but not kill him. Duncan watched patiently for an opening. From the corner of his eye, he saw his older brother Ian doing battle with the MacLeod Chieftain. From behind Ian came a MacLeod with claymore ready to strike. Ian was too involved with the fight at hand to have seen the other man. Duncan took his dagger from its sheath in his boot and threw it, hitting the enemy in the neck.

At the sound of the cry behind him, Ian noticed the man for the first time and looked to where his brother was. With a small salute Ian thanked his brother, then stood horrified as he watched the young man his brother was fighting, stab Duncan with a dagger of his own. In slow motion, Duncan looked down at his chest then his deep-greyish blue eyes met Ian's similar gaze. He dropped to his knees as his claymore slipped from his fingers.

As Ian watched his brother fall in battle, anger erupted in him. He went crazy, fighting like a man possessed and bringing down the MacLeod Chieftain in one mighty blow. With blood dripping from his sword, Ian went after the lad that had killed his brother. There would be no mercy for him now. His life would not be spared this day.

One

Ian paced outside his brother's chamber. He ran a hand down over his face. Watching his brother fall in battle had been one of the single most horrifying sights he had ever witnessed. To watch Duncan, fall as he had, had turned Ian into a *Beserker*, of sorts, all wild and crazed. He had cut MacLeod men down one after another until they had retreated to the sea.

Now, back at Dun Akin castle, he waited while the old wise woman from the village tended his brother. He had been joyous to find Duncan alive after the battle.

His cousin Aidan strode down the corridor toward him. "What news is there, cousin?" Aidan stood with hands gripped in angry fists at his sides as he looked at the door where his other cousin lay, possibly dying.

"I've nay word yet," Ian growled then turned to the door and burst into the room. "Tell me old mother, how does he fare?" Anger etched Ian's chiseled face. The old woman bowed her head, "Laird, I do all that I can, but I am afraid his wound 'tis to sever for my knowledge. Yer brother's life slips away."

The room was stifling as the fire raged in the hearth. Ian roared his displeasure. "I'll be damned, if I'll lose him!" Ian kicked a chair in anger, splintering it. With his hands hanging limply at his sides, he bowed his head in sadness. Slowly, he raised his head and turned to look at the wise woman as she cowered in the corner of the room. "Tell me old mother, is there aught that can save him?"

She twisted her gnarled old hands, "Laird, there may be a way." She flinched as he stepped forward, "'Tis said that the clan Brodie has a woman who is said to be a *bana-bhuidseach*, a healer of some great repute. She is said to have the touch of miracles."

"Is she a witch, or a healer, woman?" Ian roared in anger.

"I have heard tales of her healing touch and 'tis said she has saved men who were aught but dead." The old woman spoke softly.

Ian studied the old woman for a long moment. If there was a chance to save his brother, he could not pass it up. "I will return within a fortnight. I leave my brother in yer care. Best ye keep him alive until I return with this witch." He turned on his heels and headed for the door.

"But Laird, what if he should die?" She called after him.

"Best ye pray he does nay." Ian growled then strode from the room leaving the old crone nearly swooning after his departure.

Raven tossed and turned in her bed as the dream wrapped around her, so much blood and death. She could hear metal striking metal and the screams of men dying. As she stood there, she saw men wrapped in plaids fighting all around her. Was he here? Was he in this fray? Her eyes scanned the area around her and her bluish-green gaze met the familiar deep greyish-blue gaze, but this time there was pain and sorrow. Her breath seized as she felt the pain that he was feeling race through her.

Tears coursed down her cheeks as she tried to reach him, but her feet would not move. No matter how hard she willed them to. His pain, was her pain, and she woke holding her chest, a cry of anguish on her lips.

Raven sat there staring into the pale morning light with tears running down her cheeks, even as the pain from the dream faded. The man from her dreams was dead and she had been unable to save him. The thought tortured her.

Throwing back the covers she slipped from her bed and walked to the window of her room. Opening the shutters, she looked out at the Scottish-Highlands around her. This was not her home, she thought as a tear slipped down her cheek, where was her home? She wondered. Raven dried her tears on the sleeve of her nightdress.

On a shuddering sigh, she turned away from the window. Her hopes of escaping the Brodie laird were now gone. When she had first begun dreaming of the Scotsman with the long dark hair, full of war braids scattered throughout his locks and beautiful greyish-blue eyes, she had thought he would be the one to save her from her prison.

It had been a little over three years since she had washed up on the shore of the Brodie lands. She had been grateful for their help and when their chieftain had been wounded mortally in battle, she had used her special gifts to save his life. That had been her mistake, for as soon as Ewin had awakened he had confined her to her room until she'd told him how she had healed him. Now, she could go nowhere without guards. She had tried to escape once, but it had proved to be useless as Ewin had brought her back and punished her severely. For weeks, she had borne the marks from that beating on her back, as she was unable to heal herself.

Sitting on one of the chairs in her room, she pulled her knees up and encircled them with her arms. Laying her head upon them, she allowed her sorrow to fill her. She would be stuck with the Brodie clan forever.

Ian had ridden hard for five days to reach the Brodie lands. He had taken only five men with him and had left the Dun Akin in Aidan's care. As they came within a few leagues of the Brodie keep, but just out of sight from their sentries, Ian pulled up rein. He had found the Brodie stronghold, and now all he needed was to find the witch herself.

Sitting atop his horse, Ian surveyed the land around him. He turned to Shane on his right, "Scout the area, we'll make camp o'er yon ridge." Ian gestured toward a ridge nearly a league away and to his left.

"Aye Laird," Shane sent his mount moving toward a wooded area that, as far as they could see, stretched all the way to the sea.

Ian took the other four men and went to make camp. He itched to get his hands on the witch and make haste for MacKinnon lands. Once he had the woman within his own castle walls, he would force her compliance, and his brother would be saved.

They made no fire, and only lay on their plaids that night. When Shane returned to the group, he gave them the lay out for the castle. Ian sent Giles to watch the castle through the night and into the wee morning hours. They had an idea of what the witch looked like. However, the tales they had heard were sketchy at best.

One story told that the *bana-bhuidseach* was truly a daughter of one of the mystical Fae, who had seduced her mother. It was said that this witch was a small beautiful woman with flowing black hair, but her eyes were as odd as could be, 'twould appear that no one knew exactly what color they were. There had been arguments of emerald green and sea blue, others had argued that her eyes had been a silvery shimmer that had changed hue. Ian didn't give a blithering hell about her beauty, or her eyes, he just wanted the woman to save his brother.

Ian lay beneath the brilliant stars and longed to know how his brother fared. Was Duncan yet alive, or was he dying even as Ian lay here looking up at the heavens? His chest ached with the thought of losing his brother. He wasn't sure if he would be able to handle the loss of Duncan.

As Ian looked at the stars above, Raven looked out over the land of the clan Brodie, she could hear the surf pounding on the shore. She looked at the stars shining up above and sighed, how she wished she could remember her life before she had been found by the Brodie Clan. Her memories were full of mists and shadows. There was nothing clear about her world prior to the one she found herself in now.

How she wanted to leave this place, leave this keep and castle. She wanted to walk free through the hills of Scotland, she wanted to find where she belonged.

At least she had gotten Ewin to allow her to venture into the forest tomorrow to gather herbs she needed to help the Brodie people. Though she knew she would not be permitted to venture there alone.

Ewin would not take the chance of losing such a treasure as herself.

As she thought of the Brodie Chieftain, she frowned and shook her head. The man was lecherous with his hands. She had avoided his bed so far by convincing him that if he took her to his bed, she would lose her special gift. It had worked thus far, but she wasn't certain her luck would hold out forever.

How she wished her Scotsman from her dreams was here, then perhaps he could steal her away from this place. For a moment, she brought those eyes into her mind and focused on him. The pain seared through her making her hiss out a breath, heat bombarded her as sweat broke out on her forehead. Her bluish-green eyes snapped open. He was alive! Her Scotsman was alive! Hope and joy surged through her. Hugging her arms to herself, she gave a joyful little cry then sought her bed for the night.

When sleep overcame her, her dreams revolved around the tall dark Scotsman.

The sun was not yet up, when Ian and his men scouted the Brodie castle searching for the best way inside and to the witch. They left their horses deep within the woods about half a league away and within easy reach should they need to escape quickly.

"Bloody hell, the thing looks impenetrable." Ian sat down with his back to a tree trunk and scowled at the castle in the distance. Getting to the witch inside was looking hopeless.

If he didn't get the *bana-bhuidseach* soon his brother was sure to die, *'twas only her powers that could save him,'* Ian thought. With a sigh, he formed a plan.

Raven's sleep had been tormented by images of her dark Scot being wounded in battle, and of the pain he was suffering. He was sure he was in hell, but she thought perhaps he was burning with fever. She yearned to get to him and to heal him of his terrible wound, but alas she was stuck in Ewin's grasp.

Once during the night, she had felt the Scot's longing to let go and allow his soul to join those of his kin in Summerland. It had taken tremendous energy to keep him within his body, to convince him to fight the infection that had already begun inside of him.

By the time she woke, the sun had already risen, and the dew had long since dried. Dressing hastily, she hurried to plait her long black hair. Grabbing her basket to collect herbs and a large skin of water to give thanks to the plants with, she found her escorts and hastened from the castle.

As Raven hiked toward the forest near the castle, she smiled up at the sunshine glistening brightly above her. It was going to be a beautiful day, she thought with a smile. Now, if she could only lose the four burly Scotsmen who were escorting her on her foray into the woods, the day would be perfect. Raven tried to pretend they didn't exist. She hummed a tune and began collecting her herbs, as she made her way through the forest.

Ian couldn't believe his luck. The woman being escorted into the woods where he was standing had to be the witch. It was unlikely that this was a serving girl out on an errand for the healer. Besides, this woman fit the description that he was given of the *bana-bhuidseach*, the raven black hair, the mystic beauty and the small stature of the woman. Her four escorts simply dwarfed her, making her look more like a child than woman who was full-grown. '*Och, but she is a wee one,*' Ian thought with a frown.

He watched the five of them walk into the trees. Her escorts were fooling around and lagging considerably. Ian looked at his men spread out around him. He gestured for them to take out the guards while he snatched the witch.

Raven looked over her shoulder and saw her escorts falling farther and farther behind her, with a smile, she quickened her pace until she could no longer see them. Walking through the woods she breathed in the smell of the trees and plants as well as the sea laced air.

Soon she could no longer even hear her escorts and the thought gave her pause for a moment, but she brushed it aside. This was, after all, the first time she had more than a minute alone in the forest since her arrival. With a smile, she stopped and began collecting leaves from a fairy cup plant. She opened the skin of water and poured a bit at the base of the plant thanking it, as she finished collecting the herb that she needed from it.

In the next instant, she tried to scream as a hand clamped over her mouth, and a muscular arm slipped around her waist lifting her off the ground. Her scream was blocked by the large hand that was nearly suffocating her, she tugged at her abductor's hand desperately, but it would not relent. The trees flew by as she was carried by her captor at a running pace. She had no clue where she was. Suddenly, she saw a group of horses looming ahead of her, and she knew this man meant to spirit her away. Her escorts were surely dispatched of, and that meant she was on her own.

Ian made it to the horses and stopped running, he pressed his mouth against the woman's ear and whispered, "If ye wanna live, ye'll nay make a sound when I remove my hand. Do ye ken?"

Slowly, Raven nodded her head and took a deep breath as air rushed into her lungs, when his hand moved from over her mouth. In the next instant, her hands were being bound and a gag was secured in her mouth. She tested the strength of her bonds and found them supremely secure. In a quick motion, her abductor swung up on his large black horse taking her with him. He settled her in front of him lying across his lap. It was not a comfortable position. When he wheeled his horse around and took off through the woods it was even worse. The man was a brute! She thought furiously.

Ian rode as fast as possible desperate to leave Brodie lands before the witch was discovered missing. When she and her escorts failed to return to the castle the alarm would be sounded, and the hunt would be on. He had to spirit her as far away as possible, long before the Brodie Chieftain found out she was no longer with them.

His men were instructed to try and catch up with him, but if they were unable to do so they were to make their own way back to *Kyleakin*, on the Isle of Sky, where the MacKinnon Clan made their home. By fair, or by foul means, he would get the witch there and force her to save his brother's life.

Raven watched the forest melt away and she knew she would only have a chance if she could get off this blasted horse and make it to the woods and hide. Taking a deep breath, she thumped the horse's side as hard as she could, while sending the poor creature a bit of a shock with her magick. She caused it to stumble a bit and her captor to ease up his hand on her back.

Pushing from the horse, she flung herself to the ground and rolled with the force. The impact jarred her body making her teeth click together and the breath was knocked out of her.

Lying there on the ground, she groaned as pain racked her body. The sound of thundering hooves had her rolling over and pushing to her feet. On a stumbling stride, she headed for the trees, hoping they would protect her.

Ian slid from his horse as he neared her, "Damn it ye bloody witch! I've nay time for this." He ran after her and caught her arm just as she was going to enter the woods. She pulled her arm from his grasp and fell to her side.

Fear raced through her as the large Scotsman turned her over, the sun blinded her at first, but then he was standing over her, blocking it out with his large frame. She looked in to an incredibly handsome face, but it was not his face that startled her, it was his eyes. They were the same eyes she had seen for more than a fortnight. Slowly, she reached up and traced his cheek, as he kneeled before her, they were the same eyes but, yet different. These deep bluish-grey eyes held anguish, but not the pain she would have expected.

Ian furrowed his brows as the woman touched his face. When she reached up and touched the gag at her mouth and tugged, he frowned, "Ye want me to remove the gag?" When she nodded enthusiastically he hesitated, "And yer nay gonna scream, aye?" She made an x over her heart and shook her head. Reluctantly, Ian removed the cloth.

"Who are ye?" She asked astounded. This man was her Scot but, yet, he was not. It made no sense to her.

"I am, Ian MacKinnon, Chieftain of the Clan MacKinnon and Laird of *Dun Akin*." He informed her proudly as he stood up and helped her to sit up.

Raven frowned at him, this man was not her Scot from her dreams, but the resemblance was unmistakable. "And why do ye steal me away from my home, Laird MacKinnon?" She demanded in a regal voice as she raised her chin.

"I am in desperate need of yer healing powers, *bana-bhuidseach*." Ian informed her sternly.

Raven looked him up and down. She had felt no injury in him when she had touched him. "Why do ye need my help? Yer uninjured."

"'Tis nay me. 'Tis my brother who lies dyin'." Ian frowned in thought and prayed his brother was not dead.

"And tell me, *Laird*, what makes ye think I can save him?" Raven was giving away nothing until she knew more. "And why nay simply come and ask me to help ye, instead of spiritin' me away?"

"'Tis said Ewin Brodie keeps ye under lock and key. He would never allow me to seek yer help." Ian narrowed his gaze at her, "Does nay matter one whit, ye will return with me to my home and heal my brother."

Raven stood herself up and looked up at the man, way up, as she was more than a foot shorter than he was. Though she was small, she feared no man. Pushing the hair from her face with her bound hands she walked up to him and poked him in the chest. "Ye've nay right to be stealin' me away, and makin' demands of me. Perhaps, ye big oaf, if yer were to ask a woman nicely, she'd come along willin'ly."

Ian glowered down at her for a long moment then burst out in laughter, "Bloody hell yer a brave one." He

11

looked in to her bluish-green eyes that seemed to change hue neigh on every second.

"I may be small, *Laird*, but I can take care of myself." She raised her chin in a haughty gesture. Though the sheer size of the man frightened her, she would not let on.

"All right witch..."

"I've a name, if ye care to be askin'." She growled at him.

It took a lot for Ian not to laugh at her again, "Beggin' yer pardon, lass, but what 'twould that be?" Ian looked down at her and was swept away by her beauty once more.

"Raven," she raised her chin.

"Raven Brodie..." She cut him off once more.

"I am nay a Brodie," she told him firmly. "My name is just, Raven."

"Fine Raven, with nay clan name," Ian looked down at her then dropped to one knee, "Lass, I beg yer help, to save the life of a good man, my brother Duncan." He took her hands in his large one, "If ye grant me this, I shall grant ye any boon within my power that ye wish."

Raven was quiet for a long moment as she closed her eyes, she evened her breathing and reached out to this man's brother. His breathing was shallow and labored, but his heart was still strong. She reached outside of herself to touch him and reassure him.

Ian's eyes widened as he saw the woman before him begin to give off a faint blue shimmering glow. Her hands warmed in his and he felt the energy crackle through his hand and up his arm. She was indeed a witch, but if it took the powers of the very devil himself to save his brother, then so be it.

Coming back to herself, Raven slowly opened her eyes. "We must hasten our journey, yer brother lives, but with each sunset he weakens and gives up hope." She held out her wrists to him, "If I am to journey with ye, then I beg ye to remove my bonds."

"Aye," Ian pulled his dagger from his sheath and cut the bindings around her slender wrists. He looked in to her unusual eyes and frowned, "Are ye positive that Duncan lives?"

Raven reached out and touched Ian's arm in reassurance, "I can feel him even from this far, he lives, but we must make haste if we are to reach his bedside in time."

Ian stood up and held out his hand to the small woman. "Come, Raven of nay clan, let us begin our journey."

Raven slipped her small hand into his larger one and smiled sweetly up at him, "This time *Laird*, I pray ye dinna throw me over yer horse, like a mill sack of flour." She laughed at Ian's sheepish look.

"I must apologize for my behavior, lass, but I saw nay other way in which too secure yer help." Ian walked her over to his destrier and looked down at her, "How would ye prefer to ride lass, front, or back?"

She thought about trying to hold onto this man as they rode hell bent for leather over the Scottish countryside. "Front, for I am afraid, I have never ridden a horse in my life, that I ken." She looked at the powerful beast and shook her head, "And I've nay wish to fall off the hind end of this beastie, 'twould probably break my neck."

"Then come lass, I'll give ye a hand up, then I'll swing up after ye." Ian took her around the waist and lifted her, she weighed little more than a feather. He set her on the saddle and placed her hand on the horse's mane. "Hold on, while I mount up behind ye."

When he went to mount she got a death grip on the horse's mane and Ian was thankful his destrier was well trained. Swinging up behind her, Ian settled himself in the saddle then lifted her so that she was settled in his lap. She gave a little squeak as he set the horse in motion. "Have nay fear lass, I'll nay let ye fall."

Raven still held on for dear life as they picked up speed. When they were racing across the Scottish countryside, she began to enjoy the wind rushing through her hair, and for the first time she wondered what this giant man's home was like.

Anticipation, to finally meet the man who had been plaguing her dreams for so long now, surged through her. What would Duncan MacKinnon be like? She wondered if this laird would truly grant her the boon he had sworn to her.

Time would tell what the outcome of this journey would be. Perhaps, she would finally find herself. Mayhap, she would finally be free again.

Two

Traveling across the Scottish-highlands was not easy, Raven was glad it was early spring and not winter, for she was sure they would not have made it through.

The first night they travelled, she fell asleep against Ian MacKinnon as they rode through the night. She woke to the sun shining, and his tartan tucked around her to keep her warm. She looked down at the beautiful weave and colors. The MacKinnon plaid was breathtaking. She looked up at the man she had fallen asleep against. "Have we ridden all night?"

"Aye lass, we've nay stopped since yesterday." Ian slowed his mount and found a place where she would be afforded a bit of privacy. "Ye must be needin' a privy by now, and mayhaps to freshen up a bit."

"Aye, 'twould be wondrous." Raven sighed in thought, perhaps these MacKinnon men were nothing like Ewin Brodie.

When they stopped, Ian set her from his lap and slid off the horse then turned and hoisted her down. Carefully, he set her on her feet and caught her when she staggered. "Easy lass."

"Thank ye," Raven smiled up at him and began to hand him the plaid. Ian took it and wrapped it around her shoulders and body.

"'Tis chilly this morn' and ye've nay plaid, nor cloak of yer own." He smiled down at her.

"I thank ye for the use of yer tartan, but are ye nay chilly yerself?" Raven frowned up at him.

Ian shrugged, "If I get chilly, I shall use my own plaid, that one belongs to my brother, Duncan." He turned away and began rubbing his horse down. "Dinna wander too far away, and when ye return, I'll give ye somethin' to break yer fast."

Raven made her way about fifty feet into a stand of trees. She hid behind a bush and relieved herself. When she was finished, she combed her hair with her fingers as best she could, then removed Duncan's plaid from where she had hung it on a tree branch and wrapped herself in its warmth once more. For a moment, she stopped and lifted the plaid she held around her, to her nose and breathed. She could smell its owner, embedded in the fabric, there was a hint of soap and outdoors as well as something uniquely Duncan MacKinnon. For a moment, she could picture the man in her mind, but he was shadowed.

Pulling herself back to the here and now, she laughed at her own foolishness. 'Here she stood sniffin' a man's plaid that she dinna even ken.' She thought with a laugh. Picking the plaid up so that it wouldn't drag on the ground, she made her way back to where Ian stood waiting for her. They ate their meal in silence and once finished, Ian helped her back onto the horse's saddle.

16

By the third day of travel, she was becoming weary of riding on the blasted horse. She swore her teeth had clicked together so many times that she would have hardly a one left in her head. It was exciting, to see new places and watch villages and towns pass by, but it would have been more fun to explore them instead of watching them go by.

That night they stopped in a wooded area, but Ian would not allow them to have a fire, so she was wrapped up once more in Duncan's plaid for warmth. Ian made her a bed of pine needles and tall grass. It was soft enough, but she was freezing. She figured if the ride didn't shatter her teeth, then her chattering would.

Ian could hear her teeth chattering as she shivered from the cold. On a sigh, he moved over to where she was and lay down beside her. He pulled her into his arms and tossed his plaid over them both.

Even as she shivered, Raven snuggled into Ian's larger body for the warmth, "Thank ye, Laird."

"Ian," he lay there looking up at the stars, "I beg ye, call me by my given name."

"Thank ye, Ian." Raven felt his warmth already surrounding her.

After a short time, she was still awake. Ian sighed, "Can ye nay sleep, lass?"

She sighed, "I am nay sleepy."

A long pause ensued before Ian said into the darkness, "Can ye tell me once more how my brother fares?"

Raven sat up slowly, "I can try." She closed her eyes and took Ian's hand in one of her own, and clutched the plaid in the other. She evened her breathing and sought outside herself. The heat was nigh on unbearable, and his body was filled with agony for the infection eating away at him. His heartbeat was still strong, but not nearly as strong as before. He was tired of hanging on, of fighting to live. He wanted to enter *Summerland* with the rest of his kin who had gone before him.

Desperately, Raven held onto Duncan's spirit and tried to assure him and soothe him. She took on as much of his pain as she could, to help give him rest and make him more comfortable.

Ian began to worry when nearly half an hour went by, and she said not a word. He felt the heat rolling off her body and wondered at the way her skin shimmered with a pale bluish light. Reaching out, he touched her gently and felt the perspiration on her skin. When she whimpered slightly he jerked his hand away.

Her eyes opened and glowed in that mystical shimmer of bluish-green swirl. "He lives, but his pain is great. He wants to join his kin in Summerland. The infection is racing through his body and the heat is insufferable."

"Dinna let him die lass, tell him we're near. He must hold on." Ian spoke desperately and took her other hand and pain shot through him.

Raven jerked her hand away and released his other hand then stood up. She swayed, but caught herself. With wobbly motions, she moved a few feet away still clutching Duncan's plaid around her as she sat and leaned up against a tree.

Ian lay there and watched her for the longest time, until his eyes grew heavy and slumber pulled him into the darkness.

Upon waking in the morning, Ian found her curled on her side wrapped in the plaid sound asleep. When he went to check on her, she was so deep in sleep he could barely get her to stir. When he was ready to leave, he walked over and scooped her up in his arms. He mounted his destrier once more with Raven cradled to him. Ian settled her on his lap with her head against his chest.

It was nearly sunset when she finally awoke. She stretched languidly and was startled to see other Scotsmen riding along with them.

"'Tis good to see ye stir, lass," Ian smiled down at her. "Ye had me worried."

"I had to recover from last eve." Raven placed a hand over her stomach as it growled loudly. "Could we stop for a few moments, Ian?"

"Aye, lass, I'm sure yer needin' to." Ian turned them for the edge of a loch. "I'm afraid there 'tis little privacy to be had here, but we'll do the best we can."

When she relieved herself, Ian held his plaid up to shield her from view of the other men. He allowed her to sit for a few minutes by the side of the loch and wash up then eat some of the dried meats he had with him.

"We shall reach Inverness in a couple of hours." Ian informed her.

"Is this a village?" Raven felt excitement grow. "Aye lass, 'tis a rather large village at that," he looked her over, "Have ye nay heard of it 'afore?"

Raven shook her head, "Nay."

Rubbing his chin that was covered in a fair growth of beard, not for the first time did he wonder about her. Where had this woman come from and who was she? What kind of powers did she truly have?

Looking out over the loch she sighed, "'Tis a shame we have nay time to stop and have a glance around, but we must get to Duncan as swiftly as possible."

19

Ian looked at her for a long moment, "Tell me lass, what was it ye were doin' last eve?"

Raven was quiet for a long time then sighed, "I helped to keep him alive. I stayed with him."

"That is nay all ye did, lass." He looked at the loch spread out before them. "Ye were in pain last eve."

She looked at him, "I eased his pain to give his body a better chance, though I fear I could nay take it all away from such a great distance as this."

"Ye bore the burden of his pain, is that nay true?" He looked in to her swirling bluish-green eyes searching for the truth.

"Aye," she spoke quietly.

He looked at her thoughtfully, "Lass, I ken my brother and he would nay be happy with this. Like all MacKinnon men we treat our women with respect and protect them at all costs."

Raven turned to him, "I dinna need to be protected." Her eyes glowed in the late afternoon sunlight, "Did ye, or did ye nay bid me to save him?"

"Aye, I wanted ye to save him, but..."

"Nay," she growled, "I did what I must, to save him. If I had let him go last eve, he would have joined yer kin who has already passed on."

Ian furrowed his brows. "Ye kept him from dyin'?"

"Aye, ye big oaf," Raven turned away from him.

"I thank ye, Raven, but ken that I'll nay sacrifice yer life for my brother's. Yer a woman and I shall protect ye," he clasped her shoulders, "Yer my responsibility now."

She shrugged off his hand, "I dinna want yer protection. I want my freedom."

"Whether ye want my protection or nay, ye've it. For the Brodie will come after ye." Ian informed her,

"'Twill be myself and my clan that shall stand between ye."

Raven gasped and looked at him, "Ewin does nay ken 'twas ye who stole me. How could he find out?"

Ian scratched his head trying to find a nice way to put things to her, "Lass, between that plaid ye've got draped around ye and yer looks 'tis a bit hard to nay stick out."

They passed into Inverness as the sun was sinking from the sky. Ian decided that they needed a night's rest and some decent food. At an Inn, he secured lodging and a warm meal. Raven was thrilled when he got her a bath. For Raven's sake, Ian claimed she was his wife. This afforded her the protection and treatment of a laird's wife and she loved the royal treatment.

In the room they were to share, she stripped and climbed into the tub of hot water. It felt like heaven. She scrubbed every inch of her skin clean. Once the water grew tepid she stepped out and dried herself. The Innkeeper's wife had given her a nightdress to borrow. Slipping it over her head, she sighed at the feel of clean clothing.

Her body felt so heavy and tired that she kept yawning. She went to the table where her meal had been set out. Grabbing a lamb pastry, she took a bite of it. Hunger hit her hard and she ate the pastry in four bites. Then she ate another a bit slower. By the time she had finished the second pie, she was so tired she could barely walk to the bed.

Lying on a mattress was heaven. She curled her hands under her cheek and her eyes closed immediately. Sleep closed in around her and she surrendered to its bliss.

Sitting in the pub of the Inn drinking and eating with his men, Ian frowned at the thought of the woman above stairs. None of them discussed the woman, but he worried at leaving her alone. As soon as he was finished, Ian left the table to go check on Raven and make sure all was well with her. He knocked on the door, but there was no answer. Pulling his dagger from its sheath, he entered the room cursing himself for not putting a guard on her door.

Ian slipped into the room and spied her lying upon the bed sound asleep. Walking over, he went to flip the coverlet over her to make sure she was warm when he spied Duncan's plaid clenched in her hand as she used it for a pillow. He had the feeling that this small woman was not going to let go of that plaid very easy.

Going back below stairs, Ian sent Lieth to stand guard outside the door to Raven's room. Later he would sleep on the floor of her chamber and allow his men to seek their own beds.

Raven looked around and fanned herself. It was so hot here. The pain sliced through her even as she approached the tall broad warrior, who stood there in front of the raging fire.

"Have ye come to try and keep me here longer, lass?" Duncan MacKinnon looked over his shoulder at her with his long dark hair lying unbound over his shoulders and down his back.

"Aye," Raven raised her chin, "I have sworn to save yer miserable hide." She had come to see that the man was testy and ornery when it suited him.

22

"How close is my brother, lass?" He turned and crossed his arms over his broad chest.

"A couple of days, we are in a village, a verra large village, but I dinna recall the name." She walked over to the chair near the fire and sat down. "Please, dinna fight me this night, for I grow weary of fightin' with yer ornery hide."

Duncan walked over and pulled up a stool to sit in front of her. "And what do ye suggest we do instead, lass?" His deep greyish-blue gaze sparkled with amusement.

"Dinna fight my attempt at healin' ye." She rubbed her hands over her face and he caught her wrists.

Pulling them down Duncan looked at her, "Ye grow weary and weak woman." Duncan growled, "Do ye think I dinna ken yer shieldin' me from my own pain? 'Twill kill ye if ye keep this up, lass."

Raven's eyes snapped with fire, "Dinna presume to tell me anythin'. I ken what I can and can nay do."

"I'm tellin' ye to cease this foolishness. If I die before ye arrive, so be it. For the Gods have willed it so." Duncan shook her slightly.

"If ye die than I shall die as well," Raven protested.

Duncan studied her for a long moment, "Tell me, has my brother threatened yer life?"

"Nay," she shook her pitch colored head, "But yer the only one who can save me from Ewin Brodie." Raven tossed back at him in defiance.

Duncan sat back and frowned at her, "Then I shall live as long as possible lass, but dinna think my brother would allow Brodie to harm ye."

Raven pulled her wrist from his grasp then grabbed his hands in hers. "Yer correct, I do grow weary, so I pray ye'll make my task simpler."

Duncan stood up pulling her to her feet and walked with her to the bed in the chamber. He lay down and she knelt next to him on the mattress. He took her hands and pulled her forward so that she leaned over him, her face mere inches from his. Fingers laced, he looked in to her bluish-green eyes as her loose raven black hair formed a curtain around them shining with blue highlights in the firelight. "Dinna shield me from my pain, woman."

"'Tis thee only way to help ye," she looked in the deep greyish-blue depths of his eyes and moved slightly closer. "I must save ye." She breathed in the scent of him and recognized it as the same one on the tartan.

"Will I remember ye, lass?" He pulled her a bit closer. "Will I remember yer visits here?"

"Nay," she spoke softly sadly, "Ye will nay remember any of this."

"Then I'll have yer name," he reached up and caressed her cheek with his fingertips then traced a finger over her lips.

"Raven," she told him softly as her heart stuttered in her chest.

Duncan gave a slight nod, "'Tis fittin' for ye," he smiled up at her, "My dark saving angel, Raven." With his hand on her cheek he pulled her down capturing her mouth in a kiss.

Raven felt that kiss all the way to her toes. The feel of his lips on hers and the taste of him filled her. Never had she been kissed like this! Ewin had tried once, and it had been sloppy and had turned her stomach. This man knew how to kiss a woman. His lips were soft and delicious. Her hand had found his beard-roughened cheek and caressed it.

When at last he pulled back and looked at her, he rubbed his thumb over her kiss swollen lips, never had he seen such a beautiful sight. "I shall remember ye, Raven. A man, can nay forget the taste of such a woman." He smiled, "Tell my brother to hurry his arse up, and brin' ye to me."

Raven looked in his deep greyish-blue gaze and smiled longingly, "I wish ye would remember me, but 'tis nay possible."

"Keep me alive woman and ye shall see," Duncan gave her a cock sure smile.

"Then let us begin." She closed her eyes and began using her healing powers.

Ian knelt by Raven as she lay sleeping and looked at her. She looked exhausted and drained. The dark shadows under her eyes were deepening not easing, he thought with worry. As she slept, she was even now trying to save his brother, he was sure. Ian reached out and tucked a strand of hair that had fallen in her face behind her ear.

He prayed they reached Duncan in time to save him, and that this wouldn't cost Raven her life. Duncan would be furious if Ian endangered a woman for his sake. With a gentle hand, he shook Raven's shoulder.

Slowly she stirred and looked at him dreamily, "Duncan?" She spoke his brother's name softly.

"Nay lass, 'tis Ian." He told her with a smile. He would take it as a good sign that she had said Duncan's name.

Raven licked her lips and tasted the flavor of Duncan there. "He says for ye to hurry yer *arse* up in gettin' me to him."

Ian threw back his head and laughed wholeheartedly, for Duncan was alive for sure. Those were true words to be spoken by his brother. When at last he stopped laughing, he was sitting down on the floor with Raven looking at him as if he'd gone addle in his head. "Aw lass, ye've nay idea what good those words did for my heart. Means my brother 'tis alive for sure."

"And how long 'afore we reach him?" Raven inquired.

"Two days unless the sound 'tis bein' fickle." Ian scratched his scruff of beard, "But we'll have to go through Matheson lands, for the MacCleanan clan and their cousins the MacLeans dinna favor MacKinnons."

"I dinna care, so long as we get there as soon as possible." Raven told him, "Now, let us get this day started."

The rains set in around noon and slowed their trek through the highlands of Scotland. Raven was as desperate to get to Duncan as Ian was, so they agreed to travel through the night as well.

It took them three cold rainy days to reach the sound between *Alba* and the Isle of Skye. The rain came so hard that they were forced to take shelter for the night with a fisherman and his wife, Ian once again claiming that Raven was his wife.

They shared a single bed and Raven was afraid to reach out for Duncan this night as she had in the past few nights. She was terrified as to what the fisherman and his wife would say to see her glow in the dark, as Ian had told her, she did at times.

She slept terribly as nightmares plagued her. Her dreams revolved around Duncan dying and she wept in her sleep. At one-point Ian woke her as she lay there weeping. Her fear grew as the night went on.

By morning she was sick with worry over Duncan. When they reached the sound, the water was thrashing and crashing, and the fisherman told them it was unsafe to cross it.

Fearing for Duncan, Raven decided she had no choice, but to show her powers and walked to the edge of the sound. The sea air lifted the ends of her hair to fly all around her and kissed her face in recognition. Lifting her arms, she began commanding the water to calm for them. The clouds overhead parted and a spear of light spilled down over her then began breaking apart the gloomy clouds to allow the sun to shine down on the land. The water calmed with a wave of her hands and the breeze died down and her hair lay against her back. Turning back to look at Ian she smiled, "We must make haste, the sea is nay patient today."

Ian inclined his head and turned to the fisherman who stood gap mouthed as he stared at Raven. Putting on a laird's face he barked orders at the man and his men, who were also standing there looking at Raven as if she were a monster.

Raven pulled Duncan's plaid closer as the sea wind whipped around her. Ian was the only one to talk with her, or even came near her once she had calmed the sea.

Ian walked over and leaned against the rail of the boat. "Ye've got a death grip on that railin'." Raven looked over at him and he read her terror. "There's aught to fear lass, I could swim the distance between here and shore without even tryin' hard." He was quiet for a long moment, "Why do ye fear the sea so much?"

She shook her dark head, "I've nay idea."

"Where do ye hail from, if 'tis nay with the Brodie's?" Ian looked out at the Isle where he called his home.

"I dinna ken," Raven shrugged a shoulder, "One of the Brodie clan found me washed up on the beach after a storm."

Ian inclined his head, "And ye've nay memory of yer clan and yer home?"

She shook her head, "Nay a one." She smiled over at him faintly. "But yer's seems to be directly ahead."

Ian looked out at the Isle of Skye, it was glorious to be home. He waved a hand, "Welcome lass, to *Kyleakin.* And that would be *Caisteal Moil, or Dun Akin.*" He pointed to the tall beautiful castle with towering round torrents, on the hill overlooking the sound, "*Dun Akin* 'tis my home and yers for as long as ye like."

Raven breathed deeply, this was one of the things she had smelled when she had breathed in the scent of Duncan's tartan. "'Tis beautiful." She spoke wistfully. "'Twould be a wonderful place to call home."

Three

By the time they reached the castle proper they were all weary and exhausted, but Raven hurried to keep pace with Ian as he strode through the castle toward his brother's chambers.

Throwing open the doors, he burst into the room startling the old women. "Tell me how he fares?" Ian roared.

The old woman scurried away from him, "He was seeming better Laird, but 'twould seem he took a turn for the worst last eve." She twisted her gnarled fingers together.

Raven drew up short as she walked into the room. The heat was stifling. Walking over to Duncan, she laid her hand on his forehead, he was burning up. Leaving him, she walked over to the windows, and threw them open letting in fresh cool sea air.

The old crone gasped, "Are ye mad child, he'll catch a chill and surely die." She hurried to shut the windows.

"Dinna touch those," Raven turned to Ian, "and put out that fire, are ye tryin' to roast the man alive?" As the crone made to shut the windows, Ian held up a hand, "You can do nay more for my brother old mother, leave my castle and return home." He took a bucket of water and doused the flames in the hearth. Ian nearly groaned when Raven stripped the covers off Duncan leaving him bare. He cleared his throat, "Um… lass ye should nay be seein' him in such a state of undress."

Raven glared over her shoulder at him, "Be useful Ian, and fetch me some clean water." She went to work removing the grime the old woman had placed upon Duncan's chest.

Ian strode into the hallway stunned that someone had had the nerve to order him around. Running in to Aidan he frowned, "She ordered me to fetch water?"

Aidan looked at him and laughed, "Then order someone else to fetch it."

Ian's eyes glinted, "Then fetch it lad, and be quick 'bout it." He turned on his heels and walked back to the bedchamber leaving Aidan with his mouth hanging open.

Ian watched her work for some time. Once the water arrived, she began rattling off herbs that she needed him to retrieve for her. With a pot of hot water from the kitchen, she washed her hands and cleansed the wound that was infected. When she ordered seawater brought up, Ian ordered it fetched without haste. She made Ian and the younger MacKinnon man with him, change the bedding that Duncan was laying on. She paid them little mind except to call out orders, as time was critical to save Duncan.

Looking at Ian, she knew she could not wait for the herbs to arrive. She gave him and the man he said was his cousin, instruction on how to grind them and how to mix them to place on Duncan's wound. Duncan's labored breathing worried her. She knew he was dying.

Ian grabbed her shoulder, "And just what do ye plan, lass?"

"To keep him here with us," Raven climbed upon the bed and knelt next to him. She grabbed the basin of seawater from the stand and she chanted over it and made it glow and swirl in the basin. The water formed a mini-cyclone, while Ian and Aidan watched with amazement as the water came out of the bowl to swirl above Duncan's body. Suddenly, a blackness came out of Duncan's mouth and nose. They watched as the water began to turn dark, once it was wholly blackened the water streamed back into the bowl. The words she spoke were not of any language they had ever heard of.

Raven handed the water to Ian, "Ye must pour it into the sea." She gave him a hard look, "Nay on the ground, but in the sea and ye must make sure of this."

"Aye lass," Ian inclined his head and stepped back.

Raven closed her eyes and chanted again three times then leaned forward so that her face was above Duncan's by mere inches. One hand she placed over the wound. She began speaking and the words sounded musical almost like that of the legendary mermaid, Ian thought.

Aidan couldn't believe his eyes as she took on a mystical bluish glow. Never in his life had he seen such a thing. The sea breeze blew through the window causing Raven's hair to lift as it encircled her and Duncan. As suddenly as it started the wind died, her singing stopped, and the glow faded. She sat up and swayed. Aidan moved forward to catch her as she slipped into unconsciousness. Looking over his shoulder at his cousin, he lifted a brow.

"Lay her there beside him," Ian smiled softly as he heard Duncan mumble in his sleep, "I believe he agrees." The color had returned to Duncan's face and his breathing was normal again, and Ian felt relieved. Walking over he threw the covers over both Duncan and Raven. Picking the basin of blackened water up from where he had set it, he left to walk down to the sea.

Raven stirred and found herself trapped beneath a large muscular arm. She was lying in a strange bed, in a strange chamber that was not her own. Looking over her shoulder, she saw Duncan MacKinnon sleeping behind her, spooned with her, holding her close to him. For a moment, she closed her eyes and relished the feel of him curled around her, all warm and wonderful. After a couple of moments, she slipped from his grasp. He mumbled grumpily in his sleep and she smiled, "Glad to see yer, yer own happy self once more."

She went about checking his wound, and was glad the redness and infection was fading away. Raven checked to see if he was running a fever, and was happy to find his forehead cool. Sitting on his bedside, she took his large hand in hers and sought into his body to see how he was mending and if she could help him along.

Ian stood there with a tray in hand for a few minutes until she turned to look at him.

"Aw food, 'tis a welcome sight, I thank ye." She set Duncan's hand back down and walked over to take the tray and set it on the only table in the room. "I'll be needin' fresh water again soon."

"Yer welcome, and ye've only to ask and someone will give ye whatever 'tis ye need." Ian smiled at her then walked over to his brother. He looked down at him, he and Duncan were but a couple years apart. He couldn't imagine life without his brother. He swallowed convulsively, "Thank ye, lass, for what ye've done."

"I've nay finished, so dinna be thankin' me yet." Raven tore off a piece of bread and ate it ravenously. She was famished after the long trek through the highlands, then after using her powers to keep Duncan alive earlier, she was drained.

"I have faith in ye, lass, and 'twould seem my brother does as well." Ian looked over at her. When Duncan started to stir, Ian looked over at him.

Raven came over and sat on his bedside. When she picked up his hand, he pulled her to him and whispered. She looked up at Ian, "'Twould appear he wants a drink." Walking over she filled a mug with watered wine, swirling her hand over the mug then took it to him. Lifting his head, she helped him drink, "Slow and steady there, boy-o." She told him when he tried to gulp it down and coughed.

Duncan settled back into sleep and Ian looked from his brother to the woman sitting next to him. "I've had the chambers next to this readied for ye to stay in for now. When Duncan is well once more, ye may have nigh on any chamber ye chose."

"For now, I shall stay in here so that I may tend yer brother." Raven informed him, "But I thank ye, for yer kindness."

"Is there anythin' at all that ye may be needin'?" He looked her over and noted that she would probably enjoy a bath.

"Aye, if ye could manage to find me somethin' clean to wear, I would be beholdin' to ye." She brushed a hand over her gown, "I have been wearin' this gown for more days than I care to admit."

Ian inclined his head. "I shall have ye clothin' by morn. I can nay promise the fit of them, but I'll endeavor to do my best, lass."

"I am sure whatever ye can manage shall be just fine." Raven walked back over to her food and began eating. She was ravenous. "Again, I thank ye for yer kindness, Ian."

With that Ian inclined his head and left her to her meal.

Raven had just finished eating when a woman knocked then entered the room at Raven's bidding. She was more than a score of years older than Raven. "Aye?" She raised a brow at the older woman.

"M'lady, the Laird ordered that I prepare ye a bath," she didn't look up and kept her eyes averted. "I'll take yer tray if yer finished?"

Raven walked the tray over to the woman and handed it to her. When the woman hurried away, Raven sighed, it was to start all over again. She was to be named witch, and condemned before any of the inhabitants of the castle even knew her.

Shrugging her shoulders, Raven sat back and watched as the older woman and several young lads brought in bucket after bucket of hot and cold water. A large tub was rolled out from behind one of the doors in Duncan's chamber. The woman laid out a bath sheet and fragrant soap for her.

When they would have poured the water for her, Raven waved them away. Once they'd left, Raven looked about the chamber and saw a large chest. Walking over to the chest, she opened it and found that it was full of men's clothing. Pulling out one of Duncan's linen shirts she held it up. She would positively swim in the thing, she thought with a smile.

Taking the shirt over near the fire where the tub sat, Raven poured her bath water then stripped out of her dirty dress. Laying it aside, she climbed into the tub and sank into the steaming hot water and sighed. Lord, it felt wonderful to sink into a nice hot bath again. She quickly grabbed the soap and began wetting and washing her hair.

It was the sound of water splashing that woke him. Duncan turned his head and looked toward the fire that lit his room. For a moment, he thought it was another one of his strange dreams, about his dark-haired angel. In the glow of the firelight, he watched her as she sat on her knees in his tub washing her hair. He could see the outline of her breasts and her hard, pebbled nipples. Her body was slender and molded perfectly.

He watched her grab the cloth to wash with and lather it with soap that smelled of highland heather. As the cloth glided over her delicate skin he felt himself, hardening.

It was hard to grasp the fact that his dream angel was real. Looking at her in the firelight, he yearned to touch her. Because the tub's sides were so high, he couldn't see below her waist, but he was sure her bottom was as round, and perfect as her lovely breasts.

When she finished rinsing the soap from her body and laid back in the tub, Duncan closed his eyes and drifted off into the darkness that had been his home for far too long. His dreams were fragmented and had a dark-haired angel within them.

Raven sighed in the cooling water. It had felt wonderful to take a hot leisurely bath. She hated to leave the tub, but Duncan could use a bath as well. Grabbing the bath sheet, she stepped from the tub and began drying herself. She slipped into Duncan's shirt and began rolling the sleeves. The shirt hung to nearly her ankles. Pulling her wet hair out of the shirt, she dried it the best she could with the bath sheet, until she could sit by the fire and comb her fingers through her tresses.

Taking the warm water that was sitting by the fire, Raven poured some into a basin. She walked over and shut the windows that had allowed the night and sea breeze into the room. She didn't want Duncan to catch cold while she bathed him.

With a cloth for washing in hand, she walked over to where he lay sleeping. Carefully, she uncovered him from head to toe. For a moment, she allowed her gaze to take all of him in. Never had she seen a man so purely male. His face was beautifully masculine, even under the scruff of beard, he could make a lass melt with that dangerous smile of his, she thought, remembering their earlier encounters in the *Dreaming*.

Her eyes roamed over his body and she sucked in a breath, he was huge, with muscles roping his body. His arms even in rest were bulging with strength. His chest and shoulders were bronzed like his arms, and just as powerfully built. Her gaze traveled over his stomach that was cut into blocks of muscles and held a dark trail of curling hair that brushed over his navel and met his groin. She let her gaze rest for a moment on his manhood, surrounded in a dark thatch of curling hair. Her eyes widened, it would appear, that everything about the man was large, she thought, then nearly laughed out loud. She finished her survey taking in his powerful thighs and calves. Even the man's feet were huge.

Kneeling on the bed, Raven carefully set the basin next to her and wet the cloth. With gentle strokes, she began washing his face and neck, then moved to his powerful shoulders and his chest. She didn't notice the greyish-blue gaze watching her actions as she leaned over him to wash his left arm. Diligently, she wet the cloth once more and started on his right arm. She glanced up at his face and saw that he was asleep.

She stroked the cloth over his powerful chest then started down his muscular stomach, when she noticed his manhood once more. This time it was erect and very much aroused. Her gaze whipped to his face, but his eyes were closed and not a muscle moved giving any indication of him being awake.

Raven glared at him, "I think we shall stop there." She scooted back off the bed with the basin and set it aside while she covered him up. After she had thrown the water out the window and shut it, she studied her patient for a long moment. He could not have been awake, she thought with a shake of her head.

Walking back to where Duncan lay, she climbed back on the bed to have another look at his wound. Carefully, she removed the bandage that covered it and she winced, as she had to tug a bit to lift the bandage. The wound was still red and aggravated, but as she touched around it, she noticed that the infection was all but gone. She glanced at his face. He'd have another scar to go along with the many others she had seen in various places all over his body. The man had been lucky, if the blade that cut him had been more to the right by about three or four inches, he would have died for sure.

Wanting to help the healing in his body along, she placed one of her hands over his heart and the other above the wound. Closing her eyes, she focused and sought to enter his body.

Duncan felt the warmth of her as she began healing him once again. Her scent surrounded him and he felt the pain in his chest ease. Opening his eyes, a bit, he looked up at the woman kneeling beside him. Her hair swirled about her as a bluish aura surrounded her, causing her to glow eerily. A warm tingle started in his wound and spread across his chest and down through his shoulder into his arm.

The sound of her voice was as musical as the sea, as she sat there kneeling beside him chanting softly. When she finished, she swayed, and Duncan caught her with his right arm. Carefully, he lowered her so that her head rested on his chest and she sprawled over him. It took some doing, but he lifted the blanket and laid it over her. His hand slid over her silken black hair, "Enough lass, yer too weak to continue this." He told her as he held her to him.

Four

Ian knocked on the door of Duncan's chambers, but got no response. Carefully, he opened the door and crept in. Walking over to the bed he drew up short at the sight of Duncan with Raven sprawled over his chest. Had the woman crawled into bed with his brother? Ian took in her bare shoulder and Duncan's arm securing her to him.

He looked at his younger brother's face and deep greyish-blue eyes met like. "What the bloody hell?" Ian hissed.

Duncan got a cocky smile, "Even I am nay that virile, brother." He reached up with his left arm and traced the shadows beneath one of her eyes then looked at Ian, "She again worked to heal me last eve. Nay more Ian, 'tis too much for her."

Ian closed his eyes, "I had nay thought she would try such a thin' again." He looked at his brother, "I shall speak with her."

Duncan looked down into her sleeping face. The sunlight spilled across her, highlighting her beauty. Her ebony hair shone in the sunshine. She was tiny and delicate. He looked back at his brother, "I will nay allow her to harm herself to save me."

Raven's lashes fluttered up and she sighed, "Ye have aught to say in it, ye ornery ogre." She pushed away from him and grabbed the shoulder of the shirt to cover herself.

"I have every say in it, woman." Duncan barked at her in a hoarse voice.

Slipping from the bed, she strode across the room, and nearly laughed when Ian turned his eyes elsewhere from her in Duncan's shirt. The light coming through the windows must have made the shirt a bit thin. "Perhaps, ye should be stayin' in the chambers next door." Ian suggested casually.

"Put somethin' on for Gods sakes, woman," Duncan pushed himself up on his good arm, "And stop showin' yer *arse* to my brother."

Raven grabbed Duncan's tartan and threw it around her shoulders. She raised her chin, "There are ye satisfied?" She snapped back at him.

Duncan snorted. "I'll be happy when yer fully clothed." He looked her over and decided she looked good wrapped in his plaid. For a quick moment, he wondered what it would be like to lay her out naked upon it. "Aye, ye'll move to the chambers next to mine."

Walking across the room, Raven poured a mug of watered wine and quickly enchanted it then took it to him, "Drink this for now, and I'll make ye somethin' to help yer throat." She thrust the mug at him. "As for yer request, 'tis denied. I shall stay in this room until yer all, but healed."

Duncan erupted in a sting of Gaelic oaths. He threw the covers upon his bed back and began climbing from it. "Denied? Denied? Nay one denies me aught." He sat on the edge of the bed and as Ian strode over to him, Duncan waved him away. "If the stubborn wench will nay listen, I'll remove her from my chambers myself."

Raven crossed her arms over her chest and cocked her head and smiled as she spoke sweetly, "Yer a horse's *arse*, Duncan MacKinnon."

With a roar, Duncan pushed off the bed and took two steps toward her and would have fallen as the room spun around him, but Ian caught hold of him and put him back in the bed.

Raven walked over and pushed him back so that he was lying down and looked at the wound on his chest. "Ye big oaf, now yer bleedin' once more." She pressed a bandage to the wound.

"Damn woman, yer hurtin' me!" Duncan growled.

"Oh, stop yer whinin'," she smacked his hand as he went to remove her hand from the wound. "And stop yer blitherin' and bellowin'."

Duncan lay there watching her tend his wound. He looked at her lips, the woman was infuriating, but damn he wanted to kiss her for real and know if she tasted as sweet as she had in his dreams.

Ian stood there with his arms over his chest and looked at the two. He had never seen anyone besides himself and their parents, talk to his brother like that. Most women would be terrified of Duncan's roaring, but not Raven. Though she was more than a foot shorter than her patient, she had effectively put him in his place. It was her competent hands and her ultimate caring that made the decision for him as he spoke, "Raven stays as long as she feels 'tis necessary."

Duncan growled low in his throat, "I'll nay allow her to heal me, nay when she endangers herself."

Glaring back at his brother, Ian imposed his full laird mantel, "I am the MacKinnon, and what I say goes. Yeah gave me yer oath, and sworn yer fielty, now

41

ye'll obey." Ian looked at Raven, "If he persists in givin' ye trouble lass, ye've but to tell me and I'll tie him to his bed personally."

Raven looked from brother to brother and laughed, "'Twould seem yer out ranked, ye big oaf." She pressed another bandage in place and smiled at his hiss. "Yer mine to torture."

Duncan looked at his brother then at the woman kneeling over him, "Remember wench, retribution can be more than ye can handle." His gaze swung to his brother, "Same for ye, *'Laird'*." He looked back at Raven and smiled devilishly as he leered at her, "Remember woman, ye've chosen to share my chambers."

Raven's bluish-green gaze met his dark greyish-blue one and what she saw there made her want to shiver. If this man chose, he would have her in all respects of a woman and a man, and he would not need to force her. With this one, she didn't think telling him that she would lose her powers if she were to be bedded by a man, would work. Duncan MacKinnon was not that stupid.

Ian had a pallet moved into the room and set up near the hearth. Raven had insisted that she could sleep on the floor near the fire, but Duncan had barked orders for the pallet to be brought in.

As promised, Ian provided her with some clothing. Though they were a bit big, Raven figured she would manage with them. Looking around the room she sighed as she spied Duncan watching her. "Would it be too much to ask that ye afford me a bit of privacy by turning yer head when I change?"

"Aye," he glared at her. The woman was a trial and bossy to boot.

"Aye what?" Raven put her hands on her hips and glared at him, "Aye, 'tis too much to ask? Or aye, ye'll turn yer bloody head?"

"Have I averted my gaze, yet?" Duncan arched one arrogant brow.

Raven stomped her foot, "Ogre!" She threw the tartan back around her shoulders and turned her back to him. It was a struggle to change her clothing, but she managed. Dropping the plaid, she turned around and glared at him then stuck out her tongue.

Duncan laughed as she stormed to the windows and threw them open. Raven ignored him and leaned out to look over the sea. She breathed in the light salty air and smiled. She had always loved the sea. The thought made her freeze. She could remember standing in the brilliant crystal blue sea as a young girl playing in the water. She could almost feel the water running through her fingers. She could hear her name being called, but she couldn't make out what that name was.

"Lass?" Duncan inquired, "What's wrong?"

Raven shook herself and looked back at him, "I remember playin' in the sea."

Pushing himself up he frowned, "Sit down lass, 'afore ye fall down." He waved her to the edge of his bed.

Obediently, Raven walked over to the bed and sat on its edge, "I remember bein' a young girl and standin' in the sea."

Lifting a brow Duncan frowned, "I have lots of childhood memories, lass."

Raven shook her head, "I dinna have even one, well I dinna until now."

"*Cò às a tha sibh?*" Duncan asked with a raised brow.

"I dinna ken where I am from." Raven bowed her head.

"Where did Ian find ye?" Duncan spoke softly.

"The Brodie keep," she frowned in thought.

"Then yer a Brodie?" He raised a brow.

"Nay," she shook her head, "Three years ago, I washed up on the shore of the Brodie's lands, but I dinna ken anythin' 'afore I woke up in the Brodie keep." She looked in to his deep greyish-blue gaze. "Raven is nay even my real name. 'Tis the name the Brodie gave me, 'cause of my hair."

Duncan thought over what she had just told him. He couldn't imagine not knowing who he was for one day let alone three years. "'Tis a fittin' name, lass, verra bonnie."

She looked up at him and smiled weakly, "Dinna go and be kind to me, I might think ye like me."

"Dinna fear, lass," Duncan smiled, "I dinna like ye in the least." He reached out and tucked a strand of raven black hair behind her ear. "Until we figure out who ye are, yer a MacKinnon now." He paused for a moment then spoke, "Raven MacKinnon, seems fittin' as well."

Later as Raven sat eating her evening meal, Duncan glared at her, "Ye can nay expect a man to live on broth alone. I'm needin' real food if I'm to heal and leave this bed."

Raven stopped eating and walked over to him and laid her hand on his forehead, she noted that he was very warm and had a touch of fever. "I dinna mean to be cruel, but I can nay allow ye to have anythin' more now."

Duncan crossed his arms over his chest and growled at her, "I think ye mean to torment me."

Raven patted his head and laughed, "Dinna pout, 'tis unbecomin'."

A knock at the door interrupted her before she could go any further. Aidan MacKinnon poked his head in the door and smiled at the two of them.

Raven felt her jaw drop at the sight of the man as he strode into the room. He was beyond handsome. This man was a dark beautiful Fae. His eyes were silvery and his features looked as if the Gods had chiseled them in their own likeness and when he smiled, he stole her breath away. Just like the two MacKinnon brother's, he was tall and powerfully built and sheer male. How she had missed this man when she first arrived, she wasn't sure. She vaguely remembered him being in the room when she was trying to save Duncan. But she had been so focused on what she was doing that she had paid little heed to who was around her.

"Close yer mouth, lass," Duncan growled.

Aidan strutted into the room and stopped in front of Raven, "I dinna believe we've been properly introduced, lass." He bowed from the waist, "I am Aidan MacKinnon, cousin to this barbarian, and ye'd be?"

Raven held out her hand, "Raven," she said simply and tried to keep her knees from melting out from under her as he brushed a kiss over her knuckles.

Aidan looked in to her bluish-green eyes and felt that instant surge of power. He had never seen a more beautiful woman in all his life. "I wish to thank ye for savin', my cousin's life. As I dinna get a chance to do so the day ye arrived. If there is some boon I can grant ye to repay our debt, ye've but to ask."

45

"Oh, for the love of the Gods!" Duncan growled, "Get away from her, Aidan."

Aidan raised a brow, but before he could say anything, Raven drew his attention back to her, "If ye would nay mind, could ye sit with him for a few moments, while I seek out the garden robe? I must apologize as he is ornery and cantankerous."

Shrugging his shoulders, Aidan smiled, "He's always thus way." He walked over and sat in a chair near Duncan's bed, "Dinna fash yerself 'bout it, lass, I can handle him."

She looked from Duncan to Aidan and smiled, "Run him through if he can nay behave himself." She turned and walked to the door.

Duncan snorted behind her, "As if he could." When she left the chamber, and shut the door behind her, Duncan glared at his younger cousin. "As for ye lad, ye'll be keepin' yer hands off her. She does nay need yer lecherous self chasin' after her."

With his hands steepled Aidan looked at Duncan, "And tell me cousin, what 'tis between the two of ye that ye would warn me off."

"Aught," Duncan spoke flatly and looked away.

"Then she is fair game for tuppin'?" Aidan raised a brow in question.

"Nay!" Duncan growled as his gaze shot back to his cousin's. "Be warned and let it be ken, I will nay remain in this bed for long. If so much as a hair on her head is touched by another man, they will feel the bite of my sword."

With a grin, Aidan leaned forward in his chair, "So she is under yer protection then, aye?"

"Aye, ye blitherin' git." Duncan spat out as he sat up in the bed then swore a blue streak as the pain in his chest gripped him.

"Dinna fash yerself, cousin, I dinna plan to steal yer woman." Aidan laughed as Duncan spat a vicious oath at him in Gaelic. But Aidan could not help but to wonder how Raven would feel about this whole situation once she met Isobel.

Raven returned to find Duncan in an even fouler mood if that was at all possible, she thought rolling her eyes. When she checked his forehead for fever, she bit her lower lip.

"What makes ye bite yer lip, lass?" Duncan demanded surly.

"Ye've a fever again and it grows," she shook her head, "I need to try healin' ye once more."

He grabbed her arm and jerked her close to him, "I will nay allow it." He growled at her, "Look at ye, lass, yer still weak and tired from 'afore."

Raven raised her chin, "Dinna tell me how I feel, and dinna think I need ye to care for me." She tried to pull from his grip, but couldn't break it. "When yer brother comes, ye can tell him that ye've chosen to refuse my help. Now, let go of me boy-o, because yer hurtin' me."

Duncan let her go and glared, "I'll nay have ye hurtin' yerself to save me." She walked over and sat in the large chair, tucking her feet up under her, "As ye wish m'lord. I'll sit here and watch yer stubborn *arse* die. But remember if ye change yer mind, ye've only to call my name."

"Nay bloody likely." Duncan grumped and turned over in his bed. Sleep took him into the dark depths.

Raven sat there for hours and finally dozed off into fitful dreams, all of them revolved around Duncan. It was full nightfall before Raven woke with a start. She looked around the room and saw that the hearth was stone cold, and the room was chilly. Walking over to it she laid a fire from the kindling that was there.

The sound of Duncan thrashing around in his bed had her turning and rising. She took two steps toward him then stopped herself. He had told her he didn't want her to help him. Walking back to the chair, she sat back down and hugged her arms around her waist as she bowed her head. "Stupid fool," she hissed.

The castle was nearly settled for the night when Ian came to Duncan's chamber to check on him. When he walked in his heart froze at the sight of Raven sitting in the chair with her knees drawn up and her head resting on them. He rushed to her side and knelt, "Lass, what 'tis amiss?"

Raven lift her head and looked at him with tear filled eyes. "He forbade me from helpin' him."

Ian looked over to where his brother lay. Pushing to his feet he walked over and placed a hand on his brother's forehead and found it burning up. He looked back at Raven, "Ye must help him, lass."

Slowly, she shook her head, "I can nay." She wiped a tear from her cheek. "He forbade me."

"I dinna care what he forbade, I am Laird here." Ian growled and walked over to her taking her chin. "If he wishes to take it out on someone it can be me."

Raven closed her eyes, "I can nay unless he asks me to help him." She sighed, "I have tried to reach him, but he denies me."

Ian was furious as he strode away from her and to the bed where his brother lay. Looking down at him, Ian growled, "Damned stubborn fool, ask the woman for help blast ye." He wanted to shake his brother for his foolishness. He looked at Raven, "What can I do?"

Raven raised her chin, "Fetch me cold water." She pushed from the chair, "He may have forbidden my magick, but he dinna say I could nay help him through my knowledge of healin'." She walked over and pulled the covers off him.

Ian walked to the door and thought about the fact that he was sent to fetch water once more. On a tight grin, he walked out of the room and down the corridor heading to fetch the woman water.

After Ian had brought her fresh water, she began bathing Duncan's body in cool water continuously. Through the night, she fought the fever raging through Duncan's body. Hour after hour she would throw water out the window and get more. She kept the fire in the grate burning low and bathed his entire body.

Every time he murmured, she listened for her name, but it didn't come. She peeled back the dressing on his wound and winced as she saw the infection beginning to spread once more. All her hard work was being undone, she thought with a sigh.

Morning had dawned and still Duncan raged with fever, and still Raven fought it. Ian paced and raged at his brother as he lay in his bed wasting away. No matter how she tried, Duncan would not allow her to help him.

Through the day, she had herbs gathered to crush and mix into drinks, which they could get down Duncan's throat little by little.

By the next night, Ian took the cloth from Raven's hands and set it aside. She looked so exhausted. Ian swept her into his arms and walked her over to her pallet. Carefully, he laid her down and swept a lock of hair from her face. "Sleep lass, I'll stay with him."

Raven nodded slowly then grabbed Ian's hand, "Dinna let him die." She whispered, "If he grows worse, wake me?"

"Aye lass," Ian nodded solemnly. "For now, ye must sleep."

Raven nodded and before Ian made it back to Duncan's side she was fast asleep.

Raven looked around her and smiled, she knew this place. She wiggled her toes and felt the sand beneath her feet. Looking around she saw the sea bright and brilliant spread out as far as the eye could see. Up the beach she spied a cottage and slowly walked toward it.

As she got closer, Raven realized that she knew this place as well. It was her grandmother's cottage. On eager feet, she ran to the door. "Gram?" She called as she burst through the door. "Gram?"

"Aye child, I am here." The older woman turned from where she was cooking at the hearth. "'Tis about time ye've returned."

Raven stopped and looked around the beloved room. She could remember playing there as a child. She could remember hearing her grandmother's stories of the old days. Walking over to the old table, Raven ran her fingers over the scarred wooden table.

"Sit, sit child," her grandmother waved her to the table then came to sit across from her, "What took ye so long to return, little one?"

Raven looked at her, "I've been lost." She sighed then looked at her grandmother, "Gram, I dinna remember much about my life 'afore the last three years." Okay so that was a lie, she remembered nothing really.

"I see," the older woman smiled at her, "And ye've came here to seek out who ye are, or have ye come for advice on how to save yer man?"

Raven looked at the older woman for a long moment, "Can I nay have both?" She knew the answer to that even before the older woman shook her head.

"I can nay give ye both answers now, and some things ye must find out for yerself," her grandmother laughed softly. Raven had to admit that her grandmother didn't look very old. If anything, she looked to be no more than two or three score.

"And if I choose to learn who I am?" Raven forced the question.

"Aw, but that 'tis yer choice," her grandmother frowned, "But ken this, ye can nay find one without the other."

Raven looked in her green eyes and sighed, "I have to save him."

"Then I shall show ye what ye must do." The older woman smiled and stood. When Raven joined her, her grandmother cupped her cheek, "Perhaps, now ye'll find out who ye really are."

"I hope so." Raven let the older woman take her hand and lead her out of the cottage.

Five

Raven woke with a start, and looked around the room. Rolling over she looked at Duncan's bed and saw Ian sitting there in the chair next to his brother, with his head hung in exhaustion and sorrow in the early morning light.

Slowly, Raven rose and went to Duncan. Carefully, she laid his plaid upon the foot of his bed. Laying her hand upon his forehead, she felt the burning fever raging within him. Taking the cloth from Ian's hand, she began bathing him once more as she sat on the edge of the bed.

"I will try once more to heal him," Raven glanced over her shoulder to where Ian sat. "I make nay promises that he will allow me to help him."

"I beg of ye try, lass." Ian leaned forward in the chair imploring her to save his brother's life.

"Yer brother will nay be happy that I interfered where he dinna want me." Raven informed him, "Ye will swear to shield me from his wrath, aye?"

"Aye, I swear it to ye, lass." Ian went on bended knee in front of her and made his pledge. "Nay matter his wrath. I will take the blunt of it."

Raven inclined her head and set the rag aside. She climbed onto the bed then looked back at Ian, "When I have finished, ye shall remove me from this chamber and take me to the one ye've prepared for me."

"Aye lass," Ian suddenly had a bad feeling about what was to come. "One last thin', Laird," she looked in to his deep bluish-grey gaze that mirrored his brother's, "When ye place me in the chamber dinna allow him in the room with me, I dinna want him to feel the burden of guilt. For he denied me to do this."

Ian's stomach dropped away even as he inclined his head and gave his vow. He prayed to the Gods, he was making the right decision. As Raven turned back to Duncan, Ian reached out placing a hand on her arm. When her mystical eyes looked in to his, he felt uneasy about what he was asking her to do. "Tell me lass, can this kill ye?"

She raised a brow, "Aye, but if the Gods are kind, I shall live through it." With that said she turned back to her patient and began. Her small body glowed with the blue aura as power filled her. She chanted in a language older than any heard in the last millennium. The sound of the ocean waves pounding the shore increased and power surged through her.

Ian stood back and watched her, as the room grew dim except for Raven's ethereal glow. He prayed silently that this wouldn't cause her to lose her life. Lightening ripped across the sky as thunder shook the earth and the heavens erupted in sheets of driving rain.

Raven leaned over Duncan and pressed a kiss first to his forehead then to his lips. As she sat back up she lifted her face toward the heavens and chanted as she laid her hands on his chest. She felt it enter her, the vile sickness and the shadow of impending death.

Sweat broke out on her forehead and Ian clenched his jaw as he watched the darkness leave his brother's body and swirl around her. He wanted to snatch her away from it, but he knew it would do no good now.

She opened her arms and accepted the inky shadow that had filled Duncan's body. Giving a cry of pain, the darkness slammed into her. She swayed and began to collapse. Ian rushed to catch her in his arms.

Ian winced as he felt her body burning against him. Sweeping her into his arms, he carried her to the chamber next to Duncan's and laid her upon the bed. Quickly, he locked the door that connected the rooms from her side. In the hall, he bellowed for a servant to send for Aidan and two of his most trusted men.

Grabbing the basin of water from Duncan's room, he walked back to Raven's bedside and frowned down at her. With indecision ridding him, he finally called for a couple of the women in the castle to aid him in removing Raven's garments.

While the women dealt with Raven, Ian went to check on Duncan where he lay sleeping peacefully with Aidan standing guard over him. His fever was completely gone, and he looked as healthy as could be. Ian almost feared what would happen when his brother woke.

Aidan turned icy eyes on his cousin, "What did ye do?" He clenched his fists and frowned, "Did ye have her bargain with the devil to save him?"

Ian shook his head, "I dinna ken who the lass bargained with, but 'tis too late to undo this, now I must hope for the best." Ian scrubbed a hand over his face, "I have to keep him from her. I swore an oath to her that I would."

Aidan shook his head, "I would nay wish to be in yer boots when he awakens." He pushed from his chair and strode out the door, "Stay with him, while I see to, Raven." Aidan left the room closing the door behind him.

Ian sank into the chair near the bed and put his head in his hands as he thought over what he had done. Guilt assailed him and worry over Raven filled him.

The sound of Duncan's voice pulled him from his own personal berating.

Duncan's eyes fluttered open and he looked up at the ceiling, "Lass?" He looked around and spied his brother sitting in the chair and met his gaze.

"How do ye feel?" Ian stood up and walked over to Duncan.

"Strange," Duncan rubbed his forehead and frowned, "I had the strangest dream." He looked up at his brother and raised a brow, "Where 'tis the lass?"

"She's restin' in the next chamber." Ian looked away from his brother and cleared his throat, "Can I get ye a drink?"

"Aye," Duncan looked at his brother with suspicion. When Ian got up and poured him a mug of water, Duncan sat up and looked around the room. Something didn't sit well with him, but he was unsure of what it was.

Taking the mug that Ian offered him, Duncan drank down the contents. Setting the mug aside he threw back the covers and swung his legs over the side of the bed. He looked up at Ian, "I told the lass I would be fine. I dinna need her help."

Ian looked down at his younger brother and cursed. Walking over to the window he looked out then scrubbed his hand over his face once more. "She healed ye." Duncan's greyish-blue gaze roamed over his brother, as Ian stood with his head bent and his long black hair hanging down to cover his face.

"Where is she?" Duncan spoke softly and pushed himself up to stand. At first, he wobbled, but caught his balance. Looking at his brother he bellowed, "Where is she?" "Nay, where ye can see her." Ian turned to look at his brother. "I forbid ye to go near her." "Where is she?" Duncan gave his brother a hard look and started toward him, but a furious knock at Duncan's chamber door had him spinning and grabbing his plaid where it lay across the foot of his bed. Quickly, he donned it as Ian went to the door and opened it.

"Aye?" Ian raised a brow at the young woman standing there.

"Laird, his lordship Aidan bids ye to come at once." Her eyes darted to the door next to Duncan's.

"I am on my way," Ian turned back to his brother, "Ye must stay in yer chamber until Aidan returns to ye."

"Ye can nay keep me prisoner in my own home." Duncan's deep greyish-blue eyes held a hint of challenge and threat. "And ye can nay keep her from me."

"I can, and I will," Ian strode out the door and looked back at him, "Dinna try to defy me on this brother, for I made a vow to her." With that he shut the door and strode to Raven's door and stopped to have a word with the sentries standing guard. "Dinna allow my brother to pass this door, do ye understand me?" He would place two more men across the hall to ensure Duncan did not get in.

Entering Raven's room, he could see her laying on the bed her face pale and the sheen of sweat on her brow. Walking over to where Aidan sat on the bed bathing her forehead, Ian stopped and reached out a hand to feel her brow. "How is she?"

Aidan glared up at his cousin, "She grows worse with every minute." He bathed her forehead once more and tried to simmer his anger at his cousin. "I fear, she will nay make it through the night."

Ian and Aidan both looked up at the noise coming from the other side of the door. Duncan's roar could be heard and both men came to their feet.

"We will nay be able to keep him from seein' her." Aidan marched to the door and slipped through to help hold Duncan off.

Ian took the cloth from the basin and began bathing Raven's forehead once more. After a few minutes, he took her hand in his and held it. "I am sorry, lass." Ian looked at her, "I should nay have asked such a thin' of ye, 'twas wrong of me. I pray ye live and I can offer my apologizes, once more."

Duncan paced his room and raged as Aidan sat in the chair watching him. He was amazed that Duncan seemed so hearty after only hours before they thought he would die. Raven was amazing, he thought with a frown. Now if the Gods were kind they would allow her to live. Stopping his pacing Duncan growled, "Tell me what is happenin' to her." He looked at his cousin with wild eyes, "Tell me how she fares?"

Aidan sighed, "'Tis nay for me to tell ye. I am sorry, Duncan." He shook his head, "Ye'll have to speak with Ian, if yer seekin' information on the lass."

"Bloody hell!" He roared and headed for the door of his room. Going to the next chamber door Duncan growled at the guards, "Get out of my way, or so help me by the Gods, I shall retrieve my sword and run ye both through."

Greig blanched at his words, but Deacan frowned and spoke, "Duncan, we're just followin' yer brother's orders. If ye want to gain access to the room, ye'll have to speak with him." He glanced around, "If 'twere up to me, I'd open the door for ye myself."

Duncan blew out a breath and hung his head for a moment to calm down. Lifting his dark greyish-blue gaze to theirs he spoke softly, menacingly, "Tell the Laird, that I request an audience with his stubborn *arse* as soon as possible. And furthermore, the request is non-negotiable." With that he turned on his heels and headed back to his chamber and to where Aidan still sat.

Aidan raised a brow in question, but said not a word.

Pacing, Duncan stopped before his younger cousin, "I dinna need ye to babysit me."

"As ye wish," Aidan walked to the door and stopped to look back at Duncan, "But remember this, cousin. Ian did what was only natural. He would give anythin' to save ye, as ye would for him. Dinna think this is easy for him." With that Aidan left the chamber shutting the door softly behind him.

Walking to the window Duncan looked out at the sea and frowned. How was she? Was Raven even still alive? Why did Ian deny him to see her?

Question after question plagued his mind. Did Ian think he would hurt her? God's blood he'd never hurt a woman in his life, and he wasn't about to start now. What had it taken for her to cure him? What was she suffering because of him?

"Little fool," he spat as he turned from the window to pace the room once more, "Damn her for her interference!" His anger surged as he thought of what kind of hell she must be in.

At the same time, his anger was surging so were his worries. He wanted to see her with his own eyes to make sure she was still alive. He wanted to be there with her and let her know she could draw on his strength. Walking over to the door that connected the chambers, Duncan tried the door once more only to find that it remained locked. He had to see her, for himself.

Ian did not grant him an audience for nearly a week, but that also meant that Raven was alive, for Ian was with her nearly the entire time. Duncan kept watch on the chamber where Raven was ensconced. The few times the door was opened he tried to see within, but his view was always blocked by the guards Ian had stationed there to keep him out.

Duncan raged and ranted, but it did no good, Ian did not relent in the least. He refused to see him until he was ready. In the meantime, Ian stayed by Raven's side and worried over her condition, as she seemed to be holding on to life by a bare thread.

When at last, Ian agreed to see his brother, he was exhausted and beyond weary. Walking into Duncan's chamber, he looked at his brother's broad back as Duncan stood before the windows looking out at the sea. He was dressed in black trews, a white shirt and leather boots that laced up his calves. His plaid was fastened across one shoulder and around his waist.

"How is she?" Duncan spoke softly and tried to hide the rage that was simmering inside of him.

Ian sat in the chair and frowned down at his hands, "Nay well." He sighed and pushed out of the chair, "If I had ken what 'twould cost her, I would nay have allowed her to attempt it."

"I want to see her, Ian." Duncan spun around and gave his brother a hard look. "I need to see her."

"I can nay allow ye to." Ian walked over and stood before his brother, "'Tis nay my choice."

"Then by who's will..." Duncan growled angrily, and he paused, "Little fool." Anger built in him, pushing past Ian, he stormed from the room. Ian shook his head and wondered where his brother had gone. Sitting back down in the chair for a moment, Ian leaned his head back and closed his eyes.

When Duncan came back into the room, Ian's mouth dropped open as his brother held a battle axe. "And what do ye intend to do with that thin'?" When Duncan swung it, and struck the door that connected the two rooms, Ian started to laugh. "I guess I ken what 'tis for now."

"I'll be damned, if the wee hoyden will keep me from seein' her." Duncan swung the axe once more making a serious split down the center of the door.

"For God sakes, Duncan!" Ian growled getting up and striding over toward him.

"If ye dinna want to find an axe in yer skull stay back." Duncan growled and swung the axe with a powerful stroke once more splintering the door.

Ian reached out and caught his arm, "If yer goin' to take out yer anger on someone, it had damned well better be me."

"Oh, I am angry with ye, have nay thought of gettin' out of it," Duncan narrowed his eyes at his brother then turned to the door and ripped it out of his way.

"And ken that ye'll be repairin' that door." Ian shook his head and knew that nothing was going to stop his brother now.

Duncan was in a rage of fury as he stalked into the room. He drew up short as his gaze landed on the woman lying on the bed. She lay there in a ray of sunlight and looked ethereal. Walking slowly to the bed, he sat on its edge and laid a hand to her brow. 'She is burnin' with fever. How could she survive?' he thought, with anger and sadness filling him. "Bloody little fool." He brushed his knuckles down her silky soft cheek. Then he brushed a lock of hair from her forehead, '*she is so verra pale,*' he though sadly.

Reaching over he picked up the cloth and began bathing her in the cool water. He worked tirelessly to cool her burning skin and comfort her as he spoke softly to her.

Ian stood there for a while and watched his brother at his task. Though Duncan had always seemed gentle with women, he had never seen his brother care for one with such tenderness. On a sigh, Ian left the room and told the guards they were dismissed.

For a time, Duncan bathed her heated skin, but realized that she was still burning up. Standing he scooped her up in his arms and strode for his bedchamber. He felt the heat in her body radiating against him. '*How could a woman so small and fragile undergo such a tormentin' fever?*' He wondered.

Quickly, he laid her in his bed and left her with no covers. Taking his plaid off his shoulder and waist he covered her with it. Carefully, he settled the door between the chambers so that the portal was somewhat covered.

Returning to her side, he sat there and removed the tartan and began tenderly bathing her entire body. He took in her delicate, but beautiful features and knew he had to save her.

When Ian was alerted that Raven was removed from her chambers, he went to Duncan's door and knocked. He waited patiently until Duncan answered. When his brother opened the door, and stood there blocking the way Ian growled, "Do ye have her in there?"

"Aye," Duncan narrowed his gaze, "And I'll nay allow ye to remove her from here." He knew it was wrong, but he threw the barb on the end of his tongue anyhow, "Gods ken ye've done enough to harm the wee lass."

Ian jerked back as if he had been slapped. Slowly, he lowered his gaze from his brother, "I did what I thought 'twas best."

"Ye did what was selfish..."

"Aye, but yer standin' here, are ye nay?" Ian growled and clenched his fists.

Duncan was quiet for a long moment, "Aye, but at what cost, brother?" He turned back to go into his room.

"Forgive me, Duncan," Ian laid a hand on his brother's shoulder. "If I could undo what wrong I've done, I would."

Duncan grasped his brother's shoulder, "I ken," with that he pulled away, "But she is my responsibility now." He closed the door and went back to her side.

For two days, he bathed her body until exhaustion dragged at him. He lay on the bed next to Raven and held her, as she lay there wrapped in only his plaid. He brushed his lips over her burning forehead and whispered to her softly in Gaelic.

Sleep claimed him quickly as he held her tucked into him. That was how Ian found them when he came to bring Duncan his evening meal. He looked at the pair and realized that Raven fit his brother perfectly as if she was made for him. He prayed to the Gods that she made it through this.

Leaving the two alone, Ian set the try aside in case Duncan woke.

The surf rolled across the sand of the beach as Duncan stood watching the woman sitting at the edge of the sand as far away from the water as possible, looking out over the surf. Her deep black hair shone with blue highlights it was so dark. Walking over to her, he settled on the sand next to her.

Raven turned her head and looked at him, "How did ye find me?"

Duncan shrugged his massive shoulders, "I dinna ken lass, I ended up here."

"This is nay real, 'tis the Aslin'," she shook her head, "But I dinna brin' ye here." She searched his face as he reached out and ran a hand over her dark head then played with the ends of her hair.

"Tell me how to help ye, lass." Duncan reached out and touched her cheek.

"Are ye nay angry with me?" Raven raised a brow in question. "Are ye nay furious with me for interferin'?"

"Of course, I am angry, and ye need a sound spankin' for nay listenin' to me." He laughed at her scowl, "but right now, I dinna care 'bout any of that. Ye saved my life, lass. Now tell me how to help ye."

Raven stood up and held out a hand, "Walk with me a bit, highlander." She spoke simply. When he took her hand, stood then brought her small hand to his mouth, she smiled.

Six

Duncan woke with a start and felt Raven jerking in his arms. He climbed off the bed and felt his heart constrict as he realized if he didn't act quickly she would die. Scooping her off the bed, wrapping her in his tartan, he strode from his chambers and through the castle.

Ian quickly caught up to him in the castle proper. "What the bloody hell do ye think yer doin'?" He strode next to his brother matching his long strides.

"I'm savin' her life." Duncan growled as he turned toward the beach. His strides ate up the ground quickly. Raven was feather light in his arms.

"And just how do ye plan to accomplish that?" Ian jogged in front of him and stopped him.

"Get out of my way," Duncan growled, "I have nay time to explain myself to ye." He tried to step around Ian, but his brother stepped in his way once more. "Damn ye Ian, will ye let her die?" Duncan raged at him.

Ian narrowed his eyes, "If I allow ye to pass, then ye had better explain yerself on yer way to wherever the bloody hell yer goin'."

Duncan inclined his head and Ian stepped out of the way, waving him along. Knowing that time was scant he jogged along the path that led to the sea. "She's dyin'," he spoke flatly, "And if I tell ye how I ken to help her, ye must nay think me bent in the head."

Ian looked at his younger brother, then at the woman in his arms. "After what I have seen of this woman, ye've nay worries."

Duncan inclined his head. "I spoke with her in a dream."

"A dream?" Ian raised a brow.

"Aye, 'tis nay the first time that she has come to me in one," Duncan looked at his brother for a second. "When I was sick, she came to me from time to time as ye brought her to me."

Ian nodded his head, "I have seen her do it." He laughed softly, "She scared me witless the first time she did."

Duncan looked down at the woman in his arms, "She's slippin' away from me."

It was the look upon his brother's face that had Ian growling, "Then go, for Gods sake go."

It was all the encouragement he needed, Duncan began to run toward the sea. As he hit the beach, he sprinted into the water with her cradled against his chest. "Hold on, Raven, just hold on." He wadded thigh high and looked down at her.

Her face was ashen and her body lifeless. Looking at her, his heart stopped for a minute. She was not breathing. He put his ear to her mouth and knew he would not hear her breathing. Wading to his hips he gave a roar filled with rage and sorrow. He hugged her to him even as her hair floated around him, "'Tis nay fair!" His heart constricted at the thought of her death.

"Give her back to me!" He demanded as he looked at the heavens above.

Suddenly, the sea began to churn and pound around him. He stood, but the waves knocked him backward several steps at a time as if to spit him out of the sea. Waves beat at him until finally one snatched Raven from his hands. He fumbled for her, but he lost her in the water.

"Damn ye!" He screamed at the sea around him. He dove under water several times trying in vain to find her. He burst from the cold water for the tenth time and was exhausted. Slowly, he made his way from the sea and lay on the beach looking up at the sky as pain filled him. He threw his arm over his eyes and felt the loss of her rip through him. He had no clue how long he lay there until he heard his brother whisper, "Holy hell."

Duncan looked from Ian to where his brother was looking. The sunlight was so bright he couldn't see at first. A million diamonds sparkling on the sea blinded him, but then as he watched they became a backdrop for a small woman wrapped in his tartan. His heart thumped in his chest. 'It could nay be.' I can nay believe it!' Duncan thought, with his mind whirling.

As she made her way to the shore, he stood and strode over to her. Raven walked out of the sea and straight to him, her brows furrowed. "Duncan?"

"Aye, lass," he cupped her face in his large hands and leaned down to brush a tender kiss across her lips. When he straightened, and released her, her knees buckled. He swept her up into his arms.

"Ye're wet," she leaned her head on his shoulder.

"Aye, lass." He could nay believe she had come back to him. "We're both wet."

"Ye need to change yer clothin' 'afore ye catch sick once more." She spoke softly as she fell asleep with her head leaned on his shoulder.

Duncan threw back his head and laughed at her then pressed a kiss to her temple. "I'll take care of us both, lass, nay worries."

Ian followed Duncan back to the castle and watched him take her into his chambers and slam the door shut behind them. For a long moment, he stood there looking at the door, then a smile crossed his lips. It would appear, that his brother, the mighty warrior, had been swept off his feet by one little woman. With a mirthful laugh, he walked off to find Aidan and share the good news.

Carefully, Duncan laid Raven on the pallet by the hearth. Quickly, he started a fire then unwrapped her from the soaking wet plaid. Grabbing some linens, from his clothing chest, he began drying her carefully. He paid meticulous attention to her hair. Once she was well dried, he stood and stripped off his own clothing. Grabbing the quilt that graced his bed, he brought it over and lay down with her.

Ever so gently, he slipped his arms around her and held her to him to share his body heat with her. The feel of her cradled against him made his loins begin to ache with need. He tried to push the thoughts of her naked body away from his mind, but it was useless. As carefully as possible he ran his fingers through her dark silken hair to dry it, and free it of tangles. He watched the shiny ebony strands slip through his fingers over and over as the firelight shone off it.

Once her hair was almost dry, Duncan lay back and pulled her to him. He had to admit she felt good wrapped in his arms, almost as if she belonged there.

The room was dark except for the small dying flames and glowing embers of the fire. Raven felt warm and secure as she snuggled deep into the warmth surrounding her. She took a deep breath and smelled... Duncan? Her eyes flew open and she looked at the man lying there surrounding her. For a moment, she stared at him with her mouth hanging open.

She was lying there with him and they were both very much naked! Had they...? Could they have...? She swallowed hard. If they had made love, and she dinna remember it, what a shame, she thought as she looked at Duncan's beautiful body.

Feeling a moment of braveness, she reached out to touch him then pulled back. Quickly, she looked up at his face and breathed a sigh of relief to see him sleeping peacefully. Biting her lower lip, she tentatively reached out and traced her fingers over the muscles of his chest and marveled at the feel of him. The thin cover of hair that was on his chest was silky and it led to the narrow strip that disappeared down to his groin. She traced his shoulder and his chest then began to follow the trail of hair leading to his manhood. When she reached his navel, her wrist was caught in his strong hand.

"I would stop there, lass," Duncan warned in a husky voice, "If ye go explorin' further ye'll find that there's more there than ye bargained for."

She looked up into his beautiful greyish-blue gaze, "How long have ye been awake?"

He gave her an arrogant grin, "Long enough to enjoy yer touch." Duncan brought her hand to his mouth and pressed a kiss into her palm, then closed her fingers over it.

"Ye should have told me ye were awake." She furrowed her brows in frustration.

"Would ye have stopped touchin' me?"

"Aye," she flushed at the memory of her intimate exploration of him.

"Then 'twas best I said aught." He laughed at her when she thumped him on the chest then he rolled her under him capturing her hands and pulling them over her head. He looked down into her ethereal face and knew he had to kiss her, to taste her once more.

"Let go of me," she spoke breathlessly. The feel of his body pressed against hers started her body tingling. It made her nipples bud and her breasts ache. Between her thighs, she felt the fires of lust pooling and begging to be fanned, or put out.

Duncan looked down into her mystical bluish-green gaze and felt the familiar pull. "Nay lass," he grinned, "Nay until I satisfy my curiosity."

"What curiosity?" She raised a brow.

"If ye taste as good in real life, as ye do in my dreams." He lowered his head and captured her lips with his before she could respond. She tasted like heaven, he thought as the fire she had started while touching him, exploded in him. He changed the kiss from innocent to demanding as he changed the angle and deepened the kiss.

Raven's mind blanked at the feel of his lips on hers. She was swept away in a tide of feeling and ecstasy. The air around them crackled with electricity and it ran a current between them. She whimpered as his tongue swept across the seam of her lips, and when she opened for him, he thrust his tongue deep within the cavern of her mouth. She could feel his hard, throbbing sex pressed against her belly and she felt wicked for wanting him inside of her, deep inside of her.

She couldn't stop herself from writhing under him as he freed her hands and roamed one of his giant hands over her lithe body. Hunger for this man beat at her.

Duncan had meant to merely taste her, but the fire in him that burned for her, quickly raged out of control. He wanted this woman with every fiber of his being. His sex was throbbing for her and here she was writhing under him. His hand cupped her sumptuous breast and kneaded. He caught her moan in his mouth as he reveled in the taste of her. His hand slid down her flat stomach, to cup her woman's mound and she cried out as his fingers slipped within her silken folds to find her tiny nub of desire.

As he touched her and stroked her, Raven felt the pressure build in her until she was sure she would die from it. His thumb circled her tiny pearl of desire and she felt herself slipping into ecstasy.

Duncan left her mouth and pulled back to watch her shatter as her orgasm ripped through her. When she cried out his name, he felt himself fall just a little bit more. It was a great feeling to ken he'd given his woman pleasure, he thought as he looked in to her passion filled eyes. When his fingers slid down to encircle her entrance, he reveled in the feel of her.

At first, he didn't realize she was speaking to him, then he looked at her as she spoke to him again. He furrowed a brow, as he listened to her.

"*Gura mie ayd,*" she spoke softly as she brushed her fingers through his thick dark hair as she looked in to his greyish-blue eyes and smiled.

"What did you say?" He knew it was Gaelic, but he couldn't place the dialect.

"I said thank you," she smiled softly.

"What dialect of Gaelic was that, lass?" Duncan traced her cheek, "'Tis nay familiar to me."

Raven thought back over what she had said, and she couldn't remember what she had said exactly, just that she was thanking him for the pleasure he was giving her. That familiar ache in her head came as she tried to remember. Putting a hand to her forehead, she rubbed and hissed at the pain of trying to remember.

Duncan pulled her hand away and pressed a kiss to her temple, "'Tis nay important right now, lass." He moved off her and pulled her to a sitting position. "How do ye feel?"

"Besides a slight ache in my head, I am well." She held the blanket up to cover her breasts. She looked at him sitting there on his hunches and blushed as she looked away. Duncan laughed and rose from the pallet. He walked boldly over to the chest and grabbed another plaid out of it and wrapped himself up in it with expert skill. Now dressed in a kilt with his legs and chest bare, he grabbed one of his shirts and brought it over to her.

Kneeling next to her, he placed a hand to her forehead and was relieved to find it cool and her eyes bright from something other than sickness. "Ye must be famished."

Raven smiled shyly, "Aye, verra." She placed a hand over her stomach. "I can nay remember the last time I ate."

"Yer far too thin, lass." Duncan moved behind her and began plaiting her hair. He ran his fingers through it to help with any knots he had missed earlier, or created since they had awakened. When he was finished, he handed her the braid and got up. Walking to his chest again he pulled a tie from it and walked back. Carefully, he tied the end of the braid in a strip of leather to keep it back.

Raven looked over her shoulder at him. "*Tapadh leat*," she spoke gently in Scottish Gaelic as she thanked him.

"Yer welcome," he pressed a kiss to the top of her head. "Now, I'll go raid the larder and find us a bite to eat." He gently laid her back down and covered her up.

When Duncan was almost to the door Raven stopped him, "Duncan?"

"Aye lass?" He looked back at her as she lay there in front of the fire.

"Ye remembered me from yer dreams?" She looked at him with open curiosity.

"Aye lass," with that he left the room and her to contemplate the fact that he remembered her and the *Dreaming* where she had taken him to do her healing.

Raven wasn't sure how he remembered, but that he did was for certain. No one had ever remembered her healings before. She had to wonder if this meant something special. She could always remember what happened in the *Asling*, she even remembered him coming there to find her when she was sick.

She sat up quickly, as the memory assailed her. How had he gotten into the *Dreaming*? It was not something mere humans could do! That thought brought her pause, as she realized that, if she knew in the back of her mind that mere humans could not enter the *Asling* without aid, and what did that make her? She buried her face in her hands. Still after so long, she had no clue as to who or what, she was.

With a sigh, she lay back down and watched the flames leap in the hearth and thought about the man whose chambers she was in. After a while she got up and donned the shirt he had left her.

The shirt was huge on her and made her realize the size difference between her and Duncan even more. Raven would guess that while she had been sick, she had lost an entire stone. She rolled the sleeves as far as she could to make her hands show and still the neck of the shirt hung down to show the cleavage between her breasts. With a sigh, she figured there was naught to do about it.

Climbing back into their makeshift bed she waited another ten minutes for Duncan to come back. When he did, the feast he had brought with him astounded her. There was bread and cheese, wine and ale. He had a fresh plum in the mix and cold meats. When he showed her the sweetmeats he had pilfered, she was ecstatic.

Raven ate nearly half the loaf of bread and half the cheese he had taken from the kitchen, then she drank two cups of wine. She sat cross-legged on the pallet eating the juicy plum as she talked. "What do ye remember of the dreams, when I healed ye?"

Duncan watched a bit of plum juice slip down her chin and her finger come up to catch it. When she stuck her fingers in her mouth to suck the plumb juice off, he thought he would die. Gods help him, how he wanted to lick the sweet plum nectar off her chin and suckle it off her finger. He tried to focus on the discussion instead of how the plum juice would taste on the skin of her belly. "I remembered bits and pieces at first, but more as ye got closer."

She frowned and took another bite of her plum, and he nearly groaned. "I dinna understand it. Nay one remembers the *Aslin'*, or if they do 'tis vague and shadowy."

"Is that what 'tis called?" He leaned over and took the plum from her and granted himself a bite of it.

"Aye," she furrowed her brows, "I dinna ken how I remember this, but I do." Raven took the plum back and bit it then slowly licked her lips, "If I try to remember my head aches somethin atrocious."

"Then dinna push yerself, lass." Duncan watched that tongue dart out again and swipe at the juice of the plum and he was so hard, he was sure he would expire tonight with wanting her. However, in the kitchen he had spent the entire time lecturing himself that he could not have her tonight, or any night soon. At least until he was sure she was healed.

"But I want to remember so badly." She looked at him then smiled, "Do ye ken since I have come here, I have remembered more than the whole three years I was with clan Brodie."

"Then yer in the right place." He reached out and wiped the juice from her chin and lower lip then raised his finger to his mouth and suckled the juice off. The taste of sweet plum and sweet woman mixed to delight him.

Raven blushed and looked away. "Yer verra bold." To the best of her knowledge, she had never known a man in the womanly way.

"Dinna fash yerself, lass, I would never do anythin' ye dinna wish me too." His eyes held a hungry predatory look as he gazed at her. "I would only give ye pleasure, never pain."

She raised her chin, "And if I tell ye I dinna want ye to touch me?"

"Then I would ken ye were lyin' to me." Duncan laughed at her. "And how would ye come to such a conclusion?" She looked at him crossly.

"Because yer body and yer eyes say somethin' much different than yer mouth." He laughed at her affronted gasp.

Seven

Raven walked down to the beach and sat on the edge of the sand as far away from the water as possible. She watched it sparkle in the sunlight, but shivered as a wave crested and crashed on the shore.

Seagulls cried out as they wheeled around in the bright blue sky. For a time, she watched them swoop and circle. Some landed on the beach near her and others flew out to sea.

For a moment, Raven wondered what it would be like to be as free as those birds. She wondered where she would go and what she would get to see. The world she decided, she would see the world if she had the chance.

After a while she lay back in the sand and let the sun warm her. Closing her eyes, she dozed off. She had no clue how long she was napping until a shadow fell over her blocking out the sun.

She looked up at the enormous highlander standing over her. Shading her eyes, she smiled, "What brings ye out here?"

Duncan knelt next to her, "Ye." He spoke simply. "I returned to find ye gone." He frowned at her, "Are ye sure yer well enough to be out here?" He touched his hand to her forehead.

Raven laughed at him, "I am perfectly fine." She pushed his hand away. "Dinna be such a mother hen."

Duncan sat next to her and looked out at the sea. "Have ye remembered anymore 'bout yer past?" He glanced at her as she lay there with the sun shining down upon her.

She shook her head, "Nay." Raven had hopes of finding out who she was, but there was too much confusion in her mind. "I had hoped that while I was here, I would remember more." She shrugged then looked out over the sea.

Duncan stood up and held his hand out to her, "Walk with me?"

Raven hesitated as she looked from him to the sea and back to him. She slipped her hand in his and let him pull her to her feet.

They walked hand in hand for a few minutes as the sound of the sea played around them. The wind tugged at Raven's hair pulling it from her braid. Black ribbons of hair slipped across her face and waved in the air around her.

Duncan had yet to give her back her hand and she reveled in the warmth of his large hand around hers. Though the day was balmy the sea breeze was just a tad cool. Raven shivered as a particularly hard blast of air came off the water and rained the sea spray over them. Duncan immediately turned and blocked her from the spray.

Reaching out as the wind died down, he cupped her chin and ran his thumb over her cheek to wipe the water from the spray away. "Are ye all right, lass?"

"I'm fine," she looked up at him with her big bluish-green eyes and smiled softly, "I'm nay that fragile."

He smiled broadly down at her, "Yer a mite of a thing, lass." With that he turned them and they resumed their walk.

They were quiet for so long that Raven wondered if they would talk at all. She was nearly startled when Duncan broke the silence between them.

"How long do ye plan to stay, lass?" He didn't look at her, but kept his gaze straight out ahead of them. Raven shook her dark head, "I dinna ken." She sighed, "I have nay where else to go, yet I ken that I must find out where my past lays."

For a long moment, his dark greyish-blue gaze met her mystic one, "Where do ye think it may lay?"

Raven shrugged, "I dinna ken, but I feel as if there are pieces to the puzzle layin' all around me."

"Then we'll put those pieces together," he raised her hand to his lips and brushed a kiss over her knuckles.

Raven felt the electrical current from that kiss all the way to her toes. Looking in to his beautiful gaze she felt the connection between them. Never had a man affected her in such a way, making her want and need. She felt him pull her closer and saw him lower his head. Her eyes drifted shut as his lips brushed over hers. The taste of him exploded within her as he deepened the kiss.

Duncan felt drunk with the taste of her. She was like the sweetest of wines and he longed to go on sipping of her, forever. She was addicting. The sound of laughter had Duncan pulling back. A growl emanated from his throat as one of his MacKinnon brethren and one of the maids from the castle came into view. He set Raven from him and stepped in front of her so that she was blocked from the intruders' view.

The young MacKinnon came to a halt and looked at Duncan with something akin to fear. "I beg yer pardon, m'lord." Greig swallowed visibly. The young woman next to him hid behind Greig's shoulder and peeked at Duncan.

"Ceana," Duncan raised a brow, "I dinna believe yer Da would approve of ye bein' out here with Greig." He glared sharply, "I suggest ye hightail it back to yer Da's home."

"Aye m'lord," Ceana bobbed a quick curtsy then turned and raced back down the trail leading toward the castle.

"'Twas nay how it looked, m'lord." Greig looked beseechingly at Duncan. "I had nay intention of dishonorin' her."

"If ye had nay intention, then ye would have sought permission from her Da to walk with her out here." Duncan growled, "Ye shall return to the garrison and stay within yer quarters until I give ye leave."

"Aye," the young man bowed his head and turned to hurry toward the castle, but Duncan's next words had his mouth hanging open.

"I hope ye have intentions of doin' right by Ceana." Duncan crossed his arms over his chest and sent the lad a look that broke no argument. "Off with ye," he waved the younger man off and was relieved when he was out of sight.

Raven stood there glaring up at Duncan as he turned toward her. "Dinna ye think ye were just a tad hard on 'em both?"

He looked down at the tiny woman, "Nay in the least."

She crossed her arms over her chest pushing her lovely little breasts up higher as she readied herself to take him to task. "Ye scared the lad half out of his wits.

Could ye nay see the way the boy looked at her? He loves her, ye big oaf." She tapped her tiny foot as she looked up at him glaringly. "And who are ye to lecture 'em?" She thumped him on the chest, "Here yer kissin' me then rake their hides over the coals."

Never had a woman since his Mam taken him to task over anything. Not even his cousin's wife Kandra, who could match his prowess with a blade and stood no more than a head shorter than he, had taken him to task. And yet here Raven who was neigh on half his size was spitting fire at him and nary a speck of fear showed in those bonnie eyes, he thought. He threw back his head and roared with laughter.

"So ye think to laugh at me, boy-o," she hit him in the stomach as hard as she could when her temper got the best of her. Her tiny fist hit his hard, muscled stomach and bounced off. With indignation, she kicked him in the shin.

Duncan swore viciously and stopped laughing as he hopped around on one leg glaring at her. "Why'd ye go and do that for?" "Because yer an *arse*." She put her hands on her hips and glared, "How dare ye laugh at me!" With that she stomped back down the path leading to the castle.

The evening meal was ready to be served when Aidan escorted Raven into the great hall and to Ian's table. He seated her between Ian and himself and ignored Duncan's heated glare.

Raven enjoyed her meal and conversation with Ian. She completely ignored Duncan as he sat there glowering at her. It was a waste of time, she thought angrily, to care what he thought of her.

The meal was delicious and when it was concluding she nearly choked as a tall willowy blonde strutted over to Duncan and draped herself over him.

Duncan smiled fondly at the woman, "Isobel, my sweet." He pulled her into his lap and kissed her soundly.

Raven turned her head away in disgust. She focused on what Aidan was saying to her. "I will need to venture out and see if I can find the plants I am needin'."

"If ye would nay mind the company, I would be honored to guide ye through MacKinnon lands in search of 'em." Aidan smiled brightly at her. At Duncan's glower, he only smiled harder at Raven then picked up her hand and placed a soft kiss to her knuckles.

"I would welcome a guide," Raven smiled shyly at Aidan. She didn't even spare a glance at Duncan as Aidan stood and pulled her to her feet.

"Then let us begin yer list of needs and desires, lass." He led her away from the table aware the entire time of his cousin's gaze that followed them.

Duncan was seething with anger. The woman in his lap was beginning to sound like a yapping little dog as she begged for his attention. Looking down at Isobel he frowned.

She ran a finger over his lips then pressed a kiss to his pouting mouth, "I have missed ye greatly my lover." Isobel pressed her well-endowed breasts against his chest then nibbled on his ear lobe, "I will await ye in yer chambers if 'tis yer wish."

Duncan pulled away from her and looked down at her for a long moment. Isobel was beautiful and wanton. She was everything a man could want. "Aye, 'twould please me greatly." He set her off his lap and waved her away. He would slate his appetites with Isobel and that little hoyden Raven would not fire his blood so badly, any longer.

Ian watched Isobel sashay off and shook his head, "I would nay wish to be in yer place when Raven finds out who Isobel is."

Duncan shrugged, "I have nay care what the witch thinks." He looked at his brother, "She is aught to me."

Ian gave a snort and clapped his brother on the shoulder. "Lie to someone who will believe ye, little brother." With that Ian stood and made his way from the great hall. He planned to have a word with Aidan to make sure that his young cousin had all his wits about him. Ian wouldn't relish the thought of telling his cousin Lachlan, Aidan's older brother, why Duncan had run Aidan through. As was his habit, Ian turned and headed for the outer bailey wall.

Raven walked next to Aidan as they entered the inner bailey. She looked at the handsome Scotsman. His long black hair flowed down over his muscular back all the way to his magnificent *arse*. His powerful muscles rippled as he moved, the twin silver bands around his arms held ancient Celtic designs that were a be spelled to invoke courage and protection in battle. For a quick moment, Raven wondered if he knew what those symbols represented, but she brushed it aside.

Aidan flashed her a smile and nearly laughed at her aghast look at being caught staring at him. He shook his dark head, "Dinna fash lass, yer nay the first nor the last woman to look me over." The man was more than comfortable with his beauty. In fact, he gloried in it and how it drove women to want him.

No matter how desirable Aidan MacKinnon was, Raven was more attracted to another fine specimen of the MacKinnon males. Duncan was beyond handsome, she thought with a small smile. "I was nay looking at ye, I was thinkin'."

Aidan raised a brow, "And just what were ye thinkin', lass?" He laughed as a blush crept up her cheeks. "I have the feelin' 'twas nay me ye were contemplatin' 'bout." He stopped and ran his knuckles over her cheek.

Raven blushed and cast her gaze to the ground, then kindling her anger she looked at Aidan with fire burning in the depth of her gaze, "Hang the man, he's nay but an infuriatin' *arse*."

Aidan threw back his head and laughed, "Yer a tough one, Raven, and mayhap the perfect woman to brin' my cousin to heel." He held out his arm to her, "And I'll do my best to help ye alon' yer way."

Raven looked up at the man she was walking with, she couldn't help but to wonder what was in it for Aidan, but before she could ask, Ian strode out of the dark to meet them.

"A word with ye cousin," Ian looked his cousin over as Raven held onto his arm.

"We were on our way to visit the outer bailey walls and have a look at the stars." Aidan flashed a smile at his cousin.

"I would have that word with ye, now." Ian looked from Aidan to Raven, "If ye dinna mind, lass, 'tis imperative that I speak with Aidan."

Raven inclined her head, "Of course, Ian." She turned and looked up at Aidan, "I will see ye on the morrow."

Aidan stroked his knuckles down her cheek, "I can nay wait until the morrow." He released her hand and watched her walk away. Turning to his cousin he smiled, "Ye've requested a word?" He raised a brow.

"Aye," Ian turned and waved his cousin to follow him.

Raven had barely made it in the keep before Duncan fell in step with her, "Ye'll stay away from my lecherous cousin, lass."

Raven stopped and glared up at him as she poked his chest, "Dinna be thinkin' ye can tell me who I can and can nay be around, Duncan MacKinnon." She snarled, "Yer nay my keeper, boyo." With that she turned to stalk away, but he caught her arm and spun her back toward him.

The momentum spun her into him and he locked his arms around her to keep her from falling. He looked down into her enraged face, "Ye will obey me on this, lass."

"Ye'll release me immediately," she growled at him.

Duncan looked down into her beautiful face and felt the need in him grow for this woman, "And if I refuse?" He leaned his head forward and caught her lips in a soft teasing kisses.

"I'll... scream... like... a... *beansidhe*." She spoke the words between his kisses. "Stop...Kissin'...Me!!!" She growled up at him.

Duncan pulled back and looked down at her for a long moment, and smiled, "Ye mean a *cointeach*?"

"That's what I said ye arrogant *arse*," Raven snarled at him. "Have ye never heard of her, she'll herald yer death." She gave him a threatening glare, "And if ye nay let me go, I'll raise the roof with my screamin'."

Duncan looked at her upturned chin as a challenge, he moved them next to the staircase leading to the solar and reached behind him. When the hidden doorway swung open, he moved the two of them inside of it. The door swung closed behind them as inky darkness surrounded them. "Start yer screamin ye little *cointeach*, nay one will hear ye."

Raven pulled out of his arms and stumbled backward, she would have fallen if it had not been for Duncan grasping her arm.

"Careful with ye lass, ye'll break yer fool neck if yer nay careful." He grinned in the darkness as she threw a few choice words his way. "Where have ye taken me, ye great brute?" Raven thumped her knuckles against his chest. She looked in to the solid darkness and couldn't see a thing.

"We're in the secret passageway." Duncan informed her. Taking her hand, he began leading her down the stone steps.

As they descended farther and farther down the curving stairway, Raven could hear the sea pounding against the rocks. She surmised they were well below the castle. She could feel the cool stonewall beneath her fingertips as she traced the wall and Duncan led the way.

"Have a care, lass, 'tis the last step." He carefully guided her. They walked across a smooth stone floor. Duncan stopped them and turned toward her, "Dinna move, lass, I shall light a torch."

He let go of her hand and for a quick moment fear surged through her, "Duncan?" she groped in the dark for him as the sound of rushing water and darkness engulfed her.

"Dinna fash lass, I'm here," he took her hand once more and brought it to his lips. Softly he brushed a kiss over her knuckles. "I've got to let go of yer hand long enough to light the torch. Will ye be all right?" He was so close to her she could feel the heat coming off his body.

Raven swallowed her fear and hugged herself as Duncan released her and quickly lit the torch. As the blaze from the fire cast the cavern in a soft warm glow, she gasped as she looked at the water rushing in and out of the cavern just feet from her. She backed up a step from the dark swirling water as fear clutched at her.

Duncan lit two more torches that were held in wall brackets and it helped to light the area in a warm glow. He stuck the torch in his hand into one of the empty wall scones. Turning to look at Raven he saw the intense fear wavering in her eyes as she stared at the water.

In two strides he reached her, "What's amiss, lass?" He ran his hands up and down her arms. "Are ye nay goin' to still scream like a *banshee*?"

Raven looked up into his hypnotic gaze and tried to push aside her fear. "Why did ye brin' me here?"

"Because lass, if ye were goin' to scream like a banshee, 'twould be a place where nay one could hear ye." He grinned at her, "Scream all ye like, but aught will hear ye, but me."

Raven felt the anger surge through her, "Yer arrogance kens nay bounds!" She turned on her heels and headed for the stairs. She hadn't made it two steps before Duncan caught up to her.

Grabbing her arm, he spun her around to face him. "Dinna walk away from me, Raven."

She kicked at him, but he avoided her foot easily this time. Glaring up at him, she spoke tersely, "Let go of me ye big oaf, ye have nay right to tell me what to do."

He quickly backed her against the wall, "I have every right." He crowded her smaller body with his larger one.

Narrowing her eyes at him, she hissed, "I'm nay yer 'hore, if ye wish to command someone go find her."

"Isobel 'tis my leman, nay a 'hore." Duncan frowned.

"Call her what ye wish, but I am nay yer leman nor yer 'hore to command. I am aught to ye." Raven glared up at him even as the pain of knowing he saw her no different than he saw any other woman, lanced through her. "Now, leave me be."

"As ye wish, lass." Duncan released Raven and stepped back. When she turned, and stomped up the stone stairs, he followed behind. Reaching the door, he tripped the mechanism and let the door pop open. He placed a hand on her shoulder and stopped her from pushing the door open, "Hold a moment, I must make certain nay one 'tis around." Carefully, Duncan looked in to the hall and sighed with relief, "'Tis clear." He swung the door open and watched her march through it, her long black hair swaying around her hips.

Raven didn't turn back. She kept her head held high and strode to the stairs. For a moment, she paused and looked back at Duncan standing there. He was a gloriously handsome highlander with his long dark, deep mahogany hair that flowed over his shoulders. His body rippled with muscle as he moved, and she knew that even in sleep his body emanated raw power. At neigh on six and a half feet tall he was a man among men. His deep greyish-blue eyes could capture a woman's heart and soul, keeping them for eternity and beyond. Pulling her gaze from his, Raven walked up the stairs and sought refuge in her chambers.

Duncan felt the anger within him, damnable woman was more problems than she was worth. He had seen the hurt in her eyes and it'd flared his anger.

What did the woman think, that one woman could sate his lust? He would never be happy with just one woman. Even when he married and begot his wife with bairns he would keep his leman.

In a foul mood, Duncan closed the hidden door and made his way to his room. As he had instructed, Isobel was awaiting him in his chambers. He locked the door behind him as he watched her rise from the bed with just a sheer piece of material wrapped around her. He could clearly see her sumptuous breasts in the firelight and her blonde curls at the apex of her thighs.

As she sashayed up to him and wound her arms around his neck, Duncan pulled her into him and captured her mouth in a savage kiss.

When at last he released her, Isobel smiled seductively, "I've missed ye, lover." She pulled his head back down and kissed him once more. The witch had not managed to steal her man, Isobel thought smugly.

Eight

Raven woke in the strange room, and looked around. There was no fire burning in the hearth and she had no clue how long she had been sleeping, but she was sure it hadn't been more than a couple of hours.

Memories of the previous night came crushing in on her and she choked back her tears. Duncan MacKinnon was a horse's arse, she thought. She had laid there in her bed for nearly on two hours, listening to the sounds from Duncan and his whore, in Duncan's chambers. When at last she could no longer stand the thumping, banging, and cursing. She had fled her room and run as far as she could until she found a quiet chamber to sleep in.

Sitting up gingerly, Raven looked at the plaid she had wrapped around herself. She buried her nose in it and smelled the familiar scent of nature and man imprinted in it. One tear escaped and coursed down her cheek before she caught it. She refused to cry over a man as arrogant as Duncan MacKinnon.

Swinging her legs over the edge of the bed, she decided she had too many important things to do to waste her time on the man. Wrapping the plaid around her shoulders, she made her way back to her chambers and prepared herself for the day ahead.

Dressed in a pale blue gown, Raven quickly plaited her hair and tied a piece of leather around the end to hold it. Knowing she was late for meeting Aidan, she raced through the corridors and down the stairs into the hall. Going to the great hall, she spied Aidan straddling a bench talking to another young man. Walking over she smiled brightly, "Good 'morrow, gentlemen." She bobbed a quick curtsy.

Aidan smiled brightly, "Good morn', lass." He eyed her, but kept his survey to himself. She had dark smudges under her eyes. She looked pale and drawn, and it worried him. He waved to a serving wench summonsing her over. "What will ye have to break yer fast this morn' before we set out upon our quest?"

The serving wench came over and kept her gaze lowered as she waited for Raven to tell her what she wanted. Raven slid onto the bench beside Aidan and smiled, "Just a bit of toasted bread would do nicely and some watered wine, thank ye."

Aidan frowned down at Raven, "Ye can nay survive on such meager beginnin's." He shook his dark head, "Thank goodness I've seen fit to have us a lunch packed, lass."

Raven shook her head, "I am sure toast seems meager to ye, but for this morn' 'twill do me nicely."

She laughed at him, "That and a bit of jam will be plenty, besides I am afraid I have made us verra late."

Aidan took her tiny hand in his and smiled, "I would wait for ye lass, even if ye took until the noon meal to rise." He winked at her then brushed a kiss over her knuckles.

Raven felt her breath catch at the sight of him,

Aidan MacKinnon was the devil's own enticement. "Get on with ye, Aidan, ye'd wait for any woman."

She snatched her hand back and laughed at him.

"Ye wound me, lass." Aidan pressed a hand over his heart. "And here I was tryin' to treat ye as if, yer special."

Raising a brow Raven pointed to a young girl chasing after a hound, "I am nay more special than that wee lass there," she swung her finger over to point to an elderly woman who sat mending by the fire, "Or that grandmother there."

Aidan looked at her seriously, "But ye are, lass," he gave her a long look, "And well ye ken it."

Just then Raven's bread and jam arrived. The young maid nearly threw it down in front of Raven and left as fast as her feet would carry her. Raven sighed and began spreading jam onto her bread.

Looking at her then at the fleeing young woman, he growled harshly, "What 'twas that 'bout?"

Raven laughed softly, "Nay one wants to be too close to the witch." She shook her head and laid a hand upon his arm as he made to get up and go after the young woman, "Let off it, Aidan, does nay bother me."

"'Tis ignorance." He could not stand for anyone to be treated so wrongly by people who knew nothing about her.

"Aye," she looked at him and smiled, "but 'tis ignorant fear, and I am sorely used to it."

Aidan took her hand in his and pressed a kiss to her knuckles, "Ye should nay be treated in such a manner."

Neither one saw the man standing across the room with his fists clenched and grinding his teeth in anger. With a curse, Duncan spun on his heels and left the great hall.

Raven walked through the woods and examined many different plants. She muttered to herself as she picked and harvested what she needed. When they came to a willow tree near a stream she was overjoyed. "I need yer dirk." She held out her hand impatiently.

Reluctantly, Aidan pulled his dirk from the sheath at his waist and handed it to her. It looked so large in her tiny hand that he nearly took it away from her. "Be careful," he warned sternly.

He walked over and sat on a large rock as she carefully removed a bit of bark here and a bit of bark there. Aidan watched her work and smiled, "What are ye doin'?"

"I'm lookin' for spots where the willow is givin' up its bark for us to use." Raven flashed a bright smile over her shoulder at him, "I use the willow bark for healin'."

"Well, I'm hungry," Aidan pulled a sack of food out of the bag he was carrying. Next, he pulled his extra tartan from the bag and began setting out their lunch.

Raven gave the willow a bit of water to thank it for its offering and headed over to where Aidan was sitting on the blanket. They had been walking for hours and Raven was famished. She sat on the plaid Aidan had laid out and ran her hand over it. "The MacKinnon tartan 'tis beautiful."

"Aye," he smiled at her, "We have various tartans for various occasions, but this one 'tis my favorite."

Raven examined the colorful red tartan that was weaved with green, blue and white. The pattern was gorgeous. She looked up at Aidan and smiled. "I would love to see the other patterns," she wondered for a moment, as she looked down at the colorful plaid, what Duncan would look like in other colored tartans. Pushing that thought aside, she looked back at Aidan as he handed her a piece of roasted chicken.

The chicken was tasty, and she ate with vigor. When Aidan handed her berries, and produced cheese and bread, she was thrilled. Raven ate until she was stuffed, then laughed when Aidan ate the share of her food that she couldn't finish.

Aidan flashed her a boyish grin, "I am a growin' lad." He professed innocently.

"If ye grow anymore, ye'll touch the sky." She laughed, "Ye and yer kin are all giants to me." Shaking her head, she laid back and looked up at the blue sky. "I've always wanted to touch the sky."

Aidan leaned on his elbow and looked down at her, Raven was beyond beautiful, a man would be hard pressed not to fall in love with her. Her looks alone could bring a man to his knees, but once he got to know her, he would realize that Raven was amazing. She was warm, caring and loving, no matter what kind of *arse* a man made of himself. If Aidan were going to be honest with himself, he would fancy himself a wee bit in love with the woman. That thought brought a smile to his lips as he looked at Raven laying there with the sun shining down on her, her eyes closed and a serene smile gracing her full mouth.

Raven cracked open her eyes and looked up at Aidan, "What are ye grinnin' 'bout?" She searched his eyes and saw the seriousness there.

"Yer verra bonnie, lass." Aidan smiled boyishly, "But there is aught more beautiful than a woman in love, or one carrying a man's bairn." He reached over and swept a strand of hair off her cheek.

Raven felt the knot in the pit of her stomach. Slowly, she ran her tongue over her suddenly dry lips, as she thought of what to say to this man. Aidan MacKinnon was beyond handsome. In fact, she wouldn't at all be surprised if there was *Tuatha De Danann* in his bloodline somewhere. "I...I'm nay in love."

He reached out caressing her cheek with the back of his knuckles, "But ye are, lass," he leaned down closer to her, "I can see it in yer eyes. Yer in love with my *arse* of a cousin."

She shook her head slightly. "He's an arrogant *arse*, who is of nay concern to me any longer." She stuck her nose in the air. "If the *Ankou* himself was after Duncan, I would turn a blind eye and allow his soul to be taken."

Aidan pulled back and laughed heartily, "Yer nay much of a liar, lass." Quickly, he stood up and held his hand out to her, "What do ye say we continue on our way?"

Raven placed her hand in his and let him pull her to her feet. As she went to help Aidan take care of their picnic, he waved her off to collect her plants and herbs. Picking up the basket he had provided for her, she set out looking for passionflower or Life-everlasting for sleeping droughts.

Slowly, she made her way through the forest examining plants. As she was carefully harvesting the leaves from a Life-everlasting plant a shadow fell over her. Smiling she looked up, but just as quickly the smile died on her lips.

"Look what I've found, lads, 'tis a wee wood nymph." The man was tall and broad like the MacKinnon men, but he had dark red hair. He reached down grabbing hold of her arm pulling her up and against his large body. "What's yer name woman?"

"R...R...Raven...Raven MacKinnon," She looked in the man's brown gaze and felt fear race through her at the cruelty she saw there.

"She's a MacKinnon, lads." He looked over his shoulder at his three men and laughed. The sound sickened her. "I say we have a bit of sport with her, Aye?"

"Release me," she demanded as she glared at him, raising her chin haughtily.

"And if I dinna release ye?" He leaned down to put his face close to hers.

"Ye'll regret it when Duncan, Ian and Aidan, get hold of yer sorry *arses*." She hissed furiously with fake bravado.

"And just what are ye to them, lass?" He raised a brow.

"I am Duncan's woman." She let the lie roll off her tongue easily. "He will show ye nay mercy if ye harm me."

"Duncan MacKinnon's woman, aye?" He cupped her chin in his hand, "Then I'll have the pleasure of beddin' ye, and makin' ye my 'hore."

When Raven kicked him in the shin he bellowed in anger then drew back and slapped her across the face, knocking her to the ground. Raven lay there dazed by the blow. She cried out in pain as the brute grabbed her by the hair and hauled her to her feet.

"Unhand her!" Aidan roared as he stepped out from behind a large tree. "Unhand her, or I'll see ye in hell, MacLean." His claymore was in his hand and he was ready to kill all of them if needs be, or die trying.

"Ye think ye can take all four of us?" Baoithein MacLean laughed at him.

A dagger came out of nowhere and stuck into one of the MacLean's chest and dropped him to the ground. Baoithein stopped laughing and growled, "Show yerself MacKinnon!"

Duncan stepped out into the open, "I think the odds just got a bit better." He growled at Baoithein and the two remaining MacLean men behind him. "Release her now, yer trespassin' upon MacKinnon lands and upon my woman's person."

Baoithein pulled a knife and wrapped his arm around Raven's waist. He rubbed his cheek against her hair and ran the flat of the knife along her cheek, "Perhaps, I fancy her mine now." He laughed as she flinched away.

Raven looked at Duncan with sheer fear in her eyes and silently pleaded for him to help her. When her captor reached up a hand and squeezed her breast painfully enough to make her cry out Raven tried to bolt away from him. He grabbed her by the hair and she screamed as he dragged her back to him. "Please let me go, please." She fought him as utter terror filled her.

For the first time that he could remember, Duncan felt true fear and not for himself, but for Raven. He had to save her, but first he and Aidan had to dispatch the two remaining MacLeans. Glancing at Aidan who nodded they engaged the MacLeans as Baoithein drug Raven off kicking and screaming.

The skies overhead darkened and lightening flashed across the heavens as thunder boomed and lightening flashed across the sky. The wind began to whip as all hell began to break lose.

Panic settled over Raven as the man struck her several times with the back of his hand driving her to the ground. Twice she managed to slip out of his hands and started to run, but between her wet sodden dress and the man's sheer size it allowed him to catch her.

When he threw her on the ground and covered her smaller body with his own, Raven fought with all her strength, but had little effect upon him. She tried to call about her magick but could not summons it. Her captor grabbed her hands and held them as he quickly bound them, then he tore the front of her gown baring her breasts to him. With cruel and painful hands, he groped her. Tears blinded her as she struck him over and over with her bound hands.

The sound of Ravens screams had Duncan's heart pounding with fear and he couldn't stay focused on the fight at hand. Anger surged through him, when she screamed for him. Twice the MacLean he was engaging got in a good swipe with his sword.

When Aidan gave a cry of victory and came to assist him, Duncan growled, "Ye deal with this bastard, I'm goin after, Baoithein." Aidan smiled and nodded as he engaged the MacLean with relish.

Duncan raced through the woods as fast as his legs would carry him, as he leapt over fallen logs and rocks. He followed the sound of Raven's cries. He spied them not but a few feet ahead of him. With a roar of rage, he saw that the damned MacLean had her skirts pushed up to her waist and her bodice ripped open to his groping hands.

Raven struck her attacker in the face with her hands, but it had little effect. As he leaned down to put his mouth to her breast again, he was suddenly flying off the top of her. She gave a cry of relief and tried to move away as she watched Duncan pummel the other man in a fury of rage.

The only thought in Duncan's head was to kill the MacLean bastard that would dare to touch Raven. His fists were raw and bloody by the time Aidan grabbed hold of him. Rage lit his eyes as he looked upon his younger cousin. It was the sound of Raven's sobs that brought him out of his rage.

He released Baoithein and quickly stood. Slowly, he walked over to Raven, where she sat with her head on her up drawn knees rocking and sobbing. Carefully, he knelt beside her and ran a gentle hand over her dark head, "Aww lass, yer safe now."

Raven looked up at him with teary eyes and flinched when he pulled her into his arms and onto his lap. When his arms closed around her protectively, she sobbed her heart out.

Duncan held her close to his heart and rocked her asshe cried. He pressed kisses to her dark head and spoke soothing words to her in Gaelic. Before long the sobs turned to sniffles, carefully he lifted her chin and surveyed the damage. The sight of her split lip and bruised face had the rage roaring through him once more.

When Aidan knelt beside them his eyes were full of sorrow, "Raven lass, I am so verra sorry. I should nay have let ye outta my sight." Slowly, he took her bound hands and cut them free with his dagger. Raven was exhausted and in pain. She laid her head, on Duncan's shoulder, "'Twas nay yer fault, Aidan." She spoke softly then bit her lip and hissed in pain. She opened her eyes as Duncan pushed her away from him and quickly removed his extra tartan from the satchel he was carrying. When he wrapped her in it carefully, she snuggled into the familiar warmth and scent it held.

Aidan stood and looked down at his older cousin as he sat there holding Raven to him. The fool was besotted, Aidan thought with a small grin. He sobered and held out his arms, "Let me carry her back to the castle."

Duncan's greyish-blue gaze shot up to Aidan's, "I dinna think so." He growled as he carefully stood with the woman securely in his arms. "Retrieve my dagger and deal with things here. I shall see to Raven."

They had been walking for about ten minutes when Raven though exhausted, looked up into Duncan's handsome face, "I can walk." He said not a word, but continued, on their way. She sighed then frowned up at him. "Put me down, Duncan." She commanded.

He stopped and looked down into her battered face, "Nay lass, I shall put ye down when yer safe within the confines of my chambers." He continued walking through the forest. At least now the storm had died down, he thought with a frown. Both remained quiet until they reached the castle.

As they entered the keep, Ian appeared before them. "What the bloody hell happened?" Ian demanded as he strode alongside Duncan.

"Raven was set upon by MacLean's that were trespassin'." Duncan growled, "Aidan and I dispatched of them, but ye may wish to send out a party to help Aidan." Duncan took the steps two at a time heading to the solar. "Ye'll find them about oneand a half league to the west of here near the border."

He stopped in front of his chamber door and raised a brow at his brother.

Ian sighed and opened the door for him, "Dinna ye think she would be more comfortable with a woman tendin' to her?"

"I shall tend her." Duncan walked over and carefully set Raven upon his large bed. He turned to his brother and glared. "I killed, Baoithein MacLean."

Ian let several oaths fill the air, then ran a hand through his long hair, "His father will be livid," he looked at Raven, "But the bastard was trespassin' upon more than just our lands, he trespassed against one of our women. That deserves death." He looked at his brother, "I will inform his father of his crimes and we'll deal with this." With that he turned and left the room.

Duncan turned back to Raven where she lay on his bed. Walking over he stroked a gentle hand down over her cheek, "How are ye farin', lass?"

Gingerly, she sat up and swung her legs off the bed, "I want to go to my own chamber." She would have gotten off the bed, but his large hand stopped her.

"Nay lass, ye need to be looked after." He carefully removed his tartan from around her and helped her stand. With gentle hands, he removed her ripped and torn clothing until she stood before him naked.

Duncan surveyed the damage until she covered herself with her hands. Wrapping her back in his tartan he set her back on the bed and knelt before her, "How 'bout a bath?"

Raven looked down at her hands and nodded her head. She hated to see that look in Duncan's eyes. It bordered on pity, but also held disgust and contempt. She swallowed hard as he rose and went to his chamber door to bellow for a servant to bring up heated bath water and wine.

He, himself set out the large wooden tub by the fire. When the servants brought the water, he stopped them at the door of his chamber and retrieved the buckets himself, to fill the tub. Once the tub was set to his satisfaction, he walked back to the bed and removed the plaid from around her and scooped her up in his arms.

Deftly, he placed her in the tub and picked up the cloth to wash her. Raven said not a word as he washed her body and her hair. When he let her soak in the warm water and brought her a goblet of wine, she drank it down quickly and held it out for more. She sipped the sweet wine and stared into the fire before the tub, lost in thought, as a storm rumbled off in the distance.

When the water grew tepid, Duncan lifted her from it and wrapped her in the bath sheet. Taking her to the bed, he dried her thoroughly then dried her hair with another bath sheet. Carefully, he laid her upon the bed and grabbed a tin of salve, made with Life-everlasting, willow, and rosemary. As gently as he could he began treating her bruises and scratches with the balm. There were angry scratches on her breast and arms. The bruises were on her face, and neck. As Duncan looked her over, he noticed a scratch on the inside of her thigh and stared at it for a long moment then looked up into her face. "Did he..." He spoke harshly making her flinch. Duncan closed his eyes and tried for clam. "Tell me lass, did he touch..." the words wouldn't come out.

Raven couldn't hold back her tears as she rolled onto her side and curled into a ball. Her sobs were silent as she remembered the feel of his hands touching her.

Duncan sat on the bed and stroked her hair. When he pulled her into his arms, he rocked her once more. "Hush lass, ye must tell me, did he enter ye?"

Slowly, Raven looked up at him with tears running down her face and Duncan knew he had never seen such a heartbreaking sight. He leaned down and kissed her tears away. Slowly, she pulled back from him. "He touched me, but he was unable to do more, because ye saved me," she spoke hoarsely. Reaching up she cupped his face in her small hands then pressed a kiss to his mouth, "Thank ye, Duncan."

Duncan brushed a kiss over her lips tenderly once more then pulled back. He didn't want to frighten her with his own lust. He looked, into her tired bluish-green gaze, "Ye need some rest, lass." Carefully, he tucked her into his bed.

When she reached out for him, he linked his fingers with hers and looked in to her beautiful eyes as she spoke, "Please dinna leave me alone."

He pressed a kiss to her palm then crawled into the
bed with her and held her until she fell asleep.

Nine

Raven could feel his hands on her again digging into her flesh and ripping at her clothing. His breath was foul and teeth painful as they bit her breast. She struggled to get away from him, but he was too big, and she was not strong enough. She screamed and screamed for Duncan, but he wouldn't help her this time.

Duncan woke to Raven in the throes of a nightmare. He held her to him as he tried to calm her, "I'm here Raven, I'll nay let anyone harm ye." He stroked her back and her hair. He felt her hot tears on his chest and his heart tore at her agony. "Raven love, wake up. Yer dreamin' 'tis nay real, sweetin'." He shook her slightly. "Wake up for me, love." When she began to calm, he looked in to her tear, filled gaze. "Yer all right love, I'm here." He pulled her to him as she began to sob uncontrollably.

When her tears subsided, he lifted her chin and kissed her wet cheeks, "Better?" He asked gently.

She nodded hesitantly, "I want to forget, what happened." Raven looked in to his deep greyish-blue eyes. "Please Duncan, make me forget." She kissed his hand then moved closer, and kissed his chest.

Duncan hissed out a breath, at the feel of her lips on his skin. His hands ached to fill themselves with her and his hardened manhood throbbed to be inside of her. But he knew she would regret it in the morning if he took her. Gritting his teeth, he looked down into her beautiful face. Slowly, he traced the line of her nose and brows, then her jaw. He would dim the nightmare and lay a sweet memory over the top of it. He gently pressed a kiss to the end of her pert little nose then to her forehead as he whispered, "Are ye sure this is what ye want, lass?"

"Aye," she ran her hands over his broad shoulders and relished the feel of him touching her.

Duncan growled deep in his throat. He would pay hell to keep from taking her, and he would be in hell after he touched her intimately. However, the price of it was worth it, if it meant it would dim the nightmare for her. He captured her mouth in a searing kiss as he gently ran his fingers over her cheek and down her throat. When his fingers grazed her breast, she stiffened, "Hush lass, I'll nay harm ye."

Raven relaxed as he swirled his fingertips over her skin making her tingle everywhere he touched. When his hand brushed her other breast, she didn't stiffen, instead she wove her fingers through Duncan's silken hair and brought his mouth to meet hers again.

Duncan caressed her and stroked her. He toyed gently with her nipples, bringing them to hardened peaks. Dipping his head, he lightly ran his tongue over one taunt nipple, and heard her gasp in pleasure. He lavished attention to both of her breasts equally. His mouth suckled, and his tongue caressed as his hands enticed her body.

Raven watched everything he did to her as she wanted to focus on him, and drive the nightmare away. She watched his mouth move over her breasts and his tongue flick her nipple and she laughed. This man could never be monster enough to harm a woman and she reveled in the feeling of him touching her.

The sound of her soft laugh was music to his ears. He looked up at her and flashed her a wicked grin, "Are ye ready to touch heaven, lass?"

Raven raised a brow, then grinned when she felt his own rumbling laugh against her belly. Then she felt the heat of his lips scorching a path across her stomach, his tongue flicked into her navel and she felt the pool of need deep within her.

When he moved down and tried to spread her thighs she resisted at first. Duncan looked up at her, "Trust me, lass." Reluctantly, she allowed him to part her creamy white thighs.

She gasped as he pressed kisses to the inside of her thigh and swirled his tongue around the soft skin there. He nibbled, and he toyed with her driving her wild, but for what she didn't know. All she knew was that she wanted more.

Duncan bent his head and placed a kiss to her dark woman's mound and laughed as she pushed at his shoulders. When his tongue parted her soft feminine folds she gasped, and grabbed his hair trying to pull him away. When he ran his tongue over her tiny jewel she moaned in pleasure. Soon her fingers were woven through his dark locks and braids, but instead of pushing him away she was pulling him closer.

Raven had never felt anything so decadent, so amazingly wonderful. The feel of him tasting her, and his tongue doing amazingly, sensuous, magickal things had her arching up to meet his mouth and the coil of heat inside her winding tighter and tighter. She bit her lower lip and whimpered as she tried not to scream in pleasure.

Duncan could sense her struggle to withhold her climax. Gently, he pressed a finger, then two inside her tight sheath. He drove her higher and higher, until at last she had no choice, but to allow her release. The sound of his name on her lips nearly drove him over the edge of reason. For a second, he thought about moving up her body, and thrusting himself deep within her, but sanity won out.

Raven felt the explosion of pleasure rip through her as she cried his name. White lights burst behind her eyes and she truly touched heaven. When at last she came back to earth, she was panting and spent. Her body was boneless and malleable.

It took a couple of moments to notice that Duncan was lying next to her. She could feel the tension in his body. Slowly, she rolled over and looked at him, he was beautiful, she thought as she reached over and traced his cheekbone. "'Twas amazin'." She smiled. When her fingers went down over his chest, she could feel the muscle bunch and coil, and that excited her.

As her hand slipped lower, he caught her wrist. "Nay lass, 'tis nay a good idea." He looked at her, his eyes nearly as harsh as his voice. By bare threads, he was holding on to his sanity. Turning he pushed the blanket between them then turned her back to his chest and spooned her to him.

"But Duncan..."

"Hush lass, go to sleep, now." He pressed a kiss to her temple then tucked her under his chin.

It wasn't long before she drifted into a confused, but sated sleep.

Duncan woke to an empty bed, and looked around his chamber, but there was no sign of Raven except his tartan folded neatly over the end of the bed. 'It took him nigh on half the day to find the blasted woman. It was as if she was avoiding him.' He thought mulishly. Aidan had finally told him, she was sitting in one of the torrent rooms on the window seat. Sure enough, that was where he found her hiding out. Her knees drawn up and her arms rested atop them as she looked out at the churning sea.

Raven knew the moment he entered the room, but she didn't want to look at him and see the same thing she had seen the day before. She could handle the sadness, but pity and disgust were not things she could cope with right now.

Duncan cleared his throat then walked into the room and sat on the edge of the seat, "How are ye this day, lass?"

"Fine," she frowned at the discontented sea.

Slowly, Duncan reached out capturing her chin forcing her to look at him. He looked at her and surveyed the bruises and her split lip. Anger filled him once more. He wanted to take away her pain, but he didn't know how to. He couldn't abide her sadness.

Suddenly, an idea came to him and he smiled, "I dinna want such a thing to happen to ye ever again, lass." He told her firmly. "So, I am goin' to teach ye to defend yerself."

Raven pulled her chin away from him, "Dinna jest." She laid her head on her knees again and sighed forlornly.

Duncan stood and growled at her, "First thin' on the morrow, we begin yer lessons." When she only looked up at him dispassionately, he smiled wickedly down at her, "I'll teach ye lass, have nay doubt, size means aught. I ken a woman who can nigh on best me with a sword."

Raven raised her brow, "Who is she?"

"Kandra MacKinnon," he grinned in thought of the woman, "Aidan's brother's wife." Though Kandra was more than a foot taller than Raven, it didn't mean Raven couldn't learn to defend herself.

"Surely ye jest." She shook her head, "How could a woman hold her own in a sword fight with ye?" The thought intrigued her. And she would dearly love to be able to defend herself, but she didn't see how it could happen.

"She may be smaller than I, but where she lacks size and strength, she makes up for it in agility and skill."

He promised her then sat back down and took her hand, "I swear to ye, Raven, what happened yesterday, shall never happen to ye again. After I am through with ye, ye'll be able to fight back."

Raven looked at him for a long moment then slowly she inclined her head. "I'll try." Duncan released her hand and cupped her face, he pressed a kiss to the top of her head and stood once more, "Then we begin on the morrow." With that he strode from the room and sought out the black smith.

Raven was in the herb garden near the kitchen attending some of the plants when Isobel stalked over to her. She glared down at Raven, "I ken what yer doin' witch, and I'll have none of it."

Looking up into Isobel's face Raven frowned, "Just what am I doin'?"

"Yer tryin' to bewitch Duncan away from me." She accused Raven, "I warn ye witch, I shall have none of it. If ye dinna stay away from what 'tis mine, I shall make ye verra sorry."

Raven felt the anger in her bubble up, "Dinna threaten me." She spat at Isobel.

"Ye may have been in his bed last eve, but I have always been his favorite." She shoved Raven, "He will lose interest in ye, witch."

Raven doubled her fists, "Dinna touch me, ye filthy 'hore." She shouted back at Isobel.

"'hore!" Isobel screeched and went to push Raven again, but Raven punched her.

Suddenly, they were on the ground rolling around, hitting, scratching and screaming at each other. Raven wasn't about to bow down from this woman. As quickly as the fight started, Raven was plucked off Isobel.

Strong hands held her to kept her from leaping back on Isobel and tearing her hair out. She looked up at Ian and growled, "Let me go, I'm nay finished with the filthy 'hore." She fought his hold.

Duncan had hold of Isobel who was screeching about how Raven had attacked her. When he gathered her against him and walked off with her, the fight went out of Raven. She sagged back against Ian.

"Are ye all right, lass?" Ian turned her to look at her. He picked a couple of leaves from her hair and then smiled down at her when she merely nodded. "I should reward ye for knockin' Isobel around."

When Raven looked up at him in surprise he laughed, "Between ye and me I can nay abide the woman. I've wanted to throttle her many a times." Putting an arm around Raven's shoulders Ian walked her back into the keep.

The next morning, Raven woke to Duncan rummaging through her room and her clothing, "What are ye doin'? Have ye gone addle in the head?" The sun wasn't even up yet. She had, had another restless night because she had seen Isobel slip into his chambers when she herself had been heading for bed. She had lain awake most of the night listening to the sounds coming from Duncan's room.

Duncan grumbled as he looked at piece after piece of her clothing and discarded it. "Dinna ye have a single pair of trews, lass?" He looked over his shoulder at her for the first time. "Never mind," he threw a gown of dark green at her, "Wear this for now, I'll see to it ye have a pair, or two of 'em made for ye." With that he stomped out of her room then reopened the door, "Be lively lass, meet me in the courtyard in ten minutes."

Raven dropped back on her pillow and groaned, "The man's insane!" She threw an arm over her eyes. After a couple of minutes Raven threw back the covers and grabbed the gown Duncan had tossed to her.

Nearly ready for the day, Raven grumbled her way through the castle and out into the courtyard. In the gray morning light, Duncan paced and cursed. So, he was in a foul temper as well, she thought smugly. She stopped a few feet away and crossed her arms under her breasts. "Are ye deranged, ye git?"

Duncan stopped pacing and looked at her standing there in the green gown, with annoyance filling her lithe little body. Her eyes snapped beautifully with anger. Her loose hair blew in the light breeze and her arms crossed under her magnificent breasts made his loins ache. Though she looked beautiful, she was at her most glorious when she was truly annoyed with him. "Perhaps, but if I am, 'tis women who drive me addle brained." He held out his hand to her, "Come lass, I've a surprise for ye."

With a sigh, Raven walked over and placed her hand in his. She hated to admit how good her hand fit in his and how wonderful it felt. She allowed him to lead her to a nearby bench. He picked up a long cloth wrapped package and handed it to her. Sitting on the bench, Raven carefully unwrapped it, and looked down at the claymore in her lap. Carefully, she traced her fingers over the shiny metal. There was an engraving down the blade in Latin. Slowly, she read the inscription. It read *'Audentes Fortuna Juvat'*, translating the inscribed words they read, *'Fortune Assists the Daring'*. Her eyes met his in question.

"'Tis our clan motto," He ran his fingers over the etchings, "Turn it over."

She turned the blade, and thought she would cry as she saw her name etched there. 'Raven MacKinnon' ran down the length of the blade. "'Tis mine?"

"Aye lass, I had it crafted for ye." He sat down beside her, and placed her hand on the hilt of the sword wrapping her fingers around it. "'Tis light weight and 'tis smaller than my own claymore, but designed to look like it." Carefully, he pulled his own claymore from its sheath on his back. He held it out for her to examine.

Her sword was nigh on half the size of his and narrower, she thought, but as he had said it looked identical to his own, except their names. The sword was not as light as he proclaimed, "I can nay imagine how heavy yers is. Mine 'tis heavy enough."

Duncan laughed, "That's because ye've nay built up yer sword arm, but soon 'twill weigh nay more than a feather." He stood and held his hand out to her. "What do ye say we go put it to use?"

At first Raven could barely lift the sword. After Duncan had shown her how to hold it and how to stand, he dealt her a couple of practice blows. Both times the sword flew out of her hands and her finger stung from the contact. "I dinna ken that was how it was meant to happen."

"Ye just need to build up yer sword arm and learn to hang onto the thin'." Duncan grinned then laughed at her. "Perhaps we should work on something else for a time." He took the sword from her hand and placed it back into the cloth it had been wrapped in. "Come lass, let us take a walk."

They made their way out of the castle and to the field beyond. When they reached an old oak tree, Duncan stopped and looked up at the tall tree.

Pulling his dirk from the sheath at his waist he flipped the knife so that he held it by the blade. "'Twas here that my own father taught me and my brother to throw our daggers with deadly aim, when I was just a wee lad." He grinned, "Though I do believe this tree has gotten a bit wider, since then."

Raven had her doubts on this, but she was willing to try if Duncan was willing to teach her. She walked about ten feet from the tree and watched Duncan as he threw the knife at the tree and hit it dead center. He pulled the knife from the trunk and brought it to her. Demonstrating several times, he showed her how to hold the knife and how to release it. Her first attempt ended up at her feet and she squeaked as she jumped back. Four of her other tries ended up in the dirt a few feet away.

"Ye need to release it thus," Duncan tried to demonstrate, when she threw the knife and did no better, he sighed and picked it up. Stepping behind her, he placed the knife in her hand and wrapped his arms around her to demonstrate what he was speaking of. "Ye must release the knife, at this point, lass." He stopped her where she would need to release the dagger. Going through the motions a couple more times he had her release the knife on the third try. It flew just below the base of the tree and stuck in the ground. "Now, ye try it on yer own, lass."

Raven picked up the knife and went back to where she had been standing. With the blade of the dirk in her hand, she took a deep breath and threw the knife at the tree. Her mouth hung open when it struck the trunk and bounced off. She looked at Duncan who was smiling, "I hit the tree!" She clapped her hands bouncing up and down happily.

"Aye, lass." Duncan retrieved the knife and gave it back to her. "Try it once more, but this time see it going into the tree and sticking." He stepped back, "And give it a little more power, lass."

Taking aim once more, Raven took a deep breath and visualized the knife going into the tree trunk. Pulling her arm back, she threw the knife and watched it fly and stick into the tree for a moment then wobble and fall out. "I did it," she cheered herself, "Well only for a moment, but I did it."

Duncan stroked a hand over her shiny black hair and smiled, "Aye, lass. Ye did well." Taking her hand, he brought it to his lips and brushed a kiss in the center of her palm.

Her smile faded, as she saw the hunger in his greyish-blue eyes. She would not allow this man to seduce her again. Duncan wanted more than his due, he wanted her and his leman, and that, Raven would not accept. She would not allow him liberties again. Slowly, she pulled her hand from him and turned away. She walked over picking up the dagger. With anger swirling through her, she walked back to her place where she had been throwing the knife from, this time she hit the tree and the knife stuck.

Duncan had a bad feeling when he saw the knife stick into the tree and stay. Anger swirled in the depths of Raven's mystical gaze and somehow, he was sure it had to do with him.

Ten

For a whole week, Raven had gotten up before the sun to work with Duncan on her sword skills, and her knife throwing. In between those two, he taught her how to fight.

"All right lass, we'll give it a go." Duncan walked up behind her and grabbed her.

As Raven felt his hands slip around her waist, she wanted to snuggle back into him, instead of fight with him. She thought of what he had taught her and didn't see how it would work against a man as large as Duncan. Then she thought of the MacLean man who had grabbed her. She stomped on Duncan's inner foot then rammed her elbow in his stomach. When his grip loosened, she slipped away from him and pulled her sword holding it to his neck.

The sound of clapping had both of their gazes snapping to the woman standing about ten feet away leaning against the archway watching them. Her blonde hair was pulled back into a braid and she wore men's garb as if it were made for her. The first thing Raven noticed about her was her beauty.

"Bloody hell!" Duncan pushed Raven's sword away and jogged over to the woman who was only about a head shorter than he was. He pulled her into a fierce hug and spun her around then set her on her feet and gave her a resounding kiss. When he released her the woman held out her hand and gripped his in a warrior's embrace wrist to elbow, "What are ye doin' here, lass? 'Tis Lachlan with ye?"

She laughed, "The whole damned family is here." She looked over at Raven. "Introduce me to your lady Duncan, before she runs us through."

Raven blushed and lowered the sword as Duncan pulled the woman over to her.

"Raven, I'd like ye to meet, Kandra MacKinnon." Duncan slung an arm around her shoulders and beamed, "She's a hellion with a sword and can damn near best me."

"I can best any man, I cross blades with." She said in a clipped English accent as her blue eyes twinkled with fire and determination.

A snort came from behind them, "I dinna think so, *Sasunnach*." Raven turned to see a tall broad-shouldered Scotsman standing with his arms crossed over his chest and booted feet spread in a ready stance. He had stunningly handsome features much like Aidan, but his hair was shorter as his raven black mane flowed over his shoulders. His eyes were a startling green that missed nothing. His body, like Duncan's, rippled with muscles. He was as tall as Duncan and emanated the same raw power that the other three MacKinnon men walked around with.

Kandra turned and strolled over to him. She ran her hands up his chest and entwined her fingers around his neck. "Is that a challenge, my lord husband?" She stood on her toes and brushed her lips over his, "Because I will win."

Lachlan put his hands around her waist and kissed her back, "Ye ken I'll nay cross swords with ye ever again, *Sasunnach*." He brushed a kiss over her temple, "And in yer condition, yer lucky I allowed ye to accompany me on this journey."

Duncan raised a brow, "Dinna tell me yer with child, lass?" He walked over and looked her over then looked at Lachlan and shook his head, "Braydon is nay yet a year."

Lachlan smiled mischievously, "'Tis all Kandra's fault, I assure ye." When his wife pinched him, he laughed, "She can nay resist me."

"So, I see," Duncan smiled. He had a flash of Raven and him much like this, happy and in love, but put it aside for the moment.

Kandra slipped out of her husband's arms and turned to Raven, "You are both being rude. Raven, this is my husband, Laird Lachlan MacKinnon, War Chief to clan MacKinnon." She smiled up at her husband, "Lachlan this is Duncan's woman, Raven."

With a smile, Lachlan let loose of Kandra and stepped forward holding out his hand. "A pleasure lass," when he took her hand he raised a brow, the oddest sensation filled him.

"The pleasure 'tis mine," she smiled up at him and for a second Lachlan was blown away by her beauty. She pulled her hand from his and held out her hand to Kandra, "A pleasure to meet ye as well m'lady."

"Please, call me Kandra," she took Raven's outstretched hand and her smiled faded for a moment.

"Congratulations on yer son." Raven smiled brightly. She had felt the baby though small, healthy, and hail, in its mother's belly. For a second she got a picture in her mind of a child with pitch colored hair and bright blue eyes, the image shifted into a young man who was devilishly handsome then into a man. The man would be important and powerful one day. Raven released her hand and stepped back from her. She was ready for the reaction most people would have to her powers. She would be accused of witchery and shunned.

Kandra looked the smaller woman over and smiled warmly, "I shall enjoy my time here and my time getting to know you, Raven. For now, you must excuse me, as I must find our daughter, Bryanna and our son, who is sure to be in his Gran's arms." With that she turned to her husband, "Come my love and pry Bry from around your brother's ankles, or wherever she has attached herself."

Lachlan laughed, "She will have a fit, for she has sorely missed her uncle." He took his wife's hand and laced his fingers through hers then lifted them to his lips and brushed a kiss across her knuckles. "I think ye should rest."

Kandra shook her head and laughed, "I am fine, Lachlan, and the babe is fine. You've no need to worry about us." She cupped his cheek.

"'Tis my duty, yer my life, Kandra MacKinnon." He ran the back of his knuckles down her cheek. Kandra smiled up at him, though it had been more than a year that they had been married, she still adored the sound of him calling her by her married name, because the good lord knew it fit her perfectly, just as this man did.

Raven watched the couple walk away and she sighed, how she longed for that kind of love. When she noticed, Duncan looking at her, she raised a brow. "What?"

"What was that sigh over, lass?" He stepped to her and lifted her chin so that he could look in to her eyes and noted that her bruises were all but faded away.

"Ye've a good family, Duncan, a verra good family. Yer a lucky man." Raven pulled away from him, "So are we finished for today?"

"Aye, I'd like some time to spend with my cousin." He looked her over and thought how he would like to spend the night with her naked in his bed, this time he wouldn't be so damned noble.

"Can I borrow yer dirk?" She smiled up at him sweetly, "I feel the urge to throw it at somethin'."

Duncan laughed and handed over the dirk. He watched her tuck it into the waistband of the trews she was wearing and walk away with her sword in hand. She was a small delicate woman, and she was every inch a hellion as Kandra.

Raven was out by the oak tree practicing with Duncan's dirk. Anger simmered through her as she thought over the way Isobel had been blatantly swishing her tail in her face about the fact that she was spending nearly on every night in Duncan's room.

The knife flew and hit its mark solidly. As she retrieved the knife, she spied a figure heading her way. On a sigh, she lined up her shot again and threw. She did this several times before Ian walked over and sat atop a large log laying on the ground.

"Good shot, lass," Ian crossed his arms over his broad chest, "If ye must ever fight a tree yer sure to win."

Raven couldn't help but to smile over that, "And a sorry tree it'd be." "Want to learn to hit a movin' target?" He raised a brow in question.

Raven bit her lower lip, would it be wrong for Ian to help her since Duncan was teaching her? Quickly, she decided to hell with Duncan, if he could sleep with Isobel at night then try to seduce her during the day, she could allow others to teach her the skills she needed to be able to fight. "I would be verra happy."

"Then let us go find our target." He stood and took her arm pulling her after him as he headed for the forest. Once there, he sought out a branch then took a length of vines and tied it around a log. The other end went around a tree limb. He stood back and admired his handy work. "My Da, used rope instead of vines."

Raven smiled, "I believe it shall work just as well."

"Now lass, the trick to a movin' target," he gave the log a push to start it swinging wildly back and forth. He walked back to where Raven stood and before she could blink he threw his own dagger and hit the log dead center. "Yeah must anticipate where the target will go. And meet it with the dagger."

"Oh my," she smiled over at him, "That was amazin'!"

Ian shook his dark head, "Nay amazin', lass," he walked over and stopped the swinging log, "Skill and patience and wantin'." He smiled at her, "Remember Raven, aught is impossible if ye wish for it badly enough."

She had the feeling he was talking about more than just the knife throwing, but she didn't want to talk about her situation with Duncan. "How do ye ken when to throw and where?"

Ian walked back to her and smiled, "Anticipation, lass." He had set the log swinging again. "See yer target, determine where 'tis goin' then meet it in the middle." He threw his dagger again and hit the log.

Rubbing her hands together impatient to try, Raven pulled out Duncan's dagger.

Grabbing her wrist, Ian looked at the dagger, "Where did ye get that?" He looked in to her eyes.

"From Duncan, 'tis his," she frowned down at the dagger, "He gave it to me to use, I have kept it on my person, except for when we practice with swords or..." she looked away from Ian, "When he teaches me how to escape from men like the MacLeans."

Ian smiled softly, "Did he tell ye it was our fathers?"

Slowly, she nodded her head, "If it was not his to let me borrow, I will gladly give it back to whomever it belongs too." She didn't want to admit she liked the feel of it in her hand, because it made her feel safer.

With a smile, Ian closed his hand over hers on the dagger. "'Tis where it belongs, lass. 'Twas his decision as to who he allowed to use it."

Raven was puzzled, but when she tried to question it farther, Ian refused to speak of it. Instead he had her begin her lesson in throwing a knife at a moving target. By the end of the lesson, she had nicked the log several times, but had yet to stick it.

"Patience lass," Ian told her as they walked back toward the castle. He looked down at the small woman walking alongside of him. "Patience, and study yer opponent to figure out where to strike."

"Mayhap, I can find a worthy opponent in the castle that I can practice upon?" Raven grinned up at him. "Do ye happen to ken where Isobel is?"

He threw an arm around her shoulders and laughed, "Yer a spirited one, Raven MacKinnon."

They had just entered the castle when Duncan stalked up, "Where have ye been?" He sneered as he looked from Ian to Raven.

"In the forest," Ian glared right back at his younger brother.

Duncan felt the rage billow through him, "And just what were ye doin' in the forest alone?"

"Dinna say somethin' ye'll sorely regret." Ian thumped his brother on the chest, "And if ye make such an implication again, I'll gladly kick yer sorry arse."

Duncan looked from one to the other then turned on his heels and marched away.

Raven looked from him back to Ian, anger surged through her. She ran after the retreating man. She managed to get in front of him, "Ye arrogant *arse!*" She accused.

"Get out of my way woman." Duncan growled. Raven moved closer and stood on her tip toes, "How dare ye make such suggestions 'bout me." She pulled back and hit him in the stomach hard enough to make him grunt. "Ye blackguard," she bellowed up at him. "Ye truly, are a horses' *arse.*" With that she stomped on his foot then turned on her heels and showed him her back.

And what a lovely back it was indeed, he thought as he watched her trew clad *arse* as she walked away from him with her hips swinging. His loins fired with want, and his body yearned for him to catch up with her and throw her over his shoulder. He wanted nothing more than to ravage her gorgeous little body. He had to tap down the urge to take her and make her his.

Ian clapped him on the shoulder, "Ye owe her an apology," His hand squeezed slightly, "Ye hurt her."

Duncan pinched the bridge of his nose between his thumb and forefinger. He was exhausted. Since

Raven had come to Dun Akin, he had not had a decent night's sleep.

Looking over at his brother he shrugged, "I guess I am truly the *arse* she calls me." He grew serious, "I am sorry, I 'twould think such a thin' 'bout the two of ye." He was quiet for a moment, "But what were the two of ye doin' all this time?"

Ian smiled broadly, "Teachin' her to hit a movin' target with her dagger." He laughed at Duncan as he swore under his breath about how his *arse* was in serious trouble now.

Raven dressed in a gown of aqua then plaited her hair so that her black tresses encircled her head like a crown. She slipped the jeweled dagger Duncan had let her borrow into its sheath and hung it from the sash at her waist.

The knock at her door had her hurrying over to answer it. She opened the door to find a young girl standing on the other side of it. From the dark hair and the beautiful green eyes, Raven knew who she was, "Hello, ye must be, Bryanna."

Bryanna's eyes grew wide, "How did ye ken my name?"

Raven put a finger to her lips, "Hmm, mayhap 'tis because I have met yer parents and they spoke of ye." She laughed at Bryanna's crestfallen expression.

"Oh," she sighed heavily.

"Do come in, Bryanna," she nearly laughed as the girl took a hesitant step into her room. Raven smiled at the young girl, "And just how did ye think I would come by yer name?"

Bryanna looked around the room and was unimpressed. She looked over her shoulder at Raven, "Yer verra pretty, but I thought all witches were ugly."

Raven felt the girl's word to her core, "Bryanna, where did ye hear that I am a witch?"

Bryanna sat upon Raven's bed, "From the lasses in the kitchen, then I heard my Mam and Da talkin' 'bout it," she ran her hand over the coverlet. Looking back at Raven, she smiled, "But yer too bonnie to be a witch."

Feeling sick to her stomach, Raven walked over and sat next to Bryanna. She looked down at the little girl. "Why did ye want to ken if I was a witch?"

"Because I wanted ye to make the bairn that my Mam has in her belly, a girl so that I can have a sister this time." Bryanna smiled brightly up at her. "I ken that she'll be wee for a time, but like Braydon, she'll get big and I can play with her."

Raven carefully picked up Bryanna's hand, "So my being a witch would nay scare ye?"

Bry held Raven's hand and smiled, "Nay, I like ye."

Raven smiled and read what was inside the girl. "I like ye too, Bryanna." She saw images of the girl in a few years, sword in hand teaching a younger girl with blonde hair and the same big green eyes. Raven raised her brow at the next image of a handsome young man. She frowned as she saw him again, but this time he was fighting with Bryanna, both their swords had blood on them. The last image to shift through was of Bryanna as a beautiful woman and the same man from her battle kissing her with utter passion. The couple looked happy.

Bry smiled brightly, "So can ye?" Her words brought Raven back to the present.

"Nay lass, I'm afraid I can nay work that kind of miracle," Raven stroked a hand down over Bry's silken hair, "But be assured wee Bryanna, that ye shall have a sister before ye ken it, nay this babe yer Mam has in her belly, but soon enough." Raven looked at Bry and spoke seriously, "But now ye must make me a promise Bryanna MacKinnon, ye must swear nay to breathe a word of what I've told ye to anyone."

Bry crossed her heart, "I swear it to ye," she threw her arms around Raven's waist and hugged her soundly.

Raven hugged the little girl back and held back her tears. If the women in the kitchen were still discussing her, it meant the whole of the castle was, and she would be shunned once more, and she wasn't sure if she could face that.

Bry and Raven visited for a time, but when at last Raven cried off their visit pleading a headache. Bry left and promised to visit with her again soon.

Alone once more Raven took down her hair and changed into a nightdress. She sat in front of the fire and slowly brushed her hair as she stared into the orange, red and yellow, flickering, flames. She thought about the people she had befriended in this castle and smiled softly. Ian and Aidan were wonderful, and now with Kandra, Lachlan and little Bryanna the castle was so lively.

For a brief second, she thought of Duncan and wondered what their bairns might look like, would they be as beautiful as Bryanna? On a sigh, Raven pushed those thoughts from her mind.

When she had missed the evening meal, Duncan headed for Raven's chambers. He knocked lightly at the door, but got no answer. Quietly, he entered the chamber and spied her lying on her bed, sound asleep.

On silent feet, he walked over and looked down at her where she lay slumbering. On a sigh, silently Duncan moved a chair near the bed and sat in it.

For a long time, he watched her sleep. When she mumbled in her sleep, he carefully soothed her. Sitting there he wondered about this woman. As the gray of morning was filling the room, Duncan slipped from her chamber, into his own, through the connecting door.

Eleven

She was home! Raven looked around the familiar room. This was her bedroom. She knew from the sound of the tinkling sea coming through her window and the four-poster bed that had seashells carved into it. Slowly, she ran her fingers over the carvings and felt the cool smooth wood and smiled. Her Da had had the bed carved just for her.

Raven gasped, her Da! She could remember what he looked like. He had sea green eyes and pitch colored hair. He always smelled wonderfully of the ocean.

Turning in a slow circle, she examined her bedroom. So many familiar things! Walking over she picked up a large cockleshell. Holding it to her ear she heard the music of the sea in it. She laughed out loud, she could remember the day she and her Da had found it walking along the beach.

Setting the shell down, she spied a shell necklace and reached for it, but her hand passed through it. Frowning she reached for it again, but once more her fingers slid through it. It had been her mother's and Raven knew she had been wearing it the day that she'd left.

Left? Left for where? She thought wildly then clutched her head as the sight of the angry sea and swelling waves, filled her head. Terrified, she screamed as she fought the waves pounding at her, trying to drag her under the surface forever.

Duncan had only just fallen asleep when he heard Raven scream. He was out of his bed, grabbing his sword, and bursting through the door to her room before she could let out the second scream. He raced to the bed and grabbed hold of her, "What's amiss, lass?"

She fought him as she dreamed on.

Duncan saw the glazed look to her eyes and knew she was in the throes of a nightmare. He pulled her to his naked chest and held her as he said her name and tried to reassure her.

Slowly, Raven came awake and looked around the room, she wasn't in the sea, she was in her bedchamber and she was pressed against Duncan's naked chest.

As she settled down and he felt her start to get hold of herself, he set her away from him. He looked down into her pale face, "Are ye all right, lass?"

"Aye, 'twas only a nightmare." She pushed a stray lock of hair out of her face with a shaky hand, as she sat there still shuttering. Her breath was labored, and she could almost feel the pressure of the sea still on her chest.

He surveyed her. "Tell me 'bout it." Carefully, he lifted the covers and slid into her bed, then pulled her down so that she was cradled against his chest. "'Twill make ye feel better."

Raven frowned, mayhap he was right she thought tiredly, "I remembered more 'bout my past." She spoke slowly, and told him of her room and of the things she remembered. Then she told him of the

127

necklace then the horrific sea storm. She had been helpless against it. "Since the day, I was found on the beach, I have nay willingly set a toe in the sea."

Duncan was silent for a long moment. His hand stroked up and down Raven's back soothingly. "Mayhap, ye need to conquer yer fear of the sea."

Raven sat up and shook her head, "No!" Her eyes were huge with fear. "I will never touch the sea again on my own. Never!"

Duncan pulled her back down, "But ye already have, *gràdh*." He rolled her under him so that he could look in to her beautiful gaze, "I took ye into the sea. Dinna ye remember? In the *Aslin'* ye told me how to save ye. Ye told me to take ye into the sea.

Raven looked at him in utter surprise, he had said as much before, but it wasn't possible. "Ye truly remember the Aslin'?"

"Aye, my sweet," he grinned, "I remember every time we have met there." He ran a finger down her cheek then across her lips, "I remember the way ye tasted."

A blush filled her face. She shoved at his shoulder, but couldn't move him, "'Tis impossible for a mortal to remember goin' into the *Dreamin'*."

"What?" Duncan rolled off her, "What did ye just say, lass?"

Raven sat up slowly, "What?" She fixed her nightdress and frowned at him, "Oh, I said there is no way ye can remember, goin' into the *Aslin'*, unless ye've got magick in yer bloodline somewhere."

"How do ye ken this, lass?" Duncan turned to her and frowned, she had spoken of this before, but he had no clue as to what it really was. "And what in the name of the Gods is the *Dreamin'*?"

Raven rubbed her aching temple as she thought. "I dinna ken how I ken, but I just do." Her head was killing her as she thought, "The *Dreamin'*, is nay so much a land, or a place, as a what. 'Tis another world that exists next to this one, side by side, like *Faery* ye ken, the land of the Fae?" She placed her hands next to each other to show him, "We can nay see the Fae who created it, and those who live there with them, but they can see us at any given time." She sighed, "As well as walkin' among us without bein' seen, if they wish it. It takes a magickal bein', or a *Fiosaiche* to see them, especially the *Tuatha de Danann*."

Duncan saw her rubbing her temples furiously and cursed himself for pushing her too hard. This was why he had stopped her from explaining before. To try to remember hurt her. He grabbed her hands and swung his legs back into the bed, so he could lie down. He pulled Raven down to him and cradled her. He carefully rubbed at her temples. "Dinna strain yerself tryin to remember, my sweet."

Raven sighed at the feel of his fingers massaging her temples. She relaxed slowly and felt herself begin to drift off. One thought still stuck in her mind. "There must be magick... in yer... bloodline." She yawned and drifted off.

Duncan lay there looking down at her. She looked so young with her soft smooth skin that was just kissed by the sun from their hours spent outside training. Her black lashes formed crescent moons on her high regal cheekbones. Her dark brows arched elegantly over her mesmerizing eyes that swirled like the sea from bluish-green too greenish-blue. Her mouth was full and lush and damned kissable. Reaching out he traced a finger over her straight pert little nose and smiled as she brushed at his hand. 'Twas nay wonder he had become obsessed with her, she had bewitched him with her beauty and spirit. He thought with a frown.

He stroked a hand over her inky black hair then picked a handful up and brought it to his nose. It smelled of wild Scottish heather. Duncan let the silken strands flow through his fingers like water. He wanted this woman and no other and he would have her, soon.

Duncan carefully turned her over so that he could spoon her to him and cradle her smaller body in the curve of his, where she belonged. He buried his nose in the curve of her neck, wild heather and woman filled his senses. This tiny woman had no clue what she did to him. How she made him feel protective and possessive of her. Duncan could never let her know that she made him weak kneed with feelings for her.

Duncan wrapped his arms around her securely and let himself drift into sleep and the rightness of holding her. The sun was just kissing the sky as he slipped into slumber.

Raven snuggled into the familiar warmth of Duncan's body. She reveled in the feeling of him wrapped around her. Looking down at his large brawny hand cupping her breast possessively, she smiled. This man was pure male and pure sex god, she thought as she held back a laugh. And she had tasted the pleasure he had to offer.

She smiled at the thought, he had taken her to heaven more than once and she had been breathless from the pleasure he gave her.

The smile faded, as she thought about Isobel. Had he pleasured her in the same ways, or more? Had he taken her to the heavens, and drove her breathless with pleasure? The thought of Isobel in his bed, had her gritting her teeth.

She knew that being jealous of Duncan's whore was useless, but she just couldn't help it. Raven detested the fact that Duncan took that woman to his bed.

Slipping from his arms carefully, Raven climbed out of bed gently, so as not to wake him. She stood there at the edge of the bed and looked at her highland warrior. He was a brawny man, with wide shoulders laden with muscles and his arms were roped with strength. His head was nearly touching the headboard and his giant feet where nigh on hanging off the end.

She looked at his dark hair that was plaited into a multitude of braids and tiny gold beads pressed at the ends. His face was tanned darkly from countless hours in the sun training with his mighty claymore and every other weapon imagined. She took in his dark slashing brows and his large but perfect nose that fit his Celtic features. His cheekbones were sharp and defined, but his mouth was a temptation with his firm, but gentle lips. His chin with a shadow of beard on it, was strong and determined.

She looked down his chest at the massive muscles and had to resist the urge to touch him and stroke him. She wanted to feel those muscles ripple and bunch under her fingers.

Turning away from him, Raven quickly grabbed one of the pairs of trews, Duncan had, had made for her. She donned a white shirt, then stepped into her boots and laced them to the knee. Finished plaiting her hair, she grabbed a piece of rawhide that he had given to her and tied the end of her braid.

Raven picked up her smaller claymore and looked back at the bed biting her lower lip. She had no right to be jealous. Duncan MacKinnon was not hers, oh he certainly wanted her, he wanted to bed her, but that was where it ended. He was not the type of man to give up his bevy of women for the likes of her. She was a woman with no past and no future.

Just because she loved him... Oh Gods above, she was in love with him. She wanted him to be her highland warrior, her love, but that would never happen. Raven pushed back a sob that bubbled in her throat. Turning on her heels, she slipped from the chamber without a sound.

Raven was sweaty, and determined to perfect the moves Duncan had taught her recently. She had to think her problems through, and this was the only way she could think of doing it.

Kandra watched for a time. Raven's form was good and her moves mirrored Duncan to a fault. He'd trained the smaller woman well. Kandra read the pain etched on Raven's beautiful features, and decided that she could use a friend.

With her sword in hand Kandra hailed the other woman, "Good morrow' Raven."

Raven lowered her sword and inclined her head, "Good morrow' Lady Kandra." She looked at the taller and more elegant Englishwoman.

Kandra frowned, "And I had thought we were becoming friends." She tisked with her clipped English accent, "I did not think formal address was required between friends."

"Of course, nay..." Raven was cut off by Kandra as she continued. "Mayhap, I will have to fight you for your friendship and your respect as an equal." She raised her sword and flashed a smile.

"Oh nay, I dinna mean any disre..." Raven didn't get to finish that as Kandra swung her sword and Raven was forced to block.

Raven grinned and met Kandra thrust for thrust and par for par. She quickly learned Kandra's style of sword fighting, it was much like that of Duncan's, yet very different.

Kandra was enjoying herself, Raven lacked the intense skill she, herself possessed, but she was no tenderfoot either. "You are the first woman I have ever crossed blades with." The thought made Kandra laugh.

"Yer the second person, I have had a chance to spar with." Raven laughed and ducked Kandra's blade. She met Kandra as she swung around. The clash of metal against metal rang in the morning air. It was a sweet sound, Raven decided.

"So, what are you going to do about Duncan, you are in love with him, correct?" Kandra smacked Raven on the bottom when she just stood there gaping.

Raven quickly got back into the thick of things and defended herself ardently. "What makes ye think, I'm in love with the blackguard!" She swirled away from Kandra's blade once more.

Kandra laughed heartily, "You would have to be blind not to see the way you look at him." She had to jump back to miss being flayed by Raven's blade. "Now, don't get angry."

"I'm nay angry," Raven fumed, "and I dinna look at him, in any special way." She grunted as her sword blocked a viscous blow from her opponent's sword. "And I'm nay, in love with him." She spat as rage bubbled inside of her, "And how can anyone be in love with the giant lumberin' oaf, when he has his 'hore, right here to keep him company?" She growled as her swings became much more violent and uncontrolled.

"Why not do something, about the wench?" Kandra blocked and prodded at the same time. "Why not take what it is you want, and put the wench in her place?"

For a moment Raven considered it, "Because, I'm nay a violent person." She nodded sagely even as she hacked at Kandra's sword.

Kandra snorted, "So, 'twould appear." With that Kandra decided that the fight was over, she met Raven's sword then ran her blade in quick circles around Raven's blade until she popped it out of the smaller woman's hand and flipped it through the air.

Raven stared at her as she held her throbbing hand. "How did ye do that?" She was awe struck.

"To be honest my husband once did that same thing to me." Kandra flashed a brilliant smile. "What do you say we find ourselves a bite of something to break our fasts?" She picked up Raven's sword and held it out to her.

"Aye, but only if ye promise to teach me that trick." Raven smiled and held out her hand, "Friends?"

"I think this is the beginning of a wonderful friendship." Kandra grabbed Raven's arm in a warrior's greeting. She smiled when Raven returned it.

The two women sat at a long table in the great hall. Three men who sat at the far end got up and moved. Kandra pretended as if she had not seen them, but she wondered as to the reason. She was used to men having an aversion to her, but they had looked down right frightened. Kandra looked at Raven and the blush on her face, "Men claim that women are fickle creatures, but I do believe it is they that are fickle."

Raven looked up at her, "They're movin' 'acause of me." She tucked back a stray lock of hair and frowned, "They fear me, 'acause I am said to be a witch." She watched her finger as it traced a knot in the wood.

Kandra raised a brow, "And who here have you harmed to make them fear you?"

"Nay a soul," Raven's gaze snapped up to hers. "I've never harmed another person, well except for fightin' with Isobel, but she provoked it."

Kandra spied a serving girl passing by, "Girl," she called out and waved the girl over who walked as if she were forced, "I require eggs, bacon, bread, and watered wine."

Straightening her shoulders and raising her chin, Raven looked at the girl who would not meet her gaze, "I'll have the same." The girl scurried away as fast as she could as soon as Raven finished speaking.

Kandra watched the young woman all but run away. She snorted and shook her head as she spoke, "I would most certainly love to have that kind of power over people." She tapped her chin, "Perhaps, I shall tell people I am a witch."

Raven looked back down at the table, "'Tis nay as fun as ye seem to think." She met Kandra's sky blue gaze with her own bluish-green one and shrugged, "Can be a might lonely, and makes people hate ye for nay reason."

Reaching over, Kandra covered Raven's hand with her own. "Oh Raven, I am so sorry." She looked at her for a long moment, "How old are you?"

"Nay one kens for sure," Raven smiled at her, "I was found three years ago, by the Brodie Clan." She looked in to Kandra's face as she spoke, "I dinna ken my real name, let alone my age."

"Oh, you poor thing," Kandra frowned in thought. It would be terrible not to know where one hailed from, "And you don't know if you have family, or not?"

Raven smiled softly, "I ken I have family, I just dinna ken how to find 'em." She laughed at Kandra's stricken look. "Dinna fash 'bout me, I plan to find my way home soon enough."

Before either one of them could say more the girl returned with their food. She set Kandra's in front of her then dropped Raven's plate in front of her not getting any closer than she possibly had too. When she tried to set the tankard of watered wine down, it spilled all over Raven. The girl screeched and dropped the tray she carried then ran as if the hounds of hell were on her heels.

The men who had moved burst out laughing. Kandra handed a wet cloth the girl had dropped to Raven and pushed to her feet. Striding across the hall, she walked over to the men at the table. Without a word to them she picked up two of their tankards and dumped the contents over two of the men's heads. Both men roared with fury.

Stepping back to allow the men up, Kandra looked over and was proud to see a wine soaked Raven next to her. When the three men advanced, Kandra drew her sword. "I would not take another step closer gentlemen, if you value your lives that is."

Raven pulled her sword as well, she wasn't in Kandra's league with a blade, but she would do her best to defend her friend's back. As the three Scots drew their claymores, Raven said a quick prayer to the Gods.

The first man swung his blade and Kandra met him, the second man turned to help his friend with Kandra, as the third man advanced on Raven. She remembered what Duncan had taught her and side stepped the first powerful swing. She was smaller and more agile then this man. She gave him a merry chase, blocking and rebuffing his sword, as she moved away from him. This man was not showing her any mercy, and she was sure he would slice her in half long before she could tire him out. Raven ducked under a table, but waited for him to leap across the table then came out the same side she had gone in and smiled up at the Scotsman.

"I'll kill ye, witch!" The Scotsman growled at her.

Next, she kicked a chair in his path making him stumble. "Ye'll have to be catchin' me first."

She glanced at Kandra and saw that she had the two men on the run. Both were bleeding, while she had but one little cut. Letting her attention veer was her mistake. The man grazed his sword along her upper arm. Raven winced, but moved away from him in a hurry.

At first, the roar that filled the room didn't register with either of the women, as they were intent upon their own battles. Raven ducked under the Scot's sword and struck out with her own slicing his sword arm. When the Scot brought his sword up and began to bring it down at her, Raven knew she was too close to move. All she could do was block and pray for the best. Metal clashed with metal, but his sword never struck hers. She opened her eyes and saw Duncan had blocked the blow and was now driving the man backward. It was only moments until the three angry Scots men were disarmed.

Ian, Aidan, Lachlan and Duncan stood there glaring at the three men. Lachlan was the first to explode. "Ye would dare to raise yer swords against MacKinnon women?"

"My lord," one of the men bowed his head, "We dinna realize..."

Duncan walked over and grabbed the man by the front of the shirt lifting him to his toes, "Ye dinna bloody realize they were women?"

The third man snorted and scowled at Raven, "She's nay a woman nor a MacKinnon, she's a filthy witch." Before he knew what hit him, he was laying there looking up at Duncan's angry face.

"Ye'll be apologizin', for yer ignorance." Duncan growled with his fists clenched.

Raven knew she shouldn't have been hurt, but she felt the Scotsman's words burn her through. She bowed her head and looked down at her beautiful sword. Though it said MacKinnon, it was a lie. She was not a MacKinnon. This place and these people would not be any different than the Brodie Clan. This Clan's hatred and distrust was obvious. They would treat her more and more as if she were some fearsome creature that would attack them at any second. Raven looked at her beautiful sword once more. She would never be a MacKinnon. Tears blurred her vision as pain seared her heart.

The third man remained stubbornly mute. Ian stepped forward. "All three of ye shall pay for this. Nay matter if the women are MacKinnon or nay, women are to be cherished. Ye three shall pay the penance for yer crimes." He waved his guards forward, "Take them to the dungeon and let this one think on his mouth, he can remain there until he has found it in his heart to apologize to Raven."

Lachlan walked over to Kandra and growled down at her, "Dinna look so smug, *Sasunnach*. Yer nay out of trouble yerself." He tucked a lock of golden hair back behind her ear, then cupped her cheek, "Ye'll have penance of yer own to do."

Kandra raised her chin defiantly. "Care to cross blades with me, my husband?" When he shook his head, she continued with anger bubbling inside of her. "I was not in the wrong, those men treated Raven abominably."

Duncan walked over to look down at Raven, "Is that so, lass?"

Raven looked up at him, then looked away. She felt the tears prickle at the backs of her eyes, but she would be damned if she would allow anyone to see them. She pushed past him and strode from the room then ran to her chambers. The first tears fell as she fumbled with the latch. Inside her room, she locked the doors then threw down her sword, and fell onto her bed, bursting into gut wrenching tears.

Duncan looked after her then turned to Kandra and raised a brow.

Kandra narrowed her eyes and scanned the hall. "All these people treat poor Raven as if she will turn them into toads, at the blink of an eye. Raven is a kind, sweet person, if any of you would bother getting to know her. You would know that for yourselves." Disgust laced her voice.

Isobel strolled in and sneered at Kandra, "Oh aye, ye would stick up for her," she walked over to Duncan and placed her hands on his arm. "She's a monster, just look at what she did to me." She pointed to the bruises and marks from Raven's nails. She snuggled up to Duncan and laid her head on his arm. "She's a crazy witch."

Glaring at her, Kandra growled, "Be glad 'twas not me, Isobel. For I would have torn your hair out and plucked your eyeballs from their sockets." She stepped closer causing the woman to flinch, "And make no mistake, I am going to teach Raven everything I know about war. Fair and foul." She looked up at Duncan and glared, "I did not take you for such a fool, Duncan MacKinnon." With that she turned on her heels and strode from the great hall.

Twelve

Raven cried herself to sleep as the confusion and hurt washed over her. The day had already been trying and it was not even half over.

When she woke an hour later to the pounding on her chamber door, she lay there and listen to Duncan ranting and raving. As he made his way into his chamber and tried that door, Raven got up and grabbed her sword as she slipped from her chambers and raced down the hall. She hurried down the stairs and collided with Lachlan.

He held her for a moment and looked in to her tear stained face, "Where are ye off too, Raven?" He studied her eyes and watched them shift back and forth between blue and green.

"I am goin' to the stables to spend some time with the horses, they are gentle creatures and I could use their calmin' affect." She lied easily.

"Be careful with such powerful beasties." He frowned after her as she raced away on her mission. He continued up to the solar and ran into Duncan striding down the hall.

"Have ye seen the infernal woman?" He barked sourly. Lachlan smiled, "Raven?"

"Aye, she's bloody disappeared again." He growled. "She was headed for the stables."

Lachlan bowed from the waist as his cousin brushed past him without a word of thanks, "And yer welcome."

Duncan marched down to the stables, but found nothing. Raven was nowhere to be seen. He checked the tower room and the practice field. He also stood on the outer bailey walls and scanned the surrounding land, but couldn't find her. When he did find the infernal woman, he was either going to beat her or kiss her, but he wasn't sure which would come first.

Raven sat upon the large boulder with her knees drawn up to her chin. She didn't hear Ian approach her until he sat next to her. She gave a scream and nearly fell off the boulder, but he grabbed her arm and pulled her back up. She pressed a hand to her heart and she spoke, "For the love of saints, ye scared the day lights out of me."

Ian laughed, "I thought ye heard me approach." He looked her over, "Ye need to work on those warrior skills."

Raven sighed, "I'm nay a warrior," she snorted, "I'm a witch, remember." She laid her head on her knees once more.

Ian shook his head, "People have to be shown yer nay a witch, but a special woman, Raven." He looked out over the sea, "I, myself made that mistake and for it I am eternally sorry."

Raven looked at Ian and smiled, "Ye did aggravate me with the whole witch thin'." She sighed, "But yer nay different than any of them," she gestured toward the castle, "Because I have special powers, and I dinna ken who I am, I can nay defend myself against what they accuse me of." She looked at Ian for a long moment, "Ye promised me a boon, if I could save yer brother."

"I remember lass," Ian looked at her for a long moment, "And if 'tis within my powers, I shall grant it."

Raven looked at him for a long moment, "Release me, and allow me, my freedom to leave here."

Ian shook his dark head, "I am afraid lass, I can nay grant ye that..."

"Ye can release me, 'tis within yer power..." Ian placed his fingers over her mouth to silence her, "I can nay grant ye that which ye already have, lass." Ian looked in to her bluish-green eyes and smiled, "Raven, ye have a home here always with clan MacKinnon, if ye choose to remain here 'tis yer choice, if ye choose to leave, that again 'tis yer choice." He smiled at her and cupped her cheek. "But if ye leave and find what 'tis yer looking for, and find that ye wish to return here to my clan, ye shall be welcomed with open arms."

"Ye would let me go?" Raven looked at Ian with wide eyes, "Ye would grant me, my freedom so easily?"

"I never held yer freedom from ye." Ian smiled down at her. "Ye've been free to leave whenever ye wished it, lass."

"Thank ye, Ian." Raven wiped at a stray tear. "Dinna be thankin' me for somethin' I dinna do." He used his thumb to wipe away another tear.

They sat in silence for a long time. Finally, he spoke, "Tis bonnie here." He nodded to the sea, "I come here often to think."

"Aye, 'tis a perfect place for just that." Raven looked around the area.

"Many a times, I wonder what 'twill look like in a hundred years." Ian grinned, "I oft times wonder if my grandchildren and great-grandchildren will sit here and think as I do."

143

Raven reached over and took Ian's hand in her own. She closed her eyes then frowned as images passed through her mind. She saw a beautiful dark-haired woman walking beside Ian on this very beach, and three dark haired boys playing in the sand. She watched time shift as they grew to become fine looking men. She had a sense of more years passing, but what shocked her was the number of years she sensed, it was beyond that of mere mortals. Suddenly, the image of a young blonde woman with lovely curly hair walking down the beach to this very rock had her smiling. She watched as Ian now with shorter hair and odd clothing hugged the girl to him. Her eyes fluttered open, "Aye, much like ye, yer family will come to this very place to clear their minds of their problems."

Ian smiled softly at the thought of family, "Tell me this if ye can, Raven. What will they be like, my family?"

"Bonnie," she whispered, "More than any man can hope for." She smiled at him, "Yer wife 'tis verra bonnie. Yer children a joy and even more handsome than ye."

A smile graced Ian's face as he looked at her. "Is there nay more?"

"Aye, ye will have a granddaughter, fair haired and I sense a special bond between the two of ye." Raven looked over at the spot where the woman had stood, "Ye shall be her rock in troubled times."

Taking Raven's hand in his, Ian pressed a kiss to her knuckles. "I thank ye, Raven. And ken that I still have the boon to fulfill if ye wish to ask it."

"Yer an honorable man, Ian MacKinnon." Raven smiled up at him then looked out over the sea.

"'Tis nay easy to be in love with a man like my brother." He looked out over the water himself.

"Nay," she shook her head and sighed, "I'm findin' it nigh on impossible." She laughed lightly, "Could ye nay banish Isobel forever from MacKinnon lands?"

He laughed, "'Tis a thought, lass." Looking from the sea to the woman next to him, he smiled softly, "Perhaps, 'twould be best to get the wench out of the picture, but I ken yer much smarter than she is. Outwit her at her own game."

Raven shook her head, "I dinna understand."

"Think on it, lass, ye'll soon figure it out." Ian pushed up from the rock, "Remember lass, I owe ye a boon of yer choosin', but to wish me to banish Isobel, would nay be a wise choice." With that he smiled then walked away from her, leaving her to stare at his broad retreating back.

For a long time, Raven sat there staring at the sea trying to puzzle out what Ian had been telling her. She frowned when she saw Duncan trudging through the sand toward her, with a scowl on his handsome face. Today, he looked dark and dangerous with his hair lose to blow in the sea breeze around his powerful shoulders. His muscular chest was bared as were his powerful legs as he wore his tartan in traditional kilt style. His sword was strapped to his back in the usual Scottish way, with the leather band going across his chest. She took in his handsome Celtic features, as well as his warrior's body and felt that familiar pulling in her neither region. Her breasts ached as her nipples harden. She licked her suddenly dry lips.

When he stopped in front of her scowling, she shaded her eyes and looked at him. She schooled her features and hoped she gave away none of the desire she felt for the man.

"I have been searchin' the entire damnedable castle for ye." Duncan growled down at her. "Why the bloody hell are ye hidin' out here?"

Raven pushed up to stand on the rock, "'Tis none of yer damned business, ye stupid ogre." She thumbed him in the chest as he stood in front of her. "Ye dinna own me."

She would have leapt off the rock, but he grabbed her wrist turning her back to face him. "Wait a damned minute."

"Nay, ye wait a damned minute," she tried to pull from his grasp, but it was unbreakable. "I have had enough of yer games, and I'll play nay more."

She glared at him and he could see her bluish-green eyes begin to change. The sunny day began to turn dark and storm clouds built from out of the sea. The waves raised and crashed in rhythm to her heartbeat. "Let me go," she spoke and lightening slashed across the sky as thunder boomed.

"Ye dinna scare me, lass." Duncan growled at her.

"Then yer a bigger fool than I thought," she spat as lightning struck the ground not ten feet from Duncan.

He didn't even flinch as it made the earth tremble under his feet. When the rain pounded from the sky soaking them both and he growled, "Throw yer temper tantrum, lass. But ye'll talk to me when yer finished."

With a slash of her hand the rain eased, and the lighting quit striking the beach around them, but flashed brightly in the sky. "Say yer piece then release me, MacKinnon."

"Dinna give me commands, lass." Duncan yanked her forward into him and caught her around the waist as he pulled her off the rock and held her trapped against him. His large hand fisted in her hair pulling her head back as he crushed his mouth to hers. His kiss was brutal, punishing and completely hungry. He devoured her with that kiss as he tempted and thrilled her at the same time.

She tried to fight against the desire he built inside of her, but there was no use. He made her blood heat and her heart pound. She was surprised to find her arms wrapping around him of their own accord. What the hell, she thought, as he branded her with his kiss and she kissed him back then reveled in his hungry moan.

Before she knew it, Duncan pulled her completely off the boulder and she wrapped her legs around his waist as he pressed them together intimately. Her fingers were buried in his long, thick, wet hair as she kissed him with as much desire as he kissed her. His hands roamed over her small body, creating fires in their wake. When she felt his hand on her bare skin, she jolted at the shock of sensation she felt that raced from him into her. She moaned into his mouth as his tongue swept the inside of hers and slid along her own tongue.

Duncan knew he would not be able to stop this time. He wanted her like no other woman, he had ever wanted before. Hell, he needed her, and he would have her here and now, he would lay claim to his woman. He would bind her to him for all time, he thought wildly. Setting her on the rock again he quickly discarded her shirt, and laid her breasts bare before him. Dipping his head, he rasped his tongue over one of her taunt nipples and felt her quiver in pleasure. When he suckled one of her rosy nipples into his mouth, he heard her moan her joy. His fingers worked on the laces of her trews and he cursed himself for having them made for her as he merely tangled them.

Raven was lost in sensation as she felt Duncan's mouth and hands on her body. Her fingers were buried deep in his rich dark mahogany hair as he suckled her and laved her breasts, until she thought she would scream with pleasure. When he jerked on the laces of her trews snapping it then started on her boots, she laughed at his cursing. She tried to help him, but he brushed her hands away. He removed the offending clothing as swiftly as possible, throwing it aside then tugged off his tartan and quickly laid it out. She thought it sweet that he laid it out for them, then scooped her up and placed her upon it gently.

Duncan knelt looking down at her laying there gloriously naked and wanting him. He ran his callused hands over her body feeling her soft silken skin under his palms and fingers. Her breasts were full and perfect. Though she was small, Raven was curved and rounded in all the right places for a man to enjoy her. He looked in to her beautiful face and whispered softly in Gaelic. "Yer so verra bonnie and I want ye."

Raven opened her arms to him offering herself up to him and his loving. When he knelt over her nudging her thighs apart, she thought he would seek his pleasure. She was surprised when he merely brushed a kiss over her mouth then brushed kisses over her breasts on his way down her body. His mouth moved over her abdomen and she felt her stomach clench with need as he dipped his tongue into her navel. At the top of her downy black curls he brushed his lips back and forth teasing her.

Duncan laughed as her fingers buried in his hair tightened and pushed at him to move down. He planned to make this last, he thought with a wicked grin. He lifted her left leg and ran kisses down to her ankle causing her to break her hold on his hair, then he kissed his way back up the inside of her thigh and brushed his mouth over her woman's mound. Duncan tortured her the same way with her right leg as he pressed slow steady kisses down it and back up.

She was sure he was trying to slowly kill her with his unhurried deliberate torture. Her fingers fisted in his hair once more, she tugged at him as she hissed, "Please Duncan, yer killin' me."

He laughed softly and bent his head to his target as he slipped his hand under her bare bottom and lifted her to meet his mouth. His tongue ran up the seam of her neigh lips. He could taste her essence and he reveled in her honeyed sweetness. His tongue slipped between her soft folds and flicked over her tiny bud of desire making her moan loudly as pleasure rocked her.

Raven was sure he would kill her, as his slow deliberate movements made the coil inside of her winding tighter and tighter, as desire filled her. When his tongue stroked her slowly and intimately. She clutched her fingers in his hair, begging him to bring her to release. His mouth closed over her to suckle and she thought she would die from the sheer bliss of it. A scream of pleasure built in her throat.

Duncan wanted to give her pleasure as well as ready her body for him. Slowly, he slipped one finger into her tight hot sheath. There was no doubt within his mind that she was a virgin, she was so tight around his finger. Carefully, he slipped a second finger inside her stroking and stretching her to help ready her body for his invasion.

It was the combination of his tongue and his skilled fingers that pushed her over the edge into the abyss of ecstasy. She screamed his name as she found her release. Lightening ripped across the sky as thunder shook the world around them.

Duncan lift his head to look at her and smiled at the pleasure on her face. Her body quivered, and her breath came in panting little sighs. Moving up her body he suckled one of her nipples as he nudged her thighs farther apart to accommodate his hips. His mouth found hers as he captured her lips in a fiery kiss. He nipped at her lower lip then pulled back to look at her.

"Ye've never been with a man, lass." He told her honestly.

She shook her head, "I dinna ken if I have, I dinna remember..."

"Ye've never been with a man, this I ken." He brushed a soft kiss over her lips. "There will be a bit of discomfort when we join, but I shall do my best to be careful. Do ye understand what I am sayin', Raven?"

Raven cupped his face in her small hands and pulled him down to her as she pressed a kiss to his lips and spoke. "I trust ye, Duncan MacKinnon, with all of my heart."

Those words made Duncan's heart soar. He kissed her once more then pressed the head of his shaft into her tight sheath inch by slow inch, allowing her to adjust to his sheer size.

Raven felt the pressure and at first the uncomfortable feeling of him stretching her, but nothing was painful. She ran her hands over his rippling muscles and felt his strain to move slowly. When he stopped pressing forward, she raised a brow in question.

Duncan looked in to her questioning gaze then cupped her cheek. He ran his thumb over her cheekbone as he looked in to her swirling bluish green eyes as they shift back and forth between the two beautiful colors. He brushed his thumb over her lower lip and spoke softly. "Hold on to me *gràdh*, wrap yer arms 'round me." When she complied, and wrapped her arms around his powerful neck, he looked down into her face. "Forgive me," he whispered in Gaelic as he captured her mouth in a hard, dominating kiss.

Raven reveled in the kiss, she felt him withdraw slightly and whimpered, but when he surged forward ripping through her maidenhead, she cried out. He captured the sound in his mouth. Though the pain burned inside of her, she felt him freeze, she felt the cords in his neck band, as he struggled to hold absolutely, still. As the burning pain lessened, she let loose of his shoulders where her fingers had dug in.

Duncan was holding on by a bare thread as he held himself still as a statue. He didn't wish to hurt her any more than he already had. When she wiggled under him he growled, "Dinna move, lass, I dinna want to hurt ye further."

Raven ran her hands over the hardened muscles of his chest, shoulders and arms. "I'm fine Duncan," she laughed, "It hurts nay more." She moved under him once more.

On a groan, Duncan pressed himself forward filling her completely and heard her gasp. He looked down at her and saw her soft dreamy smile. Testing the waters, he withdrew and surged forward softly. Her sigh of pleasure gave him all the encouragement he needed to begin the age-old dance between man and woman. Slipping a hand under her bottom, he raised her hips to give him better access.

"Ohhh," Raven moaned at the change in the angle and way it made him inside of her, feel even more arousing. She ran her hands over his hardened body as he plunged into her over, and over again. She pressed her lips to his chest in dozens of spots and reveled in the sound of his groans, as she touched him and tasted him. The feeling of need that coiled, winding tight inside of her had her whimpering and writhing under him.

Duncan felt his own need for release beating at him mercilessly. He would be damned if he would seek his own pleasure and leave her wanting and unfulfilled. Slipping a hand between their bodies, he used his thumb to stroke her tiny jewel of desire until she was hovering on the abyss of rapture. He watched her as he nudged her over the edge and she shattered in his arms. The feeling of her hot wet sheath tightening convulsively around him had him slipping over that edge along with her.

Raven swore she could reach out and touch the heavens as he took her to completion. She felt the power of their joining sizzle between them. She saw the pure blue aura swirling and mingling as it wrapped around them then it shifted to a multitude of colors.

He threw back his head and shouted his completion as release ripped through his body. Duncan had never felt anything like this in his life. He saw the swirl of colors wrap around them, then felt the crackle of energy their joining created. No woman had ever made him feel so very right. He heard the storm give one last earthshaking boom, then felt the sun beating down on his back once more.

Gently, he laid his forehead against hers. They were each breathing hard and fast. He mumbled nonsense words to her in Gaelic, as he pressed soft kisses to her face. She was stunningly beautiful, he thought as he pulled back to look down at her. "Ye will marry me, Raven. Be mine forever." The words were on his tongue before he could stop them from coming forward.

Raven's eyes snapped open. She looked at his handsome face. "Nay," she pushed at his chest. His words had brought her back to reality. "Dinna say that."

Duncan saw the wisdom in not pushing her. He simply rolled off her pulling her with him, so that she was sprawled on top of him. "Fine, we'll nay speak of it now." He pressed her head down to lay upon his chest.

Raven gave up the idea of fighting him and lay there listening to his heartbeat, a strong tattoo in his chest. She ran her fingers through the soft light smattering of hair on his chest. She thought over all that they had shared and felt the little ache between her thighs, but knew it wouldn't last long. A shiver raced up through her, as she remembered the feel of his hands on her body and the feel of him filling her so completely. The pleasure he had given her was beyond words.

She took his large hand in hers and held it as she concentrated on his future. She frowned when there was nothing. She slipped her fingers in between his linking them together and concentrated hard to see his future, but again it was blackness in her mind.

Puzzled by this, she kept their hands linked and listened to Duncan's deep even breathing as he dozed. She relaxed and let her mind drift, hoping she would catch a glimpse of his future. Eventually, she dozed off in a sated slumber with her lover.

Thirteen

Raven stood at her window and looked out at the clear star filled sky and sighed. This afternoon had been amazing, wonderful, and beyond her wildest dreams, she thought as she felt the warm tingle spread over her again. Duncan was a splendid lover. She could not see how any man could pleasure a woman more.

The sound of a knock at her door had her turning her head to look over her shoulder, "Enter," she called out.

As if her thoughts had conjured him, Duncan stepped through the door. He looked at her standing there in her nightdress. Her hair was still damp from her bath and he could smell the scent of wild heather coming from her skin and hair. She was beautiful, he thought, as she stood there in the soft glow of the firelight from the hearth.

"What can I do for ye?" She turned around and walked half way across the room toward him, then stopped unsure of herself.

"Why are ye ready for bed, lass? Ye've nay yet had yer evenin' meal." Duncan raised a brow, as he looked her over once more. Worry crossed his face, "Are ye ill?"

Raven slowly shook her head, "Nay, I'm nay ill." She could not bring herself to admit that she didn't want to face his clansmen in the great hall. She would have her meal alone in her room as she had many nights since she had arrived at *Dun Akin*. A tray would arrive outside her door and the girl would knock then leave before Raven could open the door.

Duncan looked at her then walked over to the chest where her clothing was stored. He dug through, found a pale green gown and pulled it from the limited number of gowns she now owned. "We'll have to see about havin' more gowns made for ye. Mayhap, one of the village lasses can create a few, until we can travel to Inverness, that 'tis." He walked over and held the gown out to her.

Raven kept her hands straight at her sides, "I am nay goin' down there."

"Ye are," he glared at her. "Ye'll nay cower in yer chambers." He took a step forward and when she only raised her chin, he threw the dress aside as he grabbed her nightdress pulling it up and over her head. Her small luscious body was bared to him. His gaze wandered over her for a long moment as his loins clenched with need, but he pushed his own desire aside. He quickly dressed her in the gown. Turning her, he fastened the laces at her sides though she gave him not a bit of help. He had to admit it would be much more fun stripping her out of the gown later, than putting her into it now.

"Yer wastin' yer time," she spoke with resignation in her voice. "I dinna plan to allow ye to escort me down to the great hall."

Duncan grabbed her chin forcing her to look at him, "Then I'll be carryin' ye, lass." He turned her and ran his fingers through her silken tresses then began quickly plaiting her hair. He tied it off with the piece of leather string he had given her.

"Please dinna do this, Duncan," Raven looked down at her hands, "Yer kinsmen dinna accept me, and like the Brodie they fear me."

Duncan placed a finger under her chin forcing her to look up at him once more, "Mayhap, but this time ye have me by yer side, lass." He leaned forward brushing a kiss over her lips, "I'll nay allow anyone to be unkind to ye."

Raven looked in to his deep greyish-blue eyes and smiled softly, "All right, but if one person is bothered by my presence then I shall leave, with nay a word of denial from yer lips."

Duncan held out his hand, "Agreed," when she slipped her hand in his, he pulled her forward into him and captured her mouth in a searing kiss.

With her hand on Duncan's arm, Raven walked into the great hall beside her Highlander. When the room grew quiet, she glared up at him.

Kandra stepped forward, "You look lovely." She eyed the green gown and smiled, "Such a wonderful color on you."

"Thank ye," Raven took the hand she offered. "Ye look a vision yerself." She took in Kandra's light blue gown that matched her eyes. She said not a word as Duncan left her with Kandra and made his way over to speak with his brother.

"I hate gowns," Kandra leaned forward to impart her secret to Raven, "I feel uncomfortable in them, but Lachlan likes them." She winked at Raven, who laughed.

"I must say, I sympathize with ye, since I've begun wearin the trews Duncan gave me. I adore 'em." Raven grabbed a handful of skirt and shook it, "These would be a might awkward to cross blades in."

"Yes, they would." Kandra laughed.

"What are the two of ye whisperin' 'bout?" Lachlan walked over and slipped his arms around his wife. "I must say yer the two most fetchin' women in the entire *caisteal*."

Kandra looked up at him and smiled, "*Tapadh leat, my lord husband.*" She cupped his cheek and pulled him down for a long passionate kiss.

Raven watched the two with a spark of longing. How she wished things were like this between Duncan and her. She was no fool. She knew that Duncan wanted her right now, but in the end, he would tire of her and have no use for her any longer, then he would return to Isobel's bed.

When Isobel appeared in the doorway of the great hall, Raven gritted her teeth. She watched the other woman glide into the room in a beautiful blue gown that matched her eyes. Jealousy reared its ugly head, but Raven fought to keep it in check.

Isobel spied Duncan talking with Aidan and Ian. She saw Raven across the room and gave her a sly smile as she sidled up to Duncan and wrapped herself around him. She wrapped her arms around his neck and pressed herself to his large hard body wantonly. "Hello lover," she gave him a sultry smile as she stood on tiptoe to nibble on Duncan's chin. "I've missed ye so."

Seething, Raven watched as Duncan's hands went to rest on Isobel's waist. She felt the tug on her sleeve and looked over at Kandra.

"I would knock her on her ass, if I were you." Kandra smiled, "Would you like me to hold her, so you can wallop her? I would be more than happy to."

"Apparently, Duncan wants her." Raven felt her heart sink at the thought. She knew what he was and, yet she felt her love for him burn inside of her, she longed for him to requite her love.

"The hell with that," Kandra spoke venomously, "What do you want, Raven?" She nodded as Raven's gaze went to Duncan, "Then fight for him."

Raven looked back at her friend and smiled wickedly. "If I had my sword, I would run her through, but since I dinna have it, magick will have to do." She shrugged then looked at Isobel and whispered a small chant. A serving girl who was passing by with a tray full of tankards of ale was perfect for Raven's revenge. The tray tipped out of the girl's hand and the tankards spilled down Isobel's back.

Isobel let out a screech and turned on the girl who looked horrified. She would have gone after the girl, but Duncan grabbed her. "What's wrong with ye? 'Twas an accident, she dinna mean it." Duncan admonished sternly.

"The clumsy…" Isobel trailed off as she spied Raven standing there smugly next to Kandra. She picked up her skirts, wrenched her arm out of Duncan's grasp and strode across the room as she glared at Raven, "Ye filthy, rotten, witch!" She screeched at Raven, "Ye did that!"

Raven raised a brow, "And?" She smiled wickedly, "Shoo before I turn ye into the snake ye are." She leaned closer to Isobel and growled, "I may be a witch, but at least I am nay a *siursach*."

"How dare ye call me a 'hore! Ye'll pay for that!" Isobel screeched and stomped her foot.

"Stupid *Baobh*!" Raven clenched her fists as anger boiled in her at the strumpet calling her a bitch, "If ye wish another fight, I shall be willin' to oblige ye, *strapaid*!"

When Isobel swung, Raven grabbed her wrist and shoved her backward. Tripping over the back of her gown Isobel fell on her backside. She succeeded in pulling Raven down with her and the two engaged in their second fight. Raven managed to pin Isobel down as she sat on her back. She got a fistful of the other woman's blonde hair and yanked for all she was worth and heard her screech. Leaning down Raven whispered in the other woman's ear. "*I've had enough of ye and yer wickedness, bother me nay more, or pay three-fold for the trouble ye give me. With heartache and headache ye'll pay with sickness. And ye shall feel my wrath in yer worst of times. As I will so mote it be!*" Isobel shrieked as the curse was delivered.

Suddenly, Raven was plucked off Isobel by Duncan, "Let go of me," she struggled against his grip. She watched Aidan pick up a sobbing Isobel, but still tried to reach for the woman. She would tear the other woman's golden hair out of her head.

Isobel looked at Raven in Duncan's arms and lunged for her, but Aidan grabbed hold of her restraining her. The two women exchanged degrading insults in Gaelic.

Lachlan looked at Raven and raised a brow, but kept quiet as both women were removed from the great hall. He walked over to Ian and clapped him on the shoulder, "The pre-meal entertainment was certainly worth it."

Ian threw back his head and laughed, "I do believe Isobel suffered the worst of that encounter. Raven has a wicked temper." "Aye, Raven's a tough one," Lachlan shook his head, "And where did she learn such words in Manx?"

Ian looked at his cousin for a long moment, "Ye ken what all she was sayin'?"

"Aye, 'twas Manx Gaelic." Lachlan shrugged, "I ken a bit of the language, as I spent some time on the Isle of Mann in my younger years."

"Raven must be from the Isle of Mann." Ian clapped his cousin on the shoulder, "The mystery of where she comes from is beginnin' to unravel."

Duncan tossed Raven over his shoulder as he took her from the great hall, as she would not cease her struggles to get at Isobel. When she pounded on his back swearing in Gaelic, he slapped her bottom making her cry out. "Ye've a filthy mouth, lass." He took the stairs to the solar two at a time.

"The 'hore deserved everythin' I did to her and more." Raven heard him struggle with his chamber door. Walking through it, she watched him kick it shut and then turn to lock it. "Put me down ye, *tha thu cho duaichnidh ri èarr àirde de a' coisich deas damh.*" She beat on his back. He deserved much more than to be called 'as ugly as the north end of a southward traveling ox.'

Duncan laughed as he strode across the room and threw her up in the air. She landed on the bed with a bounce and her mystical eyes fired with anger. '*Tha i bòidheach,*' he thought, and she truly was beautiful. "Dinna even think it, lass." Duncan stood there with his hands on his hips.

"Ye've nay clue as to what I was thinkin'." She spat as she slowly sat up and watched him walk a few feet away. "But it would certainly serve ye right if I acted upon it." She swung her legs off his bed then raised a brow. "And what do ye think yer doin'?"

"Undressin'," Duncan smiled as he pulled his shirt over his head, "What do ye think?"

"I think yer daft, 'tis what I think." Raven snorted as she pushed off the bed and walked across the room. She would have walked right out his door, but he caught her around the waist and pulled her to him.

"Aye, I am daft, lass," he pressed a kiss to her mouth, "Ye make me completely daft." Duncan nuzzled her neck pressing kisses to her pounding pulse.

Raven clenched her fists and tried to ignore the sensations that he stirred in her belly. She couldn't stop the little sound of pleasure that built deep in her throat and slipped past her parted lips. Of its own accord, her head tipped to the side to give him better access to her throat. Before she knew it, she had her fingers tangled in his long silken hair. Her mouth was devouring his in a matched heat.

Duncan felt the throb of her body and it matched the ache in his own body. As he kissed her, his hands wound her long braid around his hand over and over. Taking the end of her plait, he quickly untied it and began unplaiting her long, black silken hair. Scooping it into his hands he let it slide through his fingers like silken water. His hands slid to her sides and his skillful fingers worked urgently to undo the laces. He traced his hand down to her hip and onto her thigh, quickly bunching up the material until he felt her bare skin under his knuckles. Pulling back, he tugged the gown up over her head and off then threw it aside.

His hungry gaze roamed over her naked body. He took in her lose waterfall of shiny black hair that skimmed over her shoulders and across her luscious breasts. He thought once more about, how beautiful she was, as his heart lurched at the sight of her. Reaching out, he moved the silken strands aside so that he could see her in all her glorious splendor. Her coral nipples were pebbled and hard, her breasts were luscious and full enough to fill even his large hands. Her skin was milky white and delicate, and he planned to taste every inch of her. Hunger for her knotted in his gut. Reaching out once more, he tugged her to him and encircled her waist with his large hands, as his head bent to capture her mouth with his own.

She tasted of woman and of something that was uniquely Raven, perhaps it was power, he thought as she moaned into his mouth and he swallowed it. Whatever it was, he relished every ounce of it. She shivered in his arms and he ran his hand over her chilled skin, then pulled back to look down at her. "Yer chilled."

Slowly, she shook her head, "I'm nay cold," she ran her fingers over his broad shoulder.

"I'll start us a fire," he picked up a strand of her hair and rubbed it between his fingers. "I dinna want ye to become ill."

Raven pulled away from him and padded naked across the room to the hearth then smiled wickedly over her shoulder at him. She turned back to the hearth and knelt, she cupped her hands and spoke the words to call upon the element of fire, "*Great Dragon who guards the element of fire, grant yer gift to me. As I will so mote it be!*" She blew on her hands and a flame danced from her palms into the hearth and lit the wood. In seconds, a fire burned brightly in the hearth. She looked back over her shoulder to where Duncan stood looking at her. For a moment, she thought he would denounce her, reject her, and she would die of a broken heart.

Duncan flashed her a bright smile, "Yer a handy one to have 'round on a cold winter's night, lass."

Holding his hand out to her, he wiggled his fingers, "Come here, lass."

Slowly, Raven pushed to her feet and walked to him. She stood there still uncertain of how he felt. She looked in his deep greyish-blue gaze and thought of a beautiful loch.

He ran his knuckles down her cheek, "What 'tis this look?" When she looked away, he put a finger under her chin to make her look at him. "Do ye think yer gifts frighten me, or make me uneasy?"

"Aye," she whispered knowing what people thought of her and praying he would not sink into that ignorance.

On a sigh he frowned, "I guess I must show ye how much I still want ye, how much ye make me ache." He took her smaller hand and placed it on the front of his trews where it bulged from his heavy erection. "Does this show ye how much I want ye, ache for ye, need ye?"

Her fingers closed over him and he groaned as she looked up at him. "*Gura mie ayd.*" She thanked him. "Nay one has ever said such bonnie words to me." She stretched up on tiptoes as she reached up and tugged him down to her for a long slow kiss. With all the love she felt, Raven kissed him. When they were both breathless she pulled back and looked up at him. Slowly, she pulled away from him, but took his hand in hers as she tugged him toward the bed.

Following her wasn't a hardship for him, as Duncan watched the sway of her curvaceous hips as she walked. Her long inky black hair glistened in the firelight and made her skin appear even more pale. When she stopped and turned toward him, he wouldn't have doubted her to be a water nymph, as she stood there so tiny and ethereal, with her swirling bluish-green eyes. Reaching out he cupped her cheek and watched her close her eyes as she pressed her cheek into his palm.

Gods how she loved his touch, every time his hand brushed hers, or they made contact in any way, she felt the zing of it through her entire body. This large man, this highland warrior, was meant for her and her alone. How could he not feel it? Feel the energy between them? Raven vowed she would make him want only her, she would show him what they were together, what the universe had meant them to be.

Opening her eyes, Raven turned her head and pressed a kiss to the center of his palm. His fist closed over the kiss sealing it in his hand. Slowly, she reached out and ran her fingers over his rippling muscles and watched them contract under her touch. She traced the plains of his chest and shoulders then began her journey over his shoulder to his broad back. Laden with muscles and strength, Raven began her quest to learn every inch of this man. Leaning into him, she brushed her lips over his bronzed skin then flicked her tongue out to taste him. As she traced with her fingers, she pressed open mouthed kisses in their wake to his heated flesh.

It took all his warrior's will not to turn and grab the woman, throw her on the bed and ravage her. He clenched his teeth and fists, as her hands ran over his buttocks and her teeth nipped at his side. "*Aon, dà dhà, trì, ceithir, còig, sia, seachd, ochd, naoi, deich.*" Duncan counted slowly to ten in his head, but it didn't seem to help, as his control threatened to snap if he didn't get his hands on her soon. When at last she made her way around to his chest once more, Duncan nearly sighed in relief, but when her hand went to the laces of his trews, he growled deeply, "Dinna do that Raven, ye tempt me too far."

Raven looked up at him, her eyes glowing a mystical swirling blue-green. "I have nay begun to tempt ye yet." She unlaced the last of his trews and allowed his hard shaft to spring forward. Taking him into her hands she stroked the silken hard length of him.

His greyish-blue eyes closed as a moan sounded deep within his throat. He was sure she would snap his control with this new torture. Once more he gritted, his teeth and bore her torturous pleasure.

Raven saw the pleasure on his face and smiled, she leaned in and pressed soft kisses to his chest then began to work her way down his hard washboard stomach. Once she knelt in front of him, she looked up at him and figured if he could taste her intimately then she could do the same. Leaning toward him, she flicked her tongue over the tip of his manhood. She heard him suck in a hissing breath then she covered him with her mouth.

Without a doubt, he was going to die he thought, then reached down and pulled her away from him. He looked down into her beautiful face and shook his head. "Dinna do that, lass." His voice sounded husky and a bit breathless even to his own ears.

"Have I done somethin' wrong?" She furrowed her brows in thought.

Duncan cupped her chin, "Nay lass, but yer a lady, and ladies, dinna do such thin's."

Raven flashed him a quick grin, "This one does." With that she took to torturing him once more with her innocent, but skillful mouth.

Having no choice, Duncan plunged his fingers in her hair and threw back his head as she drove him damn near over the edge. The feeling of her tongue swirling over him as her hot wet mouth stroked him, suckled him as she drove him closer and closer toward the edge of insanity. He knew he couldn't hold on much longer. He pulled away from her, "Enough. I can stand yer sweet torture, nay longer."

He pulled her to her feet then into him. His manhood pressed against her stomach and she could feel his pulsing heat. The taste of his mouth on hers was a bit of heaven. Her body heated as flames licked over her skin in the wake of his hands exploring her. Moving her backwards, he lowered her onto the bed. His naked body pressed her down into the feather mattress and his weight was glorious.

Breaking their kiss, he raised himself up on his arms to look down into her passion filled face. "I want ye, I need ye." He bent his head to tease her lower lip with his teeth. His mouth moved to her jaw to nibble, then down her neck. His teeth grazed over her collarbone, making her sigh. When his tongue flicked over her nipple, she cried out. As his mouth closed over her breast, she arched toward him, her fingers plunging into his hair holding him to her.

Duncan laved and pleasured her breasts until she was whimpering. His hands urged her on until she was wound nearly as tight as he was. His fingers sought her feminine mound and ran through her silky black curls. Slipping a finger between her soft folds, he found her wet and ready for him. With skilled fingers, he drove her need higher and higher, until she was nearly screaming her need for him.

Raven was sure she would die from the pleasure he gave her as he drove her so high. Her hands raced over his body as need filled her. When her release came at last she cried out his name as she buried her face in the crook of his neck and held on to him.

Looking down into her passion filled face, he slipped inside her and watched her eyes slowly open. Their bluish-green depths were filled with her pleasure. Pressing himself deep within her, he strained to hold back his own need for release. Slowly, he withdrew then pressed forward.

Purring deep within her throat Raven threaded her fingers through Duncan's silken hair, she brought his mouth down to her own for a long breathy kiss. Wrapping her legs around his waist she met him thrust for thrust and urged him on.

Ecstasy wrapped around the couple as they moved in a dance as old as time itself. As pleasure spiraled through her, Raven allowed her hold on her magick to slip. The blue glow that filled their chamber lit the room and danced around them.

Duncan felt the tingle of it and allowed it to flow through him freely. The feeling of their combined pleasure raced through them heightening the sensations they felt. As he felt his own release racing forward he reached between their joined bodies and found her tiny jewel of desire and caressed it with his thumb. As he felt her inner muscles clench and grip around him signaling her release, he threw back his head and roared as he fell over the edge into the abyss of sheer pleasure.

Fourteen

Raven looked down at the babe in her arms and smiled, Braydon was adorable, he had the look of his father, Lachlan. His thick black mane and beautiful green gaze made her all but melt when he smiled, or laughed. She looked up from the babe she held to Kandra and Bryanna as they came out of the water together. The child would be nigh on the same height as her mother.

"Has he begun to fuss yet?" Kandra called to Raven as they approached.

"Nay, he's an angel." Raven couldn't help but to think of how lucky Kandra was to have such a beautiful family and a man who loved her so completely.

Kandra flopped down next to Raven and looked over at her. "Tell me what 'tis that look?"

Placing a smile on her face Raven shrugged, "I can nay help but to admire yer family, ye've wonderful children."

"Yes, I do." She looked at the other woman and laughed, "It was not easy for me to get here, Lachlan was not the man you see now. He was terrified to fall in love with me." Kandra wove her story of how Lachlan had taken her prisoner and how he had wanted her even though he argued with himself about the fact. She told Raven how she had no idea how a woman was supposed to act, or the pleasures of being a woman, for she had been raised in a castle filled with men. When she spoke of her brother Jonas, her face glowed and Raven could see her love for her brother. She went on to tell how she had been carrying Braydon when she left Lachlan.

"But ye left him," Raven shook her head, "How could ye nay tell him about the bairn ye were carryin'?"

"Because, he had made his choice." Kandra reached over and took Braydon to hold him and play with him. "And I was too stubborn to fight for what I wanted." Smiling over at Raven, she laughed, "In case you have not figured this out yet, all MacKinnon men are hardheaded and dense in the matters of love."

Raven snorted, "He's dense all right." She picked up a stone and rolled it around in her hands. "He's aggravatin' to say the least. One moment, I think he's done with..." She looked over at Bry, then spoke softly, "Isobel, but in the next I am nay so sure."

"I think 'tis time we paid her a visit," Kandra smiled wickedly.

"Perhaps 'tis time I turned her into a miserable rodent." Raven narrowed her eyes, "Mayhaps one of the castle cats shall have a feast."

"Can you do such a thing?" Kandra gave her a wide-eyed look.

Raven shrugged her shoulders, "I am nay sure, I've nay tried before." She looked at Kandra raising her brow, "I would be willin' to try on her though."

Kandra threw back her head and laughed, causing Braydon to laugh and Raven to smile as the sound warmed her heart.

"Aunt Raven, Mam, look what I've found." Bry brought them what she had dug out of the sand. Raven reached out and took it.

"Amazin'," she whispered as she studded the blue hue to the glass. "I wonder where it came from?" Kandra ran a finger over the smooth glass. "Looks like a heart in the center."

"Aye," Raven traced the heart, "'Twas formed from lightnin' strikin' the sand." She smiled up at Bry, "'Tis a gift from the Gods, lass." Looking at the glass Raven whispered a soft chanting spell. The blue glass in her hand began to glow a soft pink. "Now 'tis even more special, for it can tell true love and it will glow red when true love 'tis near it." Carefully, Raven handed it to Kandra, "I've one more gift for ye." She spoke to the stone in her hand then blew across it. Raven held out the stone, she had been rubbing between her hands.

Bry clapped her hands then held them out, "What does the stone do, Aunt Raven?"

"'Twill protect ye, 'Twill warn ye when danger 'tis near at hand." Raven ran her hand down Bryanna's dark head, "Keep it with ye always Bry, my love."

"I will," she promised as she clutched the stone, "Can I take the stone to go show, Da?" She begged Kandra.

"Yes," Kandra smiled at her daughter, "But we'll bring your glass heart back with us."

Bryanna kissed her mother's cheek then Raven's before she raced off to find her father and show off her new treasure.

Kandra looked back at the woman next to her, "That was kind of you."

"'Twas nay kind," Raven shook her dark head, "'Twas meant to be." She looked at Kandra, "I created the glass heart." When Kandra raised a brow, Raven laughed, "'Twas the first time Duncan and I made love, here on this beach."

"Does that happen every time you make love?" Kandra laughed at the thought.

"Nay, but I was angry with him and I called upon the elements, one of those being lightnin'. I made it strike the ground nay more than ten feet from where he stood and 'tis how the heart was created."

"And how long will the heart and the stone keep the magick, you've given them?" Kandra looked at the heart sitting between them.

Raven's mystical eyes looked in to Kandra's blue ones, "Until I perish from this world, I believe."

Bryanna showed everyone her magick rock. Lachlan looked at the plain stone and frowned, "I dinna see how 'tis magickal." He turned the stone this way and that.

"Mayhap, there 'tis a faery inside it." Ian suggested as he gave the stone a look see. "Nay," Bry growled at the four men looking at her stone.

"'Tis magickal, because it protects me from danger." She put her hands on her little hips, "Aunt Raven said 'tis so."

"Then it must be," Aidan snatched her up and held her upside down by her ankles, "I'll hold her and ye run her through, Duncan."

"Aye," Duncan reached for his sword as he gave a growl. All four men froze as the stone began to glow blue. "Holy..." He trailed off as he threw a glance toward Bryanna even as Aidan set her on her feet. Duncan's gaze whipped around and found Raven standing a few feet away.

"See I told ye 'twould glow." Bryanna bounced up and down with joy.

"So, we see," Duncan looked at Raven for a long moment then back at Bryanna. He scooped the little girl up in his arms, "'Twould appear the blasted thing saved yer hide this time."

Bry threw her arms around Duncan's neck and kissed him soundly on the cheek, "I ken ye would nay have hurt me, Uncle Duncan."

"I'm a fearless highlander, lass, dinna ye forget that." He handed her to Aidan then ran a loving hand down her dark hair. He looked at his cousins and brother then turned toward Raven.

Raven took in the fearless highlander in all his splendid glory. He was tall, nigh on six and a half feet of him. His hair was dark brown, and he wore it to flow down to the middle of his back as braids were woven through it with golden beads decorating it. His greyish-blue gaze looked predatory and hungry. His face was as handsome as sin with his strong nose and chin. His sensuous lips that made her body burn for him were set in a smile. She looked at his corded neck and broad shoulders, his arms that rippled with muscles and held golden armbands with the same spell of enchantment that Aidan, Ian and Lachlan all wore. His chest and arms were bare, as he wore nothing, but his kilt and knee-high boots. A washboard stomach that rippled when he moved had her nearly sighing. He was sheer male and was filled with untapped power. She nearly stepped back when he strode up to her, but instead she only raised her chin.

That was one of the things about Raven that he adored, her bravado. Though she was nearly half his size, she could take on the world and stand her ground.

Reaching out, Duncan ran his knuckles down her cheek. "'Twas a neat trick, lass."

"'Twas nay a trick, 'twas magick." She smiled up at him. Reaching up she laced her fingers with his and sent her magick humming through him.

His greyish-blue gaze fired with longing, "Dinna start somethin' ye can nay finish, lass."

"Who says I can nay finish it?" Her bluish-green eyes swirled with power and desire.

Duncan didn't give her a second to think it over. He grabbed her, throwing her over his shoulder then turned and saluted his kin as they stood there smiling. His long legs ate up the ground between the inner bailey and his chambers. Once he had her above stairs he reached up and began fondling her as he made his way to his chambers.

Raven was breathless at his barbaric behavior, and she relished the idea of making love to him in the middle of the afternoon. As he fondled her on the way to his chambers, she got revenge of her own as she grazed her lips over his bare back. Her teeth nipped, and her tongue soothed as she tasted him. She laughed when he threw her onto his bed.

A sensuous smile graced her face as she watched him strip out of his kilt.

The evening meal was ready to be served and once again Raven was on Duncan's arm as they entered the great hall. All eyes turned toward her, and the conversation came to a grinding halt. Raven clutched Duncan's sleeve and looked for a friendly face.

Through the crowd, Kandra once more came to her rescue. "Raven, you look beautiful in that gown."

Kandra took in the aqua that nearly matched the swirl in Raven's eyes.

"Thank ye," Raven smiled then turned to Ferran MacKinnon, "Lady MacKinnon, ye look wonderful." She took the older woman's hand in hers and smiled as Ferran pulled her in for a hug.

"As do ye lass," Ferran cupped her face in her hands and studied the younger woman, aye, she would do for Duncan most certainly. "But ye must simply call me Ferran, as I have told ye these past weeks."

"Thank ye, Ferran." Raven lightly squeezed her hands in return. She looked around the room and caught the stray glances and sighed. These people would never accept her as one of them.

"Dinna fash yerself about it, lass. Ye've friends aplenty." Ferran smiled brightly.

Kandra placed her hand on Raven's shoulder, "Yes and that is all that matters." As Aidan made his way into the great hall all the females seemed to bubble. Kandra rolled her eyes, "Sure he's a sight to look at, but I don't think the man could ever love just one woman. And all these women seem addle to drool over him."

Raven smiled and tucked her arm in Kandra's, "It will take a fiery redhead to capture his attention, but trust me, she's waitin' for him."

Kandra raised a brow and looked at Ferran, "Do you suppose there is such a woman out there who will capture the rogue's attention and hold it?" Ferran cupped both of Raven's cheeks in her hands again, "Praise ye lass, for givin' an old woman hope." She kissed Raven's cheek even as they all laughed. "And what are the three of ye conspirin' about this time?" Aidan looked down at all three women then bent and brushed a kiss over his mother's cheek. "Mam, ye look fetchin'."

Ferran cupped her son's cheek, "Thank ye Aidan, yer a charmer just as yer father Magnus was, the Gods bless his soul." She had that sad look in her eyes that she always got when she thought of her late husband, Magnus MacKinnon. Tentatively, she reached up and touched the necklace she had worn since the day her husband had given it to her.

Aidan wrapped his arm around his mother's shoulders and gave her a quick gentle squeeze. "I ken Mam, Da was a good man."

Raven looked at the two of them and felt her heart go out to them for their loss, but, yet she was happy to see the love and affection that mother and son shared.

Her gaze drifted over to where Duncan was laughing with Lachlan and Ian. She wondered what it would be like to hold his bairn in her arms and ken the magick of real love. As if he could feel her eyes upon him, Duncan turned his head to look at her with that greyish-blue gaze. The smile that he gave her was full of sexual heat. Raven blushed to the roots of her hair.

She was seated next to Duncan throughout the meal. He touched her often, a brush of his arm, or his hand on her thigh under the table, stroking caressing and teasing her. Duncan shared a trencher with her, cutting meats and offering her the best morsels. She had no choice, but to allow him to feed her.

Laughter ran up and down the head table and Raven felt like she was family with these people. She watched the way the MacKinnon's interacted with each other and saw the love they shared for one another.

When the meal was finished, Ian called for the tables to be cleared and moved. Soon, music filled the great hall and people danced and laughed. As the music filled the room Raven was clapping and tapping her foot along with the revelry in the hall.

She watched Ian dance with Ferran and Lachlan sweep Kandra into his arms. Aidan had maids aplenty lined up to dance with him. She laughed as she watched an older man sweep his wife into his arms and twirl her around.

Suddenly, Duncan was in front of her, "Would ye care to dance, lass?" He held out his hand to her.

She looked in his beautiful greyish-blue eyes. "I would love to." Placing her hand in his, she felt his large warm hand close over hers. Her heart pounded as he led her to the dance floor. As he swept her into his arms, Duncan smiled down at her. Her silky black hair swirled around her as he spun her in time with the music. Her laughter washed over him as her eyes sparkled with pleasure.

He whirled her and turned her as they moved to the beat of the music. She felt as if she could dance with him forever.

When the reel came to an end, he placed his hands on her waist and guided her to the sidelines.

They stood together and watched as one of the lasses preformed an intricate sword dance. Raven clapped along with the music and cheered as the girl's feet flew over the swords never touching the blades. She was amazed by the girl's agility and skill.

As the sword dance ended, Raven clapped and cheered along with the rest of the MacKinnons. As couples began to drift back onto the dance floor once more Raven smiled as Aidan came over and offered her his hand. She placed her hand in his and allowed him to sweep her onto the dance floor. It was a lively reel, but fun.

"My cousin looks fit to be tied." Aidan smiled at her. "I dinna believe he is happy 'bout my dancin' with ye."

Raven looked over where Duncan spoke heatedly with Lachlan and Ian. Rage was in his body language as he gestured. She shook her head, "I dinna understand him. He acts as if he is jealous."

"The fool is besotted with ye, luv." Aidan winked at her, "He's fit to be tied with the jealousy coursin' through him right now." He caught the glare Duncan sent him and smiled brightly back at him. The fool needed to lay his claim to Raven before someone else came along and stole her away, Aidan thought wearily. Gods knew if he had a woman like her, who could love him for more than his looks, he would brand her, his and never let her go.

Duncan grumbled and growled as he watched the two dance and he knew one thing for certain, Aidan was a dead man, for he flirted with Raven openly. Raven was his woman and no other man should be touching her, Duncan thought as jealousy raged in him.

"What are ye doin' standin' here grumpin' and growlin' for?" Ferran MacKinnon frowned at him, "If ye want the woman, then go claim her, dinna let Aidan put yer dander up, as he is doin' this to goad ye, lad." She tugged at his long hair, "I ken yer father well, and Alistair would nay have let another man, family or nay steal his woman, lad."

"Can I break his body into little pieces?" Duncan smiled at her hopefully.

"Och lad, dinna ye be hurtin' my bairn." Ferran smacked his muscular arm, "But ye may go steal yer woman away from him."

"Aye, I think I will." Duncan flashed a wicked smile at his Aunt Ferran then strode to the dance floor. Walking up to the dancing couple he looked down at Raven, "I've come to steal ye away from this rogue, lass." With that he spun Raven out of Aidan's arms and leaned down as he grabbed her waist and tossed her over his shoulder.

"Ye can nay be stealin' my woman?" Aidan groused.

"Aye, I can, 'tis tradition," Duncan grinned at him as Raven gasped, "Besides she is nay yer woman, she's mine." With that he turned on his heels and strode from the great hall with Raven draped over his shoulder.

"Put me down ye, big oaf," Raven smacked his broad back. "Have ye lost yer bloody mind?"

"Aye, I've bloody lost my mind." Duncan laughed then swatted her on the bottom playfully. "Now, hush woman."

Raven stopped swatting him and her mouth hung open, "Hush?" She was appalled.

"Aye, hush." Duncan laughed and pulled her back over his shoulder so that she dropped in his arms as he strode down the corridor to his chambers. "And stop tryin' to bite me, lass, or I'll have to be bitin' ye back." He glared wolfishly down at her.

"I should put a dark spell upon ye and make ye sorry." She groused and glared at him. Duncan stopped a few doors down from his chambers and looked at her with a raised brow. "Can ye do that, lass?"

Raven glared at him, "I dinna ken, but I'd be willin' to try, Gods ken ye deserve nay less."

Throwing back his head, he roared with laughter. "Yer a wicked wench, Raven." He shook his head and continued to his chambers.

Striding into the room, he kicked the door shut behind him with a thud. Near the bed, he gave her a toss and had her landing on the bed with a bounce.

"Yer pushin' yer luck, Duncan MacKinnon." She growled at him. "What the bloody hell are ye 'bout?" She glared at him from where she lay upon the bed.

He stood over her looking down at her lying there so small and beautiful. Her raven black hair spread gloriously around her, her bluish-green gaze glared up at him furiously. She was tiny in comparison to him, but she was as tough a woman as he could hope for. Without a doubt, he wanted to take this woman to wife, have bairns with her and grow old together. "I'm claimin' my woman." He spoke gruffly.

She snorted, "Ye've gone addled in the head, I'm thinkin'." Pushing up on her elbows, she raised a black aristocratic brow, "And pray tell, what 'tis that puppy dog look, upon yer face 'bout?"

He flashed her a wicked grin, "I'm just thinkin' how nice 'twill be when I have ye beneath me beggin' for me to love ye." Turning he sat upon the bed and began unlacing his boots.

"Yer thinkin' 'tis wrong," she spoke softly as she snagged hold of his long dark hair, tugging it until he lay back upon the bed. As he lay upon his back, her mouth fastened over his. She poured all her love and desire for him into that one kiss.

Hunger for this man clawed at her. She wanted to feel his hands upon her bare flesh, his mouth feasting upon her breasts as his manhood was buried deep within her. Her hands clawed at his shirt as she tried to get to his bare skin. Impatient, Raven pushed up his kilt as she straddled his hips.

Duncan growled deep in his throat as his mouth fastened onto her breast through her linen gown.

When she settled herself over his engorged shaft, he thought he would lose his blessed mind.

She smiled wickedly down at him as she lowered herself onto his thick engorged shaft. She nearly purred with satisfaction, as he stretched her and filled her completely. Slowly, she raised herself up until he nearly slipped out of her warm, wet, tight, sheath and he growled low in his throat. Raven laughed wickedly, as she began to explore her sexual power over him. She rotated her hips as she moved over him and he moaned softly. *'Oh aye, this man would beg for mercy 'afore she was through with him,'* she thought.

When at last Duncan was straining under her and she had driven them both to a wild frenzy, she began to move faster as she rode him. Multi-colored lights swirled and magick hummed in the air around them. His hands slid to her hips as she rode him into completion.

Fifteen

They made love several times through the night, each one was slow and leisurely. Their last time to make love was during the gray of dawn. Raven was so sated, she was sure she would sleep for the next week, but Duncan was not about to allow her that pleasure.

"Wake up woman," he patted her rump soundly and smiled at her groan. "By the Gods yer a stubborn wench."

"Bugger off," she groaned and swatted at him as he shook her again. "Can ye nay see I'm sleepin' here, ye great oaf? Let loose the covers, I'm cold." She fought with him for the covers.

When she lost her hold on the blanket, he smiled down at her naked body curled up on the bed. Kneeling upon the bed, he began running his hands over her body. Soon she was anything, but cold.

Raven glared up at him as fire lit her body, "Yer a cruel man, Duncan MacKinnon, a verra cruel man."

Duncan threw back his head and laughed, "I'm a great man lass, and dinna ye be forgettin' it." He smacked her bottom as she rolled away from him, "Now, get yer arse out of this bed and dress woman, we've plans for the day."

Raven watched him through narrowed eyes as he climbed off the bed. "Ye'll pay for that, dearly." She rolled off the bed and padded naked across the room to the washstand and began to cleanse herself.

Duncan watched her and felt his loins stir painfully, "I'm payin' already, lass." He spoke under his breath.

Raven frowned down at the cold rag in her hand, "I'd like a bath 'afore we hire ourselves off anywhere." She glanced over her shoulder and saw the raw desire upon his face. She flashed him a smile and turned around. Dropping the cloth back on the stand she walked slowly toward him.

He swallowed hard as he watched the bounce and sway of her breasts as she glided across the floor toward him. The curves and hallows of her body made him ache with need. His cock stirred to life and throbbed with wanting to thrust inside of her. As she came to a halt in front of him, he nearly groaned.

Raven looked up into his greyish-blue gaze and she saw his hunger, hunger for her. His dark hair was loose save for the two braids that hung down on either side of his face. His chest was bared except for his tartan that was wrapped around his waist and thrown over his shoulder. One of the MacKinnon clan badges fastened the plaid in place. Reaching up she ran her fingers over the pewter badge, then up to touch the ends of his hair. Finally, her fingers traced his jaw that was smooth from his shave that morning. She traced the shape of his lips and smiled when his tongue flicked out to touch the pads of her fingers. "Yer a right bonnie man, Duncan MacKinnon."

Duncan gave a low chuckle at her words as he reached out and cupped her face in his large hands. Slowly, he bent his head and brushed his lips over hers.

She sighed with pleasure at the feel of his lips on hers. As he pulled back, she laid her hands over his.

"The true beauty here 'tis ye, lass." He rubbed his thumbs over her cheeks.

She turned her face into his palm and pressed a kiss to his sword-roughened hand.

"Now, ye best get dressed lass, or we'll end up havin' at each other once more, and we'll be verra late for our outin'." He winked down at her, "Though I can nay say I would be mindin' more bed sport with ye this mornin'."

She laughed then turned and padded back toward the washstand. "Tell me where we're goin'."

"'Tis a surprise." He leaned back against the wall and watched her finish washing.

She glanced over her shoulder at him, "If ye dinna tell me where we're goin', how will I ken how to dress? Breeches, or a gown?"

"How about aught, at all." Duncan raised a brow.

Raven laughed, "I dinna think yer brother and the rest of the men in the castle would like such a thin'."

"Aye, yer right on that account, a'cause I would have to kill 'em." He pushed away from the wall and strode to the armoire in his room and pulled open the doors. Inside there were several of her dresses. Reaching in he pulled out a gown of light blue then shook his head and placed it back inside. Frowning he scanned the dresses, then pulled out a pale green one and smiled. "I like this one." He held it out to her.

"And why this one, 'tis nay a day dress." She raised a brow, but took the dress deciding she would play along with him and find out what he was up to. Duncan just smiled down at her, "Put it on woman and let us nay tarry."

Without a word, Raven donned the gown then turned to him expectantly. With a sigh, he fumbled with her laces. "Blasted things are easier to undo than to redo." He growled as he struggled to tie them.

When she was trussed up in her laces, she looked at him with a raised brow, "And my hair?"

"Leave it down, I prefer it thus." He reached out and took her hand dragging her toward the door. "If we dinna hurry the entire castle shall be stirrin'."

"But Duncan, what 'bout me feet?" Raven tugged at his hand trying to stop him.

He drew up short in the hallway, "What of yer feet?"

"I've nay boots on." She lifted the hem of her gown and showed him her bare toes. Looking back up at him she laughed at his puzzled gaze. "I'll be needin' my boots, won't I?"

He looked from her feet to her face, "Nay," He reached out and swung her into his arms. "Where I plan to take ye lass, ye'll nay be needin' yer boots." He strode to the stairs and hurried down them. Through the great hall and into the kitchen he went.

A lad of no more than ten, stood there with a basket in his hands waiting for them. "Here's what ye requested m'lord." He held out the basket and hooked it in Duncan's hand.

"Thank ye, Henry," Duncan smiled down at the boy, "Tell cook, to give ye a slice of her sweet bread with honey this morn."

"Thank ye, m'lord." The boy beamed with pleasure. With that, Duncan strode from the kitchen and back through the great hall. Raven frowned when he stopped at the door to the secret passageway.

"What are we doin' here?" She looked at him wearily as he set her on her feet then looked back at the door.

Reaching out, he cupped her chin and made her face him, "Trust me lass, there is aught to fear down there."

Slowly, Raven inclined her head. "I trust ye, Duncan."

With that Duncan released her and reached around her to release the latch of the secret door. When it swung open, he helped her step inside. Torches were already lit to light their way down.

As they descended, the stairs grew slick and the sound of waves were distant this time. When they wound their way around a curve, Raven could see the end of the stairs. She hesitated a moment as she looked in to the darkness beyond them.

"Dinna fash, Raven, 'tis safe, I swear it to ye." He frowned down at her when she still didn't move. "How 'bout if I go first?" When she only inclined her head, he took her hand in his and felt her terrified grip.

When they reached the last step, Raven clung to him as darkness engulfed them. The sound of the waves grew more intense and fear clawed at her. "I beg ye, Duncan, dinna make me go down there." She gripped his forearm with both of her hands as her voice came out in a hoarse whisper.

"I swear, I'll nay let anythin' hurt ye, *gràdh*." He leaned down and whispered the words against her ear. "Ye said ye trust me, now show as much."

Slowly, Raven inclined her head and allowed him to lead her through the dark. She swore as they walked the black changed to gray. She was sure her mind was playing tricks on her and squeezed her eyes shut. The cavern floor was slick, but soon it gave way to what felt like sand beneath her feet. When at last Duncan stopped walking, Raven realized she was shaking with fear.

"Open yer eyes and look, gràdh." Duncan's warm breath brushed against her ear.

Swallowing her fear, Raven slowly opened her eyes in the early gray light of the morning and saw part of the sea spread out before her with the gentle waves dancing toward her feet. Large rocks enclosed the bay so that it was hidden from the world. She could not see where a ship could get through the rocks, but she was sure if one knew how, they could do just that. Looking up at the blanket of stars above her head, had her smiling. When at last she looked back at Duncan she sighed as she spoke, "'Tis a bonnie place ye have here."

"Aye, 'tis one of my favorite places to watch the sun rise in the morn." He gestured toward the east. "And I thought, perhaps ye would enjoy havin' an early mornin' picnic here." He set the basket of food upon the sand and took the blanket from the top of the basket and spread it out.

Raven watched him for a long moment then turned back to the sea and wrapped her arms around herself as if she were cold. She knew how cold the sea could be, how dark and dangerous it was. A shiver ran through her as pictures flashed through her mind, images of dark angry waves crashing over her and the anger of the sea as it tried to drag her down into its watery depths.

"Do ye want to take a swim 'afore we eat?" The question Duncan posed to her, brought her out of her flashes of memory.

Raven gasped as she looked down to where her toes nearly touched the water's edge. She stumbled back into Duncan as he stood behind her. Fear quaked through her as she stared wide-eyed at the water. Duncan wrapped his arms around Raven, holding her to him. "Dinna fear lass, the water can nay harm ye so long as I'm with ye." He pressed a kiss to her temple. "I'm a verra, verra good swimmer."

"'Tis a good thin' to ken." Raven smiled weakly up at him. "But I have nay plans to set foot in that water." She frowned over at the sea as its waves kissed the shore and a sudden memory assailed her. A man with raven black hair, blue eyes and a blonde woman with lovely green eyes lying upon the beach in the sun, they were so in love with each other. She closed her eyes and let the memory take her, and she knew deep in her heart it was a memory of her parents.

"What 'tis it, *gràdh?*" Duncan felt her elation and turned her to look in to her face.

She reached up and cupped his jaw, "I remember. I remember my parents." Pushing up on her tiptoes as she pulled him down to her to brush a kiss across his mouth.

"'Tis wonderful," he hugged her to him. The feel of her arms sliding around him had him smiling. Though she was slight, Raven was a powerful woman. He set her away from him and took her hand, "Now let's break our fast, shall we?"

"I'm famished," Raven spoke honestly as she placed her hand over her stomach. She had gained at least a stone since she had been with Duncan, she was sure. Shaking her head, she laughed, "If I am around ye much longer, I'll be fat as a cow, the Gods ken I eat neigh on as much as ye do, now."

"I like a woman who can hold her own at eattin'." Duncan smiled down at her, "And if yer to get as big as a cow, I'll change yer name to Bessie MacKinnon to suit ye." He laughed when she punched him in the arm and stuck out her tongue.

"Yer a blackguard to the verra bone." She shook her head then squealed with delight as Duncan picked her up and carried her to the blanket.

When he sank to his knees with her in his arms. Raven took advantage of the situation. She kissed him soundly on the mouth, Gods how she loved this man. When at last she pulled back, she was seated in his lap and her hands were in his dark silken hair. Her breath was heaving and her body was afire with desire. Carefully, he set her aside and began unloading the basket of food and drink.

Raven watched him make a trencher with cheese and fresh bread. Thick slices of salted pork were added to the trencher. Apples and a plum were placed upon it next. He poured her a tankard of sweet watered wine and handed it to her. Using his dirk, he cut the meat, bread, cheese, and fruit. He held a piece of salted pork to her lips for her to eat and Raven took it eagerly.

As he fed her from the one trencher and she sat there on the blanket sipping sweet watered wine, she felt cherished. She felt as she had never felt for a man the she could remember. She was completely seduced by his affection.

When the food was gone, and the wine was all but finished Duncan stood and took her hand. Without a word, Raven went with him to near the water's edge. When he settled against one of the cavern walls and pulled her down, she laughed. Once she was nestled between his bent knees, she settled back and looked at the sky to the east where the first tinges of morning were creeping across the sky.

His chin rest atop her head and she was surrounded completely by his warmth as he held her.

She could feel his heartbeat at her back as she slipped her hand into his. He raised her hand and brushed a kiss across her knuckles.

Raven snuggled into him and watched as the sun crested the horizon washing the world in blues, pinks and gold. "That 'tis true magick," she whispered reverently, "'Tis the bonniest thin's to see."

"Aye," Duncan agreed, "I can only think of a handful of thin's bonnier."

"Like what?" Raven looked up at him. "Wakin' up next to ye every mornin' for the rest of my life." He brushed a kiss over her lips. "Growin' old with ye, and havin' wee bairns together."

Raven gasped, "What are ye sayin', Duncan? Speak plainly now, for I think my brain is addled." He could nay mean what she thought he was getting around to, she thought with her mind whirling and her heart hammering.

"What I'm sayin' Raven MacKinnon, is that I'm askin' ye this time to do me the honor of becomin' my wife." Duncan took a ring off his pinky finger and held it out to her. "I want to spend the rest of my life with ye. I want to have wee bairns together. I want ye to make me complete. I've asked ye once before and here I am askin ye one last time to be my wife. I love ye, Raven MacKinnon."

She turned and knelt in front of him. "Yer serious?" She narrowed her eyes at him, "Yer askin' aye, nay demanding and yer through with Isobel?"

"Aye, never more serious. I'm truly askin' ye, lass. There aught between Isobel and myself now." He took her hand and held the ring to her finger, but didn't slip it into place. "So, will ye do me the honor?"

She looked down at the golden ring posed at the tip of her finger. The sapphire in it winked in the morning light and made her think of the sea and the eyes of the man she loved. Celtic symbols wound their way around it and Gaelic words encircled the sapphire. "Two hearts woven together make one life." She read the inscription and tears filled her eyes. Looking back in to his deep greyish-blue gaze Raven smiled, "Aye."

Duncan slipped the ring on her finger then frowned, "It does nay fit."

"It fits perfectly." Raven took the ring and put it on her thumb for now. "See, we have it fixed later, but fits here!" She looked at the man sitting before her and threw herself at him, "Oh Duncan, I'm so happy." She pressed a kiss to his mouth.

The kiss was filled with passion and met with passion. Before long both lay naked in the sand as they made leisurely love, each sating their hunger for the other.

When at last, their passion was spent, they lay curled together in the sand and dozed. Finally, Duncan stirred and looked down at his snoozing bride to be. Tracing her nose with his fingertip, he smiled as her eyes fluttered open. "Let's take a dip in the water and clean all of this sand off from us." Panic filled her eyes as she shook her head. He laid his finger across her lips to silence her, before she could protest. "I would give my life for yers, and I would let aught, or nay one harm ye. Ye said that ye trusted me, now show me that ye do and come into the water with me."

Raven looked away from him, "I'm afraid, Duncan."

He caught her chin and made her look back at him. "I ken love, but ye must face yer fears if ye wish to ever overcome 'em."

"Swear to me, ye shall keep the water from takin' me away." Raven looked in to his eyes and saw his honesty.

"Come in to the water with me and I shall make certain ye shall come out once more." Duncan pushed to his feet and held out his hand. "Do ye trust me?"

Raven placed her hand in his, "Aye."

Together they walked to the edge of the water and Raven's heart hammered in her chest. Duncan stood before her and took both of her hands, "The water will nay harm ye."

Raven looked in his eyes and allowed him to tug her into the water. The first feel of the water hitting her toes made her want to run away, but Duncan held tightly onto her hands, and coaxed her in farther. Before long, she was knee high in the water, then hip deep.

"That's it, keep comin'." He smiled down at her, "We've a long way to go 'afore I can touch bottom nay more."

She laughed, "That would be because yer giant compared to me." She was almost chest high in the water now and she felt the energy flowing through her.

"Stop," she cried and frowned down at the water. Something called to her, but what it was she had no idea.

"What's amiss, lass?" He searched her face, but couldn't tell what was wrong.

Raven tugged her hands free of his and laid them on top of the water. "Can ye feel it?" She looked up at him and heard his gasp.

Her eyes had turned a translucent aqua and glowed, even her skin glowed with the shimmer of blue. She was ethereal, as she stood there in the water with the tops of her breasts showing and her black hair floating around her. "Aye," he spoke hoarsely, and yes, he could feel the magick shimmering around them.

Suddenly she smiled, "I can swim." She laughed and then she dove under the water only to resurface a few yards away from him. "'Tis it nay great, Duncan? Come catch me if ye can." She was gone again and Duncan dove after her. His hand skimmed over her ankle as he swam under water after her, but she was as quick in the water as a dolphin and as slippery as an eel.

The game went on for some time, with Duncan catching her from time to time and stealing a kiss. Then she would slip out of his grasp and flittered away through the water. They were nearly across the cove from one another when Duncan surfaced. The sound of Raven's laughter had him turning around and glowering, "Ye cheated lass."

"Nay," she shook her head, "Yer just slow." Her laughter rang across the water and had him smiling.

"When I catch ye, ye'll pay for such an insolent remark." He smiled wickedly at her. "Well first ye must..." Right before his eyes she was suddenly ripped under the water before she could finish. Panic washed over him as Duncan pushed away from the rocks and swam as fast as he possible could toward her with one thought ripping through his mind. He had failed her, and he had let the sea take her away.

Reaching the spot where she had been he dove under the water to search, but found nothing. He began searching through the water for any sign of her, staying under the water until his lungs nearly exploded and he was forced to the surface.

Raven coughed the water from her lungs as she felt the floor beneath her palms. Her wet hair clung to her as she pushed herself into a sitting position. Looking around the chamber she recognized it from her past. A smile flittered across her face as she spied the two thrown chairs on the platform. Pushing to her feet, she walked across the room, she was now wearing an iridescent pale blue gown, with shells at the shoulders and waist. She knew the gown to be one of her favorites. "Mama," she whispered and ran her hand over her dress.

Suddenly, the memories came crashing in. She knew her real name as well as her mother and father's names. Rhiannon was her mother and Toslar was her father. Ishna was her grandmother. She held her head as her whole life came rushing back at her. Her head pounded with all the information that overwhelmed her and she wept.

The feel of loving arms wrapping around her, had her turning into her mother, "Mama, oh Mama." Raven cried.

"Oh, my baby," Rhiannon rocked her daughter as she whispered in Manx to her. "The troubles and trials ye have gone through."

When at last, her tears subsided Raven looked up at her mother, "But how am I here, Mama?"

"We tried so long to reach ye and to bring ye home, but ye turned yer back upon the sea and we were powerless to help ye." Rhiannon wiped at the tears still on Raven's face. "But ye are home now, and happy 'tis that we have ye back."

"I have missed all of ye so much, though I dinna remember any of ye, my heart was empty without all of ye." Raven smiled watery, "Where is Da?"

"I am here," Toslar stood from where he had sat watching the two women he loved most in the world as they cried together and held one another. He strode toward his daughter and wife. "I am nay sure if, I should scold ye, or hug ye." He told Raven. "But I'm thinkin' I shall settle for huggin' ye for now, then shall scold ye later."

"I will take the scoldin' later for my foolishness, but for now, tell me that ye love me, Da." Raven wrapped her arms around her father.

"With all my heart and soul," he pressed a kiss to the top of her head. "I could almost hug that mortal who helped us get ye back." He laughed.

Raven pulled away from her father and looked down at the ring she still wore on her thumb. "Duncan, oh Gods Mama, he must be worried sick." She pressed a hand against her stomach.

Rhiannon took her daughter's hand and led her to one of the shells filled with water, "Show us what we seek." She waved her hand over the water and it glowed for a second then showed Duncan sitting on the edge of the water with his head in his hands. "Oh, the poor man, he is so verra sad, for he blames himself for lettin' ye down." Rhiannon frowned into the water.

"I have to go back to him." Raven looked at her mother, "I have to let him ken that I am well, and tell him who I am."

"I forbid it!" Tosler roared from behind them. "We have only gotten ye back. I refuse to allow ye to leave our home ever again." He huffed as he stormed around the throne room.

"But Da..." Raven cried.

"Nay!"

"I love him!" Raven raced to her father, "I love him with all of my heart." She pressed her hands to her chest.

The sight of the ring on her finger had her father's rage boiling to the surface and the waters of the sea reacting. "What is that?" He pointed to the ring.

Raven looked at the ring on her hand, "I have agreed to marry him." She looked her father squarely in the eyes, "I have given my word."

Before her father could say more, her mother brushed past her, "Tosler enough! They are bound together, I have seen this with my own eyes. Only they, or the Gods can tear them asunder. 'Tis nay for us to interfere." She raised a brow at her husband daring him to contradict her. "Ye ken my visions are never wrong."

"Aye," Tosler swiped a hand over his face. He raised his eyes to the heavens above, "Then who am I but a concerned father to argue with the Gods?" He looked at his daughter, "Go back, but ken that I shall be watchin'. Warn yer young man, that I'll tolerate aught untold from him. And I expect that if there is to be a weddin', it will be held with yer family in attendance."

"Aye, Da." Raven swallowed hard then turned to her mother. "I have to go back Mama, but a part of me does nay want to. I dinna wish to leave either of ye."

"But ye must," Rhiannon cupped her daughter's cheek. "'Tis yer destiny, he is yer destiny."

Raven noticed the sad look in her mother's eyes, but before she could question it her mother was sweeping her toward the center of the room once more.

"Ye must hurry back to him," Rhiannon pressed her cheek against her daughter's. "Remember love is nay an easy road to travel, but 'tis worth fightin' for."

She gripped her daughter's hands as she stepped away, "Hurry back home, my sweet."

"I love ye, Mama." Raven watched her father speak the words that would send her back to the man she loved.

Sixteen

Duncan held his head in his hands as guilt washed over him. He had promised to keep her safe then he had lost her. Duncan searched, until his body had nearly given out in the effort. His muscles were weary, and he ached with every fiber of his being. His heart broke with the knowledge that he would never find another woman like his Raven. There would be no bairns, no mornings of waking up next to her and keeping her in their bed to make long leisurely love. He would not see her eyes fire with temper, or hear her sweet voice ever again.

"Twas nay fair, that I should lose her so soon after finding her,' he thought wearily. *'Why are the Gods punishin' me?'* Duncan looked to the sky and let out a bellow of rage. Lying back on the sand he threw and arm over his eyes. He had begged and pleaded while he searched for her. Duncan had offered up his own life in place of hers and, yet the Gods hadn't listen to him.

"Why?" He asked the gods once more.

She saw him lying there as she rose from the water. What a miserable sight he was, it broke her heart to know that he was distressed over her. She stopped as she stood on the water looking at him. "Poor Duncan," she spoke softly.

At first, he thought he was hearing things. That perhaps he was losing his mind. Raven had been swept out to sea. She was gone. Was his mind playing tricks upon his poor heart?

"Duncan, oh Duncan." Raven walked toward him across the water.

Duncan sat up looking out over the water watching the image of her walking toward him. "Yer nay real." He whispered hoarsely.

She inclined her head and smiled, "Aye Duncan, I am verra much real. I assure ye." Raven laughed as she walked to the water's edge. "I'm verra much alive, Duncan." She reached out, and he pulled away. She laughed lightly.

"I saw ye go under the water, I searched for ye." He held up his hands and frowned. His eyes were filled with grief, "I swear to ye, Raven, I tried to save ye. I'm sorry I dinna keep my word to ye."

"I'm nay dead, ye great oaf," Raven knelt beside him and grinned as she reached out cupping his face then pressed a kiss to his lips. She laughed against his mouth as he sat there frozen. "Are ye goin' kiss me back, or must I do all the work?" Raven whispered against his lips.

Duncan pulled back and cupped her face in his large hands. His thumbs brushing over her cheekbones then her lips. "By the Gods, yer alive?" He searched her eyes and raised a brow, "How?"

She looked down and didn't meet his gaze. "'Tis a long story and one that will take a bit of explainin'." She sighed.

"I dinna give a damn 'bout any of it," he pressed a kiss to her lips then rained them over her face. "I only care that ye've come back to me."

When he pulled her into his lap she wrapped her arms around his neck and met him in a passionate kiss. His hands roamed over her as if to make sure she was whole and hail. Before she knew it her dress was laying a few feet away and Duncan's mouth was exploring her bare flesh. Her fingers curled into his silken hair and she pulled his mouth back up to hers for a long erotic kiss. But Duncan was not to be sidetracked as he pulled from their kiss and leaned down to run his tongue across her taunt nipple. The sound of her moan drove him to taste every inch of her. His mouth roamed from one breast to the other then down over her stomach to her hip.

The feel of his lips on her skin burning a fiery trail, had her nearly screaming. Her hands were buried in his hair as she held on for dear life. He was driving her beyond control.

He wanted her beyond reason, but he longed to taste her sweet essence. As his tongue thrust deep inside of her, she screamed his name and he reveled in her pleasure. He drove her higher and higher then allowed her to come down a bit only to drive her higher still. When at last she spent her release, he moved up her body to cover her with his own and thrust deep within her.

It had almost killed him, but he held himself still and looked down into her beautiful face. When her black lashes fluttered opened to look up at him, he smiled down at her. "Will ye take me to husband?" His voice was husky with need and desire.

Raven reached up and cupped his cheek. "Aye, I will take ye to husband, Duncan MacKinnon." "Here with nature and the Gods as our witnesses, I will take to ye wife, Raven MacKinnon." He leaned down brushing a kiss across her lips. "For the rest of our lives we will be man and wife." He began to move within her making her moan with pleasure.

"I love ye, Duncan." Raven raised up pressing a kiss to his lips.

"And I love ye, Raven MacKinnon." He returned her kiss. Together they loved and fulfilled each other until both were completely sated.

Duncan wasn't sure how long they lay there wrapped around each other, but the sun was much higher in the sky now and he could catch the echoes of activities from the castle above them. He looked down at the woman who lay in his arms and admired her beautiful face. Her breaths were even, and her lashes formed half-moons upon her cheeks as she slept. Duncan had thought his life over when he had lost her, but to have her back in his arms was a blessed miracle.

He traced her lips in her sleep then her cheekbone and she stirred. Duncan took a lock of her hair and let it fall like silky water through his fingers. Never had a woman made him feel the way this woman did. He could never allow her to know the full extent of the power she held over him, least she bring him to his knees.

"Why do ya look so somber, my love?" Raven traced her fingertips over his cheek as she searched his greyish-blue gaze.

"I was contemplating what a lucky man I truly am, *gràdh*." He dipped his head and took her lips with his own. Just then her stomach rumbled, and he laughed.

"Mayhap we should curb our ways and find ye a bit of food." "Mayhap." Raven blushed up at him, she loved it when he called her, *gràdh*, the endearment meaning love, made her feel cherished. She took his hand, when he stood and allowed him to help her up. With a wave of her hand she clothed herself in the gown she had worn down from the castle. When she looked up at Duncan, he stood there with his brow raised in shock. "I can explain." Raven offered lamely.

Duncan closed his mouth and turned to pick up his trews and put them on the mortal way. When at last, the laces were done up, he looked back at her. "I think 'twould be prudent for ye to explain that little trick." Raven stepped forward then frowned, "Mayhap, we should sit down and eat while we talk." She walked over to the sheet and knelt upon it.

Duncan sat then opened the basket and found it all but empty. "I'm afraid we've eaten all but a heel of bread." He held it out to her.

Raven looked at him for a moment, then over his shoulder. "If ye'll allow me, I can remedy this." Duncan waved her on and she closed her eyes and held out her hands over the basket. The blue lights swirled then faded.

Duncan reached into the basket and pulled out cold meats and cheese. When he looked at her he saw her flinch and realized he had not allowed her to explain. "Pray, explain all of this to me as I seem to be at a bit of a loss."

Raven bowed her head and her thick black hair curtained her face as she tried to figure out a way to tell him all that had happened to her. When he stuck his fingers under her chin and forced her to look at him, she swallowed hard. "The best way would be to meet this head on and start at the beginnin' if ye can, *gràdh*," Duncan smiled gently at her.

Raven looked unsure, but she took a deep breath and began her tale. "My name is nay Raven, 'tis truly

Relia and I am the daughter of King Tosler and Queen Rhiannon." When she saw the bafflement in his eyes, she surged on. "They are the rulers of my people." She looked down at her hands, "I am half Irish Sea Water Guardian and Manx witch." She allowed a blue ball of energy to fill her hands. "My home was on the coast of the Isle of Mann." She glanced up at him, "That 'tis where my parents live."

"So how did ye end up with clan Brodie?" He frowned thoughtfully.

Raven laughed softly. "I had an argument with my father and I left my home to find my own place in the world." She snorted and shook her head, "How wrong I was. I wanted to be a mortal, so I packed my belongin's and ran away from home."

She shook her head, "I was on a ship and the storm came from nay where, a hurricane that threw the ship 'round and I could nay stop it. The boat broke apart in the water and I was tossed in the dark churning waves, where I hit my head and nearly drowned. I was terrified when I awoke. I swam as long, as I could, until my body was exhausted. I found a piece of the ship floatin' in the water with me and I grabbed onto it. The next thing I ken, I had washed ashore near the Brodie keep where they took me in and I became the Laird's prisoner and I was given the name Raven, 'cause of my hair."

Raven sighed, "The rest ye ken except that when we were swimmin', my parents summonsed me to one of the underwater castles. There I began rememberin' and now..."

She shrugged her shoulders and looked at him for a full minute before she dropped her eyes.

"Relia," Duncan turned the name over as he looked at her, "'Tis a bonnie name, but it does nay suit ye, I prefer, Raven." He smiled at her, "So yer a princess, are ye? And do yer parents ken about what 'tis between us?" When she nodded, he laughed hardily, "I bet yer father 'tis fit to be tied, as I'm far below yer station."

"To tell the truth, he would be unhappy with any man. Especially a mortal." She smiled at him. "But 'tis my choice."

His greyish-blue gaze caught hers, "And do ye choose me, Princess Relia?" Duncan's face was somber and serious as he stared at her.

Raven felt her indignation raise, "Did I nay just choose ye?" She gestured toward the place where they had made love, "Did I nay choose ye, when ye asked me if I will take ye to husband?" Her eyes swirled dangerously like a storm at sea. "When we made love."

Duncan inclined his head, "Aye, ye did." He reached out pulling her across the blanket to him and kissed her. He pulled her into his lap and looked down at her. "So yer immortal?"

"Aye," she whispered as she snuggled into him. "So ye'll stay young forever, while I'll grow old." Duncan thought this over, "Why would ye want to be with me, when I'm a dodderin' old man and yer a young bonnie woman?" He pressed a kiss to the top of her head.

"Because I plan to grow old with ye," she pressed a kiss to the underside of his jaw.

"How 'tis it possible?" Duncan frowned in thought. She moved her shoulders in a small shrug, "I will give up my immortality."

Duncan set her away from him and glared down at her, "The hell ye will." He was angry in a flash, "I'll nay allow it."

Raven's mouth opened then closed as she tried to understand his fury. "Ye have nay say in my keepin', or givin' up my immorality." She raised a brow, "'Tis my decision and mine alone."

"The hell I dinna have a say, yer my woman and I will nay allow ye to give up yer life for me." Duncan grabbed her shoulders and shook her slightly, "What if I were to die in a month, a year, what would ye do then?" He tried to check his anger, "Mortal means ye shall die one day, and I will nay have ye die on me."

"I have nay plans of dyin' anytime soon," Raven smiled at him, "We've bairns to make together and raise." Leaning into him, she brushed a kiss over his lips.

He set her back from him once more, "Promise me, Raven, ye shall wait, and ye will nay do such a thin' without my agreein' with ye. Promise me?" His gaze pled with her.

"If it means so verra much to ye, aye, I promise." She inclined her head. Raven didn't understand why it was so important to him, but if it meant that much she would keep her word. Her heart sung with happiness that he seemed to be able to accept her as she was.

Duncan inclined his head then stood, "I think 'tis time we were gettin' back to the castle 'afore Ian sends out a search party." Reaching down he helped her to her feet then pulled her into his arms and looked in to her bluish-green gaze, "Ye'll be wantin' a proper weddin' I expect." He brushed a stray lock of hair away from her face as he smiled down at her. "What exactly is proper among yer people?" He wondered aloud. "We'll settle for a mortal weddin' as long as my family can be in attendance." Raven wrapped her arms around his waist and held onto him. The sight of a couple standing near them had Raven turning her head.

"Do ye see them?" Duncan whispered in shock. "Are they ghosts?"

"Nay, they are images from the future. 'Tis a rare thin' we're seein', for 'tis a stitch in time." Raven spoke with a smile, for the couple looked very much in love, yet sad at the same time. The man was nearly as tall and broad as Duncan, with long black hair and bright blue eyes. The woman was tiny in comparison with long curling blonde hair and big brown eyes. And if Raven wasn't mistaken she had a bit of Elf in her. The odd thing about the vision was that they seemed to be studying each other, as Raven and Duncan looked at the couple they looked back and even more strangely Duncan could see them. Raven looked up at Duncan, "Ye can see them?"

"Aye, I can see them, yet, I ken that if I were to walk over there they would nay be standin' there." He took his eyes from the couple and looked down at her. "Who are they?"

"I dinna ken," Raven shook her dark head and smiled, "But I ken the lass belongs to yer brother somehow."

"And how do ye ken this?" Duncan raised a brow. The woman had been fetching and she had reminded him of his own kin, for there was something in her looks that had said MacKinnon, but the man with her had been a stranger.

"I have visions of the future." Raven looked back at the spot where the couple had stood. "I have seen her before, the lass, in a vision of Ian's future."

"Aye, she has the look of a MacKinnon." Duncan inclined his head proudly. "Perhaps, she is to be Ian's daughter." He smiled in thought. He would give anything to have bairns of his own. Ian was going to be one lucky man.

When at last Duncan and Raven returned to the real world going about in the castle above, they were met with grim faces.

Ian met them with a scowl, "We've to talk brother." He ground out, "'Tis serious."

Raven looked from brother to brother and smiled wanly, "Pray excuse me, I must seek out Kandra to have speech with her."

Duncan turned to her and looked in to her beautiful face, "I shall seek ye out later."

She smiled lovingly up at him, "Until later." Raven inclined her head then walked away. Something was wrong. Something, that Ian didn't want her to know. She would see what Kandra knew of the situation.

Duncan followed his brother to his study, where Lachlan, and Aidan were already seated. Ian walked over to the hearth and leaned against it as Duncan leaned against the desk frowning at the group, "Tell me, what has got ye all with such long faces?"

"Gordon MacLean, their Chieftain, has decided that he wishes to talk before any more blood is shed." Ian growled, "He wishes ye and yer lady to pay yer respects at his home, within the next sennight, so that ye may discuss his departed son and his actions, and mayhap avoid further bloodshed." Ian snorted in disbelief.

Duncan's greyish-blue eyes hardened, "I'll nay allow Raven to go there." He would not place the woman he loved in peril, it was out of the question.

Ian's mouth hung open for a seconded then he snapped it shut, "Do ye hear yerself, Duncan?" He pushed away from the hearth to pace "Ye've nay one concern for yerself, ye dolt."

Duncan raised a brow, "I will nay put the woman I love in danger." He looked at his brother and cousins, "Ye can nay ask of me, what ye would nay do yerselves. And if my payin' a visit to the MacLean will stop a clan war, then so be it." He looked at each man as he spoke, "But nay a one of ye, shall speak a word of this to Raven. I'll nay have her upset."

"Are ye daft man?" Aidan leaned back in his chair and shook his head, "Ye'd be walkin' into a slaughter."

Duncan inclined his head, "Aye, 'tis possible, but if 'twill save the bloodshed of our clan, then so be it. But I shall stand before the MacLean and announce that justice was served when Baoithein, laid his hands upon my woman."

Lachlan steepled his fingers, "I must agree with, Duncan." He raised a hand when Ian and Aidan would have protested, "I would do nay less for Kandra, or my bairns. I would nay allow any of them to accompany me, but I would stand for her and my clan, to avoid useless bloodshed." He looked at Duncan. "Ye must go, but nay without a plan, if things should go awry."

"I thank ye," Duncan inclined his head then looked at his brother and other cousin, "There can be nay other way, without harm to our people."

Ian sighed, "Yer a fool, but yer a good-hearted fool." He looked at his younger brother, "I suppose, we've a plan to make."

Duncan flashed his brother a smile, "Aye, we do, but we're MacKinnon's so nay worries."

Though Raven was worried about what Ian was so upset about, she was happy. She had her memory back, the man she loved, and even now she was seeking out Kandra to tell her the happy news of their upcoming nuptials. Humming to herself, she walked down one of the hallways, where Kandra and her family were staying.

On her right, a door stood slightly ajar and Raven felt the sickness within. She heard a moan and felt her heart lurch. She could not stop herself from walking over to the door and pushing it farther open.

On the bed across the room lay a figure under a comforter. A small pitiful groan came from the figure. Raven walked over and looked down at the woman lying there. Her golden hair lay limp and sweat soaked. Her pale skin was nearly translucent from her pain and sickness. Raven felt her heart sink, she had done this, she thought as her words came back to haunt her. "*I've had enough of ye and yer wickedness. Bother me nay more, or pay three-fold for the trouble ye give me. With heartache and headache ye'll pay with sickness. And ye shall feel my wrath in yer worst times. As I will so mote it be!*"

Dropping to her knees next to the bed, Raven took Isobel's hand in hers, "Oh Isobel, I'm so sorry. I dinna mean for this to happen."

Light blue eyes looked in Raven's face, "I'm sorry, Raven, I should nay have been so cruel to ye." Isobel winced in pain and coughed. "I hope ye can forgive me?"

"Oh Isobel," Raven stroked her forehead that was burning up with fever, "I can help ye if ye'll let me."

Isobel looked at her with such hope, that Raven prayed she wasn't wrong. "Ye will nay let me die?" She rasped, "I dinna want to die." Tears welled in her eyes and coursed down her cheeks.

"Of course, I shall nay let ye die." Raven stroked her forehead and smiled, "Close yer eyes and rest." She sighed as Isobel did as she requested, "*What I have done,*

I undo. Undo the heartache, headache and sickness, I cursed upon ye. What I have done, I undo. As I will so mote it be!"

Isobel sighed in her sleep as Raven touched her forehead once more and found it cool. She smiled and pushed up from the bed. She froze as the old crone stood in the doorway.

"Witch, ye cursed her with yer evilness." The crone pointed a finger at her. "I ken what ye are." She accused.

Raven narrowed her eyes, "And I'm sure ye've been sharin' yer views with the rest of the castle." She shook her head, "Yer ignorance amazes me." Raven spat, "Ye of all people should understand the old ways, and revere the magick around us, crone."

The old woman gasped as Raven began to glow a vibrant bluish-green and the windows of the chamber flew open blowing Raven's black locks around. The old woman turned to flee out the door, but the door flew shut and locked. The crone turned around fear marring her face, "Who are ye?"

"I am Manx Undine," Raven informed the woman. "Irish Sea Water Guardian?" The old woman gulped, and when Raven inclined her head the crone nearly fainted. "I dinna mean any disrespect." She bowed her head and waited for this magickal being to strike her down for her lack of respect.

"Ye did mean great disrespect," Raven's eyes glowed in an iridescent bluish-green. "I should strike ye down for yer ignorance, and yer lack of faith."

"I beg ye to spare me." The crone dropped to her knees. For she knew that with little more than a flick of her wrist, Raven could end her existence. "I dinna ken who ye were." "Is this how ye treat all others of magick? Would ye be so ignorant as to look down yer nose at a *Tautha de Danann*?" Raven narrowed her eyes at the woman, "I am nay less, for I do the biddin' of *Manannan, the Sea God.*" "Aye m'lady," the crone groveled at her feet, "I have disrespected ye, but I beg yer forgiveness and another chance."

Raven looked down at her bent grey head and sighed, "From this day forth ye shall respect all magick, even that which is foreign to ye. For I could have verra well been *Unseelie* and ye could have met yer end." She reached out her hand to help the crone up, "On yer feet, I charge ye to take care of Isobel and see to her needs. If she should grow worse, then send for me immediately."

"Oh, thank ye m'lady." The crone lumbered to her feet even with Raven's help. "I swear to ye, I shall nay disrespect any magick again."

"Ken the old ways are still verra much alive." Raven smiled softly at her, "Ye have nay forgotten them and ye'll pass them down."

"Aye m'lady." The crone bowed her head. "I shall take my leave of ye if ye've nay further need of me." Raven inclined her head to the old woman. When the old woman smiled wanly at her and assured Raven she had no need of her assistance, Raven took her leave to continue her journey to find Kandra.

Seventeen

Raven was asleep in his chamber by the time Duncan found her late that night. He looked down at her beautiful sleeping form. Even in the tiny hint of moonlight from the last stages of the waning moon, she seemed to glow with her beauty. Duncan watched her for a time as she slumbered. He memorized her features, etching them into his memory.

When at last he couldn't stand it any longer, he stripped his clothing and slipped into the bed with her. His fingers traced over her silken skin, his lips followed the same path, as he tasted her skin.

"Duncan?" Her voice was husky with sleep.

"Who else do ye think 'twould be, *gràdh*?" He laughed softly against her skin.

"Mayhap 'twould be my lover, he would nay wish for ye to ken of him." She rolled over toward him and wrapped her arms around his neck. "For he 'tis verra handsome, verra virile." She sighed heavily, "And his kisses neigh on make me swoon."

Duncan rolled her under him and gave her a cocky smile, "He sounds as if he's verra handsome, and a rouge of a lover." He brushed his lips over hers.

She laughed softly, "Aye, that he is." Raven ran her fingers over his cheek, "Where have ye been so long?" He captured her mouth with his. "Thinkin' 'bout ye, lass," Duncan spoke as he pulled back from their kiss leaving her breathless. She frowned up at him, "What's amiss, Duncan?"

He slipped his fingers between them and found the curls at the junction of her thighs and stroked her. "Ye talk too much, Raven, my love." Duncan captured her mouth once more as she moaned. He made love to her that night until she was so sated, she was sure her body floated up off the bed. There was such a hunger to his loving that she had been swept away by it. She snuggled into Duncan and decided that they would talk in the morning about what was worrying him. For now, sleep was pulling her under and she surrendered to it.

The sunlight streamed through the window and Raven blinked in annoyance. She tried to snuggle in closer to Duncan, but found that he was missing. Slowly, she sat up and found herself naked in his bed with Duncan's tartan wrapped around her. Looking around she spied a piece of parchment on Duncan's pillow. With a sinking feeling she picked it up and began to read the masculine script.

Raven,

I had to leave and dinna wish to wake ye, lass, for ye looked so peaceful, like a bonnie sleeping fae. I shall be gone 'bout a week. Watch yerself lass, and dinna wander to far from Dun Akin, for 'tis nay safe. Stay near Kandra, for she can help ye if the need arises. Keep my dagger with ye, always. If either ye, or Kandra should have a problem, go to Giles or Shane, for Ian, Lachlan, Aidan and myself, have left them in charge of Dun Akin until we return. Stay safe, and await my return, then we shall announce our union and make plans for a formal celebration. Dinna worry, lass, I shall make haste in my return to ye.

Duncan

Raven read the note twice and scowled. She threw back the covers and Duncan's tartan as she climbed out of bed. She stomped around her chambers as she performed her morning absolutions.

Half an hour later, Raven was pacing in Ian's study as Kandra sat watching her. "How dare he be so high handed!" She growled then read the note to Kandra.

Kandra sat up when Raven finished, "Oh my goodness." She got to her feet and hugged Raven, "You're betrothed?"

Raven looked up into Kandra's excited face, "Aye, but he may nay make it long enough to fetch a priest." She shook her head, "I dinna understand this, where have they gone?"

Kandra hugged her again then laughed, "I fear MacKinnon men are all high handed." She sat back down and shook her head, "I got a similar note this morning as well." She narrowed her eyes, "I was not very happy myself. When I find out where they've taken off to, I plan to go after my husband and show him the sharp edge of my tongue."

Raven sighed and sat in the chair next to Kandra, "I fear somethin' 'tis terribly amiss." She shook her head, "I dinna like this."

Kandra sat up, "Can you see where they've gone?"

Raven shook her head, "Nay, for they are nay in a place I can see them, or I am blocked, for I am only Undine, nay Fae."

Kandra looked at her and frowned, "What is this Undine?"

Raven smiled softly at her, "'Tis a long story and one for another time."

Raven knew she should be angrier at Duncan, but she reasoned with herself that Duncan wouldn't have slunk off in the night to only the Gods knew where, if something wasn't terribly wrong.

"I've nothing but time," she laughed and sat back more comfortably in the chair and placed her hands over the tiny swell to her belly where her babe lay.

Raven sighed and began her story of how she regained her memory and how she visited with her parents. She got up and paced as she told Kandra everything that had happened.

Kandra smiled affectionately at Raven, "So you're an Irish Sea Water Guardian with a dash of Manx witch." She laughed, "Well isn't that amazing."

"Aye, but it does nay help with our problem of findin' our wayward men." Raven growled as she flung herself into the chair next to Kandra. "I already tried to find them this morning, but am somehow blocked. They must be far away from the sea."

"No, it does not help, but I think I have an idea." Kandra pushed up from the chair, "Come, we'll go seek out those who do know where they are and try our hand at persuading them into telling us what we wish to know."

Raven smiled up at Kandra, "Shane and Giles, what do ye have in mind for 'em?"

"We'll talk on the way." Kandra rubbed a hand over her stomach. "Men get nervous around pregnant women."

"Yer an evil woman, Kandra MacKinnon." Raven laughed, "I can nay wait to see this bairn of yers born. He will be an amazin' man, with an amazin' life."

Kandra ran her hand over her stomach and smiled, "I hope you're right."

"I've seen it." Raven smiled at her then linked her arm through Kandra's. "I think when they return, or we find 'em, we give those men hell for leavin' us without nary a word." She tisked, "They act as if we're fragile, or some such thin'."

Kandra gave an unladylike snort, "I may be carrying a babe, but I am far from delicate." She looked down at Raven, "And Lachlan damn well knows it."

"Aye, but I would nay want ye to be strainin' yerself. It could cause great harm to yer bairn." Raven smiled then placed a hand against Kandra's stomach and was rewarded with a powerful kick.

Her blue gaze caught Raven's, "I would not allow anything to happen to any of my children."

"I dinna doubt it," Raven laughed, "Yer a wonderful Mama." She reached over and squeezed Kandra's hand lightly, "And yer a wonderful friend. The best I've ever had."

"I feel the same," Kandra wiped at her eyes as tears filled them, "I'm afraid I am a weeping willow with this one."

"I pray I never get in such a way if I were to have a bairn." Raven shook her head as they continued down the hall.

"I think you shall be a wonderful mum," Kandra laughed, "And Duncan will be a doting husband and father."

Raven's eyes went all dreamy, "Aye, that he would be." She sighed, "I do love the man so."

"It has been obvious for some time." Kandra laughed, "You have the look."

"I dinna have such a look." Raven shook her head and laughed.

"Yes, you do." Kandra grinned, "It's in the way you look at him, or how your eyes go soft when you think about him."

Raven gave a hearty laugh, "Aye, mayhap I do."

Half an hour later the two women had Shane cornered in the great hall. Kandra's fists were on her hips, "Tell me where they've gone, and I'll not run you through."

Shane shook his dark head, "I'm afraid I can nay tell ye, m'lady." He sighed heartily, "If I were to tell either of ye, the Lairds would strin' me up, cut out my tongue then cut me to pieces a bit at a time."

Raven narrowed her eyes at him, "We would nay allow them to do such thin's."

"Ye could nay stop 'em," Shane frowned and got a horrified look in his eyes, "The men ye fought with here in the great hall, do ye ken what happened to 'em."

Raven looked at Kandra who shook her head then she looked back at Shane, "They were punished of course."

Shane looked at her with surprise, "They were put in the dungeon and they're still there. The Laird and his brother deemed that they could die in there for all they cared, for they attacked MacKinnon women." He saw Raven's horrified face, "They were whipped 'afore they were put in there."

Raven gasped. "'Tis outrageous!" She cried then turned to Kandra who was pale, "'Tis nay right, we must do somethin' to free those men." She could feel her anger bubbling at Duncan and his cohorts. She looked back at Shane, "We're nay through with ye." She waged a finger at him, "But for now ye'll take us down to the dungeon to fetch those men." When he started to deny her request, she placed her hands flat on the table where he sat and leaned toward him. "'Tis nay the Laird and his cohort ye should be fearin' here and now, believe me, boy-o 'tis me." She stood up straight and created a blue ball of energy in her palm, "I could destroy this castle and all who reside in it in the blink of an eye." When he stood, and stepped away, she looked at Kandra, "Duncan MacKinnon shall rue the day when he returns, or I find his sorry, *mas*."

Kandra fought to hide her grin and choke down the laughter that wanted to bubble out. Without a doubt, Duncan was the ass Raven had called him, but she wasn't the only one who was steamed over the misdeeds of her man. When Ian, Duncan, Lachlan and Aidan returned, or she and Raven found them, they were in for an earful each.

Raven went to the dungeon with Kandra on her heels. They found the men in a cell together and none of them were in very good shape. Raven was steaming when she ordered them taken to chambers up in the solar.

She had some of the men bathe the wounded men then she and Kandra began washing and tending their wounds that were infected.

One of the men named Dorstan was in grave shape. Raven ordered seawater and sea kelp along with several other herbs. She tended his wounds with a special mixture then used her healing powers to begin drawing out the infection that had set in. By the time, she was done she was swaying on her feet.

Kandra touched her arm, "You're in need of rest."

Raven looked at her and inclined her head, "Aye, but these men are in sore need of care."

"Yes, they are, but Shane and his men can care for them, while you rest." Kandra ushered her out of the room and down the hall to where Raven's chamber was. "Get some rest, we've a rough evening, for we must badger Shane for the whereabouts of our men."

"Aye that we must," Raven laughed softly then turned to her chamber door. "Wake me in nay more than a couple of hours, I'll surely be myself by then." Kandra promised to wake her then left Raven to crawl wearily into her bed. When her head hit the pillow, she was already asleep.

Two hours had passed in the blink of an eye for Raven. For when Kandra had awakened her, Raven had felt as if she hadn't rested one bit. Dark smudges were under her eyes and her body was weary. With heavy feet, she walked to the great hall and met Kandra for the evening meal. She had no appetite and pushed her food around her plate more than anything.

"Tell me what is wrong, Raven?" Kandra placed a hand over her friend's. A worried frown creased her brows.

Raven forced a smile, "Truly, I am fine." She shook her head, "I just need a bit more rest."

"Perhaps, we shouldn't badger Shane this evening." Kandra frowned as she looked at Raven, "Mayhap you should sleep."

"Oh nay," Raven shook her dark head, "I want to ken where Duncan has scurried off to that he could nay tell me 'bout." Anger simmered and her weariness was pushed aside slightly.

"When we figure out where they have gone, I say we ride out after them and give them what for when we catch up to them." Kandra narrowed her eyes in thought, "Lachlan, will be lucky if I ever speak to him again."

Raven held up her hand, "Ye mean we shall take a coach after them, aye?"

Kandra laughed and shook her head, "A coach will be far too slow. We shall ride horses."

"Horses?" Raven squeaked.

"Aye, horses are the fastest way to catch them." Kandra raised a questioning brow, "Can you not ride?"

Raven shook her head, "Nay, I'm terrified of such large beasties."

Kandra laughed, "Horses are gentle and sweet." She gave Raven a determined look, "Then we shall spend the next few days teaching you to ride."

"Nay," Raven squeaked with a terrified look upon her face, "Ye can nay be serious."

Kandra raised her brow, "I've never been more serious," she frowned, "You are dependent on a man if you do not know how to ride, or fight."

Raven only smiled weakly at her and prayed she would live through the lessons. When the evening meal was finished, Raven hurried through the castle to where the wounded men lay.

She smiled as she saw that Dorstan was awake. She walked over to the bed and reached out to feel his brow. "Ye've a touch of a fever." She tisked, "But at least ye'll live."

Dorsten looked up at her, "Shane, told me that ye and the Lady MacKinnon freed us from the dungeons." He swallowed then continued in a rough voice from his parched throat. "I'm beholden to ye, Lady Raven, ye've saved our lives. I'm sorry, for what we did. We had nay cause. I beg yer forgiveness."

Raven smiled down at him, "There is aught to forgive, ye made a mistake and 'tis nay but human to error." She cupped his cheek, "But I beg of ye to learn from yer mistake."

"I shall m'lady." Dorsten closed his eyes, "But I fear the MacKinnon, or Duncan shall banish us from here, or execute us."

"I will nay allow it." Raven raised her chin. She was determined that she would not allow Ian, or Duncan to harm these men in anyway, they had paid for their crimes dearly, already two of them had nearly died.

When at last she had Dorsten settled and asleep, she slipped from the room and met Kandra in the hall. Worry filled her eyes as she spoke, "How do the others fare?"

"They are gaining their strength back and healing, how is Dorsten?" Kandra peered over her shoulder at the closed door, Raven had come through.

"Not well, but he has awakened and spoke to me." Raven sighed, "I fear he is nay improvin' as fast as I had hoped. The sepsis in his wounds is verra severe." She glanced at the door over her shoulder. "I think I should perform another healin' on the morrow."

Kandra eyed her carefully, "I don't think that would be wise, you look tired." She laid a hand on Raven's shoulder, "Are ye unwell?"

Raven smiled, but it did nothing to dispel her weary look. "Nay, I am fine, just a wee bit tired." She sighed, "I am in sore need of rest."

"Then why do we not seek out our chambers," Kandra smiled at her, "Besides, I want to go look in on the children." Kandra adored her children and couldn't wait to see them.

Raven read her longing in her eyes and smiled, "Agreed, we shall seek our chambers and meet on the morrow."

"Yes, so that we may start your riding lessons." Kandra grinned then turned and walked away.

Raven scowled at her back, "I am feelin' a wee bit ill after all." She called after Kandra and the sound of her laughter floated back to Raven.

Eighteen

Raven scowled at Kandra as the taller woman drug her out to the stables. "I dinna want to be doin' this." She informed Kandra who didn't even break stride. "I hate big beasties."

"They are not beasties." Kandra shook her head. "They are amazing animals. Strong and powerful, beautiful and swift."

"And huge," Raven wailed, "Kandra, have ye nay noticed that I'm a verra wee woman?"

Kandra stopped and eyed her, "I have, but what is your point?"

"That those beasties could kill me." Raven growled up at her and placed her hands upon her hips. "I can nay ride a blasted horse, on my own!"

"I did not take you to be a weakling. I apologize, if you are too scared to learn." Kandra put her hands on her hips and narrowed her eyes at Raven in challenge.

Anger ignited in Raven and she was ready to argue. "I am nay a coward." She spat at Kandra, "Ye may be bigger than I, but I'm just as tough."

"Then prove me wrong." Kandra issued the challenge. Raven waved her on as she spoke, "Fine, pray lead the way."

Kandra smiled as she walked toward the stables and Raven stalked next to her. She had the feeling that once she got Raven upon a horse and showed her the freedom of riding, Raven would be thrilled.

At the door to the stables Raven's steps faltered. The beasts beyond this point were large powerful animals, where she was small and lacked the physical strength to stop one if it became out of control.

Kandra looked back at her as she stood in the doorway, "They'll not hurt you, Raven." She walked over and stroked the white nose of her destrier, Hadwin, as he poked his head out of his stall. "Hello my darling." She fed him a half of an apple as a treat.

Raven watched in awe at the way Kandra was nuzzled by the horse with pure affection. Hadwin as she called the beastie, seemed overjoyed to see his mistress. Kandra laughed as Hadwin nuzzled her satchel and nibbled at her clothing. "Scoundrel," she scolded him softly, "You love me merely for the treats I bring you." She pulled the second half of an apple out of her satchel where the horse had been nibbling. Hadwin took it with a look of pure bliss.

Finally, Kandra turned to Raven, "Come in and meet one of my best friends." She beckoned Raven forward and laughed as Raven shook her head, "I swear, he'll be a perfect gentleman." Kandra assured her.

With a sigh, Raven stepped into the stables and slowly walked up to stand beside Kandra. When the horse moved her way snorting, she jumped back hiding behind Kandra, who laughed heartily.

Reaching behind her Kandra grabbed her hand and thrust it forward so that Hadwin could smell her.

As the horse nibbled her palm, Raven laughed and peered around Kandra at the great beastie. "What's he doin'?"

"Getting to know you," Kandra smiled, "and if you would step out from behind me he would see you as well as be able to smell you."

Gingerly, Raven stepped from behind Kandra and faced the horse. When he moved his massive head, and tried to nuzzle her, he nearly knocked her off her feet and she laughed. "Yer a bit enthusiastic, there boy-o, I'm but a might of a thing, ye've to be more a mite more, gentle." Raven wagged her finger at him and Hadwin nodded then tried once more, gently this time.

Kandra stared at her, "How did you do that? Usually he only listens to me."

Raven looked back at her and laughed, "I simply spoke to him the way I would a sea creature." She looked back at Hadwin enthusiastically. "Can I ride him?"

"No," Kandra laughed and shook her head, "He's not the type of horse you could control at first." Kandra smiled to soften her words, "You lack the strength and skill it takes to control him."

Raven looked at her then at the horse, "Aye, ye'd ken best." She was determined to ride him before long though. For he was a beauty of a beastie, she thought as she stroked a hand down his soft nose. "Aye, yer a beauty, are ye nay?"

Kandra smiled and walked down the row of horses. She passed where Lachlan, Aidan, Ian and Duncan's horses had been stabled. She couldn't wait to get her hands upon her husband, because her wrath would know no bounds.

Walking down the aisle, Kandra found a nice friendly mare and stroked her soft nose as she butted Kandra looking for attention. "This one is the one for you, Raven. She will be gentle and careful with you." Kandra stroked the mare's head and laughed as she nibbled on her shirt. "Sorry, but Hadwin ate all of the apple. I'll bring you some later if you are good this morn."

Raven walked down the aisle and looked the mare over. She was black with a white star on her forehead. Her big brown soulful eyes looked back at Raven with gentleness. "She's a pretty thin'." Raven reached out stroking a hand down the mare's head. "Do ye think she'd let me ride her?" Raven looked at Kandra hopefully.

Kandra looked at the horse then back at Raven. "I believe she would be the perfect horse for you to learn upon. She's very docile, and has a good heart." Kandra looked back at the horse, "Let's get her saddled." She opened the stall door and led the mare out of the stables.

Kandra taught Raven how to saddle the mare that they discovered was named Star. Once the saddle was on, Kandra taught Raven how to mount the horse.

"Always mount from the left." Kandra instructed and demonstrated as she mounted the mare. She smiled down at Raven as she spoke. "You probably will need to find something to help you mount. Here in the stables you can use the mounting block, or the fence. But outside of here, you will need to find a rock, or a tree stump." Kandra stepped back and allowed Raven to lead the horse over to the mounting block then waited for her to climb up.

Raven ran a hand over Star's flank then looked at Kandra, "I'm still nay sure I can ride her. She's a bundle of muscles and power."

"You shall be fine, and I am right here to help you should you need it." Kandra assured her. She knew that Raven could handle anything that came her way and that truly she had no real need of Kandra, except perhaps to give her instructions as to how to ride. Before she mounted, Raven took the horse's bridle in her hands and lowered the horse's head until she was looking the beastie in the eyes. "I expect ye to be mindin' yer manners, Star." She stroked a hand over the horse's head then smiled, as the horse seemed to nod her head in agreement. Taking a deep breath Raven stepped up on the mounting block and carefully mounted the mare.

Settling herself upon the horse, Raven finally let out the breath she had been holding. When the mare danced anxiously under her Raven smiled. "She's wantin' to run in the fresh morn air." She looked at Kandra and raised a brow.

Kandra laughed and shook her head, "Absolutely not." She walked over and took the mare's bridle. "Let's walk before we run, shall we?" She gave a shrill whistle and Hadwin her large destrier came trotting over. Grabbing his mane, Kandra sprang onto his back in one graceful movement.

"Should ye nay be careful with such movements when yer carrin' yer wee bairn?" Raven raised a brow and scolded.

"I began riding a horse before I could walk." Kandra flashed a brilliant smile in return, "And I rode nearly every day that I carried Braydon. Trust me, we're fine."

"If ye say as much." Raven shook her head. "What are we about now?"

Kandra moved Hadwin next to the mare and she showed Raven how to use the reins and her heels to spur the mare into action.

"Does that nay seem a bit mean, can I nay simply ask her to begin walkin'?" Raven frowned in thought.

"It doesn't usually work that way." Kandra laughed softly.

"Aye, but it does." Raven leaned forward and spoke in Gaelic to the horse. Star inclined her head twice then began to walk calmly forward.

Kandra stared in awe, as she watched Raven and the mare move forward. She had never met anyone else who could simply speak to a horse and have it do as she asked. "You can truly speak to the horse?" She bit her lower lip then confided, "I thought I was one of the only people who could do so."

Raven looked over her shoulders, "'Tis magick that allows us to do so." When Kandra raised a brow, Raven frowned, "Do ye nay believe in magick, or the old ways?"

Kandra shook her head, "I've never thought about the possibility of magick truly existing, until I met you, Raven, and saw it with my own eyes. I thought horses were just very smart and that was why they understand me."

"It does. It exists in every livin' thin' around us." She held up one hand and opened her palm where a blue sphere floated there then left her palm to circle around Kandra and return to Raven's palm where she closed her fingers around it making it disappear. "Each of us has magick within us, but we must believe in ourselves and our own magick to harness and use it. Ye've magick in ye I can feel it."

Kandra held up her fist, opened her palm and laughed when it remained empty, "I don't think I have any magick, you are very much mistaken."

Raven shook her head, "Ye must believe in yerself, to create yer magick." Looking at Kandra, Raven knew she had powerful magick inside of her, if only she would allow herself to bring it forth. "Each of us has a different magickal talent. I am a healer."

Kandra frowned in thought, "What would I be?"

"I've nay idea." Raven smiled as she shook her head, "When ye learn to bring it forth and harness yer magick, ye'll ken."

"Would you teach me?" Kandra was intrigued with the idea of using magick.

"Aye, but ken 'tis a responsibility, nay always a pleasure." Raven frowned down at her own hands, "And the Gods dinna always see fit to allow us to use it." She looked up at Kandra sadly, "I've lost so many people, I just could nay save 'em."

Kandra reached out and touched her shoulder in comfort. "You cannot take the blame for such things."

Raven looked at her, "Aye, but the grief lingers."

By the end of the morning, Kandra had Raven riding at a gallop and Raven loved the feeling of freedom. She loved the feel of the wind rushing through her hair and brushing across her face. For the first time in her life she felt totally free. Kandra praised her for her skills and quickness in learning, but warned her that practice was very necessary.

In return for the riding lesson, Raven spent two hours after the noon meal working with Kandra and teaching her about magick. By the end of the lesson Kandra could create a small white ball of energy that she couldn't control. Raven deflected it more than once for them.

"I am certain yer element 'tis air." Raven smiled at her proudly.

"How can you be so certain," Kandra sighed.

Raven stopped next to her and turned to face her. "All right, give this a go. Close yer eyes and imagine the air brushin' yer face and stirrin' around ye. Can ye do that?"

"Sure," Kandra shrugged and closed her eyes and began to imagine the air moving around her brushing softly across her face. A smile spread across her lips and she laughed softly.

"Open yer eyes."

Kandra obeyed then gasped as her long loose hair swirled around her in the moving breeze. As she stiffened the breeze died down.

"Nay, keep the air stirrin' 'round ye." Raven ordered.

Kandra had no choice, but to comply and concentrated on stirring the air. She raised her hand and a small whirlwind tickled her palm. "This is amazing." Her blue gaze collided with Raven's in sheer wonder.

"Did I nay tell ye that air 'twas yer element?" Raven laughed as the air stirred around her as well. Kandra was indeed a fast learner, and had powerful magick within her.

After their lesson in magick, Kandra and Raven took the children on a picnic. With the remains of lunch spread out on the blanket between them, and Braydon crawling around on his hands and knees, Raven lay back on the blanket enjoying the warmth of the day. For the nights had begun to get colder as was apt to do in the highlands. But the days were still warm and pleasant.

Kandra lay on her side and watched her babe crawling toward Raven's black braid. "Do you plan to be married right away?" She laughed as Raven rolled over and began tickling Braydon with the end of her braid.

"I dinna ken," Raven shook her dark head and continued to tickle the bairn. Sadness crept over her face, "A part of me says to marry him quickly, but a part wishes to wait until I have been truly reunited with my family. Though we have pledged to each other, so I ken he is sincere."

Kandra touched her hand to Raven's arm, "We are your family as well, Raven."

"Aye, and I thank ye for it." Raven smiled, "For the whole of my life, I have never ken people such as ye MacKinnon's." She sighed, "Ye make me feel as if I were a MacKinnon as well, yet I am an outsider."

Kandra laughed, "You are a MacKinnon, Raven, the moment Duncan laid claim to you, I'm afraid there is no turning back, now."

"I fear yer right." Raven flopped down on the blanket dramatically and Braydon laughed wholeheartedly, causing Raven to giggle too. She couldn't wait to give Duncan wee bairns. Raven wanted at least three of each so that there would be children aplenty filling the castle.

Duncan growled in frustration, "For the last bloody time, I am nay bringin' my woman here to speak with ye." He got up from the makeshift table inside the tent that sat on the border of the MacLean and the MacKinnon lands. He ran a hand through his hair in frustration, causing the beads at the ends of the braids he wore to clank together. He turned and eyed the MacLean Chieftain. "Would ye brin' yer woman, to such a thin' and expose her to such possible dangers?"

Gordan MacLean, the Chieftain of the clan MacLean sat back in his chair, "I would nay, but 'twas nay my woman who accused a man of tryin' to rape her."

Duncan glared at the MacLean, "She dinna accuse, I saw what happened with my own eyes."

"As did I," Aidan growled.

"How do ye ken she was nay temptin' him and teasin' him with her woman's wiles?" The MacLean Chieftain's third son Parlan, accused Raven in a sneer as he eyed the MacKinnons with distain.

Aidan stood up placing his hands upon the table and leaned across it. "Ye dare to soil her name in such a manner? Perhaps, I should teach ye a lesson, the woman has more honor in her little finger than ye have in yer whole body, MacLean. Would ye care to step outside?"

Duncan was furious and gave Parlan a deadly stare and began to advance upon him, "I'll cut yer black heart out with my dagger, if ye choose to insult my woman again." Duncan roared as he stepped closer, his body tense to do battle. "Yer nay better than yer blackguard of a brother." He was ready to jump the table and tear Parlan's head off until Lachlan stopped him.

Ian stood, "Mayhaps, we should call a halt for the remainder of the day until we can regain our control?"

"Agreed," Gordan MacLean sat back in his chair and glared at his son. He would deal with Parlan when the MacKinnon's had left the tent. The boy was hot headed and Gordan was glad leadership of the

MacLean clan would not fall into his bloodthirsty hands. "We shall meet at noon on the morrow."

"Agreed." Ian inclined his head and tugged at Aidan's arm while Lachlan pushed and prodded Duncan out of the tent. They gathered their weapons and strode back onto MacKinnon lands and to their encampment.

Once in Ian's tent, Duncan began swearing in Gaelic as he stormed about. "Like bloody hell shall I brin' her here near these lecherous bastards." He wanted to destroy something and turned to glare at his brother and cousins, wondering which one was up for a round of sparing. "I shall nay allow her near that bastard Parlan."

"Consider, brother, it may be the only way." Ian leaned against the makeshift table that sat in the center of his tent. "If 'twill prevent warfare, then aye, ye shall fetch Raven and allow the MacLean to speak with her." He held up a staying hand to quiet his brother's protest. "But we shall nay allow them to harm her in any way."

Duncan roared his displeasure and stormed from the tent. Anger rolled off him in waves as he strode through the MacKinnon encampment. Going to the river, he paced and cursed at the thought of bringing Raven there and exposing her to the MacLean bastards. Hell, he ached with need for her and would have loved to have ensconced her in his tent where he could make love to her all-day long.

Sitting down by the riverbank, Duncan thought of his beautiful Raven, with her long black hair and her beautiful bluish green eyes. His loins fired and ached as he pictured her lithe little body and all its delicious curves and ripeness. If she were there beside him, he would take her here on the riverbank then wash her in the flowing water once they had recovered.

The sound of footsteps behind him had him jumping up and whirling around ready to defend himself. He relaxed at the sight of Lachlan striding toward him. "I hope ye have nay come to try to change my mind. I'll nay allow Raven near those men. I'll nay make her relive what he did to her that day."

Lachlan shook his head, "I have nay, but have come with somethin' better." He smiled roguishly and pulled two bottles of good Scottish whiskey from the bag he carried.

Duncan grinned in return, "'Tis the next best thin' to a woman."

"Aye," Lachlan tossed one bottle to Duncan then walked over to the riverbank and flopped on the ground as he pulled the cork from the bottle with his teeth. He took a long pull from the bottle then frowned at it. "And I am sorely missin' my wife." Duncan flopped next to him and nodded in return, "As am I." He took a long pull from the bottle in his hand.

"Ye miss my wife?" Lachlan deliberately misunderstood to make Duncan laugh.

Duncan threw back his head and laughed heartily, "Aye, I miss yer wife, like a toothache. The woman is forever challengin' me to a sword fight and she does nay play fair."

Lachlan grew serious, "She has nay fought with ye since we have arrived at *Dun Akin*, has she?"

Duncan sighed, "Aye, she has, but nothin' that 'twould endanger the bairn she carries." He added the last quickly.

Lachlan growled low in his throat, "I forbade her from liftin' her sword until our bairn 'twas born. She begged me to allow her to brin' her sword with her." He took a long pull from his bottle. "But she swore, she would nay engage in any sword play."

Duncan tilted his head to look at his cousin, "But she dinna lie, well except for the fight in the great hall. She has nay lifted her sword for fightin' once. But ye dinna tell her she could nay practice with it."

"The blasted woman, she twists my words at nary every turn. She makes me angry enough to throttle her." Lachlan took another swallow from the bottle and paused for a long moment savoring the taste. "But, I could nay imagine a day of my life without her. I love the damnable woman more than life itself."

Duncan was quiet for along moment. "I've married Raven," he blurted out.

Lachlan looked at him for a long silent moment, then a grin spilt his shocked look, "Congratulations are to be in order then. Why did ye nay tell us before we left?" "Because I wish to marry her in a real ceremony." Duncan took a drink of his whiskey and growled, "I wish to invite her family, I'm just nay sure how one goes about marrying an *Irish Sea Water Guardian*."

Lachlan choked on a swallow of whiskey, "She's a what?"

"Aye, 'tis what I said, when she told me." Duncan frowned at his bottle then took a long pull from it. His life had changed so much in such a short time that he wasn't sure what was real and what wasn't anymore. How had he found himself in love with a woman, who wasn't even truly human? Oh, she had every appearance of being human, but she was truly, a mystical being, that he knew little to nothing about. When he returned to *Dun Akin* he would sit her down and have her explain everything to him, about *Irish Sea Water Guardians*. He had no clue what it meant to wed, or even court a woman such as Raven. With her being a princess to boot, he was out of his depths.

"She's a bonnie lass." Lachlan smiled at him. "Wee but bonnie."

"Aye, that she is, I'm a lucky man. I can nay wait to wed so that we may start a family." Duncan smiled proudly as his thoughts turned to bairns and making those bairns. He couldn't wait to see Raven's stomach swollen with his child.

Lachlan sighed, "Are ye nay afraid she'll be a might to wee, to carry yer bairns?" He looked at Duncan and sadness reflected in his eyes. "'Tis how I lost my Kara. My son was too large for her to birth and they both died."

Duncan's brows drew together. "I had nay thought of that. She's by far too small to carry my bairns." He growled deep in his throat as he spoke, "We'll have nay bairns then, for I shall nay risk her life."

"What if she wants bairns?" Lachlan laughed, "Lasses are powerful creatures, even the wee ones. If she be wantin' a babe, I grant she'll get one from ye."

Duncan was quiet for a long moment as he swallowed more whiskey and thought. He wiped his mouth with the back of his hand, "I'll make her swear that she'll nay trick me, or try in anyway to have a bairn. Mayhaps nieces and nephews shall be enough."

Lachlan drank a healthy swallow to match Duncan's from his own bottle then laughed, "Good luck to ye, cousin. I have a feelin' that wee lass, is goin' to keep ye on yer toes."

Both men toasted to that and to having found the women of their dreams, then took a long swallow each.

Nineteen

Raven lay in her bed as dreams of Duncan surrounded her. She could see him leaning against a tree trunk snoring lightly. Kneeling next to him, she waved a hand in front of her face as the smell of whiskey assailed her nose.

On a sigh, she touched his shoulder and shook him, "Duncan, wake up." He snored loudly, but didn't wake up and she laughed. "Duncan MacKinnon, ye wake up this minute!" She pushed him over and he jerked awake.

Duncan looked in to her beautiful ethereal face. "What are ye doin' here, lass?" He sat up and reach out to touch a lose strand of her hair. "'Tis too dangerous for ye to be here."

Raven laughed lightly, "I am at Dun Akin. I have nay left there. For I sleep in yer bed wrapped in yer tartan." She tugged on his hand to get him to stand. When he did, she looked over at Lachlan. "What are ye men doin' out here?"

Duncan reached out and touched her, "If yer nay here, how 'tis it that I can touch ye?"

"'Tis the same as when I healed ye, we are in the *Dreamin'*." She smiled up at him. "Why did ye brin' me here?" He furrowed his brows.

236

She shook her head. "I did nay brin' ye here to me, ye brought me here to ye." She smiled brightly, "I take it ye must be missin' me, somethin' terrible."

Duncan slipped his arm around her waist and pulled her to him. "I have missed ye sorely, Raven MacKinnon." He pulled her up to him as he leaned down to catch her lips with his. The kiss was searing and left her breathless.

When at last he released her, she looked up into his deep greyish-blue gaze and smiled as she panted. "I have missed ye as well." She cocked her head, "Tell me why ye're here?"

He shook his dark head, "'Tis nay for ye to worry 'bout." He ran his knuckles down her cheek then brushed his thumb across her lips as he cupped her cheek. "Have I told ye what a sight for sore eyes, yer bonnie face 'tis?"

"Nay, ye have nay." She slowly shook her head and her mystical bluish green eyes glowed with love. "When will ye come home to me, Duncan? I have missed ye terribly."

He stepped back and held out his hand, "Come walk with me, lass." When she placed her hand in his, he brought it to his lips, and nibbled upon her knuckles. "I dinna wish to waste a moment of our time together here."

Raven inclined her head and allowed him to lead her along near the river. She smiled as she saw the flat rock that Aidan had sat upon and the spot where they had picnicked. Suddenly she stopped walking, "Yer here to deal with what Baoithein MacLean did to me, are ye nay?"

"I dinna wish to talk 'bout it." Duncan's lips drew a hard line, as his eyes blazed with fury and his body went rigid.

"As ye wish," Raven nearly whispered. She didn't want to be reminded of what had happened not too far from here, but she couldn't stop the shiver that raced through her.

Duncan pulled her into his arms and held her, "Let us replace those nightmares with sweet dreams," he lifted her chin and brushed his thumb over her lower lip.

A small smile graced her mouth, "'Twould surely make that nightmare fade." She reached up and tugged on his hair so that he would lean forward, and she could catch his mouth with a kiss. Her hands went to his tartan and she unfastened the MacKinnon broach holding his plaid to his shoulder. She carefully unwound his tartan from around his waist and let it slide to the ground. Her fingers tugged on his shirt and pulled it from the waist of his breeches, then slid her hands up his chest and untied his shirt.

She moaned into his mouth as his hands traced every curve, plain and hollow they could find. His thumbs caressed her breasts through the thin fabric of her nightdress, making her arch into him for more.

She pulled away from his kiss and demanded he remove his shirt. Once he did, she leaned forward and pressed kisses to his chest as her hands roamed over it. The muscles quivered and bunched under her tiny hands. She ran her hand over his muscular stomach until she found the top of his breeches. Her fingers deftly worked on the laces until his manhood sprang free into her hand. As she wrapped her fingers around his engorged staff and stroked him, he growled deep within his throat.

When at last he could take no more, he removed her hand from him. Duncan bunched her nightdress into his hands and whipped it over her head and off her. He let it flutter to the ground a few yards away and did not care. All he cared about was getting Raven naked and burying his manhood deep within her. He leaned her back against a tree as he dropped to his knees in front of her. Lifting her leg, he draped it over his shoulder opening her to him.

His fingertips caressed her legs as he kissed her inner thigh. His tongue traced circles and she moaned. When his fingers traced over her femininity then parted her to slip inside, she gave a soft cry. He stroked and teased her until she was nearly begging him to take her, but he was not through with her yet. When his mouth kissed her intimately and his tongue flicked over her tiny nub of desire, she screamed his name. As he tasted her hot moist center deeply, she clutched her fists within his hair begging him to take her into the euphoria that loomed just out of reach.

When at last she shattered, Duncan stood and turned her around. "Lean forward and hold on to the trunk of the tree, lass."

Raven did as he told her then sighed with pleasure as he pressed the head of his shaft into her warm moist center. Suddenly, he thrust forward burying himself to the hilt as he growled deeply. He pulled back then thrust just as hard into her again, making her cry out in pleasure. Soon he set a pounding rhythm of thrusts and withdraws, until Raven was sobbing with pleasure, sobbing his name like a litany over, and over again.

As Raven spiraled into her climax, Duncan thrust harder as her orgasm forced his own release. Throwing back his head he gave a hoarse cry of pleasure as his muscles strained and bunched.

His body quivered from his exertion and he could stand no longer. Duncan pulled her to the ground with him to sprawl her across his chest. Raven laid her dark head upon his chest as her hair spread out covering them like a blanket. The sound of his beating heart soothed her. Her body was still tingling, and her head was fuzzy with sleep and pleasure. She sighed then pressed a kiss to his chest.

Duncan rubbed light little circles over her back as she lay there. "How is it that I could brin' ye here?"

Raven raised her head and shook it, "I dinna ken." She bit her lower lip then spoke, "Ye must have some sort of magick in ye from those who came 'afore ye."

"I dinna ken of even one." He frowned, "Though my family has held strong to our Celtic roots and have nay yet been forced to fully embrace the Christian faith. I have heard nay even one such rumor of magick." He looked at her with a frown. Shaking his head, he denied bringing her there, "Though ye dinna ken it, ye must have brought me here."

Raven had no time to answer. Her head snapped up and she frowned. "Someone approaches."

"Where?" Duncan sat up setting her away from him as he reached for his clothing and found no sword. He had heard nothing. "Where are they, Raven?"

Raven looked at him with her glowing eyes and whispered, "Wake up Duncan, wake up now!"

Duncan woke and felt the hilt of his sword in his hand and heard the sound to his right. Lachlan was to his left, but he knew deep within him that Lachlan was awake as well. He opened his eyes only scantly and saw Parlan move closer with his sword in hand. How had he gotten through the MacKinnon camp, Duncan wondered briefly then pushed that aside as he watched Parlan move closer ready to kill him while he slept.

This was a clear act of war, and Duncan was not about to ignore it.

The sword swung down, and Duncan met it even as he thrust his foot out catching Parlan in the knee and taking him down. He came to his feet just as Lachlan came to his feet as well. A MacLean lay upon the ground with a blade wound in his belly.

Three more MacLean charged them, and Duncan met one and blocked another as Lachlan took on one himself. The battle was over in moments as MacKinnon men surrounded the three MacLean assassins. Duncan held up his hand silencing his men. Walking over to Parlan he grabbed his red hair and ripped his head back. "With yer actions, ye've declared war upon Clan MacKinnon, yer father can nay stop us from killin' ye."

Parlan glared up at Duncan, "If ye kill me, we shall seek vengeance and kill yer 'hore for it." He spat the words then was silenced as Duncan rammed his fist into Parlan's face, knocking him out cold.

"Take the bastard away and guard him well." He looked at his brother who came striding from the encampment toward him and the others.

"I see ye've survived," Ian growled then toed the bottle lying upon the ground near his foot. "We'll talk 'bout this later." He leveled a glare at his brother and cousin. "For now, tell me what's happened here."

Duncan didn't so much as flinch under his brother's brutal look. "'Twould seem that Parlan MacLean here and his cohorts tried to assassinate the two of us." He rested his hand upon the hilt of his sword and glowered down at an unconscious Parlan McLean.

Ian raised a brow, "'Twould seem that ye've put a halt to his plans." He turned to one of his men. "Send two men and watchers to the MacLean encampment. I wish to speak to their laird." He smiled devilishly. "Tell him, I wish to parlay within the hour."

"Aye," Ian's acting captain of the guards spoke, issuing the orders and sent men scattering.

"As for these bastards, we shall keep them under guard until we have reached a decision as to what to do with them." He gave a hard smile, "Parlan, best pray that his father strikes one hell of a bargain." Duncan smiled brightly, this was the key to keeping Raven from being subjected to the likes of the MacLean. "I bet we're home 'afore nightfall." He clapped his brother on the shoulder.

Lachlan grinned, "I can nay wait to see my wife and children."

Aidan laughed, "I can nay wait to see the kitchen lasses, for I'm in sore need of a woman."

Ian gave his youngest cousin a hard look. "Take care if ye choose to be tuppin' the lasses, cousin. I would nay want to see ye hand-fastened to one of those lasses."

Aidan shrugged, "'Tis careful I am."

Duncan changed the subject, "Let us break our fasts 'afore we meet with the MacLean."

It was nearly nightfall when Duncan, Ian, Lachlan and Aidan rode through the portcullis into *Dun Akin*. They were informed that the evening meal was being served. All four men chose to retire to their chambers to freshen up.

Duncan was thrilled to be home and couldn't wait to see Raven. He whistled as he strode to his chambers and ordered a bath as he went. Entering his chambers, he saw the tub already sitting in front of the hearth. When the water buckets, arrived he grinned and poured his bathwater. Stripping he started to climb into the tub when a knock sounded at his door. With a curse, he wrapped a bath sheet around him and answered the door.

Raven sat in the great hall next to Kandra enjoying the Bard that had come to entertain them. His stories fascinated and thrilled her. She laughed and clapped with the rest of the MacKinnon clan.

"M'ladies," Shane bowed to the two women, "I have been sent to inform ye of the return of the MacKinnon and his kinsmen."

Kandra and Raven looked at each other and smiled, "Where are they?" They asked in unison then laughed.

"The MacKinnon and Aidan will join everyone in the great hall shortly. Laird Lachlan and Duncan have gone straight to their chambers and have requested yer presences." Shane smiled at them even as the stir at the doors of the great hall announced the presence of Ian and Aidan MacKinnon. "Excuse me ladies, for I must see to the rest of my instructions."

Raven pushed back her chair, and smiled at Kandra as she stood as well. "Shall we?"

"After you." Kandra waved Raven ahead of her.

Raven picked up her skirts and stepped down from the dais that held the laird's table. Before she took more than two steps a set of large hands swept her up and she squeaked.

Ian smiled down at her, "Are ye well, Raven lass?"

"I shall be, once my heart stops poundin' in alarm." She hugged him back. "Tell me all went well?"

"Aye lass," he smiled down at her, "Duncan tells me we have ye to thank for yer quick warnin'." He hugged her once more, "I thank ye for savin' my brother's life again, lass."

"'Twas my pleasure." She looked at Ian levelly, "I could nay allow him to die."

Ian bent down and brushed a kiss across her cheek, "My brother is lucky to have ye in his life, lass."

"Aye, he is," Raven laughed then inclined her head, "Now, if ye'd be excusin' me, Ian, I'd like to go see him."

"Aye lass, I'm sure he is eager to see ye." Ian winked at her then turned to greet his Aunt Ferran.

Raven hurried through the castle to the stairs that led to the solar. She quickly went up the steps and headed for Duncan's chambers. Her heart sped up with her eagerness to see him. How she had missed him.

A smiled graced her face as she walked to his chamber door and opened it. "Duncan..." Her words trailed off and the smile slipped from her face.

The sight of Duncan with Isobel in his arms had her heart stopping and her breath catching. When he set Isobel away from him and started to her, Raven held up her hand stopping him in his tracks. "Dinna come near me." The skies outside darkened, and the winds began to whip through the skies.

Raven took the ring from her finger, the one he had given her when he had asked her to marry him. She looked down at it sitting in her palm.

"Raven, 'tis nay what..." Her slashing hand cut off Duncan even as he struggled to move and break the spell she had placed around him. She clenched the ring in her fist.

She looked at him standing there with his bare chest and his long dark braided warrior's hair, with its golden beads shinning in the candlelight. There was a couple of days' worth of whiskers upon his face and his greyish-blue gaze begged her stop what she was doing. "I loved ye." She opened her hand and let the ring fall to the ground. Raven looked at Isobel who also could not say a word, and frowned at her. "I should nay have saved yer worthless life." With the first tear streaming down her face, she turned and ran out the door.

The moment Duncan was free of her spell, he began spitting out curses in Gaelic as he grabbed his breeches and fled the room after Raven. He ran down the corridor yelling her name as he opened door after door searching each, and every room. Soon Ian, Aidan, Lachlan and Kandra were searching the castle for her as well.

Rain slashed outside beating at the castle, the wind roared in fury, as thunder shook the ground. Lightening ripped through the sky striking the ground all around the island, but Raven was nowhere to be found.

Ian looked at Duncan. "We've check everywhere, but the tower rooms." He was beginning to get worried that Duncan was right about Raven venturing out in this storm.

Duncan brightened, "The tower rooms, I've nay checked there, and she loves those rooms." He turned and raced off. He ran up the stairs to the first tower room and frowned at the empty room as he burst through the door. The lightening lit the room and he gazed around at the room's emptiness. She had to be in the other tower, he thought with a smile.

Raven sat in the tower window seat. Tears streaked down her cheeks as her sobs racked her body. The sound of Duncan's voice calling her name carried up the stairs to her. She slid onto the cold floor and quickly created an invisibility cloak around her.

As the tower door crashed open, Raven jumped but held her breath, even as her heart sped up at the sight of him and her stomach quivered at the thought of him touching her.

Duncan's eyes scanned the room, looking for any sign of Raven. "Where the hell have ye gone too, gràdh?" He spoke softly as he ran a hand through his hair. She had been there he could smell her scent. He had searched the entire castle. "Damn it." He cursed then he turned on his heel, he strode from the room.

Raven allowed her tears to begin to fall once more. Sliding down to sit upon the cold stone floor, she sobbed her heart out until she fell asleep.

A chill swept through her, as Raven woke and pushed herself up off the cold stone floor where she had ended up curled into a ball. She was stiff and cold.

Pulling her knees up she laid her head upon them. She was cold and hungry, but neither of those compared to the pain in her heart.

She knew she couldn't stay here at *Dun Akin*. She didn't want to see Duncan again. She couldn't handle any more heartache. Pushing up from where she sat, she knew what she needed to do.

Pulling her cloak closer around her. She slipped into the darkened room. Walking over to the bed where the figure lay sleeping, silently she stepped up to the side of the bed and reached out. Suddenly, she was lying flat on the bed with the man pinning her to the mattress with his larger body. Her hands trapped over her head, she was helpless.

"Ian, 'tis me, Raven." She gasped out.

He spat out a curse. "What are ye doin' in my bed?"

"Ye pulled me into yer bed, ye great oaf." She hissed up at him. "As for the rest, let me up and I'll explain myself."

"Close yer eyes." He growled at her.

"What?"

"Close yer eyes, lass, unless ye wish to see more of me than my brother would be happy 'bout."

"I dinna care what makes yer brother happy." Raven bit out, but she closed her eyes. "Hurry up with ye now." She hissed at him.

Ian let loose of Raven, and moved away from her grabbing a pair of breeches. Stepping into them, he quickly laced them up. Turning to her, he frowned. "Where have ye been, lass? We nigh on turned the castle upside down searchin' for ye."

Raven sat up on the bed, the hood of her cloak falling back to reveal her dark inky black hair and her ethereal face. "It does nay matter where I was. I have come to collect my boon."

"Yer boon?" He frowned down at her.

"Aye," she inclined her head regally.

Ian crossed his arms over his muscular chest and looked down at her. "And what 'tis it ye'd be wantin'?"

"I wish to return home." Raven raised her chin, "And I wish that nay MacKinnon be allowed to stop me from leavin'." She looked past him.

"If that 'tis yer wish," he inclined his head. They were both quiet for a long moment. Finally, Ian broke the silence. "Duncan has been searchin' franticlly for ye. We had to stop him from goin' out in this storm to look for ye."

247

"I dinna care." She raised her chin stubbornly. "I dinna want Duncan anywhere around me." She huffed.

He gave her a level look. "Ye've my word that nay one shall stop ye from leavin' here, for ye have always been free to leave whenever ye wished." He sighed in frustration, "But I insist that ye agree to take an escort with ye. I shall have a few of my men take ye home. I will nay allow a woman to travel alone through *Alba*."

"I agree." Raven stood and walked over to him, she reached up tugging his hair, when he leaned down, she planted a kiss to his cheek. "Yer an honorable man, Ian MacKinnon. 'Tis been a pleasure to ken ye. I thank ye for all ye've done for me."

"There is nay need to be thankin' me, lass." Ian smiled down at her. "We're family, Raven MacKinnon."

The morning air was chilly as Raven finished packing her clothing. She picked up the satchel and then turned back and grabbed the tartan lying on the end of the bed and stuffed it into her satchel. On a sigh, she stepped from her chambers and headed down the hallway. She had considered returning home using magick, but had decided the mortal way was better. Then she had time to think and for her heart to heal before she returned home.

Below stairs she went through the great hall and out of the keep. The sound of her name being called had her turning around and smiling.

Kandra came jogging up to her. "Raven, I have been so worried about you." She hugged the smaller woman.

"I'm fine," Raven spoke softly. "'Tis sorry I am that I worried ye."

Kandra looked down at Raven searching her face. "Ian told Lachlan and I that you were leaving. Are you, all right?"

Raven's face crumbled at Kandra's words, "Nay, I'm nay all right." She sniffed and looked up at Kandra with tearful eyes. "I found Duncan and Isobel together after he returned." She shook her dark head, "I was a fool to think the man would choose me over someone like her."

Kandra hugged her again, "I am so sorry, I thought the two of you had finally settled things. I would not have thought Duncan would break a promise. Are you sure they were being intimate?"

Raven laughed bitterly, "He was wrapped in a bath sheet and she had her arms around his neck." A tear sparkled in her eye and she waved it away.

"Oh my," Kandra gasped, "That is bad." She bristled with indignation. "You wait until I see his sorry hide, I'll give him a tongue lashing he will not soon forget."

Raven laughed sadly, "He's nay worth it. He's a liar and a cad." She shook her head, "I dinna think he told ye of what happened last eve."

"He neglected to tell us that part of it." Kandra growled. "He should be run through." She jumped to Raven's defense. Then she looked at Raven, "But I am going to miss you, for you are my first real female friend."

"Oh Kandra, I shall miss ye as well, but we're nay so far apart when I am on the Isle of Mann." Raven took her hand and squeezed it. "I'll come visit ye as soon as I can." Raven and Kandra hugged once more, "I'll miss ye sorely."

"As I shall miss you my friend." Kandra sniffed as they hugged one last time. "Goodbye."

"*Mar sin leat.*" Raven said her goodbye then turned and fled to where Ian was standing.

"Are ye sure ye wish to do this, lass?" Ian asked with a frown. He took in her long lose black hair and her heavy cloak for traveling. Last, but not least, he saw the satchel she carried. Reaching down he took it from her.

Raven looked in to his bluish-grey gaze and frowned, "I have to do this, I've nay choice. I can nay stay here with Duncan near at hand." She looked away with tears sparkling in her bluish-green gaze.

"Well if ye insist, I've somethin' for ye." Ian waved to where a black mare was being led out of the stables.

"Star." Raven whispered as she turned and ran to meet the horse. Star nuzzled Raven affectionately. "I'm sorry, I've nay treats for ye."

Ian walked over and hooked Raven's satchel to the saddle. He looked down at her, as she stroked the horse's nose. "Can I nay talk ye out of leavin' us, Raven, lass?"

Raven shook her head, "'Tis time I go home, my parents are likely worried 'bout me," she sighed, "But I thank ye, Ian, for the kindness ye showed me and the home ye provided me. And I must thank ye for freein me from Ewin Brodie and his brutish clan."

"Ye've nay reason to thank me lass, ye did me a wonderful service by savin' my brother's life." Ian smiled down at her. "Besides Lachlan and his family, Duncan 'tis all I have left."

Raven frowned, "I'm nay sure ye should be thankin' me for savin' his miserable hide. I feel I have done ye a disservice instead of a good deed."

Ian laughed heartily over that, "Yer a spirited one, lass." He hugged her to him. "Ken that yer welcome back to *Dun Akin* forever, Raven MacKinnon, and ye'll be missed greatly." He pressed a kiss to the top of her head and set her away from him. "If ever ye find yerself in need of help, ye've but to call upon us MacKinnons and we'll answer."

"I thank ye." She smiled up at him then she stepped back and leaned down to pick up a stone from the ground. Holding it between her hands she chanted quietly. Her hands glowed and she smiled. Opening her palms, she handed the stone to Ian. "If ye ever have need of me, Ian, ye but to hold the stone and call my name, Relia, three times and it shall send me the message of yer troubles. I shall come as quickly as I can."

She placed the stone in Ian's hand then closed his fingers around it. "Take care of yer brother, I would hate for ye to call me over him."

Ian laughed then inclined his head, "I thank ye, Princess."

"*Mar sin leat*, my friend." Raven walked over to the horse, but before she could mount it, Ian picked her up and placed her in the saddle. Then he adjusted the stirrups to fit her shorter legs. Looking up at her, he smiled, "I wish ye luck and the best, lass."

Ian whistled and six men on horseback all wearing cloaks came riding up alongside of her. Raven furrowed her brows and wondered for a moment, but Ian spoke in Gaelic and the men took off and her horse went with them.

Twenty

About an hour of riding after her escorts made land fall on Scotland, they set out at a fast pace. As the group rode over a hill five of the men peeled off and headed back toward the Isle of Sky and *Dun Akin*. Raven slowed as she gaped at them and yelled at them. "Where are ye goin'? Come back here!"

"They left, lass." Duncan pulled back his hood and smiled at her as he slowed his own mount. "I told 'em too."

"What are ye doin' here?" She spat icily as she glared at him.

"Ye wish to go to the Isle of Mann dinna ye?" He raised a brow.

She reined in as she spoke. "Aye, and Ian promised nay MacKinnon would try to stop me."

He reined in beside her, "I dinna intend to stop ye, *gràdh*, I'm goin' with ye."

"Dinna call me that!" She snarled at him. "I will go on my own, I dinna need the likes of ye with me. Nay, I will nay allow ye to accompany me."

"Ye can nay go on yer own." He countered. "I've a right to stop ye, or to go with ye."

"Ye dinna have any rights where I am concerned." Raven yelled at him. "I hate ye, Duncan MacKinnon!"

"Hate me or nay lass, yer stuck with me." He countered evenly as he took in her pitch, black hair that shone blue in the bright sunlight and the hurt swirling in her eyes.

"And why is that?" She huffed out at him with tears shinning in her eyes.

"Because, I am yer husband and yer my wife, for a year and a day." He spoke softly knowing she would not be pleased.

Raven gasped, "'Tis nay so, ye lie." She shook her head. It couldn't be true, she thought desperately. "We were nay handfasted."

"Aye 'tis lass, when we made love on the beach, ye spoke the words pledgin' yerself to me." Duncan grinned at her, as he relived that day on the beach with her. Raven's mind spun back to that wonderful day on the cove and she groaned. Duncan was right they were married, not just promised to each other.

"Aye ye remember," he grinned, "In accordance with Celtic law, we're married. So, wife do ye wish to go on to the Isle of Mann, or do ye wish to return home to *Dun Akin*?"

Raven glared at him and the sun began to be blocked out by clouds and the wind picked up as lightening ripped across the sky. "I hate ye, Duncan MacKinnon. I want aught to do with yer sorry hide. Yer a cad and blackguard." She growled at him as the wind whipped her hair and thunder rumbled. "Mann 'tis my home, nay Dun Akin."

"And yer a coward, lass." Duncan narrowed his eyes at her.

Raven's own eyes widened as she sputtered. "I... I am nay a coward!" The nerve of the man!

"Aye yer a coward, 'cause ye will nay fight with me, without usin' yer magick." Duncan sat there and raised a brow in challenge.

Raven raised her chin, "I dinna need magick to fight with the likes of ye." The wind immediately ceased blowing and the sun came back out. "Yer an *arse*, Duncan MacKinnon." She turned her horse toward the inland and began to ride at a leisurely pace.

Duncan rode up beside her, "And where do ye think yer goin'?" He grabbed her reins.

"I'm goin' home, ye oaf." Raven tried to yank the reins from his hands, but only succeeding in upsetting Star. "Let go of my horse." She smacked at his hands.

"Stop bein' a fool, lass." Duncan growled and tried to contain the horse.

"A fool..." She was cut off as Duncan grabbed her and swept her off Star just as the horse reared and took off running. He set her in front of him on his own mount. "Now, look at what ye've done." She glared up at him.

Before she could move he leaned down and brushed a kiss across her lips. "Have I told ye lately how bonnie ye are, my lovely Princess?"

Raven hissed up at him, "Put me down, or I shall scratch yer eyes out." She threatened.

Duncan laughed, "I am nay 'ascared of ye, lass." He nudged his horse to follow in the direction her mount had run.

Raven glared up at him with her swirling bluish-green eyes. "Ye should be." She raised her chin once more and gave him a harsh look. "I am goin' home and I dinna want ye to accompany me."

"Wish it, want it, or nay, we shall travel together." He growled down at her, "I will nay allow my wife to travel by herself." When she would have argued, he captured her hair in his hand and forced her face up to his. "We can either return to *Dun Akin*, or go to Mann, lass, 'tis yer choice, but ken 'tis one or the other and we travel there together."

Raven narrowed her eyes up at him, "I wish to go to my home on Mann, but sorry 'tis ye shall be for travelin' with me." She gave him a wicked smile and Duncan knew she could easily make him sorry.

He was already sorry in more ways than one. He was sorry he had hurt her, but had he been unable to explain what she had seen. Perhaps, she would not have acted so hasty as to request leave of *Dun Akin*, if he had just had a chance to talk with her. Now, he would have to force her to listen to him. He had not realized how very much he loved her, until he had lost her, now he would never let her go. To make him further sorry, the little hoyden rode in his lap and it was having a profound affect upon him already. When she wiggled her bottom, he hissed between his teeth and she smiled.

After an hour of riding double, and Duncan cursing under his breath for the hundredth time, they found Star grazing in a field near a loch. Reining in his mount, Duncan was about to help Raven dismount when she slipped from his lap. "Damn it lass, ye need to be more careful."

Raven ignored him and ran over to her horse. She cupped the mares face in her hands and spoke to it. "Star, I was so worried 'bout ye. Ye should nay have run off like that." She pressed a kiss to the beast's head. "Are ye all right?"

When the horse whinnied, and nodded her head, Duncan gaped. "Ye can talk to the blasted beast?"

Raven frowned over at him, "Of course I can. She's an intelligent creature." She turned back to the horse. "I'm so sorry we frightened ye." The horse whinnied once more and rubbed her head against Raven. "He certainly does bellow a lot."

Duncan frowned and growled, "Yer makin' that up." "I am nay makin' it up." Raven glared at him, "Ask her yerself, if ye, nay frightened her."

"I can nay ask a horse like that." Duncan shook his head.

"Aye ye can, if ye'll but come over here I shall help ye." Raven held out her hand then wiggled her fingers. "Are ye a coward?"

Duncan bristled then dismounted from his own destrier and marched over to where Raven and the mare stood. He took Raven's tiny hand in his and looked at her.

"I hear aught."

"That's because ye are nay touchin' her." Raven placed his other hand on the horse's neck as well as her own.

Images raced through Duncan's mind, he jerked back taking his hand off Star and nearly knocked Raven on her bottom. "What the bloody hell?" He looked from Raven back to the horse. "What the bloody hell was that?"

The horse sounded as if it was laughing at him and he watched Raven smile then start laughing. "She was talking to ye, ye oaf." Raven laughed so hard that she had tears running down her face. "The look upon yer face was amusin'." She wiped at the tears but when they just wouldn't quit coming she turned away as images of Duncan and Isobel wrapped in each other's arms flashed thorough her mind.

When she turned away and continued to cry, Duncan frowned, "Raven?"

She shook her head and ran toward the loch. She knelt there and wrapped her arms around her waist and bowed her head. The ache she had tried to bottle spilled out, and consumed her. She rocked back and forth as she sobbed.

Duncan walked up silently behind her. The sound of her sobs ripped at his heart. He had no clue how he would fix this, but he knew he could not live without this tiny woman, for she held his heart in her small delicate hands.

He sat down next to her on the ground. Staring out over the loch, he frowned and waited for her sobs to lessen a bit, because he was afraid if he tried to touch her, he would only make it worse. "It was nay what ye think, Raven."

She looked at him with red rimmed eyes as tears slipped down her cheeks. "I was a fool. I let myself fall in love with ye. I gave ye my heart, Duncan MacKinnon, and ye threw it back in my face." She shouted at him. "I hate ye! Leave me be!" With that she stood and ran back to where Star still grazed.

He sighed, she wasn't ready to listen to what he had to say. Hanging his head, he thought for a moment, his only choice was to wait her out, but he wouldn't stop trying. Before long he would convince her to listen to him.

He gave her a few more minutes then stood and walked over to his destrier. "'Tis time we were on our way." He spoke gruffly to her. "Do ye need help mountin' yer horse?"

Raven glared at him then inclined her head coldly, regally. When Duncan walked over to her, she sucked in a breath as his hands slid around her waist. Her hand on his shoulders, she could feel his muscles bunched under his shirt as he lifted her. His scent wrapped around her and made her heart pound as yearning for him pooled deep in her belly.

Duncan sat her upon her mount and looked up at her. Her long silky black hair hung over her shoulder, her bluish-green eyes held the same desire that swirled inside of him. She was beautiful with her petite ethereal features. There would never be another woman he would love as much as Raven MacKinnon. Making sure she was settled, he turned and vaulted onto his large black destrier. Raven's mount was nearly half the size of his own powerful horse and he had to keep his mount, Quinlan, at a slow pace.

Raven urged her own mount into a trot to keep pace with Duncan's horse. She couldn't help but to admire the man next to her. Her husband, she thought with a sigh. What was she going to do with him? She didn't relish the idea of traveling all the way down the Scottish coast to reach a crossing for the Isle of Mann. It would take more than a week to make the journey and she honestly didn't know if she could be around him that long without giving into her desire for the man.

Duncan found a place to camp for the night. It was wooded and offered a bit of shelter from the cool autumn evenings. He dismounted and tethered Quinlan. Quickly, he walked over and helped Raven from her own mount. She yawned widely as he lowered her to the ground. He looked down into her beautiful face and frowned, "Yer worn out, *gràdh*." He traced his finger over the shadow under her eye. "Take a seat over there and I shall see to our mounts, then I shall make us a fire for the night."

Raven wanted to argue, but she was so very tired. Stumbling over to a nearby tree, Raven sat down and leaned back. Her body ached, and she was exhausted. Her stomach rumbled, but she was too tired to even think about eating. She watched Duncan for a time then slipped into a light slumber.

With the horses rubbed down, watered and grazing, Duncan grabbed some nearby wood to make a campfire. He looked over to where Raven, sat sleeping. He sighed, she was not made for a rough journey like this. Laying the wood for a fire, he started the tinder then fed the fire until it was nice and toasty near it. He reached into his bag and pulled one of his tartans from it. Laying out the plaid material he walked over and scooped his wife into his arms. Carefully, he laid her out on his plaid and covered her with it.

Taking his bow, he looked down at his sleeping wife then slipped away for a few minutes to hunt.

Raven woke to the most delicious smell. She rubbed her eyes and looked at the warm fire where her broad Scottish warrior sat roasting meat on a spit. Her stomach rumbled loudly, and she yawned.

"'Tis nigh on finished." Duncan smiled over at her, "'Twould seem just in time." He pulled the rabbit from the fire and cut into it with his knife. Cutting a large piece off, he handed it to Raven who took it and blew on it as she juggled it from hand to hand.

She took a nibble of the meat and smiled. "Mmm, 'tis verra tasty, thank ye." She ate the meat with appreciative hunger. When he handed her more, she smiled brightly, "Where did ye get this?"

Duncan shrugged, "I went huntin' while ye were sleepin'."

Raven frowned, "I should have taken care of my horse." She looked to where Star grazed. "I thank ye for takin' care of her, and lettin' me sleep." She wiped her hands on her breeches and shook her head, "'Twould seem ridin' takes its toll upon me, for it seems to tire me easily."

"Ye'll get used to it." He smiled and handed her more meat. "Give it a few days, and ye'll be sturdier in the saddle."

Raven chewed on a bit of their dinner as she thought this over. "Do ye truly think 'tis so?"

"Aye, it takes time to build the strength and endurance to ride great distances." Duncan shrugged then smiled, "Ye were nay born ridin' horses, princess."

Raven was quiet for a long moment then finally looked over at him sitting there in the firelight. "Go home Duncan, and allow me to return to my home alone."

He shook his dark head and the beads in his hair glistened and flashed in the firelight. "I can nay do that, Raven. Yer my wife, and I shall nay leave ye by yerself." He took a deep breath, "We need to be talkin' about what happened..."

Raven pushed up from where she sat and glared down at him. "I dinna want to talk 'bout this." She turned and fled into the darkness.

Duncan was sitting back whittling a stick as she returned to the campsite. Walking over to the plaid, she lay down upon it and curled her hand under her cheek and watched the flames dance, instead of looking at the man who claimed to be her husband.

She closed her eyes when she heard him move, but said not a word. When she felt him lay down beside her she gasped and looked over her shoulder at him. "What do ye think yer doin'?"

"I'm layin' upon my tartan to go to sleep." He rolled so that his front was to her back.

"This is my bed." She hissed at him, "And I've nay wish to share it with the likes of ye."

Duncan snorted. "'Tis my tartan, if ye'd be wishin' nay to share it, then ye can go sleep by the tree."

Raven narrowed her eyes, "Fine, I shall." She got up and walked over to where her satchel sat and pulled the MacKinnon plaid from it then walked to the tree where Duncan had sat earlier. Sitting down, she wrapped the tartan around her shoulder and around herself then leaned back against the tree.

She sat there and shivered as the fire died down. She leaned her head back against the tree then forward onto her up drawn knees trying to find a comfortable way to sit and sleep. Her body still ached from the long day's ride.

Duncan lay there watching her as she shifted from position to position and shivering in the cooling night air. He was not a man to sit by and watch a woman suffer. On a sigh, he rose and walked over to her.

Raven looked up at him looming over her. When he reached down and picked her up, she squeaked. "What are ye doin'?"

"I'll nay sit by and watch ye shiver yerself apart, then catch cold." Duncan knelt and laid her upon his plaid then lay down behind her and spooned her to him.

"I dinna want to lay with ye!" She spat and struggled in his arms. She gasped when he pulled her under him and loomed over her, pressing his sex between her legs.

"Cease." He growled in a voice that broke no argument. "Yer my wife and my word is law." He pinned her hands beside her head. "Try to hit me again, and I'll turn ye over my knee."

"Get off me," Raven hissed. "I have nay wish to lay with ye, nor be near ye." She struggled under him then gasped as she felt his manhood grow against her, pressing firmly into her, she stopped her struggles.

"Aye, ye feel what ye do to me, Raven." He growled his next words, "I want ye, lass." His mouth, was inches from hers, "Yer my wife, 'tis my right to make love to ye."

Raven sucked in a breath then whispered, "Nay Duncan, I shall nay willingly again give my body to ye, ye shall have to force yerself upon me." She felt the breath whoosh out of him. She knew he was too honorable to force her into such an act. He was not a man to hurt women purposely.

Duncan moved off her, but turned her on her side so that he could lay behind her and wrap his arm around her and spoon her to him. He grabbed the edge of his tartan and threw it over them. "Go to sleep, wife." He spoke gruffly against the top of her head.

Raven lay there and reveled in the heat coming off his larger body. She snuggled into him and sighed as she began to drift off to sleep. She felt and heard him inhale her scent, but she was too tired to berate him. She drifted into a warm peaceful sleep with dreams of her large handsome Scotsman.

Duncan lay there for a long time gritting his teeth as he fought his own body's impulses. He wanted Raven so badly it hurt him, but he wouldn't force himself upon her. He wanted her willing and ready to accept him with open arms. He inhaled the sweet scent of her and nearly groaned out loud. As the night was drifting into morning he finally drifted off to sleep.

Raven woke and looked around at the trees. She furrowed her brows and inhaled the masculine scent of Duncan enveloping her, the scent made her smile softly. Suddenly, her stomach rolled, and she knew she would be sick again this morning. For the last few weeks she had been ill. Her energy lacking, she often found herself nauseated for no apparent reason.

She wiggled out from under the heavy arm that held her trapped and stumbled to her feet. She made it just past a nearby tree and knelt. The sickness was violent and always wore her out, but she knew it would ease once her stomach was empty. She cursed herself for eating so much the night before as she was sick again.

When she felt her hair being lifted off her neck and felt the arm around her helping to hold her up, she tried to push Duncan away as embarrassment set in. Her stomach hurt from her sickness and her head was light.

Duncan held her and spoke soothing words. He wet a cloth and held it out to her so that she could wipe her mouth when she was finished being sick. He left her long enough to get the skin of water and give her a drink to allow her to rinse her mouth out. Then he picked her up and carried her back to the plaids and laid her down.

"Rest *gràdh*," he soothed the hair from her brow and took in her pale complexion. His brows were furrowed as he studied her. "Did the hare make ye sick?"

Raven looked away from him and sighed, "It must have." She closed her eyes and placed a hand over her stomach, "I think I just need but to rest a few and I'll be fine."

Duncan cupped her cheek. "Sleep for a bit longer and we shall see." He stood and left her side long enough to walk into the woods and perform his morning absolutions. By the time, he was back she was sound asleep.

Duncan watched Raven sleep, as the morning became nearly noon. The sun was high in the sky and the day was warming. When at last, her eyes fluttered open once more she was still very pale, and it worried him. Walking over to her, he knelt, and brushed his knuckles over her cheek, as he looked in her intriguing eyes. "How do ye feel?"

Raven smiled weakly up at him, "I seem to be a bit better."

"Mayhap we should return to *Dun Akin*, until yer well again." Duncan suggested softly as worry creased his brow.

Raven laughed softly as she sat up, "I am well enough to continue on." She carefully gained her feet with Duncan's help.

"Do ye nay think, 'twould prove worse upon what ails ye, to ride as far as Mann?" Duncan hovered over her as she walked toward the woods to relieve herself.

Raven shook her head and walked farther into the woods. When she heard him behind her, she stopped and turned to him. "Do ye mind?" She waved to the woods around her then laughed as he gave her a questioning look. "I need to relieve myself and I fear ye can nay help me with that."

Duncan grunted and turned his back. "Fine, but I'll be here if ye have need of me."

"I will nay need yer help," she smiled behind him. "Off with ye." She shooed him away then laughed once more as he grumbled stomping through the woods. When she came back to the campsite, Duncan had both the horses saddled and ready to go. He turned to her and glared, "Are ye sure ye wish to undertake this foolhardy journey to Mann?"

"Aye," she inclined her head and walked over to Star. Stroking her hand over the muzzle she began to chat with the mare. "Even Star agrees 'tis nay a foolhardy journey."

Duncan growled low in his throat, "And what does a horse ken of this?" He fastened her satchel to his horse. Turning he stalked over to Raven and turned her so that he could look down upon her, she was still pale, and her eyes had dark circles under them. "Why must ye insist upon this journey, lass?" He cupped her cheek, "I wish to return to *Dun Akin*, to assure ourselves that yer well enough to travel. I dinna want somethin' to happen to ye."

She laid a hand upon his and frowned, "I will nay return to *Dun Akin*." She looked away from him then removed his hand from her cheek. "I dinna plan to ever return there." She looked up at him with fire in her eyes. "I loved ye, and ye dinna care..."

"Yer wrong *gràdh*..." She cut him off before he could finish what he had to say. "Nay, ye cared more for Isobel..." Her eyes held fire, "I dinna want to hear yer lies..."

Duncan covered her mouth with his large hand too quiet her. "Is goin' to Mann yer wish?" She nodded. "Will it make ye happy?" She nodded again. "Then we shall continue this bloody journey." He turned her and took her around the waist placing her upon Star. Walking over to his own mount he swung up into the saddle, looking over at her with his greyish-blue gaze, he inclined his head then nudged his horse into a trot.

Raven followed behind for more than an hour, before she started to get lonely. Whispering to Star she moved up beside Duncan and looked around. The countryside was beautiful and beginning to burst with colors as autumn took a firm hold. "'Tis verra verra bonnie."

Duncan inclined his head, "There is nay place, bonnier then Alba." He smiled at the Scottish-Highlands with pride.

"Have ye traveled many other places?" Raven wondered with a smile. Wouldn't it be wonderful to see the world and what was out there waiting to be explored, her father had never allowed her to leave Mann, as he was, by far, to over protective.

"Aye, I've been to many places, far from here." He smiled over at her. "I have been to the *Eire*. Ye would like it there, 'tis so verra green and we've kin there." He sighed, "I have been to the Germanic countries as well. They are a bit strange over there, but likeable enough people. But aught beats *Kyleakin*, for 'tis my home." A smile graced his face as memories of his life there flashed before him.

"It must be verra nice to travel and return home." Raven laughed, "I can nay wait to return home, to walk in the sea and to see my family and friends, for I miss them greatly." She had a faraway look in her eyes and it made Duncan's gut clench.

"Tell me about yer home, lass." Duncan frowned as he spoke. He looked at the autumn leaves and wondered if they would be stuck on the Isle of Mann for the winter, or would he return home alone. If he couldn't win Raven over and convince her to stay with him, he would give her what she wanted, even if it meant his heart would be broken forever. The thought made him sick, but her happiness was the most important thing in the world to him, because he loved her with his whole heart.

Twenty-one

After nearly a week of riding from midday until dark, they made slow progress. Duncan knew that Raven couldn't handle riding much farther on horseback, for it was wearing her out. He decided to seek shelter with his cousin Alistair MacKinnon on the Isle of Mull, then see if there was a ship they could take that would drop them on the Isle of Mann. Making the detour, Duncan stood next to a fisherman named Selig, who had agreed to take them across the sound to the Isle of Mull. They would cross on the morn.

Raven and Duncan shared a simple, but pleasurable meal with Selig and his wife Nora. The older couple was polite and treated Raven and Duncan like friends.

Raven ate the fried fish and simple fried potatoes with relish. When she spied the loaf of bread at Duncan's elbow she smiled at him, "Could I have a piece of that bread, for I feel as if I'm half starved to death!"

Duncan furrowed his brows, she had been violently ill that morning, and now here she sat eating like she was starving. In the entire time, he had been around her she had eaten like a bird, though he had joked with her about changing her name to Bessie, she hadn't truly been that big of an eater. He cut the piece of bread and she took a big bite and complemented Nora as she chewed.

When the meal was finished, it was rather late so both couples retired for the night. Raven and Duncan had insisted on taking the loft and not sleep in Selig and Nora's bed.

Raven climbed the ladder first and Duncan smiled as she climbed. The sight of her derriere swinging back and forth fired his loins. When she had reached the loft, and stepped onto the wooden floor, Duncan began his climb.

Looking around the loft Raven sighed as she unbraided her hair. The bed was small, but she would sleep upon the floor. She turned to tell Duncan as much and laughed hysterically as he bumped his head on the ceiling when he climbed off the ladder.

Duncan rubbed the top of his head as he stooped. "Think 'tis funny do ye, *gràdh*?" He advanced upon her and she scurried backward and ended up falling onto the bed. Before she could utter a word, Duncan was on top of her pinning her slight body with his massive one. "Perhaps, ye will nay think it so verra funny if I torture ye." He rubbed his bearded face against her neck and cheeks causing her to laugh uncontrollably. He had discovered a few days before as he lay with her next to their campfire that she found his beard ticklish.

"Duncan stop," She laughed and tried to push him away, "That tickles." She gasped for breath as she laughed. "Mercy!" She cried and wiped away tears.

Duncan stopped and looked down at her. She was so beautiful with her black silky hair spread out behind her and a smile upon her face. "*Tha gaol agam ort.*" He whispered then leaned down to capture her mouth in a searing kiss that left her breathless and her head spinning.

Raven looked up into his beautiful greyish-blue eyes then closed her own eyes. "Dinna say that, please." She shook her head and pushed at his chest to get him off her. "Dinna say that you love me, when ye dinna mean it." She looked at him and tears slipped out of the corner of her eye before she could stop them.

Duncan let her push at him, but he didn't relent as he held her there trapped upon the bed. "Damn it Raven, 'tis time ye listened to me." He gave her a hard look. "I love ye Raven Relia MacKinnon, more than life itself. There has been aught between Isobel and I, after ye arrived."

Raven glared at him, "Dinna try to play me the fool. Yer an arse if ye think I'd be dense enough to believe that." She heaved a breath. "I saw ye with her with my own eyes. I heard the two of ye, together night after night, the sounds ye made together. She was the first one ye choose to see when ye returned to *Dun Akin.*" She put her hands against his chest. "Get off me." She growled up at him. When he didn't move, she let a bit of her magick hit him in the chest.

The shock bit into Duncan's chest and he merely gritted his teeth against the pain it caused. His greyish blue gaze looked down at her as magick crackled in his eyes. "I have had aught to do with Isobel, since my brother dragged ye to my home, believe me or nay, for 'tis the truth. I've nay clue what ye thought ye were hearin', but I have nay bedded Isobel, since I met ye."

"I heard ye and her the thumpin' and noises coming from yer chambers, night after night." Raven frowned at him. "I ken that ye were with Isobel. Then I saw ye with her."

Duncan frowned down at her, "What ye heard *grádh*, was me working with my sword, trying in vain to wear myself out until I could sleep. Night after night, I laid in my bed and all I could think 'bout was ye and how much I wanted ye." He sighed heavily, "What ye saw between me and Isobel, was not what ye thought. Ye can believe me or nay, but I swear to ye, it was innocent. Now, pull back yer magick, *Princess*."

Raven gave a soft cry as her powers snapped back at her as if they were met by another magick. His hand went to her throat, "I shall tell ye this once and only once Princess Relia, dinna use yer powers on me ever again. Princess or nay, wife or nay, ye shall be sorry if ye do."

Slowly, and with a bewildered look, Raven inclined her head. She didn't understand what had just happened, Duncan was a mortal and he should not have been able to use his magick, for he was not druid trained, or anything else she was aware of. Perhaps, there was more to these MacKinnon men than she thought.

Duncan released her then grunted as he moved around the room, laying out his tartan and settling himself upon the floor. Raven made to protest that she was planning on sleeping upon the floor. However, one look at his angry face, had her mouth snapping shut. She crawled into the bed without another word.

Laying there in the darkness Raven listened to Duncan tossing and turning. Her mind whirled around the possibility that Duncan could be telling her the truth. But she had seen him and Isobel standing there with their arms wrapped around each other. How could she argue against what she had witnessed? The Gods could only know how much she wanted what he said to be true, because she loved him with every fiber of her being.

Rolling onto her side, she looked down at the floor where the man she loved lay on his side facing her. She frowned in thought, he had traveled this far with her to grant her wish to return home. He had held her and cared for her when she was ill. She owed him the bed at the very least.

On a sigh, she created a small ball of soft blue energy in her hand. She looked down into his greyish-blue eyes that seemed to glow in the light of her energy ball. "Why dinna ye take the bed?" She climbed from the bed and stood looking down at him.

Duncan smiled softly wickedly. "Only if ye'll share it with me?" There was a mischievous glint in his eyes.

Raven snorted, "I think nay. I ken ye, Duncan MacKinnon," she shook her finger at him.

He gave her an innocent look that looked anything but innocent. "I would behave like a gentleman. Ye've my word of honor." He crossed his heart.

Raven shook her head and smiled, "Ye'd act more as a rogue gentleman than aught." She shook her head, "My virtue would nay be safe with ye." Duncan gained his feet. "I believe ye already gave me yer virtue, *gràdh*." He ran a finger down over her cheek and the energy ball grew brighter. It was a telling sign and made Duncan smile brightly. He still affected her, and she still cared for him. "But I shall decline the bed, for I dinna relish an empty bed." He made to lay upon the floor once more.

"If ye promise to act like a gentleman, I shall share the bed with ye." She tilted her head, "But I am nay yer leman, so ye keep yer hands to yerself."

Duncan waved her to the bed and she frowned, "Ye can go first." When he inclined his head, and climbed upon the bed it groaned as he settled himself. He patted the bed next to him and Raven walked over and sat upon the edge. She extinguished the energy ball and lay down on the straw mattress as far from him as possible.

When Duncan snagged her waist, and pulled her back to him then rolled her under him, she gave a small squeak. She then was silenced by his lips catching and keeping hers. His tongue swiped across her lips demanding entrance and Raven couldn't help herself as she opened to him. He caught her moan of pleasure and desire in his mouth and reveled in it. His tongue mated with hers in a sensual arousing dance.

Raven felt the heat coil in her belly as his large, strong hands stroked over her body igniting fires everywhere he touched. Need pulled in her lower regions as her hands stroked over his muscular body. The taste of him was like a sweet drug she had been denied for far too long and she hungered for him, like she hungered for life.

Why had she denied herself for so very long, she wondered. All that mattered was Duncan and being with him.

Duncan stroked his hand over her and felt his erection press into her. She wiggled against him and he groaned with desire for his beautiful wee wife.

Finally, he pulled from the kiss, that left them both panting and filled with need. "Yer nay my leman for I have nay need of one. But yer my wife, *gràdh*, dinna ever forget that." Then he did the hardest thing he had ever had to do. He rolled off her and tucked her into him spooning her. His erection pressed into her bottom and he nearly groaned. The scent of her hair made him ache to run his fingers through her tresses. Her enticing body called to him, to worship it and love it, but he would deny them both and hope it caused her to want him more.

Raven lay there puzzled about his actions. He had kissed her like he was drowning in her and as if she were the only one who could save him. She pressed her fingers to her lips then sighed. Perhaps she had over reacted. Mayhap he hadn't been with Isobel when he had been with her. The image of the two standing there flashed through her mind and she stiffened. She was wrong, he had been caught being intimate with his leman.

Duncan leaned down and pressed a kiss to the side of her neck and his silky hair caressed her cheek. He had felt her stiffen and knew she was thinking about him and Isobel. Somehow, he would convince her that she was the only woman for him. That he could not live life without her. He would convince her of the truth.

Soon he felt her relax in his arms and listened to her breathing even out. He picked up a handful of her hair and smelled it, then rubbed it against his cheek. How could he live without her? How would he go on, when no other woman could satisfy him? Or make his stomach clench with need the way it did when Raven laughed, or smiled at him? How could he go for long without seeing her bluish-green eyes swirl with passion, or fire? To all his questions he had one answer. He couldn't go on without her in his life. So, he would fight for her, even if it meant fighting her, to keep them together.

He pulled Raven deeper into him, wrapping his body protectively around hers. His face snuggled into the crook of her neck where he could feel her pulse beating. In sleep, she murmured then reached up to stroke his cheek and wiggled into his warmth even more. For a moment, he swore he heard her whisper the words *Mo ghaol ort*, Duncan. She loves him? Gods help him he was sure she whispered the words in her sleep. He pressed another kiss to her neck then let himself relax for slumber to take him, for he had new hope running through his veins and he knew he could win her back.

The sun was barely peeking through the house when Raven woke sick once more. She slipped out of Duncan's arms and down the ladder. She stumbled out the door and around the house then fell to her knees as the sickness overwhelmed her.

A hand upon her shoulder had her jumping. "Easy m'lady, I wish ye nay harm." Nora smiled gently down at her. "I heard ye leave the house, and wondered what was afoot." She looked at Raven with concern.

Raven shook her head and proceeded to get sick once more. Nora stayed by her and rubbed her back as Raven emptied her stomach. She leaned against Nora as the sickness left her weakened. "Thank you." Raven whispered.

Nora stroked her black silky hair and rocked her gently. "'Tis nay my business m'lady, but are ye with child?"

Raven just stared at her horrified. She quickly shook her head then asked, "Why do ye ask?"

"Well m'lady..."

"Please call me, Raven," She laughed weakly as she sat herself up, "After that, 'twould only be proper."

Nora laughed lightly herself. "Raven, how long has it been since ye've had yer curses?" She laughed at Raven's shocked face. "Aye, ye dinna remember, huh?"

Raven shook her head then placed a hand over her stomach. "I dinna think 'tis possible." But she couldn't remember when her monthly had come last.

"Do ye become ill each morn?" Nora inquired and when Raven nodded she went on. "And by the midday 'tis gone, aye?" Again, Raven nodded. "Has yer body increased yet?"

Now Raven bit her lip and shook her head. "I dinna think so." She sighed, "Are there other signs?"

"Aye many," Nora smiled, "Have yer breasts been painin' ye?"

Raven's eyes widened as she slowly nodded. She covered her stomach with one hand as her head grew light. How could she be pregnant? What would she do? She could not tell Duncan. She looked at Nora and took her hand, "I beg ye, please dinna tell my husband."

"'Tis nay my place. 'Tis somethin' special between the two of ye." Nora hugged her, "But I am happy for ye, Lady Raven." She leaned back and looked at the young woman in front of her. "Firstly, ye'll be needin' a bit of mint to take with ye. Chew a few of the leaves and it'll help too calm yer stomach. Or ye can brew it into a tea." Nora helped Raven up and into the house where she gave her a few leaves to chew upon and a sack of them to carry with her.

By the time Duncan awoke, he found Raven sitting at the table sipping tea and eating toasted bread. She was pale again this morning, but she looked better than she had in days. Relief filled him at the thought that she was overcoming whatever illness she'd had. Sitting down at the table across from her he smiled at her. "Are ye feelin' better, *mo ghaol*?"

"Aye," Raven smiled over at him as she took another sip of her tea. "I think things shall be better from here on." She smiled at Nora and Nora smiled back. For some reason that he couldn't understand, Duncan felt as if he were missing something.

"'Tis good, then ye shall enjoy visitin' my cousin Alistair." Duncan smiled over at her, "'Twill be the first time I have met his wife, for I missed the weddin' as I was away." He smiled up at Nora when she set a plate of eggs and bread in front of him. "Thank ye."

"Yer welcome." She patted him on the shoulder and sighed. "I'll see if Segil will be ready to take ye to Mull soon." She slipped out of the cottage to find her husband.

Duncan looked at Raven, "Is there somethin' that I'm missin'?"

Raven laughed, "Yer a man, ye miss much." She spoke cryptically then set her tea down as she got up from the table and headed for the ladder that would take her up to the loft.

Duncan watched her go up the ladder and disappear all the while humming a tune he had never heard before. He shook his head and turned back to his food.

The crossing of the sound was fairly, easy. The horses seemed relaxed once Raven spoke to them, and still Duncan couldn't understand how she did it. He watched her standing there on the deck of the boat, wrapped in one of his tartans. With her silky black hair blowing around her in the breeze, she stood there smiling, lost in her own world of thoughts. He studied her soft smile and realized he hadn't seen that type of smile on her face before.

Striding to her, he wrapped his arms around her and pulled her back against him as he stared out at the Isle of Mull coming closer.

"It looks like Skye, yet different, smaller mayhap." She looked up at Duncan and smiled, "Is yer cousin's castle as grand as yers?"

Duncan shook his head, "Nay, Alistair does nay have the coin we possess. But I hear his wife is fairly, good at gettin' coin."

Suddenly, a chain net came up out of the water, in front of the boat and it stopped them with a thud. It nearly threw Raven to the deck. Duncan cursed under his breath. "What the bloody hell is this?" He set Raven to rights then strode forward with Segil. They both shook their heads in wonder.

Duncan looked up as three smaller boats with men in them haled them from the other side of the neat. "Who are ye?" Duncan called to them, "And what the bloody hell is this?"

The man who seemed to be the leader here came closer to the boat. "There's a toll to be paid by anyone crossin' through the MacKinnon sound." His red hair reached his shoulders.

Duncan looked from the net to the man, "Then I'm damned lucky, I'm a MacKinnon, ye fool." Duncan indicated his tartan. "My brother's the MacKinnon, Ian and I am Duncan MacKinnon of *Kyleakin*." He growled to the man, "Where the bloody hell is my cousin, Alistair?"

The man's eyes grew wide. He stammered not knowing what to do. This man before him was the brother to the MacKinnon of their clan and was from the Isle of Skye. Finally, Duncan drew his sword and pressed it to the man's chest. "Tell yer men to get yer Laird's ugly *arse* out here to take care of this foolhardy business."

The man before him yelled out the orders and knew if he made one wrong move he was a dead man. He stood there, for a moment fearing for his life. Then yelled for the net to be lowered and the boat allowed through. Word quickly came that their laird would meet them upon the shore.

Segil moved his boat forward slowly and watched the men around him nervously. He made it to shore as fast as possible. When Duncan stepped off the boat he glanced back at Raven worried about her.

Raven smiled at him and tried to assure him that all would be well. She didn't bother to tell him that if these men did decide to attack that she could take care of them easily, for they were floating upon the water and she was an *Irish Sea Water Guardian*. The waters were hers to command.

Though as Duncan followed one of the men and left her on the boat, she felt a bit nervous at first. It was unlike Duncan to go so far from her and leave her alone. She didn't worry for herself, but rather for him, as earth was not her element, she could not help him on land as well.

Raven felt relief when Duncan and a fair-haired man came back out of the woods laughing and talking. The man was slightly smaller than Duncan and very fair, with his long blonde hair that brushed his shoulders. His skin was sun kissed, but much lighter than Duncan's and he wore the same armbands, but in a bronze color. She had noticed that all the head MacKinnon men wore them, Ian and Duncan wore gold, Lachlan and Aidan wore silver and now this stranger who was a MacKinnon wore bronze. She would have to ask Duncan the meaning of these bands.

When Duncan stepped back on the boat and took her hand, she glanced at Segil and Duncan looked at the older man. "Ye are under the protection of Duncan MacKinnon, should one hair upon yer head be harmed, or ye are threatened I shall kill yer assailant." Duncan inclined his head, "Our accord has been met, and ye shall never have to pay a toll through these waters, ye have but to mention my name."

"I thank ye, m'lord." Segil inclined his head in return then looked at Raven, "Take care Lady Raven, both of ye." He saluted Raven then watched as the MacKinnon men helped to unload the horses and their belongings. Raven bid Segil farewell and asked him to thank Nora once more for her help then turned and allowed Duncan to take her off the boat.

Duncan swept Raven into his arms and carried her onto the shore where he set her down carefully. He looked down at her to make sure she was well. Running his knuckles down her cheek he raised a questioning brow, "Are ye well, lass?"

Raven smiled up at him, "Aye, never better." She stepped back from him and looked at the MacKinnon men standing around them. These men were all fairer and some smaller than Duncan. The man who had been walking with Duncan earlier strode up to them. Duncan turned to greet him and pulled Raven into his side wrapping his arm around her waist possessively.

"Well cousin, are ye goin' to introduce me to your lovely bride?" The fair-haired MacKinnon stood there looking down at Raven.

"Aye," Duncan inclined his head, "Raven this is my cousin Alistair MacKinnon Laird of the Isle of Mull, Clan of the MacKinnon." He looked at Raven, "And this is Raven MacKinnon also known as Princess Relia of the Isle of Mann."

Raven watched the man's eyes widen at the word princess. He seemed to straighten up then bowed formally to her. She laughed then held out her hand. "Please just call me, Raven."

"Aye yer highness, I mean Lady Raven." Alistair smiled widely. "My wife Màiri, she will be pleased to meet ye." He looked at Duncan, "I'll give up my chambers to ye and yer wife."

"That will nay be necessary." Duncan assured him, then smiled down at Raven when she jabbed him in the ribs and mouthed 'we shall talk later'.

Duncan insisted that Raven ride Star as he and his cousin walked toward the MacKinnon keep. She listened to the conversation that flowed between the cousins, then tuned them out. She began looking at the castle in the distance and surveyed it. It was smaller than *Dun Akin* and looked as if it was in sore need of repairs. The village outside of the castle was bustling as people worked getting stores ready for the coming winter. She smiled at the people who stared up at her as they passed.

When she came by a hut, she pulled in the reins on her mare and slid from the saddle. Death pervaded the hut and the people around it looked as if to be in mourning. Raven walked over to the door and placed her hand upon it. She looked at Alistair, "What 'tis amiss here?"

He shook his head and spoke to the man standing nearby. "Their daughter 'tis dyin'. She has an ailment that can nay be cured." He hung his head. Raven raised a brow, "May I?"

He inclined his head in puzzlement, but entered the hut with Raven. She looked at the women standing around in the house. "Where is she?"

One of the older women shook her head, "There is aught to be done, we have tried all that 'tis possible." She gave Raven a dismissing look.

Raven pulled herself up to her full height and put on her regal domineer. "I am Princess Relia of the Isle of Mann, I *dinna* ask ye if I could see her. I asked ye where she is, now kindly point the way."

When the older woman looked at her laird, he inclined his head. She pointed to the room on the left then shook her head. "A visit from a princess shall do her aught good."

Raven turned around and raised her hand making the water in a bowl on the table boil. "I am nay ordinary, princess." With that she went into the young girl's room.

She saw the mother kneeling by the bedside. She laid a hand upon her shoulder. "I have come to help ye."

"M'lady, if there is aught ye can do, I beg ye to try and save my daughter. Lillian 'tis all we have." The mother was distraught over her daughter.

Raven removed her tartan and placed it on the end of the bed. She looked at the other woman, "I ken yer tired, but I shall need yer help." Then smiled at her. "Aye, I need a bowl of seawater and some clean beddin' for the lass."

The laird sent everyone scrambling to do Raven's bidding. She knelt by the side of the bed and took the girls hand. A blue aurora shimmered around Raven. "Hello Lillian, dinna be frightened my name is Raven, and I need ye to stay with us. Dinna let go of me nay matter what happens."

The little girl whispered to her and the laird and the mother gasped. Duncan stood with a tightlipped expression. He knew how dangerous this was for Raven to do. Raven was already weary, and this would drain her so much more that it scared him. He could see that she was taking some of the girl's pain already.

Unable to stand seeing Raven strain anymore, Duncan knelt beside Raven bending his head to her, "Ye can nay do this, now. Ye are too weak already, this could kill ye." He looked in to her bluish green eyes that swirled endlessly as she worked her magick.

She looked at him and smiled softly, "I have to, 'tis who and what I am." She reached up and caressed his face, suddenly she shared the pain without meaning to. Duncan hissed, and she pulled back. "I'm sorry, I dinna ken how that happened."

Duncan looked at her and grinned, "Let me help ye lass, I'll take some of the pain ye bare."

"Nay 'tis too dangerous."

He reached over and cupped her cheek the pain spread through him, but this time he was ready. Closing his eyes, he got a handle on the waves of pain rippling through his body. He opened his eyes and looked at her, "I can do this, let me help ye. Yer far too tired to do this alone."

Raven bowed her head, "If it gets to be too much pull away from me." She looked at him. "Thank ye."

"Dinna fash, my love." He leaned over and pressed a kiss to her lips. "I have nay helped ye all that much yet."

Raven smiled, "Yer takin' more of the pain then ye ken." She frowned as the seawater was brought in. "Promise me Duncan, nay matter what happens, ye'll let me finish this and nay interfere, promise me."

Duncan didn't like the sound of that, but he slowly inclined his head, "Aye, I promise." He looked back at the girl lying upon the bed. Saving a child was important, but could he risk Raven to save the girl? As he considered that question Raven placed both of his hands upon the child and released her hold upon the girl, the waves of pain increased ten-fold within him. He wanted to shout and curse as the pain ripped through him.

Raven looked down at him and smiled slightly setting his heart to tripping. "I ken ye were magick, I just dinna realize how powerful ye were."

Duncan raised a brow and smiled up at her. Then he watched Raven climb onto the bed with the bowl of seawater and knelt next to the girl. She began chanting in a language he had never heard before. The blue aura around her began to grow brighter and brighter. The water in the bowl swirled around and around until it came up out of the bowl and hovered over the little girl. Suddenly, the dark sickness began coming out of the little girl's mouth and nose. The pain was ripped from his body and plunged into the now black water cloud.

The black sickness finished coming out of the child's mouth and nose and was sucked up into the swirling water. The blackened water swirled then leapt into the bowl once more. Duncan still had his hands on the girl and could feel her weakness begin to abate as if he were feeding her strength. He looked up at Raven, marveling at his wife.

Duncan saw her waver as he pushed to his feet he snatched the bowl out of her hands and handed it to his cousin. Turning back in time he caught Raven in his arms as she fell back in exhaustion. He looked down at her pale face and watched her eyelids flutter open to reveal her mystical eyes. Deep dark circles were smudged under her eyes and her skin looked nearly translucent. "They must dump the water into the sea, nay other place but the sea." She whispered to Duncan then closed her eyes as sleep claimed her.

Duncan turned to his cousin, "Ye heard her, dump that into the sea, nay where but into the sea. Send a trusted man to do this."

Alistair turned and left the house then called one of his men forward and sent him on the errand to dump the water in the sea. He turned to Duncan who still carried a sleeping Raven in his arms. "Let us take her to the castle and find ye chambers to make her comfortable." As he and Duncan started walking once more he turned back to his cousin. "She'll be fine, aye?"

"Aye, she's stronger than she looks." Duncan grinned down at his beautiful wife. Until today he hadn't realized just how strong she was.

Twenty-two

Raven awoke to find herself lying in a large soft bed, in a room she had never seen before. She frowned as she looked around. Her gaze finally collided with something familiar, a pair of deep beautiful greyish-blue eyes filled with worry. A frown creased his brow as Duncan looked down at her.

"How do ye feel, lass?" He reached out stroking a piece of hair from her cheek.

Raven smiled softly at him, "I'm well enough." She slowly sat up, "How's the girl?"

"On the mend," Duncan sat up as well, from where he had lain with his head propped upon his palm as he watched her sleep. He pushed off the bed to pace around the room, "'Twould seem yer a bit famous now with these MacKinnon people."

Raven furrowed her brows, "I have nay intentions of bein' famous. I was merely savin' the child's life." She sniffed with distain. "Besides 'twas nay as if I did this alone. I had help from a certain dark magickal warrior."

Duncan seemed to consider this as he rubbed his hand over his whisker covered cheeks. "'Tis the truth, mayhap I should take the credit." When she smacked at him, he laughed.

"No one needs take credit except the Gods." She informed him bristly. Taking one of his large hands in hers she placed her hand upon his open palm. "I can feel the power surging through yer veins. It has increased as ye've used it. But ye must nay only learn how to use it, but ye must learn to handle it so that it does nay escape ye if ye lose control."

Duncan closed his hand around her much smaller one, "Do I look like a man who loses control?"

Raven looked in his greyish-blue gaze then away as she pulled her hand from his. "I dinna believe ye have lost control of aught. Ye always ken what ye are doin'." She slipped from the bed and walked across the room to look out the windows as she crossed her arms over herself hugging her waist.

Duncan padded up behind her looking at the scenery outside the window, as he wrapped his arms around her pulling her into him. He leaned his head, on top of her dark head and sighed. "What will it take to get ye to believe what I am tellin' ye, Raven?"

She looked up at him, "I dinna ken." She slipped from his grasp and paced to the other side of the chamber. "I ken what my eyes saw, but I ken that my eyes can be deceived." She bowed her head and looked at her clasped hands then laid one small hand upon her chest and looked in to his greyish-blue gaze, "'Tis my heart that does nay believe yer words."

He sighed, "Raven, I..." She cut him off with a wave of her hand.

"I dinna wish to discuss this yet again with ye." She frowned at him. She placed her hand over her stomach, "For now I am ravenous and in need of food."

"I believe they're 'bout to serve the evenin' meal in the great hall." Duncan inclined his head, "I shall send word that we shall attend the meal." Turning on his heel he strode from the room.

Raven sighed and bowed her head, she had not meant to hurt his pride, but her heart did not yet believe him, so she couldn't forgive him yet. Walking over to where her satchel lay upon the floor she removed her brush and began brushing out her hair so that she could put it up and wash up for the evening meal.

Half an hour later, Raven sat upon the bed waiting for Duncan to appear and escort her to the great hall for dinner. When at last Duncan appeared in their room again, he was stiff and quiet. She could tell he was angry with her, but she said not a word about it.

Raven walked beside him as they entered the great hall. She greeted Alistair and was introduced to his wife Màiri. The woman before Raven stood about five and a half foot tall, with golden ringleted hair and big blue eyes. She was busty and curvy in all the right places.

"'Tis a pleasure to meet ye m'lady. I must thank ye for yer generous hospitality." Raven inclined her head and nearly laughed as Màiri, curtsied and addressed her as yer highness. "Please dinna call me yer highness, Raven, or Lady Raven shall do nicely."

"Aye, yer ... I mean Lady Raven." Màiri smiled brightly seeming not as flustered. "'Tis a pleasure to have ye and yer husband stay with us during yer travels." She smiled at them both, "If there is aught, I may do to make ye more comfortable, please let me know."

"That 'tis verra kind of ye m'lady." Raven smiled once more. She thought perhaps they would become fast friends.

Màiri turned to the man standing just behind her. "M'lord and m'lady, I am pleased to introduce you to my little brother, Borden." She smiled up at her brother as he stepped forward. The man was huge compared to his sister. He matched Duncan in height and had the same broad muscular shoulders, but where Duncan was hard and fit for war, Borden was beginning to run to fat.

Borden shook Duncan's hand then took Raven's and brought it to his lips, "'Tis very much my pleasure, m'lady." He held Raven's hand a moment longer than necessary.

Raven tugged her hand out of his grasp and tucked her hand behind her back where she carefully rubbed off the kiss he had slobbered there. Before she could speak, Duncan hooked an arm around her waist pulling her back to him and tucking her under his chin. "How does the child fare?" Duncan asked his cousin ignoring Borden completely and showing his possessiveness.

Alistair looked from Duncan to Raven, "She is better than she has been in sometime. Her mother expects a full recovery." He smiled brightly, "And we've ye to thank for it, m'lady, is there somethin' ye will take for payment?"

Raven shook her head, "I require aught, but yer thanks." She smiled at the laird and his wife, but ignored the way Borden was looking at her, for it caused her a feeling of foreboding.

"Ye have our thanks, lass, that of my whole clan." Alistair inclined his head. "Dinna be surprised if others come seekin' ye out."

Before Raven could speak Duncan spoke up for her, "My wife is here to rest, she will nay spend her time here healin'. Call yer usual healer."

Alistair looked taken aback, but only inclined his head and changed the subject quickly. "How have yer brother and our low-land cousins been farin'?"

"Lachlan 'tis married to a spirited English lass," Duncan spoke of Kandra fondly as he described her to Alistair and explained how they ended up together.

"Ye must be jokin'." Alistair shook his head. "I can nay believe it. 'Tis a bet she'll give him fine strong sons to fight for the MacKinnon."

Raven gasped at his comment. "Kandra is more than a broodmare. She is a fine warrior and could most like best any man ye put against her." She felt the need to defend her friend.

Duncan turned to her and looked down at her. "Aye, yer right lass, she's anythin', but a broodmare. Kandra is a fierce warrior, as well as a good wife and mother." He looked in to Raven's swirling bluish-green gaze and wondered what their children would be like, what would it be like to watch his child suckle at her delicate breast. He had thought of this often since sitting on the riverbank with Lachlan. Even though he was worried about Raven birthing his bairns, he couldn't help himself, he wanted children with her. Now, if only he could get Raven to believe him.

Raven inclined her head, "I am glad ye see her as so much." She gave him a hard look, "Women can be so much more than mothers and wives." Duncan grinned, "Aye, that they can, *mo ghaol*," he ran his knuckles down her cheek, "Ye have proven as much."

Raven looked in to his deep greyish-blue gaze seeing his love shining there. She pulled back from his touch and looked away. "Thank ye," she murmured as she looked at the floor.

Duncan sighed and was happy when the meal was called to begin. He was seated to the right of his cousin and Raven was seated to his right and Alistair's brother-in-law was next to her. He talked with Alistair and his wife Màiri who sat on Alistair's left.

Raven was left to her own thoughts for most of the meal. When Borden turned to her and studied her for a long moment, she forced herself to keep from shivering under his intense gaze.

"What are you, besides a princess?" He spoke directly to her in his heavy Nordic accent.

Raven looked at him for a long moment. "I am *Irish Sea Water Guardian* by my father and *Manx Witch*, from my mother." She frowned at the look upon his face, "My father is King Toslar of the Guardian people."

"Is Raven, your given name?" Borden looked at her shinny raven's black hair. She smiled and shook her head, "Nay, my true name is Relia." Raven studied the man next to her. Perhaps she had misjudged Borden, she thought.

"'Tis a beautiful name, Relia. How 'tis it you have come by the name Raven?" He raised a blonde brow in question as he took a bite of the venison upon his plate. Cutting off a very lean piece of meat from his trencher he set it upon hers.

Raven looked down at the meat then back at him. It was not right for a man besides her husband to share food with her. Perhaps, their customs were different she thought for a long moment. She cleared her throat and decided to answer him. "I was in a ship wreck and lost my memory, I had nay clue as to my true name, or where I was from. 'Twas the Clan Brodie that found me washed upon their shores. 'Twas Ewin Brodie, that gave me my name, because of my long black hair."

"Raven, 'tis a beautiful name as well." He smiled over at her, "It fits you well." He took a drink of his wine then grabbed the flagon and refilled his own as well as hers. "So, which is it that gives you your magick, your mother or your father?"

Raven thanked him for the wine then took a sip of it. At least this man was treating her kindly, whereas Duncan ignored her completely. "'Tis from both of my parents, but mostly from my father." She smiled, "I inherited the vision from my mother."

Borden raised a brow once more, "You can see the future?" She shook her dark head, "Nay exactly, I can usually see images of people's futures."

She frowned, "Only some people I can nay see theirs and I've nay clue as to why." She glanced at Duncan.

"Perhaps they have nay future." Borden spoke softly as he looked at Duncan as well.

A shudder ran down Raven's spine at the thought. Could it mean such a thing when she could see only darkness when she tried to see his future? If they were meant to be together, why had she not seen images of their children, she thought laying a hand over her stomach. "Perhaps," she whispered. She looked down at the food upon her trencher and lost her appetite.

The meal was over, and Raven looked over to where Duncan sat, she tugged on his sleeve. When he turned to look at her, she could swear she saw anger flash in his eyes for a brief second.

"I'm tired and wish to retire to my chambers." She sighed when he furrowed his brows, "I am well, dinna fash yerself." She looked in to his deep greyish-blue gaze then pushed her chair back. With that she fled from the great hall.

Above stairs she paced their chamber as she thought. The words that Borden spoke raced through her mind. Was it possible? She wondered with worry filling her. Crossing her arms over her waist she hugged herself. Walking over to the washstand she picked up the urn of water and poured it into the gray stone bowl until it filled the bowl half way.

She looked down into the water and waited for it to settle. "Show me what I seek to ken." She spoke softly as she waved a hand over the bowl. She waited for the images to appear, but nothing came. Raven tried three times, but it would show her nothing. She gave a soft cry and flung the bowl from the stand sending it crashing to the floor. This could not be! Her mind cried.

The chamber door crashed open and Duncan stood there ready to do battle with his sword drawn. He looked around the room. "What 'tis amiss, lass?"

"Aught 'tis a miss," Raven quickly shook her head as she took in this rugged island warrior, all six and a half feet of him. His long hair held multiple braids with golden beads at their ends. Golden armbands fit snug around his powerful biceps and a golden torc wrapped around his neck emphasizing his broad muscular shoulders. He had the body of a God, and it was sun kissed golden from hours of training and honing his skills outside.

His gaze took in the broken water basin and the water spilled upon the floor. Sheathing his sword, he stepped into the room closing the door behind him. "What happened here, *gràdh*?" He strode across the room. Standing in front of her, he looked down at her then reached out tucking a stray lock of silky black hair behind her ear.

"Aught 'tis wrong." She shrugged and avoided his eyes as she spoke. "'Twas but an accident." She started to turn from him to clean up the mess, but he placed a hand upon her arm stopping her.

He looked down into her pale face, "Ye've nay to fear, for I shall protect ye with my life, Raven MacKinnon. For ye are my wife and *Tha ghaol agam ort*." He bent his head and claimed her mouth with his own.

Raven sank into the kiss and pushed her fears away. She was overreacting, she thought firmly. When she reached the Isle of Mann she would consult her mother and grandmother about her lack of visions. The taste of him, made her heart yearn to forgive him and let him make love to her, but her mind stood firm as the vision of him and Isobel flashed through her mind.

Pulling back from his kiss, Raven spoke softly, "Let me go." She could not meet his eyes as hurt raced through her.

Duncan looked down at her and sighed. She still did not forgive him, or believe him about Isobel. He was beginning to think he would have to tie her to the bed and gag her to make her listen to everything he had to say over and over until she believed him. "If that 'tis yer wish," he growled down at her, "but look at me, and tell me that ye detest my touch." Raven could not lie to him. She couldn't tell him that she hated his touch, when in fact she loved it and even craved it. "I can nay think when ye touch me thus." She whispered softly.

He smiled wolfishly down at her, "I dinna see that as a bad thin', lass." Sobering he frowned, "We need to speak of it sometime, *gràdh*." With that said he released her and strode for the door. Stopping with his hand upon the handle he looked over his shoulder at her. "Let me ken when yer ready to listen to and believe what I have to say."

She watched him walk out the door of their chamber closing it softly behind him. She stood there for a long moment then walked over to the bed and crawled upon it to lie down. Confusion, fear, anger and hurt filled her as she cried herself to sleep. For she was losing the man she loved. She could not help but to wonder now, would she lose him, no matter what happened?

Duncan made his way down to the great hall and found himself a cup of whiskey. Sitting at a table by himself he ignored the bantering going on around him. He lost himself in his cup of whiskey as he tried to drown his problems with Raven. How could he make her listen to him, other than truly tying her to the bed and making her?

He had drunk five tankards of whiskey when Alistair and Borden sat down on either side of him. His cousin frowned at him, "What are ye drownin' cousin?"

"Woman problems." Duncan sighed.

"Would ye care to speak of it?" Alistair refilled Duncan's cup. "Perhaps I can help ye."

Duncan raised his cup to his cousin, "Perhaps ye can." He spilled the whole story and how Raven caught him with Isobel and how she left Dun Akin, heading for the Isle of Mann. "I dinna ken how to make her listen to me and understand that the only damnedable woman I want 'tis her."

"Aye that 'tis a problem." Alistair shook his head, "Women are such fickle creatures."

"Aye." Duncan frowned down at his pint.

Borden had not spoken a word until now. "Perhaps, you would be better off to force her to accept your word." He looked over at Duncan, "Make her listen to you, even if she does nay wish to, for she is your wife and she belongs to you. A wife must obey her husband."

Duncan gulped down his cup of whiskey and nodded to Borden, "Aye, ye've the right of it. She's my wife and I'll be damned if I'll allow her to order me 'bout." He pushed up from the table and strode away from the great hall heading for his chambers and his wife.

Alistair looked at Borden and frowned, "'Twas nay good advice ye just gave him. He'll get his arse handed to him for sure." The laird laughed and shook his head, "I pray he passes out 'afore he reaches their chamber. Borden drank deeply of his cup, "The man's a fool." He spat then pushed up from the table himself and left the great hall.

Duncan strode up the solar stairs with purpose in his steps. He reached his chamber door and thrust it open. Raven sat up from where she had been laying in the middle of the bed. Her dark hair was disheveled and flowed over her right shoulder. Her face was flushed from sleep and beautiful, but it was her red-rimmed eyes that tore a hole through Duncan's heart.

"Duncan?" She spoke softly in a husky voice. "What 'tis amiss?" Her mystical gaze searched his.

Borden's words came back to him and had Duncan closing the door behind him as he strode over to the bed. He looked down upon his ethereal wife and felt his loins fire. Duncan reached down grasping her arms and pulling her up upon her knees to face him. "'Tis time ye listen to what I have to say to ye." He shook her slightly.

"Release me, for yer drunk." She pressed her hands against his stomach.

He pulled her up to stand before him at eye level. "Drunk I may be, but I have had enough of this foolishness. Yer my wife and ye'll obey me." He growled at her. "I shall speak plainly and ye shall listen to what I have to say. Once I have spoken, we shall nay speak of it again."

Raven gave him an icy look as she spoke, "Yer drunk." She hissed, "Release me, or ye'll be sorry."

Duncan laughed harshly, "Do ye think I fear ye?" When she just gave him a hard look he shook his head. "We're playin' nay more of yer games. What I've to say, ye'll listen to."

Raven stood there stiffly, "Dinna do this Duncan, for it matters nay what ye say if I dinna believe those words in my heart." She softened and bowed her head as she spoke her next words. "If ye feel such a need to speak then by all means speak yer peace and get it over with."

Duncan was quiet for a long moment. Taking a deep breath, he finally spoke. "Since the moment ye arrived at *Dun Akin*, I have nay tupped, Isobel." He shook her slightly, "The night ye found Isobel and I together, we were sayin our goodbyes, for she wished to leave for Inverness to find another protector."

Raven spoke not another word only stared into his deep greyish blue gaze. She tried to pull from his grip, but couldn't. "Release me, yer hurtin' me." She whispered as she stared at him.

"Did ye nay hear aught that I told ye?" He shook her once more and furrowed his brows as she hissed in pain.

She glared at him, "Aye, I heard every word ye spoke, but that does nay mean I believe every word ye said. Now yer hurtin' me, please let me go." When he finally released her, she rubbed her arms where she knew his hand would leave bruises.

Duncan stared at her for a long moment. "Will ye never forgive me and love me once more, Raven?" The hurt was plain in his eyes, but it did nothing to sway Raven.

"I can nay help but to love ye, but that does nay mean I shall ever forgive ye." She glared at him, "If yer plannin' upon sleepin' in this bed, I shall find another chamber in which to sleep."

Duncan frowned at her then turned upon his heel and strode from the room. Had he made things worse between them? Should he have waited until she was ready to listen to him?

Making his way to the great hall, he found it all quiet. He settled himself into a chair near the hearth and there he began to think upon his problem with Raven and the huge mistake he had just made with the woman he loved.

As the early morning light began to fill the castle, Duncan finally drifted off.

Twenty-three

The morning found Raven sick once again. She blessed Nora for her advice and the mint the older woman had sent along. Chewing the mint, Raven sat upon her bed and stared at the window where sunshine poured in. She wondered where Duncan had slept last night, then pushed that thought away. What should she care where he slept?

She placed a hand over her stomach, covering her tiny babe. Though Raven knew she should tell Duncan, she had no plans to at that moment. For if she did, Raven feared she would never get rid of Duncan MacKinnon. He would force his way into her life for all times, and at this point Raven wasn't sure that she wanted him in her life at all.

Raven ventured into the great hall when most of the castle had already broken their fasts. She sat at an empty table and ordered dry toast and tea to break her fast. When her food arrived, she ate it slowly as her thoughts swirled around the man she loved and her bairn.

Duncan had a right to know about the baby she was carrying, but after his actions last night she refused to tell him about their child. He had treated her as if she was a possession instead of the woman he loved.

When Borden sat down next to her, it jarred her out of her thoughts. She looked over at him and smiled, "Good morrow'."

"Aye, 'tis a good mornin' indeed." He smiled brightly at her. "'Tis always a good morn when a man gets to sit next to a beautiful woman."

"Thank ye," she inclined her head.

Borden studied her for a long moment then inquired, "After you've finished breakin' your fast would you care to tour the castle with me?"

Raven thought for a moment, "I'd be happy to." She took another sip of her tea and finished off her toast quickly.

Raven walked beside Borden who was nearly twice her size. He showed her the library and let her wander around reading titles on the spines of the leather-bound books.

Borden walked over and pulled a book from the shelf. "'Tis one of my favorites." He held the book out to her.

Taking the book Raven read the title. "'*Homer, The Odyssey*'. I've never read this before." She looked at him and when he held his hand out she placed it in his hand.

"'*Sing to me of the man, Muse, the man of twists and turns driven time and again off course, once he had plundered the hallowed heights of Troy, Many cities of men he saw and learned their minds, many pains he suffered, heartsick on the open sea, fighting to save his life and bring his comrades home. But he could not save them from disaster, hard as he strove -the recklessness of their own ways destroyed them all, the blind fools, they devoured the cattle of the Sun and the Sun God blotted out the day of their return. Launch out on his story, Muse, daughter of Zeus, start from where you will - sing for our time too.*" His baritone voice filled the room as he recited the opening of the Odyssey to her.

Raven sat on one of the comfy couches as he began to read and thought how *Dun Akin* could benefit from a library such as this one. She wondered for a moment if Ian and Duncan would let her turn one of the many rooms into such a grand library? She pushed that thought from her mind, for she planned never to return to *Dun Akin* again.

When he finished reading, Raven sighed, "That 'twas bonnie. Ye've a wonderful voice."

Borden bowed at the waist and replaced the book. "I thank you, m'lady." He smiled down at her and offered his hand to help her stand. When she took it, he pulled her to stand and stepped close to her at the same time. He looked down into her mystical swirling eyes and frowned, "Your husband does nay deserve you."

Raven looked away from him, but didn't pull her hand away, immediately. "Yer right he does nay." She looked up at him, "That's why I plan to return home and find a way out of my marriage to him." She pulled her hand out of Borden's and turned walking to the door of the library. She stopped and turned back to him. "Thank ye for showin' me this place, 'tis a place to lose oneself when they are troubled." She opened the door and fled from the library.

Raven sat in her room and prepared herself for the evening meal. She hadn't seen Duncan the whole day long, but now she waited in their chambers for him to escort her to the great hall for the evening meal.

She sat upon the bed and waited. An hour passed, and he did not come for her. Raven sighed deeply, she wouldn't go to the hall by herself for it would be embarrassing to find him sitting there dining and having not cared enough about her to escort her to the meal. She sat in front of the fire for a long time just staring at the flames. Her heart loved Duncan, but her mind told her, he was not worth her love. A tear slipped down her cheek. How she wanted to believe him, that he had no love for Isobel any longer, and only love for her, but she couldn't, not with the way he had been before and the way he had acted last night.

Placing her hand over her stomach, she made the decision not to tell Duncan about their bairn, ever. She would return to the Isle of Mann and she would raise their child by herself. Their child would not lack for love, she knew her parents, her brothers and her grandmother would love her child completely. A smile slipped into place as she thought of her family, an ache panged in her heart with missing them. She couldn't wait to see them.

A knock at the door sounded and brought her out of her revere. Standing and brushing her skirt down on her aqua gown she walked to the door. Opening it her frown turned into a smile. "Good evenin'."

Borden stood outside her chamber door, "Good evenin', m'lady." He frowned down at her. "Are you sick, m'lady?"

"Nay," she shook her head, "I'm well, thank ye." Borden leaned against the doorjamb crossing his arms over his broad chest. "Can I ask, why you've missed the meal?"

Raven looked down at her hands, but spoke the words quietly as tears filled her eyes. "Duncan did nay come to escort me down to the hall."

Borden placed a finger under her chin and made her look at him. He wiped away a stray tear with his thumb. "The bastard should be whipped for the way he treats you. 'Tis as if he does nay give a damn about you and your welfare."

Raven turned away from him and wrapped her arms around her waist. "I dinna care what he does, I plan to leave here as soon as possible, and return to my home on Mann."

Borden stepped into her room, "If you wish m'lady I will help you to find your way home." He touched her shoulder then slowly turned her, "but for now, you can nay go to bed hungry."

She waved him away, "I am nay hungry..."

"Of course, you are," he smiled down at her. "The meal is neigh on over, why nay allow me to escort you down to get a bit of somethin'."

Raven gave a soft laugh as she thought of the baby, "I suppose 'tis wiser to eat somethin' than naught." She wiped her tears away and turned to Borden, "I would be honored to allow ye to escort me below stairs. Thank ye."

"'Tis my pleasure, m'lady." He smiled down at her.

"Raven." She inclined her head.

"Then, 'tis only fair you call me, Borden." He held out his arm to her.

Taking his arm, she smiled up at him. "Yer a kind man, Borden."

Raven entered the great hall with a smile upon her face. She pulled to a stop and the smile slipped turning into a frown as hurt filled her face. Across the hall, she watched Duncan and a serving wench as the girl flopped in his lap and he laughed and took a gulp from his tankard. Her stomach turned, and she felt her heart stop, when the woman threw her arms around Duncan's neck and kissed him soundly on the mouth.

Anger filled her as power snapped in the air around her. She released Borden's arm and marched across the room. A hush fell over the room as all eyes turned to look at her and the angry snap of energy that crackled around her. She stopped in front of Duncan just as the kiss ended.

Duncan looked up at her and his eyes sobered. "Raven..." He croaked, but she cut him off with a wave of her hand. Duncan looked up at her and saw the hurt in her eyes as well as the anger.

"Dinna say anythin'." She hissed at him. Reaching out she grabbed his tankard of whiskey and poured it over his head. "Stay away from me, Duncan MacKinnon." She turned on her heels and stormed from the great hall brushing past Borden and his sorrowful look. He removed the serving girl from his lap, and would have stood, but the fist that hit his face had him knocking backward out of his chair. He looked up at his cousin, Alistair.

"I've nay clue what the hell is wrong with ye, but ye've nay cause to hurt that woman in the manner ye just have." His hands settled upon his hips. "Ye dinna deserve her, ye damned fool." With that said he turned upon his heel and stormed away.

Raven paced her room as anger surged through her. He had lied to her, Duncan MacKinnon was a heartless bastard, she thought angrily. Raven threw a spell over the door as she heard the pounding footfalls in the hallway. She wouldn't allow the blackguard to enter her chambers for she had no wish to see him.

"Raven?" He tried the doorknob then beat upon the door. Silence met his pounding. "Damn it Raven! I ken yer in there."

"Go away and leave me alone." Raven hissed through the door.

Duncan sighed at least she would yell at him, "'Twas nay what it seemed..."

"Liar!" She yelled through the door at him. "Go away and leave me be, I hate ye!"

He placed his palm upon the door and jerked it back as the magick shocked him. "Raven, I'm sorry. Please allow me to come in and speak with ye."

"Get away from my chambers, and leave me alone. For I have aught to say to ye." She called through the door at him.

"Dinna make me stand out here in the hall and discuss this with ye." He frowned at the door. "Open the door, Raven."

"Or what?" She sneered, "Ye'll beat me? Ye'll go back to one of yer 'hores? Or ye'll send me back home and have aught to do with me ever again?" He was quiet for a long moment.

"*Gràdh*..."

"Dinna call me that!" She growled at him through the door. "For I am nay yer love. Ye can nay love someone and treat them as ye have me."

He could hear the tears in her voice and it broke his heart. What an ignorant *arse* he was to have hurt her and not once, but twice. Somehow, he had to find a way to fix this. Aught had worked so far, but he wouldn't give up, he thought stubbornly. "I am sorry, lass." He sighed, "Let me come in to our chamber and we shall talk this through."

305

Raven walked to the door and frowned, "Nay Duncan, I have aught more to say to ye. Go away, return to Dun Akin, I have nay wish to ever see ye, or speak to ye again. *Mar sin leat*, Duncan!"

"Nay! Dinna say that, Raven. Ye can nay mean that!" Duncan felt his heart stop. He refused to let her tell him goodbye. She sounded so final that his heart hurt with the thought of losing her. He felt panic raise in him, he couldn't lose her, for he would be nothing without her. No other woman would ever do for him.

When only silence met his words, he waited for a few more minutes, "Raven *gràdh*, talk to me." More silence met his words. "Damn it! Fine, have it yer way, but I shall stay outside this door until ye have nay choice, but to come out then we shall talk."

Raven shook her head, but said not a word as she heard him settle down beside the door. She could almost imagine his stubborn hide sitting upon the cold stone floor with his large muscular arms crossed over his broad chest. Gods how she had loved the man! Tears began pooling in her eyes and falling as she felt her heart break once more.

Walking over to the bed, she crawled upon it and curled up in its middle. Sobs broke over her as she felt her heart ripped apart once more by the man she loved. What a fool she was to allow him near it once more.

Duncan sat there and listened to the storm building in the night, raging as the rain poured against the castle. It was her tears that rained outside, and the thunder were her sobs, while the lightening was her anger. He sat there with his head in his hands and his heart aching with the pain he felt radiating from her broken heart.

As the night raged on, her tears pulled her down into the blissful darkness of sleep. While the whiskey Duncan had drank pushed him into the oblivion of darkness and troubled sleep.

The morning dawned gray and dreary. Duncan sat up from where he had fallen asleep looking around. He stood cursing under his breath. He tried the door to their chamber and furrowed his brows when he turned the knob freely. Pushing open the door he walked into the chamber to all of Raven's belongings missing. He cursed under his breath and left the room to find his cousin.

Alistair was in his study with his steward going over the castle's business. He looked up when his cousin burst into the room.

"Where is she?" He growled as his eyes filled with anger.

"I can nay tell ye." Alistair shook his head solemnly and looked back at the books before him.

Fury erupted in Duncan. He reached over and grabbed his cousin yanking him over the desk to him. "Tell me where the hell my bloody wife is." He would kill any man who stood in the way of him finding Raven.

Alistair looked up at his cousin, "Do ye think this will make me tell ye? If ye do, yer a bigger *arse* than I thought." He pulled away from Duncan then dismissed his steward. Once the older man was gone and they were alone, Alistair frowned at Duncan. "I shall nay tell ye where Raven's chambers are. She has requested that I dinna tell ye and I have chosen to honor that request."

"Damn it Alistair, how the bloody hell am I to work things out with my wife if I can nay talk with her?" He ran a shaky hand through his hair as he paced the room. He stopped and gave his cousin a frustrated look, "I can nay lose her."

"Ye should have thought of that, before ye acted the fool." He narrowed his eyes at his older cousin. "For now, yer wife has asked for my help, and I shall give it to her."

Duncan stepped over to look his cousin in the eye, "Ye've nay right to keep my wife away from me."

Alistair frowned at his cousin, "Yer in need of a bath and cleanin' up cousin." He stepped back from Duncan and frowned, "Mayhap, if ye can show a bit more remorse than addled brains, then I shall perhaps give ye some information 'bout where yer wife is currently."

Duncan could only stare at his cousin with his mouth gaped open. He snapped his mouth closed then turned on his heel and stormed from the room. Once in his chambers, he looked at his reflection in a basin of water. Damn did he look bad, he thought with a grimace. He looked like a wild man.

First, he ordered a bath and his clothing to be washed. While he waited for his bath to arrive, he scraped the whiskers from his face and neck until he was left with soft bare skin. Once his bath was in place he scrubbed until he was clean as a whistle. There was not much he could do with his red-rimmed eyes, but some sleep that night would probably not hurt.

Dressed in his clean kilt and a white linen shirt, he strode down the stairs to the great hall and over to where his cousin stood with his wife and younger brother. He smiled at Riordan, Alistair's younger brother who was nearly ten years Duncan's junior. He gripped forearms with the younger MacKinnon in a warrior's handshake. "Where have ye been lad?"

"A bit of here and there, most recently I've been to visit your cousin Brady in Ireland." Riordan smiled brightly, "He married an Irish Princess."

His smug look made Duncan laugh. Duncan leaned in and whispered to him, "Aye, 'twould seem 'tis goin' around in this family. For so did I. Princess Relia from the Isle of Mann."

"Are ye jestin' me?" Riordan pulled back, "Well, congratulations." He smacked Duncan upon the back. "Where is she?"

Duncan straightened and frowned at Alistair, "I'm afraid I've had a misunderstandin' with my wife and yer brother has decided to help her hide from me."

Alistair glared at Duncan, "Aye, and 'tis yer fault and yer fault alone."

"I want to ken where ye've hidden my wife from me." Duncan growled at Alistair.

"I shall ask her if she wishes to speak with ye 'afore she sets sail." He frowned at Duncan, but then nearly smiled as his cousin's face went pale under his dark tanned complexion.

"Sail?" Duncan repeated lamely. "Yer helpin' her sail to the Isle of Mann?"

"Aye, she has petitioned me for my aid and I have granted it." He narrowed his eyes at Duncan, "Someone has to look out for her and..." He stopped himself and shook his head. "If ye lose her, Duncan yer a bloody damned fool."

"I have nay intentions of losin' her, if I must rip yer bloody home to pieces searchin' for her." He turned on his heels and left the great hall on his mission to search for his missing wife. She had to be somewhere near at hand, there was no way Alistair would hide her too far away, so the village was out of the question.

Alistair smiled as Raven walked through the door into the great hall for dinner. "Lady Raven, may I introduce my younger brother, Riordan." He took her hand and seated her at the table next to his wife. They enjoyed a relaxed dinner as Alistair explained that he had sent Duncan searching like a fool throughout the castle and doubted he would return in time to interrupt their meal.

Duncan had searched everywhere but the dungeons for her and his temper was increasing with every step he took. The sound of her laugh below him on the stairs had him whipping back to head to the floor below. He took the stairs two at a time and reached the second floor of the keep just in time to see Borden walking toward him with a smile upon his face.

Duncan strode up to the man and blocked his path. "Which room is my wife in?"

Borden shook his head, "I've nay idea."

Duncan grabbed the man by the shirtfront and slammed him into the wall next to them. "Where is my wife?" He growled with anger sparking in his eyes. Along with that anger his magick, that Raven had somehow released in him, snapped and surged through his hands. Borden's eyes went wide then he slumped forward. Duncan backed up releasing the man and letting him fall as he stared at his own hands. He truly did have magick, he thought with his mind whirling. Duncan carefully reached down and checked Borden to make sure he was alive.

Striding down the passageway he checked every door along the hallway. Only one was locked and he pounded upon it. "Damn it Raven, if yer in there, I've need of ye. There is somethin' wrong with Borden." He growled through the door.

He heard a sound inside and frowned. "I jest nay with ye, Raven. Borden is unconscious, and I've nay clue how to help him."

When the door whipped open and his wife stood there before him, he nearly reached out and grabbed her, but she strode past him. "Where is he?"

Jealousy raged through Duncan, but he checked it, because he had to make sure Borden was going to be alright. Duncan had no clue what he had done to the man. "Down here." He led Raven down the hall to where the man lay in the middle of the hall.

Raven hurried down the hall and knelt next to Borden. She reached for him and drew back glaring up at Duncan. "Ye used magick upon him?"

Duncan would have denied it, but he knew lying was useless. "Aye, I dinna mean to. I've nay clue how I did it." He knelt beside her and held his breath waiting for her condemnation.

Raven shook her head then held her hands above the man then sighed. She dropped her hands and looked at Duncan, "He shall be fine, take him to his room and let him sleep it off upon his bed." She pushed up and stood.

Duncan stood as well. Reaching out before she had a chance to react, he pulled her into him and brought her up on her tiptoes crushing his mouth over hers in a searing heated kiss. By the time he released her, she was breathless and unsteady upon her feet. He held her a second until she backed away from him. Watching her turn and flee down the hall to her room, slamming the door behind her, he smiled, because he still had a powerful effect upon her, which meant not all was lost.

Scooping up Borden he took him to his chambers and dumped him upon his bed unceremoniously. He turned and left to go to his own chambers. There he stripped down and crawled into his empty bed. Sleep claimed him quickly.

Raven spent most of the night pacing, tossing and turning as thoughts of Duncan raced through her mind. Her heart ached to be with him, but her head told her it was over between them.

Twenty-Four

Raven was breaking her fast, when Borden strode over to where she sat. She smiled up at him brightly. In the week since she had started avoiding Duncan, Borden had accompanied her to meals and to the village to look in on the little girl, she and Duncan had saved. Though Duncan had checked upon the girl, Raven had not seen him.

"Raven, I was wondering if you would care to visit the orchards this afternoon?" Borden smiled down at her.

"I would be delighted." She smiled up at him. The idea of some fresh air excited her. Summer seemed to be hanging on, when it should be growing cold by now. The sun was shining brightly, and Raven would love to walk through it, and enjoy it while it lasted.

Later in the afternoon Borden carried a sack filled with food as he and Raven walked toward the orchard. She had come to enjoy Borden's friendship. She looked over at the tall Norseman, he was handsome and beyond polite. She felt comfortable with him now.

Borden spread a cloth under a plum tree in the shade. He helped Raven to sit and settle her skirts around her. Pulling open the cloth, he set out a loaf of bread, a hunk of cheese, fruit, smoked meats, and he had a flagon of plum wine. He cut Raven bread, cheese and meat.

Raven ate with relish and chatted happily with him. "When do ye think a trader ship shall be in?" She was excited about the idea of leaving for Mann and seeing her family once more. Though the thought of leaving Duncan behind made her heart hurt, but she knew it was for the best. Time would heal the wound he had left in her heart.

Borden looked at her a long moment then reaching over he skimmed his knuckles down her cheek. "I hope 'tis nay time soon." His fingers caressed her neck where her pulse beat furiously.

Raven furrowed her brows and spoke as she pulled away. "'Tis inappropriate for ye to touch me thus." She frowned at him. "My husband would be furious if he were to see ye touch me in such a forward manner."

"Your husband matters nay, for 'tis clear he does nay want you." Borden informed her smugly. He grabbed her arm pulling her to him. "But I do."

Raven tried to pull away, "Let go of me." She punched him in the jaw then cried out as he backhanded her across the face. Stars danced in front of her eyes as she fought Borden's hold upon her.

"You want me, and you know as much, I have showed you over and over that I want you." He rolled her under him and pressed a wet kiss to her lips. "Do nay play coy with me." He growled, and he pulled back as he captured her hands and held them above her head.

"Release me, or by the Gods, I shall make ye verra, verra sorry." She spat up at him and when he laughed she brought her knee up and hit him in the stomach making the air swoosh out of him. She pulled one hand free and pressed it to his chest as he sucked in air to replace what he had lost. Magick surged through her and hit him making him curse and roll off her to get away from her.

Raven struggled to her feet, but she wasn't faster than Borden. "Bitch." He hissed as he grabbed her by the hair pulling her to her feet. He held her head tipped back at a painful angle and relished the sound of her cry of pain. "You made me believe you wanted me." He used his free hand to punch her knocking her to the ground and smiled at her cry of pain.

He stormed over to her where she was struggling to her feet. With a snarl, he kicked her in the ribs knocking her onto the blanket where she lay doubled over holding her side coughing. Rage surged through him as he knelt beside her, his hand encircling her throat. "You're nay different than every other whore."

Raven grabbed Duncan's dagger from her waist. Borden may have hurt her, but she was anything besides defeated. Bringing the knife around quickly she stabbed him with all her might in the shoulder. His hands dropped away from her throat as he cried out in pain rolling away from her.

Raven coughed gripping her side, as she pushed herself up onto her feet. He surged to his feet as she gained her own. Raven gripped the knife tighter. "I'll kill ye." She snarled at him as raged filled her eyes.

"You would nay dare," Borden taunted her, "For all of you whores are the same, weak little bitches who are begging for us real men to have a go at you." He took a step toward her, intending to make her bow down to him.

Raven flipped the knife in her hand, holding the blade in her fingers and threw it within a blink of an eye. Borden screamed in pain and she turned and began to limp away as running was impossible with the pain ripping through her side and stomach.

The sound of Borden's footsteps coming after her and his curses had her moving faster as she cut through the rows of trees and tried to find a place to hide. The sight of the man stalking into the end of the orchard row she was in, had Raven's heart leaping with hope. "Duncan!" She screamed on a ragged breath. Her heart pounded at the sight of him, and she knew the Gods had intervened.

For a quick moment, Duncan froze at the sight of Raven limping toward him, with her arm crossed over her stomach. He could see her battered face and his stomach lurched. Her hoarse cry of agony, had him sprinting into action. He reached her in a moment and had her in his arms. "What happened? Were ye set upon?" His hands roamed over her, taking in her face that was bloody and already swollen in places. Fear and anger warred inside of him. "Who did this to ye?"

Before Raven could catch her breath and tell him, Borden broke through a line of trees and pulled up short at the sight of Raven in Duncan's arms.

Anger surged through Duncan, as he took in Borden with blood blossoming brightly upon his shirt at his shoulder. He looked for a moment down at Raven and saw the total fear in her eyes. A snarl formed upon his lips as he set Raven behind him. He looked back at Borden then began to stalk toward him.

Borden started to back away and would have turned to flee, but Duncan had him by his injured arm and spun him around to face him. The rage on Duncan's face was plain and Borden knew this man could kill him without a second thought.

Duncan glared down at the man who was only slightly shorter than Duncan's six and a half feet of height. "Did ye do this to my wife?" He growled but didn't allow Borden to answer. "Nay one puts a hand upon my wife." He pulled back his fist and rammed it into Borden's face causing the man to fly off his feet and hit the dirt. Duncan was on him before Borden could so much as blink.

Rage whipped through Duncan like heat lighting. Grabbing the man, he began hitting him in the face over and over. If it weren't for Raven calling his name and crying, he would have killed the man. The sounds of her sobs broke through the haze of rage.

Turning his head, he looked at his wife. Her pale cheeks had tears coursing down them and her lips trembled then thinned in pain. "Duncan." She whispered then collapsed.

Jumping to his feet, he raced to his wife and knelt beside her. "Raven? Wake up, Raven." He spoke and patted her cheek gently. "*Gràdh*, ye must wake up." He pressed a kiss to her forehead then to her swollen lips.

Scooping her into his arms he raced for the castle. He reached the inner bailey and was met by Alistair and his wife Màiri, who both wore concern upon their faces.

"Tell us what happened?" Riordan frowned at the sight of Raven battered and unconscious.

"Where was she set upon?" Alistair raged, "We shall send out men."

Duncan stopped in the great hall and looked at his cousin. "Find me a healer for my wife." His tone broke no argument as rage laced it. "For 'twas one of yer own, to harm my wife." With that he turned and strode for the chambers they had shared when they first arrived.

He laid her upon the bed then stripped her soiled and bloody clothing from her. With a basin of water, he washed her body and frowning at the bruises he found. When the healer arrived, she ushered him out. Duncan looked down at her with anger in his voice, "Dinna leave my wife alone for even a moment, or there shall be pure hell to pay. Do ye understand me?"

"Aye, m'lord." The older woman bowed her head then closed the door so that she could examine her patient.

Duncan strode below stairs to the great hall where Alistair and Riordan paced. He looked at his cousins and frowned then ordered a serving girl to fetch him a tankard of whiskey. After she had bowed away from him and hurried off to do his bidding, he turned to his cousins.

"Who did this?" Alistair frowned at Duncan, "Give me the bastard's name and he shall pay dearly for such an offense."

Duncan took the tankard of whiskey from the serving girl, took a deep drink from it then looked at his cousins. "Ye wish a name?"

"Aye!" Both brothers spoke in unison.

"Borden." Duncan narrowed his eyes at Alistair. "The bloody bastard attacked my wife," he pointed up toward the solar, "and did that to her."

"Nay!" Màiri shouted. "He would never do such a thing."

"Nay, m'lady?" He glared at her with death in his eyes. "Go look within the orchard and ye'll find his miserable *arse* there." Duncan shrugged, "For all I care he 'tis dead."

Màiri gave a cry of anguish. "Alistair, find him. Tell me he is nay dead."

Alistair looked grimly at his wife, "I shall send out men to search for him." He turned back to his cousin with a grim expression. "If he is nay dead, I shall have the healer see to him once she has finished with yer wife. Then 'tis up to ye if he has paid enough for his assault against yer wife's person."

"Alistair, nay!" Màiri cried behind him then started to sob. She turned and fled from the hall.

Alistair looked after her then back to Duncan, "Ye've the right to avenge yer wife, 'tis the law of the MacKinnon, we dinna lay hands upon a woman." He lowered his eyes from his cousin's. "But if his sorry *arse* is nay dead, I shall plead his life on my wife's behalf. If ye dinna see fit to grant such a request," he looked up and met Duncan's eyes, "I shall understand. For I would kill any man who dared lay hands upon my wife."

Duncan inclined his head, "I shall think upon it." He clasped his cousin upon the shoulder and squeezed. "I shall go see 'bout my wife." With that he turned on his heel and quit the great hall.

Above stairs he paced outside the chamber where his wife lay. His mind reeled as he thought of her condition. Fear clutched his heart, for as he had undressed her, he had notice that there had been blood running down her legs. Had the man raped her? He wondered as anger whipped through him. When a tapestry upon the wall in the corridor caught fire and he had to pull it from the wall and stamp it out, he knew he had to get his anger under control. As he barely had control over the blasted magick at the best of times.

When at last the door to the chamber opened and the healer stepped out he sighed. "Tell me how is my wife?"

The older woman wore a sad expression. "She shall live, but she has broken ribs, an injured arm, many bruises that will heal. She is verra sad, and it is for her to tell ye the rest." Before he pushed his way into the room to get to his wife, the healer laid a hand upon his arm stopping him, "Ye must be gentle with her m'lord, and ye must love her and let her ken such, for she shall need ye greatly." She shook her head, "All is meant to be, remember that m'lord." With that she turned and walked down the hall.

Duncan took a calming breath then walked into their chambers. He saw Raven lying upon their bed, so small and so fragile. She lay upon her uninjured side curled into a ball sobbing. His heart clenched at the sound. Striding to the bed he rounded it and knelt. He leaned over the bed and ran a soothing hand over her hair. "Dinna cry *gràdh*, for it breaks my heart." He pressed a kiss to her dark head and whispered, "*Tha ghaol agam ort*, aught could make me stop lovin' ye, Raven, ye must ken that."

She looked up at him with tears streaming over her pale cheeks. "Duncan... I... I..." She began sobbing uncontrollably.

Not knowing what else to do, he gently climbed upon the bed and pulled her into his arms and held her while she cried herself to sleep. Duncan lay there holding his wife as guilt swamped him. He pressed a kiss to the top of her head and whispered, "I am sorry Raven, I failed ye. I dinna mean to make ye so unhappy. I dinna mean to leave ye unprotected. I pray one-day ye'll be able to forgive me."

It was dark in the chamber by the time Raven woke once more. She could hear Duncan's heart beating steadily under her ear in his chest. She could smell him and feel him wrapped around her and she felt safe. She knew when he awoke, and she sighed, "Duncan," she whispered in the dark, for this was the time to tell him. "There is somethin' I must tell ye."

Duncan carefully placed a finger over her lips. "Nay love, there is much I need to say to ye first." He carefully laid her back upon the bed and lit a candle. He turned back to her and knelt beside the bed. Taking her hand in his, he looked at her sad beautiful eyes. "I am so verra, verra sorry Raven, for I failed ye, as a man and a husband..."

"Nay Duncan," she stroked his cheek with her good hand and smiled sadly. "'Tis I..."

He placed a finger over her lips to silence her. "Let me finish, lass. For I must say this, or I'm afraid I shall burst." When she inclined her head, he continued. "I failed to make ye happy, I failed to protect ye." He swallowed hard. "When I told ye I wanted ye from the first moment I saw ye, I dinna lie. I had nay interest in any other woman, nay even Isobel."

When she would have interrupted, he shook his head, "I ken ye dinna believe me, *gràdh*, but I have loved ye from that first moment. I have nay been with any other woman, because the only woman I want is ye. *Tha ghaol agam ort*, Raven MacKinnon."

He bowed his head, "I shall understand if ye dinna feel the same way." He looked up at her, "But ken I shall protect ye as I should have from the beginnin', for the rest of my life. I shall allow aught more harm to come to ye, and I pray that one day, ye shall forgive me," He lifted her good hand and pressed a kiss to her palm.

Raven pulled her hand from his and caressed his cheek. "There is aught to forgive on my part, but there is much I pray ye can find in yer heart to forgive me for." She pulled away and reached up wiping a tear from her cheek. "Ye dinna fail me, Duncan, 'tis I who failed ye." She laid a hand upon her stomach and her tears came hard and fast.

Duncan carefully climbed upon the bed and took her into his arms. "Hush *gràdh*, 'tis all right. There is aught I have to forgive ye for." He rocked her gently and pressed light kisses to her face. "Let us nay talk of forgivin' and see if we can ease yer discomfort." He laid her back upon the bed.

Raven wiped away her tears and frowned up at him. "There is medicine the healer left for me, 'tis upon the table..."

Duncan placed a finger over her lips once more and shook his head, "Tell me how ye heal?" Raven furrowed her brows, "I dinna ken what yer askin?"

"Aye ye do," he smiled down at her. "Teach me to heal ye."

Raven frowned, "'Tis nay easy, for it drains yer energy."

He grinned down at her, "I am a verra, verra brawn lad," he winked at her, "with lots of energy."

This caused Raven to laugh then hold her side as pain ripped through her. Duncan frowned and apologized, "I'm sorry, I hurt ye lass."

Raven shook her head, "Laughter is good for the soul, it helps one heal faster." She worried her lower lip, "But there are things that only time can help to heal." Her gaze met Duncan's, "I must tell ye..."

He shook his head, "Ye must tell me how to help ye heal." Taking her hand, he laced their fingers together, "Tell me love, how I can help yer pain? Dinna deny me to help ye."

Raven frowned, "It may nay work, dinna be disappointed, for healin' is a skill that takes much time to master." She let Duncan feel a bit of her energy through their connected hands, it was weak, but still there.

Duncan inclined his head, "What shall it hurt for me to try?"

"Aught." She shook her head. Taking his hand, she placed it over her injured arm that lay upon her stomach. "Ye must picture the wound and making the person better, fixin' their wounds and mendin' what is broken or injured." She placed her hand over his and he felt the warmth of her power. "Ye must focus yer energy through here, through yer hands." She looked up at him and smiled softly, "But most of all ye must believe in yerself."

Duncan nodded, "I believe in myself and in us, what we are together." He smiled down at her, then closed his eyes and began to focus on fixing Raven's injuries, on healing all that was wrong with her.

Warmth spread through Raven, she felt it in her stomach then it radiated through her whole body. She smiled as it tingled in her toes and her fingers. Duncan had so much raw unleashed power within him. She felt her bruises easing, and her ribs stopped throbbing, for moment, she even thought, she felt her sadness lift, and a butterfly sensation in her stomach.

Her arm stopped hurting completely and she could move her fingers with ease.

When at last Duncan pulled back breathing hard, she felt much better, but knew she was a long way from being healed. When his greyish-blue gaze met hers, she smiled weakly, up at him. "'Tis verra, verra unusual for one to learn to heal so quickly."

He leaned down tiredly and pressed a kiss to her forehead, "I had a verra good teacher." He shook his head, "But ye were right, 'tis tiresome to heal one. Did I help ye at all, did I ease yer pain?"

"Aye, ye did indeed." She wiggled her fingers for him then touched her face and he noticed the bruises there had faded a bit. She placed her uninjured hand over her stomach and sighed, "But 'twould help me greatly if ye could lay with me until I fall asleep, for I'm tired, but ye layin' with me would brin' me great comfort."

Duncan laughed lightly, then lay down beside her and pulled her into his arms carefully as if she were made of spun glass. For the first time since she had seen him with Isobel in his arms, she was beginning to believe him with her heart and soul.

They slept most of the night with Duncan wrapped around Raven protectively. As the gray light of dawn crept in Duncan woke to Raven's heart wrenching sobs. He pressed kisses to the top of her head, ran his hands lightly over her assuring her that everything would be well.

When at last, her sobs subsided, he decided he had to reassure her that no matter what happened to her, he would always love her. He laid her gently upon the bed and leaned over it. He brushed her dark strands of hair from her face, as the sun began to peak over the horizon. She was beautiful even with her fading bruises, he decided.

"Raven *gràdh*, do ye ken how much I love ye, lass?" He stroked his knuckles over her cheek and when she shook her head, he smiled down at her. "*Tha gaol agam ort*, more than life itself. There is aught in this world I love more." He leaned down and captured her lips in a soft tender kiss, filled with his love. "I should have told ye long before this. I love ye, Raven MacKinnon with all that I am." He spoke against her lips then kissed her once more as if to seal the words between them.

When he pulled back at last she went to speak but he shook his head, "Allow me to finish, please lass." He sighed hard, "I want ye to understand that there is aught that could change my love for ye." He looked her in the eyes making sure she knew what he was saying was true. "Nay matter what Borden did to ye yesterday. I love ye, Raven." He searched her gaze and watched it tear up. "Aww love, please dinna cry for each tear ye shed breaks my heart into tiny pieces."

Raven sniffed and looked up at him. "Borden dinna...dinna..." She sighed and shook her head when he would have interrupted her. "He dinna rape me." She blurted out and let out a sob, "He took somethin' much more precious from me." Raven tried to control her sobs, but it took her a while to get control of them and her sadness enough to tell him the rest.

"Tell me love, what did he take?" Duncan stared down at her with confusion.

She closed her eyes and ran her tongue over her suddenly dry lips. "He took...He took..." She placed a hand over her stomach and Duncan's gaze dropped there for a moment then snapped back to her face and locked his gaze with hers as she spoke her next words. "He took our bairn." She sobbed the rest, "I lost our bairn, please forgive me, Duncan, for I dinna protect our child as I should have."

He pushed up from the bed and paced the room. He spoke not a word as he stopped and looked out a window at the rising sun. Anger and pain ripped through him warring to take over. The sobs of the woman he loved on the bed broke over him and cooled his anger, though he ached with the pain of loss, he knew the woman he loved suffered twice as much as he did.

Walking back to the bed he knelt and took her hand in his, with his tear-filled gaze he looked at her, "Aww love," he pressed a kiss to her palm then laid his hand over her stomach. He had also failed to protect their unborn child and guilt washed over him. "I'm so sorry Raven, so verra sorry. I dinna protect either of ye. Can ye ever forgive me?"

Raven choked back her sobs and looked over at her mighty Scottish warrior. This man could kill and not think twice, he was strong and powerful and, yet he sat with her weeping with her over the child they had lost. She reached over and caught one of his tears upon her finger. Using her magick she turned the tear to crystal and clenched it in her fist. "*Tha gaol agam ort,*" she whispered softly to him. "There is aught ye need to be forgivin' for, *mo ghaol.*"

Duncan looked up at her, "What 'tis meant to be, love, 'tis meant to be. But I shall avenge ye and our child." Fire snapped in his greyish-blue gaze as power whipped around him. "*Tha gaol agam ort,* forever."

Twenty-five

For nearly a week, Duncan doted upon Raven, he kept her entertained as she was ordered by a very surprised healer to stay abed for a few more days. What the healer didn't know was that every day, Duncan worked on his healing skills with Raven and day by day she recovered by leaps and bounds.

The couple spent many days and nights lying in bed side by side, talking and laughing. Raven had never been happier, for her heart and her head agreed that Duncan had been innocent when she had caught him with Isobel. He had assured her repeatedly that Isobel had come to his room to say goodbye, as she was leaving the next day for Inverness to find a new protector. Raven had come in after Isobel had given him a hug and congratulated him and wished him great happiness in his marriage to Raven. As for the serving girl in the great hall below stairs, it turned out that Borden had hired her to help get Duncan drunk then watch for Raven to come in so that she could slip onto his lap.

Borden had seen the gap that had formed between Raven and Duncan, and decided that he wanted Raven for himself. He had used their misunderstanding against them and caused the two to lose something very precious to them.

Raven mourned the loss of their child greatly, but whenever she grew sad, Duncan was always near at hand to assure her it was not her fault, and that the Gods had deemed this to happen. He assured her they would have many more children.

"And how many children do ye plan to be havin'?" Raven raised a brow at Duncan.

He lay down by her feet at the end of the bed and smiled roguishly up at her, "Oh, a couple dozen at least." When she would have kicked him playfully, he caught her foot and pressed a kiss to the arch of it. "Think of all the fun we'll be havin' makin' 'em?" He laughed and rolled away from her feet as he leapt from the bed.

Raven would have gotten up if he hadn't jumped upon the bed and slid over to sit next to her. The man was gorgeous, she thought as her heart beat a bit faster from looking at him. He was well muscled, while his skin was bronzed from hours out in the sun. His face was just shy of being Godly handsome by a small bump in his nose. His laughing greyish-blue gaze danced with amusement as he looked down upon her. But under that merriment she saw the one thing that made her heart beat in synch with his, it was his undying love for her.

"I would give anythin' to bear yer bairns, Duncan MacKinnon." The sad look washed over her face for an instant.

Duncan leaned in and kissed her hungrily upon the lips. "As soon as ye are able, love, we shall make another bairn together. And another, and another, we'll have a whole bloody castle full." He kissed her once more leaning his forehead against hers. "But I want a little girl who looks just like ye, *gràdh*. She must have yer silken black hair and yer bonnie eyes. I want her to have yer spirit and yer heart." He laid a hand upon her chest and smiled softly at her. "But nay matter if our bairns be a lass or lad, I shall love 'em equally." He looked at her and she read the truth in his eyes.

"*Mo ghaol ort*, Duncan. Ye shall make the most wonderful of Da's." She leaned forward and pressed her lips to his once more. "Let us begin havin' that fun now." She tugged on a couple of his braids trying to coax him into bed with her.

"Do ye think yer ready for such a thin'?" He raised a brow in concern. "I dinna wish to hurt ye, love."

"Of course, I am ready, ye've done a wonderful bit of work healin' me." She frowned at him, "Do ye nay wish to love me again?"

Resting his forehead against hers again he sighed, "Tell me ye dinna believe that? By the Gods, I want aught more than to love ye and pleasure ye." He teased her lips once more with his, "The last thin' I shall ever do again is to hurt ye, love."

"Then love me, my husband," she pressed her lips to his and allowed him to lay her down and make slow tender love to her as if she were the most fragile thing in the world.

Raven sat in the great hall where Duncan would decide Borden's fate. She had begged Duncan to allow her to attend this. She had wanted to face Borden once more, before Duncan decided what to do with him. Raven had asked Duncan what he planned, but he refused to tell her.

Duncan paced the great hall as he waited for Borden to be brought into the room. Anger rolled off Duncan, and Raven felt his power surging through the room. All the MacKinnons present held fearful expressions as if they could feel Duncan's anger.

When at last, Borden was brought into the room by the guards, Duncan stopped pacing to turn and look at the man who would dare to lay a hand upon his wife. Borden walked hunched over as if his wounds had not completely healed. He was a large man, but now, he didn't appear the large Viking warrior they had first met. The guards sat Borden down in a chair then stood flanking him.

Alistair walked to the middle of the room and spoke, "Borden, yer accused of attemptin' to abuse this woman," he pointed to Raven and she jerked back as if slapped.

"He is nay accused. He is guilty of the misdeed." Duncan snarled. "All here kens thus, and dinna be making my wife look guilty of anythin'." Alistair looked chaste, but Borden began to laugh. He looked up at Duncan, "You think she is innocent?" Borden snorted, "Nay woman, 'tis innocent." He stood and pointed to Raven, "She led me on, made me believe that she and her husband were through and that she was lookin' for a protector."

"He lies," Raven stood glaring at Borden.

"Do I?" He growled at her. "Do I really, witch?"

Duncan stepped between the two as murmurs passed through the hall. He glared at Borden, "Dare ye now call my wife a liar?"

"Whores, liars, and witches, they're of the same ilk." Borden shouted at Duncan. "Why do ye protect her, when she threw up her skirts to me so very easily?

Would you have that piece of trash after she has cuckolded you?"

Duncan looked at the man for along moment, "Do aught but lies pour from yer mouth, Borden?" He stepped toward the man, "Mayhap, the world would be better if it were rid of the likes of ye."

Borden pulled back from Duncan as he leaned over him. "Mayhap, I should nay have let my wife keep me from killin' ye the day ye attacked her, aye?" Duncan let a little of the power he tried so hard to hold in check, snap in his eyes for Borden to see.

Borden leaned farther back in his chair. "Ye and yer wife are demons." He cried, "She tried to seduce me and steal my soul."

Duncan backhanded him making his head snap back and his lip bleed. "Nay one speaks of my wife, thus." He turned with anger on his face when he felt someone tapping him upon the back. Turning to do harm, he looked down upon his lovely tiny wife. Her eyes shone up at him with pure love and trust. "*Gràdh*." He spoke that one simple word meaning love.

"I wish to understand why he would do such a thin'," Raven swallowed hard, "And mayhap to help him understand what he took from me," she placed a hand upon Duncan's chest then to her stomach, "from us."

Duncan reached out cupping her cheek. "If that 'tis yer wish, then aye, ye may." He let Raven stand beside him as she spoke to Borden.

Raven looked at the man who had hurt her. "Firstly, I wish ye to understand two things. One yer verra lucky I dinna have my sword with me, or I'd have killed ye 'afore ye could blink." This statement earned a few snickers from the clan standing around them.

Duncan looked around, "Aye, ye'd all better believe it, I trained her myself." The pride in his voice made her smile.

"Secondly," she turned back to Borden, "I wanted yer friendship, nay yer body," she waved to Duncan indicating his body, "Why in the name of saints would I want yer body when I had this waitin' for me? Ye dinna compare." She stepped forward before Duncan could stop her and held the dagger Duncan had once given her up to Borden's throat. "Lastly but nay least, ye took away somethin' verra precious to me and my husband, ye caused me to lose our bairn, when ye kicked me and broke my ribs." She sobbed out the last part of that. "For that, I could neigh on kill ye myself." She turned and threw the dagger hitting a Celtic knot drawn into one of the beams along the wall across the hall then turned back to look in to Borden's fearful eyes. "That could be yer manhood next. Tell them true what ye did."

Borden frowned and when Raven pulled out another dagger, he began to tell the whole sordid story of how he had become obsessed with Raven. The story gave Raven the shivers, but she hid them well, as only Duncan noticed them.

When at last he finished the whole truthful story, Raven glared down at him, "Yer nay a man, yer lower than scum on the bottom of a loch. I should kill ye for rippin' my bairn away from me thus. But I'm neigh a killer." She walked away then whipped back and threw her second dagger and hit the chair between Borden's spread legs, a bit higher and he would be lacking his manhood. "As I warned 'afore, be glad I dinna have my sword." With that Raven walked over and took the dagger from the beam and sat down.

Duncan looked at his wife with utter pride shining in his eyes then turned back to Borden with ice replacing that pride. "Now that ye've told the truth, I shall pass my judgment." He looked from Borden to his wife then back at Borden once more. Death was in Duncan's eyes. "Ye deserve to die for what ye have done to my wife." He heard gasps and the sound of Màiri sobbing quietly, but ignored them. "Aye, but death 'twould be too quick and painless for ye."

He flicked Borden a disgusted look, "Besides, Alistair and yer own sister have begged mercy on yer life. 'Twas nay their pleas that swayed me." Duncan began to pace around the room angrily. "Their voices fell upon deaf ears."

Duncan stopped and looked at Raven sitting in her chair, her gorgeous silky black hair pulled back and her ethereal face was serene. Her mystical eyes swirled changing from blue too green and back, but no matter the color he could see her love for him shining there.

Oh, by the Gods how he loved this woman. "'Twas the words of my wife that granted ye a stay from execution." He turned to Borden and pointed back at Raven, "'Twas she who spared yer worthless life."

Raven could feel every eye in the room upon her and she raised her chin with pride. She wouldn't be daunted by the puzzled and judgmental stares, so instead of looking back at the MacKinnon clan, she looked at her MacKinnon man.

Duncan glowered down at Borden and spoke in a harsh tone as he spoke one word. "Exile." The sound of Màiri bursting into wailing sobs did nothing to sway Duncan. "And ye shall be branded for the lecherous bastard ye are." With that he turned away from Borden.

Rage filled Borden as he leapt from his chair dagger in hand.

Raven gasped and Duncan turned side stepping the blade. The dagger's blade ripped down the flesh of Duncan's arm and she felt her heart stop. Everything after that happened in slow motion as Duncan swung punching Borden in the face.

Before anyone could move, Borden spun around and hit Duncan back in the face causing him to stumble backwards. Borden jumped on him causing both men to lose their footing. They rolled upon the floor grappling for the dagger. Borden ended up on top and tried to plunge the blade into Duncan's chest, Duncan caught his wrist stopping him. On an angry cry, Borden used two hands and the blade inched ever closer to Duncan's chest.

No one moved, but Raven. In that second, she knew she couldn't live without Duncan in her life. She hadn't come to Dun Akin to find love, but to heal a man, and love had found her where she least expected it. Anger surged through her as she summonsed her magick, the knife was nearly touching Duncan's chest.

On a cry of anger, she flung a red ball of flames at Borden and heard his cry even as the hole blossomed through his chest. The castle shook around them as her magick surged. People cried out even as she watched Borden slump to the side, as Duncan pushed him off him. On a cry, Raven raced across the room and dropped to her knees at Duncan's side. Tears welled in her eyes.

Duncan sat up and took her into his arms. "*Gràdh*," he whispered the words against her lips, then kissed her thoroughly. He had feared his life would end as that blade had inched closer and closer to his chest.

When at last they pulled apart breathless, Alistair knelt next to them as the sounds of Màiri's cries filled the air. He clasped Duncan's shoulder, "I am sorry, I should nay have begged the bastard's life from ye. The man dinna deserve to live."

Duncan shook his head, "Nay he dinna deserve it, and I am sorry for Màiri's anguish." He glanced over at the woman weeping over her brother's body.

Alistair glanced over at his wife, "She will come to terms with it." He shook his head, "I dinna realize the man was such a blackguard." He looked at Raven, "I hope ye can accept my apology, lass."

Raven inclined her head, but kept her gaze from the man laying only a couple of feet away now. She felt bile rise, in her throat at the thought that she had killed him. Her breath backed up in her lungs. Oh Gods, she had taken a life, she thought as she looked down at her hands, never had she had that kind of power before now.

Duncan must have realized her distress and took her arm as he stood pulling her up with him to block out the body of the man lying there behind him. He laced his fingers with hers and pressed a kiss to her knuckles. "Come *gràdh*, let us seek our chambers."

Raven walked with him above stairs to their chamber. Once they reached their room Raven breathed a sigh of relief. She looked at the wound on Duncan's arm and began fussing over it. Though her hands shook as she helped him remove his shirt, he spoke not a word.

When her breath came out on a sob, Duncan who had already sat upon the edge of the bed reached out and took her hand pulling her to stand between his spread thighs. He brushed his fingers over her cheek as he stared into her beautiful swirling eyes. How he loved this woman. He cupped her cheek and brought her mouth to meet his. Her shuddering breath, told him how very upset she was. Shivers coursed through her body and Duncan knew she was on the verge of tears, but was fighting valiantly to keep them in check.

Their lips brushed over each other's, but just that small taste of her had him craving more so he deepened the kiss to plunder her mouth. His fear added to hers and their kiss turned desperate.

Duncan made short work of their clothing then laid Raven upon the bed. He knelt on the edge of the bed staring down at her. She was beautiful, her slender build that should have looked childish in size, was lush with ripe womanly curves. Her breasts were full and fit perfectly in his large hands. Reaching out, he cupped one of her breasts and rubbed his thumb over her nipple making it pearl. He felt himself grow even harder when she moaned softly at his touch.

As he leaned down and captured her mouth with his and she clutched at him desperately, he knew he wanted to slow things down and savor her. Removing her arms from around his neck, he pulled back and looked at her once more. He captured her wrists and pulled them over her head as he sprawled his long hard body next to hers on the bed.

With deliberate care, he caressed her as he held her hands captive. His mouth skimmed the underside of her breast and she writhed in need. His free hand cupped her other breast as he caught her nipple in his mouth and swirled his tongue around it.

His mouth kissed, licked and laved nearly every inch of her body as he held her hands captive over her head. Her pleas for him to release her hands, fell upon deaf ears. He was driving her insane with his slow meticulous loving.

When at last she was panting, breathlessly sated from his intimate kisses, he released her hands and positioned himself between her thighs nudging them wider to accommodate him. Then he slid slowly inch by wonderful inch inside of her, Raven gave soft cries of pleasure. As he at last buried himself inside of her to the hilt, he held still and looked down upon her passion filled face.

"*Tha gaol agam ort*," he spoke softly as he looked at her spread out underneath him, beautiful as an angel. Her dark hair was spread across the blanket and her alabaster skin glowed with passion.

Reaching up, Raven brushed her fingers over his cheek. "*Mo ghaol ort*," she returned softly.

Ever so slowly he began to move inside her, withdrawing and pressing forward. The sounds of her moans and sighs drove him on, but he kept the tempo slow and savory. Duncan reveled in the feel of her body clenched around him, caressing him.

Neither paid attention to the different shades of blue light glowing and swirling around them. The energy they created together was poured into their lovemaking, taking it to new heights and new pleasures.

As their pleasure built and crested, neither one noticed the wound to Duncan's arm heal as the blue energy caressed them and held them.

Raven and Duncan stood on the dock together with Alistair and Riordan.

"'Tis sorry I am, for what happened to ye," Alistair frowned down at Raven. "'Tis my wish, I could make it right by ye and my cousin."

Raven shook her head, "I dinna blame ye, for what happened." She took Alistair's hand and smiled. "Màiri, may nay forgive me ever, but she shall forgive ye soon enough, for she shall have much to occupy her attentions with, too be angry with ye." She leaned forward and laughed slightly, "Dinna fear, all three of the bairns shall be healthy."

Alistair paled, "Bairns?"

Riordan clapped him on the back and laughed heartily, "Ye've gone and scared him half silly, lass." He took Raven's hand from his brother's and brought her hand to his lips, brushing a kiss over her fingers. "When ye come to yer senses, and wish to get with the true gem of this family, ye've only to come back to me."

Raven smiled at him, this man reminded her of Aidan and she felt a pang of longing to return to *Dun Akin*. "I'll keep that in mind." She laughed as he took her hand and brushed a kiss over her knuckles once more while bowing gallantly. As he continued to hold her hand, Raven furrowed her brows for a moment then smiled. "Aye, 'tis apparent yer truly a gem among the family." She stepped closer to whisper, "Dinna allow yer anger to keep ye away from yer future, she loves ye verra much."

Riordan furrowed his brows, "How do ye ken this?"

"I've the vision," she spoke simply.

Duncan put his arm around her and pulled her to him, "Believe her, she's more than just a healer, lad." He looked down at his wife and smiled, for she was far more than a healer, a teller of futures and a princess, she was the woman who possessed his heart. He loved her more than anything in this world. "She is the love of my life."

"I love ye too." Raven tugged on one of his braids to get him to lean down to her. When he leaned over she stood upon her tiptoes and captured his mouth in a searing kiss.

The sound of Alistair clearing his throat broke them apart and brought them back to reality. "'Twould appear the good captain would like to set off soon." He waved to the tall man standing upon the bow of the ship scowling at them.

Duncan and Alistair, then Riordan, hugged clapping each other upon the shoulders. With their farewells spoken and promises to visit each other again soon, Duncan took Raven's hand in his, and walked her to the ship. He walked up the plank behind her then set her on board the ship even as the captain was standing there offering his hand. Duncan gave the man a hard look then turned back to Raven.

"Allow me to have ye shown to yer cabin." Captain MacKenna inclined his head to his steward and waved the couple to follow his man. "If there is aught that ye'd be needin', feel free to inquire with my steward."

Once in their cabin, Duncan locked the door and smiled at Raven when she turned to raise a questioning brow. "We have three days until we reach yer isle. Three days to lay abed and relax." He grinned wolfishly at her as he stalked her across their cabin.

She held her hands up and backed away shaking her head laughing. "We can nay stay in our cabin for the whole of the voyage. For everyone aboard shall ken what we're 'bout."

He laughed as he caught her between himself and the wall, "Aye, but nay matter, for yer my wife." He leaned down and brushed a kiss over her mouth. "I've every right to love ye, lass." With that said he began

339

stripping her clothing from her body so that he could love her properly.

Once their clothing was removed and they stood bare skin pressed against bare skin, Duncan reached up and unplaited her hair letting her silky tresses fall over her shoulders and down her back. He stepped back and looked down at her as she shook out her hair around her. The black glossy strands fell over her breasts barely veiling them and making her look delicious.

Stepping forward he cupped her face and kissed her once more. His hand slipped from her cheek to glide over her body and was soon joined by the other one to set flames of desire licking over her skin. Raven moaned against his mouth and strained against his touch craving more and begging for more.

When neither one could take the desire building between them any longer, Duncan whispered as he lifted her. "Wrap yer legs 'bout my waist, love." When she did he rubbed her soft moist heat against his hardened length causing her to moan deeply. As Raven thought she couldn't take any more and that she would lose her mind with need for this man, he thrust himself inside her causing her to cry out in delight.

Turning her away from the wall of the cabin, gritting his teeth Duncan held her bottom firm in his hands and began sliding her up and down his engorged shaft pleasuring them both. Raven threw back her head, thrusting out her breasts as her inner muscles clenched around him. When his mouth clamped over her breast, she cried out his name as pleasure griped her.

Duncan pulled back and watched her face as his movements grew quicker. He could see the pleasure upon her face and hear it being moaned from her throat as she encouraged him to help her find her release. His strokes became hard and fast as he pounded inside of her. Duncan's own pleasure built just watching her as her orgasm built then finally peaked and she slid into the abyss of ecstasy.

He surged into her once, twice, a third time and found his own release that ripped through his body. Throwing back his head he growled his own pleasure.

Twenty-Six

Raven watched, as the Isle of Mann grew closer. A chilly wind swept through the air and made her shiver. Duncan moved over to stand behind her with his own hands on the rail of the ship to block the wind from battering against her. He bent his head and pressed a kiss to the top of her glossy black hair. "Are ye excited, love?"

"Aye," she breathed the word and looked up at him. "'Tis a bonnie place, I ken ye shall love it." She sighed, "I can nay wait to see my Mama, Da, brothers and my Gram." She beamed with pride. "They shall all love ye nearly as much as I do."

He laughed, "Then I shall be loved greatly indeed." He rubbed his chin on top of her head as she looked back at her island home. "I love ye, Raven MacKinnon, more than life itself."

She reached forward and threaded her fingers with Duncan's larger ones. "And I love ye so much it nigh on bursts my heart." Raven brought their entwined hands to her lips and brushed a kiss over his knuckles. Silently, she prayed Duncan would like her home and her family.

Raven stepped off the ship with Duncan's assistance. She stepped upon the wooden pier and looked at Captain MacKenna once more. The sound of her quick intake of breath had both him and Duncan looking at her sharply. Duncan was at her side while MacKenna just raised a brow as he looked at her, with his brilliant green gaze. "Lucàs MacKenna?" She stepped toward him and Duncan furrowed a brow.

"Aye," he inclined his head sharply. Raven covered her mouth with her hands, "I thought..."

He inclined his head once more. "I ken what ye thought," he ran a finger over her soft cheek. "But as ye see, lass, I survived, just as ye did, Relia."

She smiled softly, "Ye look so different, but wonderful," she assured him with a small laugh. Walking into his muscular arms she hugged him hard. "I thank the Gods yer alive." She whispered.

Lucàs held her and rocked her. "When ye climbed upon my ship, I was nay sure if I should say aught." He laughed softly, "Ye were so enamored to yer man, I dinna think it was such a clever idea."

It was the sound of Duncan clearing his throat that had the two looking at his angry face. Lucàs set Raven from him and smiled over at Duncan then down at Raven. "Are ye nay goin' to introduce me to yer man, Relia, before he decides to run me through."

She laughed and even as she slipped an arm around the man's waist, "Duncan, I want ye to meet Lucàs MacKenna, he's been my partner in trouble the whole of my life." She laughed at the puzzled look upon Duncan's face. "Lucàs here 'tis my cousin and my best friend."

Lucàs held out his hand to Duncan and smiled. "'Tis a pleasure to meet ye once more, MacKinnon." He laughed and let his eyes turn the same bluish-green swirl that Raven's eyes were. "As ye can see I'm half *Irish Sea Water Guardian* as well," he shrugged a shoulder, "on my mother's side. My father is a MacKenna."

Duncan frowned as he shook Lucàs' hand. "Can ye read minds?"

"Aye," Lucàs laughed heartily at the scowl upon Duncan's face as they released hands. "We all have our talents, but mine are nay anywhere near to match Relia's, for she is neigh on burstin' with magick." He winked down at his younger cousin.

Raven walked over to Duncan and took his hands, then grinned up at him. "Lucàs, is the reason we met." She laughed at her husband's puzzlement. "He helped me to sail away from here and start out on an adventure in to the real world to find my place in it. Lucky for us he's a terrible ship's captain and steered us into a horrible storm, sinkin' our ship."

With that Duncan threw back his head and roared with laughter, even when Lucàs muttered and hurled empty threats at Raven, good-naturedly. He shook his head. "I guess I should be thankin' ye on two accounts. Firstly, for sinkin' yer ship and allowin' us to meet." He pulled Raven into his embrace then brushed a kiss over her lips. "Second for gettin' us here safely."

Raven laughed until tears streamed from her eyes. Then seeing the look of retribution in her cousin's eyes, she grabbed Duncan's hand and tugged at it, getting him to run with her. The word 'coward' floated through her mind and she laughed as she and Duncan raced down the pier and across the sandy beach until they went around the bend.

Panting and laughing, Raven slowed them and looked at her husband. Then he picked her up throwing her over his shoulder and ran farther as she screamed in delight. When at last he was panting, he stopped and slid her down his body seductively. A smile played about his mouth as his eyes danced with merriment. His fingers slid into her hair as he bent his head, his breath mingling with hers and the cool sea breeze.

Raven closed her eyes, as she tasted him against her lips. Her body trembled with need as she felt the brush of his lips butterfly against hers.

"Well, hello, Relia." A soft voice sounded behind them causing them to jump apart guiltily.

Raven turned and nearly sighed. "Hello, Gram." She smiled at her grandmother, but couldn't quite meet her eyes.

"And just who 'tis this?" Her grandmother peered around Raven as if she were hiding Duncan.

"This is Duncan MacKinnon," Raven smiled brightly. And then felt the nudge at her back when she didn't finish. "Oof...He's my...my...um...aaa...husband." She spat out as Duncan nudged her once more.

"Yer husband?" Her grandmother raised a brow in question. "And how is it ye've come home totin' a husband, young lady?"

"'Tis a rather long story," Raven shook her head slightly hoping to get out of telling her grandmother right then.

"Well then, I suggest, I make us a pot of tea and we discuss this back at my cabin." She smiled brightly, "Yer parents shall be there directly."

Raven let her shoulders slump as her grandmother turned to lead the way back to the cabin. Raven looked over her shoulder and frowned. "I'm sorry 'bout this."

Duncan shrugged, "'Tis by far better to have it all out in the open then to hide such a thin'. For I am afraid I could nay keep my hands from ye." He smiled down at her. Holding his hand out, he winked at her, "Shall we?"

"Aye," she spoke softly then sighed. "I'm afraid ye dinna ken my parents." She shook her head, "My mama shall be easy, but my father..." she trailed off. She looked up at her husband and shrugged. "I'm their only daughter, and I promised I would nay marry ye until the family could be together."

Duncan digested her words and looked down upon her. There was so much he still didn't know about this woman and, yet he still loved her with his whole heart. He thought over the idea if they had only one daughter and how protective he would be. Shaking his head, he knew he was in serious trouble when her father arrived.

The trio was seated at the old wooden table in the tiny cabin, drinking tea, when Raven's parents finally arrived. Duncan felt the power fill the cabin as the regally dressed couple stepped into the room. He could tell by their presence that they were royalty in the highest sense of the word. He watched the tiny woman with beautiful golden colored hair walk over to Raven and embrace her. The woman's eyes were a stunning green that sparkled with warmth. However, her parents and her grandmother, looked to be no more than a score and ten. Duncan frowned at this, it made him wonder just how old they were. Hell, how old was his wife?

"Oh, Relia darlin'," Rhiannon hugged her daughter tightly. "I have been so worried 'bout ye." The women looked more like sisters than mother and daughter, Duncan thought looking at the pair.

"I have been fine, Mama," Raven assured her and met Duncan's eyes, but before she could speak, her father spoke. The man was no more than six feet tall, but muscular in build. His hair was pitch colored and was cropped close to his head. His rich colored clothing marked him as a noble man. But it was his swirling blue eyes that made Duncan pause, for they moved like ocean currents.

"I had expected ye to call us to brin' ye home, why did ye take the mortal way?" Her father Toslar, scolded as he tugged her up from the chair and embraced her. "Ye've had yer mother verra worried, young lady."

"I'm so sorry Da." Raven hugged him quickly. She went to speak again, but he pulled her back from him and frowned, "Ye look different, more, womanly." He furrowed his brows and looked her over. He turned to his wife and snapped. "Do ye see it?"

"Aye," Rhiannon spoke softly and cupped her daughter's face. "Yer radiant." She pressed a kiss to Raven's cheek.

"Thank ye, Mama." Raven smiled softly.

"'Tis love, I'm thinkin'." Rhiannon sighed, "There is nay much, besides love that would put such a glow to a young woman."

Toslar's brows furrowed deeper as he looked from his wife to his daughter, "Love, ye can nay still be serious 'bout such nonsense?"

Raven stepped back from her mother and looked at her father, "Aye Da," She walked over to Duncan as he stood. "I want ye both to meet Duncan MacKinnon..."

"Ye've brought my baby girl home to me, mortal," Toslar walked forward offering his hand to Duncan,

"For that we are indebted to ye." He took Duncan's hand pumping it. "Tell us what ye wish for a reward."

Duncan smiled broadly, "Yer blessin's Sire."

"Aye…" Toslar continued to shake Duncan's hand smiling then frowned, "Blessin's?" He stopped shaking Duncan's hand and released it. "Blessin' upon what exactly?"

Raven slipped in next to Duncan and slipped an arm around his waist as she slid under his arm. "On our marriage, Da." She looked up at her husband, "Da, meet my husband, Duncan MacKinnon."

"Husband?" Toslar gaped from Raven to Duncan. "Husband?" He spoke again and watched his daughter nod. "WHAT?" He bellowed shaking the cabin and Duncan was sure the entire island.

"Now darlin'," Rhiannon hurried forward and took her husband's arm, "Calm yerself, dear."

Toslar turned on his wife enraged. "Married, she's married?" He turned back to his daughter furiously. "Ye made a promise that ye 'twould wait. I had hoped ye would come to yer senses about marryin' a mortal" He whipped around to face Raven, "I forbid ye to be married to this man, Relia. For ye are nay old enough to marry yet." He made to grab Raven away from Duncan, but found his wrist clamped in Duncan's iron grip.

"Dinna touch my wife in anger," Duncan looked at Raven's father with steel determination in his eyes. When the magick crackled in his blue gaze, Toslar frowned.

"Who are ye?" Toslar frowned at the younger man, but pulled back his hand.

"I told ye Da, his name is Duncan MacKinnon." Raven sighed, "He's the man I love."

Toslar looked at his daughter, but kept his hands to himself, "Yer too young to marry anyone, yer but a child."

"Da, I'm more than two hundred years old." Raven cried with outrage. She pulled away from Duncan to pace. "Two hundred may be a child to ye, but in the mortal world, 'tis many a lifetime."

"I dinna care, about the mortal world." Toslar frowned at his wayward daughter.

"Enough!" Rhiannon slashed a hand through the air. "Yer bein' rude, Toslar, in my mother's home." She looked from her husband to her daughter and her daughter's husband. "We shall discuss this at home." Rhiannon looked at her mother, "Would ye care to join us for our evenin' repass, Mama?"

The older woman inclined her head. "'Twould be lovely."

"Good," Raven's mother inclined her head then turned to Raven and Duncan, "Both of ye must be verra tired from yer journey." She held out her hand to Raven, "Let us go settle ye in the palace."

"Thank ye, Mama." Raven took her hand then held hers out to Duncan.

Duncan looked down at Raven's tiny hand and smiled as he took it. He wasn't ready for them to shift to the palace. A woozy feeling washed over him, as the room of the cabin they had been standing in changed and became an opulent chamber that appeared around them. He stumbled a bit when Raven released his hand.

"Duncan?" Raven grabbed hold of his hand again, "Are ye all right?"

He placed a hand to his head and shook it slightly, "I'm well." He looked down at Raven's worried face. Reaching out he caressed her cheek. "Truly *gràdh*."

Rhiannon smiled at the soft loving looks they exchanged. She nearly sighed at the true love that shone between them. It was nice to know that her only daughter was in love and from the look of things, happy.

Rhiannon hated to interrupt, but her husband would be back at the castle anytime and she would prefer to speak with him alone before they dined that evening. "I think it is time, for ye to retire to yer chambers and ready yerselves for our comin' meal."

Raven inclined her head, "To which chamber do ye wish me to show Duncan to?"

Rhiannon only looked at her blankly, "Why yers of course, darlin'." She smiled, "He is of course yer husband."

"But father..." Raven began. Her mother cut her off by raising her hand. "Did ye marry this man?"

"Aye, but nay in the usual way." Raven lowered her eyes.

Rhiannon raised her brow in question but before Raven could answer Duncan spoke up. "She took me to husband as I took her to wife, under the eyes of the Gods. Celtic law..."

Rhiannon's eyes snapped to Duncan's, "I ken the Celtic laws," she inclined her head, "And she is yer wife for one year and a day, for 'tis as good as a handfasten." She looked back at Raven, "But should she be unhappy, after the terms of the marriage are met, she may walk away freely."

"I shall nay walk away." Raven raised her chin haughtily. "He holds my heart, Mama."

Rhiannon inclined her head regally in understanding. She completely understood the way her daughter felt for this man. Stepping forward to embrace her daughter once more she spoke softly, "Go enjoy a few moments with yer husband, for I am sure our evenin' meal shall be dauntin'. Yer father is bound to summons yer brothers."

Raven groaned softly. "He would nay?"

"He would, and I believe already has." She smiled down at her daughter then cupped her face. "I shall intervene in any way I can."

"Thank ye, Mama." Raven pressed a kiss to her mother's cheek. She turned to her husband and held out her hand. "Let us seek our chambers 'afore our meal is served."

Duncan took her hand and allowed her to pull him from the opulent chamber they had arrived in.

"This was yer chamber growin' up?" Duncan looked around at the collection of shells and the beautifully appointed room. The bed was large, and it was hard to imagine tiny little Raven sleeping in such a large thing. Shaking his head, he walked over and flopped upon the bed. "Is yer father always so demandin'?"

"Aye, he and my brothers, believe everyone should follow their dictates and we should do aught without consultin' them." She shook her head. Raven walked over to the bed and climbed upon it. "'Tis one of the many things, I love about ye. Yer a demandin' bloke, but ye'll listen to what I've to say and to reason." She shook her dark head, "My brother's and my Da tend nay to listen to reason."

Reaching out, Duncan pulled her to him so that she straddled his hips as he lay back upon the bed. "So, they're an unreasonable lot, aye?"

"Oh aye," Raven inclined her head then leaned down to press a soft seductive kiss to his lips. She laughed as she felt his hands upon her breasts through her bodice. "But I'm sure ye can make them see reason, or at least convince them that our marriage is of the utmost importance." She ran her hands over his broad muscular chest.

He groaned then flipped them over so that she lay beneath him. "Oh aye, our marriage is of the utmost importance. And I'll make yer Da and brothers think 'tis their idea that we stay married." He pressed kisses to her throat causing her to moan and purr. "How long until the repass?"

Raven looked up at him with desire in her eyes and quickly untucked his shirt from his breeches. "Long enough I would expect."

The room held a table that could seat twenty people easily. Duncan had Raven on his arm as they entered the formal dining hall. The walls were sea green trimmed with gold as well as, seascapes and underwater scenery captured in paintings upon the walls. Duncan took Raven to one of the large glass windows and marveled as he looked out of it. Fish glided by the bubbled glass and looked back at him as they swam, dolphins played and chattered as if they were friends of his dropping in to say hello. It was like nothing he had ever seen before. "What an amazin' view."

Raven smiled up at him, "Aye 'tis," placing a hand upon the bubble, she laughed lightly as a starfish came to touch the glass. "'Tis the view of the world under the sea. My Da says if ye stand here long enough ye'll see every sea creature in the ocean at some point." She sighed, "As a child I spent countless hours here just sittin' and watchin'."

"Did ye see every creature?" He pressed a kiss to the top of her dark head as he encircled her in his arms and tucked her into his warmth.

"Nay," she shook her head, "There are so many creatures in the sea that I dinna think 'tis truly possible." Looking over at the sound of her father's voice she nearly cringed.

"Aye, 'tis possible, if ye live long enough." Tosler looked out through the bubbled glass to the sea beyond. "There are many things a person can see if they live long enough." He looked from his daughter to Duncan, "Even the death of the one ye love the most."

Raven raised her chin, "Aye, Duncan is mortal, but I am willin' to give up my immortality for a life with him." When her father just gaped at her, she looked from him to her mother as she walked up to join them, "A handful of lovin' happy years is worth more than forever alone."

Rhiannon smiled at her daughter. "Aye, for I would nay have changed things between us had I nay been given the gift of immortality." She looked at her husband, "And ye my love, what would ye have done if I had stayed mortal?"

Tosler looked in to his wife's beautiful face and sighed, "I would have cherished every moment together with ye then I would have died with ye, immortal or nay, I would nay have wanted to go on livin' without ye."

Duncan looked from Tosler to Rhiannon and frowned, "How is it ye became immortal?"

Rhiannon smiled over at Duncan, "I saved the life of a Goddess." She frowned and shuttered. "I created a spell that would free her from the mirror she was trapped in. It was a dark Fea hallow." She looked at her husband then at her children, "She granted me immortality for myself, my mother, sister and my children."

"So ye can become immortal?" Duncan frowned in thought wondering what it would be like to become immortal and wondering what he would have to give up.

Crìsdean snorted, "Aye, ye can become immortal if ye can convince a God, or Goddess or find the Fea Queen."

Raven glared at her brother then turned to Duncan, "I'd like ye to meet my brothers, Crìsdean, Seòrsa, and Deocan." She looked at her brothers and smiled tightly, "This is Duncan MacKinnon, my husband."

"What?" Crìsdean roared.

"Nay," Seòrsa scowled

"Pleasure to meet ye." Deocan held out his hand. He looked at his brother's and held his palms up in innocence, "What?" His two older brothers glared at him.

Crìsdean just shook his head. Then he turned his attention upon Duncan, "So ye've decided to marry our baby sister, aye?"

Duncan looked the other man in the eyes, "I have already married her. She is my wife." He let his temper snap in his eyes, but it didn't affect the other man what so ever.

"We dinna attend a weddin' for her." Crìsdean looked at his brothers for confirmation. "Pray tell, who married ye?" He crossed his muscular arms over his broad chest and glared at Duncan openly. Crìsdean was nearly as tall as Duncan himself, but where Duncan held the dark Celtic features, Crìsdean's ran to the fair side. He had long golden hair and sea blue eyes that shimmered like the ocean itself. His body was golden and roped with muscles and his face looked as if it had been chiseled in the image of the Gods.

"Duncan," Raven looked up at him and hissed as he would have told how it was they came to be married.

"We dinna have a formal ceremony, but we are married in accordance to Celtic law." Duncan reached out and stroked her cheek lovingly, "She took me to husband and I took her to wife, upon a beach next to my home." He looked back at her brothers, "We have nay had a chance to plan a formal weddin', yet."

"Then she is only bound to ye for a year and a day, unless ye die." Seòrsa smiled wickedly. "Perhaps, she will tire of him soon and move on to a new more pleasin' toy. Otherwise..." Unlike his older brother, Seòrsa was shorter and stockier with bulging muscles. His hair was midnight black and his eyes were pewter grey that swirled with power. And a face that could make an angel weep with envy, Seòrsa was every woman's fantasy.

"Seòrsa!" Raven admonished and when he shrugged, she grew angry. "I have had enough." She turned to Duncan taking his hand, "Come let us leave here. I thought I could come home and visit my family and introduce my husband, but 'twould appear all the men in my family are complete *arses*, and dinna care if I love ye, they only care about their arrogant pride, instead of their daughter and baby sister."

"Hey, now wait a minute. I dinna say anythin' bad." Deocan looked so dejected that Raven dropped Duncan's hand and ran over to her brother.

"Oh Deocan, I am sorry, that is so true, ye have nay said an unkind word to my husband." She hugged her much taller and broader brother. "When Mama and

Gram come to the weddin', ye may accompany them." She stepped back from her brother and turned angry eyes, upon her father and other two brothers. "As for the rest of ye, I never want to see any of ye again." She sniffed as tears welled in her eyes. "I always thought ye loved me, and wanted me happy, but I see I 'twas wrong." With that she walked back to Duncan and into his waiting arms, where he hugged her and rocked her as she silently wept against his shirt. "What have I done to deserve so much unhappiness?" She asked Duncan muffled against his shirt.

Duncan bowed his head and brushed a soft kiss over the top of her head, "*Gràdh*," he whispered against her hair. "Tell me what I can do to make ye happy once more?" He squeezed her to him. "*Tha gaol agam ort.*"

"I want to go home to *Dun Akin*." She sobbed softly.

Duncan closed his eyes for a moment and sighed in relief, she wanted to return to *Dun Akin* with him. "Are ye sure, love?" When she inclined her head, he looked up from her to her mother, "We will welcome a visit from ye at *Dun Akin*." He looked from Raven's mother to her father and two brothers that disapproved of their relationship. "I am takin' my wife home." He narrowed his eyes and allowed the magick within him to flow and crackle in his eyes. "Ye've hurt my wife. Ye've made her cry. If I had my claymore right now, I would run ye through for this." He frowned and looked at Toslar, "I love yer daughter, yer highness, more than life itself, more than I can ever put into words. She is the air I breathe, the food I eat and the entire source of my life. For I could nay live without her, and I would willin'ly give my life for hers."

Toslar shook his head, "'Tis nay that I dinna believe ye," he sighed, "But she is my little girl and I need to ken that she comes first with ye, that she shall be cherished." He looked at Raven then over at Duncan, "Without her immortality, she will age and die."

"Da, I dinna care if I will die," Raven looked from her father to her husband as she linked their fingers together. "I can nay imagine life without ye, Duncan." She sighed, "I want to live my life with ye, for every moment that the Gods give us together." She laughed softly as she reached up to touch his face and run one of his long braids through her fingers. "I dinna care if ye get wrinkles on yer face, or yer glorious warrior's hair turns silvery." She laid her hand upon his chest. "For yer heart shall grow with love and memories," she placed her hand upon his chest, "As will mine." She smiled up at him. "My world would be far too empty without ye, Duncan MacKinnon." She raised their linked fingers and brushed a kiss softly over his knuckles. "I take ye to husband, today and everyday left of my life," she whispered softly against his skin, "Just as I did that day on the beach."

Carefully, she removed the ring that was back on his pinky and would have placed it upon her own finger but he stopped her. "Nay lass, allow me." He took the ring from her tiny fingers, "I take ye to wife, Raven Relia MacKinnon, with every breath I take, and I shall love ye until my heart ceases beatin' in my chest." He placed the ring upon her finger then cupped her cheek, "My heart belongs to ye alone, *gràdh*." He breathed the last words against her lips.

When their mouths met in a searing kiss, Raven felt their powers surge and connect as if joining them together forever. The sound of clapping pulled them apart. Raven looked over and smiled as her cousin Lucàs stood there smiling at the group. "Nay finer words have ever been spoken, what say ye we eat?"

Twenty-Seven

The meal went well after Lucàs had broken the magick that had surrounded Raven and Duncan. Her brother's and father still seemed reserved when it came to Duncan, but they at least were friendlier than before. Besides Lucàs, Deacon, her mother and grandmother tried very hard to make Duncan feel welcomed.

Raven watched as her father and two oldest brothers brought up topic after topic, trying to throw Duncan. She smiled when he would jump right in and hold up his end of the conversations. When he wasn't sure about something, he would question her brothers, her father, or her cousin.

By the end of the meal, Duncan had confessed that he wasn't sure where his magick came from, nor how to use it. At once all the men rallied to help him harness it. Plans were set for the following day.

Raven looked at her mother and smiled, the older woman smiled back at her daughter knowingly. They would have plenty of time to catch up with each other, because it appeared her father and brothers were going to accept her marriage and her husband.

Two weeks later, Raven and Duncan walked hand in hand along the beach as waves crashed upon the shore. Sea gulls cried out as they wheeled through the sky.

"So, this is yer home, lass?" Duncan looked over at her watching the strands of her shiny dark hair blowing around her. She didn't even reach his shoulder, and sometimes Duncan feared he would hurt her by touching her with his much larger and stronger hands. She looked so fragile, but he of all people knew just how tough his wife was.

Raven pushed a piece of hair from her face and frowned. "Aye, 'tis my home and my family." She sighed, "I'm sorry for the way my brothers have treated ye." She shook her head and held up a hand as Duncan went to speak. "Nay, I understand if ye wish to return to *Dun Akin*, and never return, they have treated ye terribly."

He placed a finger to her lips before she could continue, "Hush *gràdh*, 'tis nay yer fault." He shook his dark head and laughed slightly, "They are a persistent lot, I'll give ye that." He looked in to her eyes. "They do what they do to drive me away because they love ye, but I think they are comin' 'round and shall stop torturin' me soon enough." When she would have spoken, he kept his finger against her lips and shook his head, "Nay love, they still fear ye'll give up yer immortality to be with me."

She pulled away from him, "I shall give it up." Pulling her hand from his, she turned to the sea.

"When ye start to age, I shall give it up." When he came up and put his hands on her shoulders she growled roughly, "There is aught ye can say to stop me and 'tis my decision. Dinna try to stop me, Duncan, for ye can nay talk me out of this." She turned to him, "I have thought this through, and I shall nay out live ye by years and centuries, for they would be empty without ye."

This had been an argument they had, he was sure nearly coming upon a hundred times and it always ended the same.

Looking down at her, Duncan brushed his knuckles across her cheek, "I dinna want to lose ye."

"I feel the same, Duncan." Raven tugged at his braids pulling him down for a kiss. "I can nay live without ye," she whispered against his lips.

He broke the kiss and looked in to her mystical eyes, "I should nay allow such a thin', but I understand what ye feel." Wrapping his arms around her, he pulled her into him, "I have waited so verra long for ye. I prayed to find the woman who belonged to me." He rocked them back and forth as he spoke. "I want bairns with ye lass, many of bairns."

"How many?" She pulled back and looked at him wearily.

"Ten or twenty." He smiled down at her and laughed when she whacked him on the arm.

"Ten or twenty? Are ye daft?" She chased after him as he took off jogging down the beach away from her. Raven ran catching up to him. "Ten or twenty my *arse*. 'Tis nay ye who must a carrin' that many babes, nay to mention birthin' 'em." When he turned, and jogged backwards just out of her reach, Raven scowled, "Come back here ye coward."

Duncan laughed and turned to jog a little faster, he knew he could out distance her if he needed to, for his legs were twice as, long as hers were. "Catch me if ye can, love."

Raven snarled at him, "Yer a blackguard, Duncan MacKinnon. Mayhap, I should allow my brothers to pummel ye."

"Aww lass, ye ken ye love me too much for that." He smirked as he turned back to her jogging backwards once more. "And ye love my bonnie face as well."

She snorted unladylike then her eyes grew wide. "Duncan..." She burst out laughing when he tripped over a small log lying in the sand, and he fell backwards landing on his backside. She walked over to him and laughed all the harder when he scowled.

"Ye think this is funny do ye, love?" He raised a brow.

When she nodded, and continued to laugh he simply reached up catching her hand and pulled her down with him.

She yelped when he yanked her down to sit upon his lap. Just as quickly she found herself rolled underneath him. She looked up at him and smiled. "'Twas most funny."

He tried to scowl down at her, "'Tis nay that funny." When she just laughed again, he leaned down and nibbled at her neck making her laugh once more.

When she could no longer catch her breath and tears streamed from her eyes. Duncan at last pulled back and looked down at her. Her dark silken hair was spread out around her and her face was flushed with pleasure and laughter. She was beautiful beyond words. She looked up at him with shining eyes. "*Tha gaol agam ort.*" He whispered the words of love as he leaned down brushing his lips over hers.

Their kiss was searing and passionate. Duncan's hands roamed over her, stroking her and caressing her while lighting fires of desire burning all over her body.

At first Raven thought Duncan's kisses were causing her ears to ring, but the sounds became clearer and clearer. Ian's voice calling her name echoed over and over in her ears.

"Duncan, stop." She pushed at his chest as Ian's voice rang in her ears calling her. "Duncan, stop. Ian is in trouble." Those words seemed to snap him back to reality and had him sitting up and pulling Raven up too.

He raised a brow as he studied her, "What do ye mean, Ian is in trouble?"

Raven shook her head and pushed to her feet. Stumbling over to a tide pool, Raven knelt and waved a hand over the water as she spoke in a long-forgotten language. Duncan knelt behind her and placed a hand upon her shoulder. Suddenly, he saw images swirling in the water's surface, his brother standing looking over the sea with the stone in his hand, then him talking angrily with Lachlan and Aidan. Next, he saw Clan Brodie troops standing outside the castle. God help them his people were under siege.

When at last Raven sat back and broke the connection she looked over at Duncan's stunned face. "Are ye, all right?"

Duncan looked at her and nodded his head grimly. "I have to return to Dun Akin."

"We shall leave at once." Raven climbed to her feet.

Duncan jumped to his feet. "Nay, ye shall stay here where yer safe." He began storming back to the castle.

Raven was hard on his heels. "Yer nay leavin' here without me," she informed him harshly. "I am yer wife and I am nay goin' to be left behind."

Duncan whirled around so fast that Raven slammed into his chest. He took her by the arms, "The Brodie are there because of ye."

Before he could finish she spat up at him, "I ken, I am responsible for what 'tis happenin'. I ken Ewin would come for me, but I had hoped." She buried her face in her hands, "I am sorry..."

Looking down at her, Duncan then pulled her to him, "Hush love," he hugged her to him, "Yer nay responsible for what Ewin Brodie does." He ran a shaky hand over her black hair, "I dinna wish ye to return with me, because yer safe here, with yer family to protect ye." He pulled back and looked down at her, "I dinna wish anythin' to happen to ye."

"Aught shall happen to me, Duncan." She smiled softly up at him. "I want to go, and I ken how to get us there with all haste."

"Aye?" When he raised his brow, she laughed and took his hand leading him back toward the castle.

Raven hugged her mother then her father. "Are ye sure ye dinna wish to stay here?" Toslar looked down at her, "Ye could stay here where 'tis safe."

"Da, I belong with my husband." Raven smiled and then patted the sword hilt that stuck up from her back, "Dinna worry, my husband has taught me well."

"I can nay say I am happy 'bout my little girl wieldin' a sword." Toslar shook his head, "But it does make me feel better to ken ye can use the thin'."

"I can, Da," Raven stretched up and kissed his cheek once more. "We shall be fine."

363

Toslar walked over to Duncan when he had set his daughter aside. "Let aught happen to her, ye ken?" When Duncan inclined his head Toslar spoke grimly, "'Tis nay favored to do, but if ye've need of troops, have Relia call and we shall answer."

"I thank ye." Duncan held out his hand to Toslar and when the man would have shaken it, Duncan took it in a warrior's grip, wrist to elbow, elbow to wrist.

When at last, the couple had said their good-byes, Raven led Duncan to the circle in the middle of the royal chamber. Holding Duncan's hand tight in hers she smiled at her parents, when she inclined her head, they spoke the ancient words that sent the couple heading back to Dun Akin.

As the sun was setting, the water rippled as Duncan and Raven walked across it to the beach. When Raven went to speak, Duncan shook his head and pressed his mouth against her ear to speak, "Be weary love, the enemy could be down here."

Raven inclined her head as Duncan led her into the dark cavern then to the stairs and passageway. Up through the darkened stairwell they walked quietly. When they reached the secret door, Raven held her breath while Duncan listened carefully. It was time for the evening repass, so with luck everyone would be in the great hall eating.

Carefully, and ever so slowly Duncan cracked the door open. He peered out then slowly opened the door so that they could slip through into the hallway. Once the door was secured back into place, Duncan took Raven's hand and led her toward his brother's study. On his way, he shocked one of the MacKinnon men by grabbing him and sending him on an errand to find Ian and send him to the study.

Walking into the darkened room, Raven walked over and created a fire in the hearth to chase the chill from the room. She stared down at the flames as the ominous feeling that had assailed her since they had arrived at Dun Akin, increased. She knew the fire would tell her nothing, as it wasn't her element. Rubbing her hands over her arms she fought the chill there.

Duncan's arms coming around her made her jump. "What's amiss, love?" When she only shook her head, he frowned down at her, "Ye've been jumpy ever since we set foot back upon MacKinnon lands."

She looked from the fire up into his devilishly handsome face. Furrowing her brows, she turned in his arms to face him. Reaching up she cupped his cheeks in her small hands. "Promise ye'll do aught that is rash."

He looked down into her worried face, "I can nay promise such a thin', but I shall promise to be careful, *gràdh*." Her eyes were shadowed, and worry furrowed her brows. He leaned forward and brushed a kiss across her lips, "*Tha gaol agam ort.*"

Raven sighed into his mouth as he treasured her and teased a moan from her lips. She could feel his hard body pressed against her softer one as he pulled her into him, she could feel his need for her growing.

The sound of someone clearing their throat had Duncan and Raven finally pulling apart. She blushed as Duncan growled at his brother standing only a few feet away. "Go away."

Duncan growled harshly. "I'm afraid I dinna summons ye little brother, 'twas ye who summonsed me." Ian shook his head and laughed softly as Raven buried her face against Duncan's chest.

"And now I'm tellin' ye to come back in a few minutes." Duncan bit out as he held Raven to him. Energy crackled around him as magick snapped in his greyish-blue gaze.

Raven pulled back from Duncan and scowled up at him. "He is nay yer servant and we've nay time to argue this out." When both men would have started bickering she held up her hand. "Tell us Ian, what has been happenin'?"

Ian sighed heavily. "We have been under siege here, for a little more than a fortnight, we have all of the villagers inside, that 'tis except for the ones we lost in the initial raid." Ian ran a hand through his hair. "We were in the beginnin' of the harvest and our stores were already bein' depleted." He looked at his brother, "Havin' the villagers here, has neigh on depleted the rest of our stores."

"Ewin Brodie, is a bastard who will starve ye out, or slaughter the lot of ye for fun." Raven shook her head. "I lived with him for three years. He's ruthless."

"What 'tis it Brodie is demandin'?" Duncan frowned at his brother. He and Raven hadn't been gone for very long, but suddenly Ian looked older and more haggard. Duncan wished there was something he could do for his brother to ease things for him.

Ian's deep bluish-grey gaze met Duncan's and silent words passed between them. Duncan suddenly began to swear as he stepped away from Raven. He paced the room, nearly turning the air blue with Gaelic curses upon the Brodie leader.

Raven watched her husband and raised a brow as she looked back at Ian, "What 'tis it he wants?"

Ian looked her dead in the eyes and spoke softly, "Ye, and he'll settle for nay less." When she paled, he shook his head, "He claims that yer his wife and the two of ye were married by a priest." Ian glanced at his brother quickly, "He claims he wants his woman back."

"The bloody bastard shall die." Duncan roared and kicked a small wooden stool breaking it in half. He whirled on his brother and Raven. "I'll kill the bloody bastard with my bare hands 'afore I allow him to touch what is mine. She is my woman, my wife." He growled low in his throat. "And nay man, but me shall touch her ever again." The castle shook on its foundation as Duncan spoke those words.

"Duncan stop this," Raven commanded him. "Yer losin' control, and ye could hurt someone." Duncan looked over at her and frowned. "I am nay losin' control, *gràdh*." A small wicked smile touched his face, "For I only lose control with ye." A blush crept over her cheeks as she growled a warning, "Duncan."

"Brodie claims ye stole his bride." Ian shook his head.

Duncan shrugged his massive shoulders, "Bride stealin' is the way of life in the highlands."

"Aye, except when 'tis a love match, as he's claimin'." Ian frowned over at his brother, "He's also calimin' the MacArthur clan is on his side should he need such forces."

Before Duncan could respond, the study door burst open allowing Lachlan, Kandra, Aidan and Ferran all to enter.

"Ye've returned?" Ferran embraced first Duncan and then Raven.

Aidan embraced his cousin, "Yer ugly face 'tis a sight for sore eyes." He released Duncan and turned to Raven, "Now this beauty, 'tis a welcome sight."

Duncan tossed an arm around Aidan's throat pulling him back away from Raven, "Keep yer hands, mouth, fingers, in fact all of ye, away from my wife."

Everyone stopped to just look from one to the other, "Wife?" "Yer married?" Were two of the comments that came from Kandra, Ferran and Aidan as they gaped at the couple. "When by the Gods did the two of ye marry?" Ferran frowned.

Kandra laughed heartily as she placed her hand over her rounded stomach. "I'm so happy for you both."

Raven turned to Kandra and embraced her. "We plan to have a more formal weddin'." She reached out and placed her hands upon Kandra's swollen belly. "And how have the two of ye been?"

Looking at the smaller woman, Kandra rolled her eyes as she ran a loving hand over her baby. "He's an active one, kicking and moving all night and day."

"'Tis a good thin'," Raven inclined her head, "Shows ye'll have a fine strong son."

Kandra laughed then hugged Raven once more quickly. "I am so happy, you've decided to return."

"I have missed ye greatly." Raven pulled back, "Tell me, how is Bry?"

"Bored," Kandra laughed, "With the siege, she is unable to play throughout the castle and is finding it very annoying. She wishes she were bigger, so she could go and slay the Brodies and be done with them."

Everyone laughed at that, but quickly grew serious once more. "Thin's are grim. We've been under siege far too long. Our stores are neigh on depleted." Ferran shook her head sadly. "We had hopes that the two of ye would return with MacKinnons and our allies."

Raven smiled at the older woman, "Dinna fear, we've help at the tips of our fingers, but we shall call upon them only if needs be." She shrugged her shoulders, "For now I believe, I shall speak with Ewin Brodie, and ..."

"The bloody hell ye shall." Duncan boomed. "We'll nay go anywhere near the bloody bastard." Duncan reached her in two steps grasping her shoulders. "'Tis far too dangerous, *gràdh*."

"I can take care of myself, Duncan," she smiled softly, "I've had a good teacher."

"It is nay a decision we've to make tonight," Ian looked around at the group. "For now, let us celebrate Duncan and Raven's homecomin' and marriage." Agreements echoed around the room. The group made their way to the great hall to celebrate.

It was the wee hours of the morning before Raven and Duncan found their chamber and settled in. The couple fell into an exhausted sleep wrapped around each other as the night was turning into day.

The sun was high as pounding upon their chamber door awoke Duncan and Raven. Groaning Raven rolled out of bed and began pulling on her breeches and shirt from the day before.

Duncan stood near the door watching her move about the room and laughed at her moaning and groaning. "Yer a warrior now, love, ye must learn to move faster on yer feet." When she threw a pillow at him, he ducked and laughed.

They met Ian, Aidan and Lachlan in the great hall. All three men had tight expressions. It was Ian who spoke up, "Brodie is bangin' at our door again this morn." He looked from Duncan to Raven, "He says he'll burn down the castle if we dinna show him, Raven."

"Allow me to go up on the ramparts and speak with him, perhaps I can persuade him to leave us alone." She looked at all the men standing around her.

"Nay," Ian rejected the idea, "He might try to kill ye."

"Why would he kill me, if he wanted me back?" Raven frowned at the thought. "It does nay make sense for him to wage war to kill me."

"The lass has the right of it." Aidan rubbed his chin in thought.

Duncan looked at his brother and cousins then down at his tiny brave little wife, "Fine, but I shall go up with ye, just in case he tries somethin'."

Raven stood upon the ramparts frowning at the lines of men standing just outside of arrow range. All these men willing to die, just because one man says he wants to go to war. She shook her head, what sad creatures some men were.

"Ewin," Raven called out, "Ewin Brodie!" She shouted again and waited for an answer.

"Two riders approaching the gate, hold yer arrows." Bellowed Ian's head guard to the soldiers upon the wall.

"Raven?" Came a shout from one of the men down below. "Is that ye, lass?"

"Aye 'tis me." Raven called down, "What are ye doin' here, Ewin?"

"I've come to take ye home darlin'. Back to the Brodie keep where ye belon'." He called out, "Now, come down love and let us go home."

"I am home Ewin, for I dinna belong with the Brodie clan. I am a MacKinnon now, I married Duncan MacKinnon." She frowned, as anger seemed to radiate off Ewin.

"'Tis nay true, I'll nay believe it, for ye were to marry me." Ewin growled, "I shall kill MacKinnon for this."

"'Twould nay matter if it were Duncan or nay, for I could nay marry ye without my father's blessin' and he would nay have given it to ye." Raven smiled, "Aye, I remember who I am, Ewin. I am Princess Relia, of the Isle of Mann."

"Is this what the MacKinnons have told ye?" Ewin shifted in his saddle. "For 'tis lies, lass." He shook his blonde head, "Yer nay a princess, yer a maid of nay consequence, but I fell in love with ye and I want ye to come home with me, now!"

Raven sighed, "The man's a dolt!" She shook her head then shot Aidan a quick smile, "But he's a way with words, does he nay?" She laughed at Aidan's snort. Looking back over the wall she called down. "Ewin, go home. I'm nay goin' anywhere with ye."

Ewin frowned and then cursed. "Raven come down to the portcullis, I wish to speak with ye face to face." He looked up at her and pleaded, "I need yer help."

"What do ye need my help with?" She called down suspecting a trap.

"Come down and I shall explain." He called up.

"Fine." She called just as Ian, Duncan and Aidan all said nay. She looked at them and shrugged, "Mayhap, he'll go away then."

Twenty-Eight

Raven was nervous as she walked toward the portcullis. For a quick second, her steps faltered as a foreboding feeling washed over her. She could see Ewan and three of his men standing around him and her feet faltered. Squaring her shoulders, she forced herself to continue toward the portcullis.

Duncan grabbed her arm forcing her behind him. "Remove all yer weapons and throw 'em toward the portcullis, out of reach." Once the Brodie men had thrown their weapons, Duncan released her and allowed her to continue forward to speak with Ewin.

"What is it ye need my help with?" Raven frowned at him.

Ewin shuffled his feet, "I need yer help to heal someone." "Who?" The word was weary, as Raven tried to look around him.

Ewin frowned and stepped aside, "Sarila."

A cry escaped from Raven as she looked upon the tiny girl lying on the pallet. Her blonde hair was damp from sweat and her skin pale and bluish. Raven's fingers curled around the bars of the portcullis, "What happen to her?"

"I dinna ken, she took sick and has been for, some time." Ewin frowned down at the girl, "Our healer tried everythin', but she could do aught for the child."

"Brin' her to me." Raven commanded then turned to Ian, "Raise the gate and let me out."

"Nay lass," Ian shook his head. "I dinna trust him."

"She could die," Raven insisted as she looked back at the little girl. Sarila's breath was uneven and her heart stuttered. "I beg ye, open the gate and allow me to help her." When he remained mute and stubborn she grew angry and turned to beseech Lachlan, "What if it were, Bryanna? Sarila is nay older." Raven wiped at a tear that slipped down her face.

Lachlan shifted uncomfortably. He peered at the tiny girl laying upon the pallet then turned away to look at Ian, "Open the portcullis, allow me to go out and retrieve the girl." When Ian and Duncan looked at each other than Ian looked away remaining mute, Lachlan growled in anger. "Ye can nay allow her to lay there and die. What if it were Bryanna?"

Duncan walked over to the portcullis and tried to pull Raven away from it. It took him a couple of moments fighting with her, to make her let go of the gate. "Stop this, Raven. Aidan take her." He thrust Raven into his cousin's arms. Turning back to the gate he looked through at Ewin, "Leave the girl and I shall allow Raven to heal her."

Shaking his head Ewin gave Duncan a hard look, "I'm nay leavin' the girl with ye. How can I trust ye to take care of her? For all I ken ye'll kill her and say that Raven was unable to heal her." He snorted, "Ye stole Raven from me, I can nay trust the likes of ye." He looked at Raven, "Allow Raven to come with us to our camp and heal the girl, then if for Gods ken what reason Raven wishes to return to yer keep, then we shall allow her to go." His gaze slipped back to Duncan's.

Duncan shook his head, "Nay a chance, Brodie. Ye'll nay get yer hands upon my wife."

"Will ye both just stop," Raven growled then smacked at Aidan's arm around her waist. "Let go of me." When he didn't release her right away, she gave him a quick zap of magick.

"Och, what ye do that for?" Aidan released her and rubbed his hand.

"Oh hush," Raven waved him away. She turned to her husband and Ewin as they snarled at each other. "Give me, Sarila." She demanded harshly as thunder rumbled in the sky. Anger at both men surged through her. "Open the gate, Ian. Duncan and myself shall go out to retrieve, Sarila." She looked at Ewin with anger blazing in her eyes, "Ye shall nay stop me. I'm brinin' that child in here to care for her."

"Nay, I shall allow ye to come out here to heal her," Ewin shook his head, "But ye will nay take her."

"Fine," Raven squared her shoulders.

"I am goin' with ye," Aidan spoke firmly and stepped forward to flank Raven as Duncan took the other side.

"As am I," Lachlan stood behind her in case he had to grab her and run back into the gate.

Ian sighed, "I guess if we're to go upon this fool's errand then I shall go as well."

"Nay," Duncan frowned at his brother, "Ye stay here, and be ready to close the gate should somethin' go amiss."

"Agreed," Aidan and Lachlan spoke at the same time.

"Fine," Ian sighed again. "But make this quick." He looked over and yelled, "Open the portcullis."

Ever so slowly, the gate opened. Raven wiped her hands upon her breeches. The foreboding feeling washed over her once more, but she pushed it away because she had to get to Sarila and help her.

The group moved through the gate slowly cautiously, and stopped about ten feet from Ewin and his group.

"Back away from the child," Lachlan growled menacingly as he held his hand to his claymore on his back.

"Drop yer weapons." Ewin countered as he looked at the sword on Raven's back. "What are ye doin' with a sword, lass?"

"Makin' sure I stay alive," she gave him a hard, narrow look. Her gaze went to Sarila as the child's body began to convulse. On a cry she started forward, but she was brought up short by Duncan's hand. "She's dyin'," Raven cried as she looked at her husband.

Duncan looked down at her, "'Tis nay safe." A movement from the corner of his eyes had him turning and stepping in front of Raven.

She heard the wiz of an arrow, flying and the thud as it hit its target. Duncan's body jerked in front of her. "Duncan?" She whispered.

Slowly, he turned and looked down at her, the arrow sticking out of his chest. "Nay!" She screamed as she watched him fall in slow motion toward the ground. She fell to her knees beside him. "Duncan?" Her hand shook.

The sound of men cursing had her looking up at Ewin who held a crossbow pointed at her. "Get up and come over here, Raven."

The breath backed up in her lungs and thunder cracked overhead as lightening streaked the sky. "Ye shot him?"

"Aye, and I'll kill ye if ye dinna come with me." Ewin growled down at her. Raven slowly got to her feet. "I came out here to help ye, and ye shot him!"

"Aye, ye dumb wench." Ewin growled, "Now get yer arse over here, or I'll shoot ye too."

Energy crackled around Raven, the earth shook under everyone, "How dare ye!" Lightening crackled and struck the ground only a few feet away. The wind howled and swirled Raven's hair around her as she walked around Duncan toward Ewin and his men, "Ye dare come here askin' me for my help, then ye shoot the man I love, and threaten me?" She stalked after them as they retreated. Rain started to pour from the heavens, and suddenly men started appearing dressed in silver armor, with swords and bows.

"Leave this place, Ewin Brodie and never return, or so help me I shall make ye pay with yer verra life." She whipped out her hand and wind knocked the Brodie men off their feet to land about twenty feet from where they had stood.

She stood there and watched Ewin and his henchmen pick themselves up and run toward the large group of men who stood staring in shock. Slowly, she turned back to where Duncan lay on the ground. Racing back to him she knelt beside him and whispered, "Duncan?"

His eyes opened to look up at her. Reaching up he cupped her cheek. "*Tha gaol agam ort.*" His thumb slid over her lips, "Ye scared them good, lass." The sound of Sarila thrashing had him looking over at the child. "Go save her."

"What about ye?" Raven smoothed the hair back from his pale face.

"Dinna worry 'bout me. She needs ye." He let his hand drop and frowned, "'Tis yer callin', and ye can nay let her die. Now go and let Ian sit here with me."

"Dinna ye die on me, Duncan MacKinnon." She growled down at him then leaned down and brushed a kiss over his lips.

"Nay yet, *grádh*." He laughed then coughed and grimaced in pain. "I'm nay ready to go."

"Good 'cause I'm nay ready to let ye go." She pushed up to her feet and strode over to where Sarlia lie writhing in pain. Death pervaded the air around them. Kneeling beside the girl, Raven place a hand upon her forehead and felt it burning with fever, then one hand over the girl's stomach and gasped as she explored her body for the sickness. Poison, Ewin had given the child poison. Raven looked to where the band of Brodie men were packing their belongings to get away from the MacKinnon castle, she narrowed her eyes and several bolts of lightning hit the ground around them. They stopped packing and ran.

Turning back to the child, Raven began chanting and drawing the poison out of her body. When a hand touched her shoulder, she looked up into her father's face and tears filled her eyes. "Can ye save him?"

When Rhiannon appeared, and held out her hand Raven felt herself grow cold. "Take her place and save the child, Toslar." She looked at Raven, "Come with me and we shall try together."

Raven knelt on one side of Duncan and Rhiannon on the other. The two women laid their hands upon Duncan and began to look at the damage done inside of him. After a few moments, they pulled back and looked at one another.

"We have to remove it." Raven pleaded with her mother.

"He will die." Rhiannon frowned, "If the arrow is pulled, he will bleed to death, but if we leave it he will die."

Raven shook her dark head, "There has to be a way?" She looked down at her husband, "I can nay lose him, Mama."

Rhiannon sat back and thought for a few moments. When Toslar settled next to her, he took her hand and thread his fingers through hers. Raven knew it was all but hopeless.

He cleared his throat and spoke, "I have a suggestion, but I can nay make ye any promises, Relia." Raven and Rhiannon looked at him. "Aye?" Raven spoke hopefully.

"Take him to the sea and perhaps the Gods will look favorably down upon ye." Toslar looked at his daughter, "I may nay be happy 'bout yer marriage, but I would never want ye to be unhappy, sweetin'." He reached out and took her hand, "If ye love him, then perhaps the Gods will be merciful."

Raven let the tears shimmer in her eyes, "Help me?"

"Tell us what to do?" Aidan spoke and waved his hand to encompass the men standing around them. She looked up not only at Aidan, but Ian, Lachlan, but her brothers Crìsdean, Seòrsa and Deocan. All of them stood awaiting her orders.

"We must carefully carry him to the sea." Raven directed them. Crìsdean, Seòrsa, Deocan and her father used their magick to create a litter to carry him easily to the beach. The precession heading toward the beach was long with MacKinnon men, women and children walking with them. Standing down on the beach were Kandra, Ferran and Bryanna.

Raven paused as Bryanna raced to her hugging her waist. Hugging her back Raven stroked her shiny black head then bent and pressed a kiss there.

Bryanna looked up at her with tears shining in her brilliant green eyes. "Ye'll save him won't ye, Aunt Raven?"

"I'm goin' to try my verra best." The words trembled as she spoke.

"Ye can, I ken ye can." She hugged Raven once more then was pulled back by Kandra who took her daughter's place and hugged Raven tightly.

"Everything will turn out for the best." Kandra hugged her best friend tightly. "Have faith, he is a strong warrior."

"I'm tryin' to." Raven sobbed softly against her friend's shoulder. "I pray the Gods are merciful, this day." When Kandra released Raven, Ferran hugged her tight. "The Gods will spare him, for he 'tis a good man, and ye deserve nay less."

When at last she made her way to the edge of the water where they had Duncan laying, she knelt beside him. Brushing a stray piece of hair from his face, his eyes fluttered open. His gaze was glassy with pain. "*Gràdh*," he whispered softly, "*Tha gaol agam ort*, forever."

"Duncan," Raven couldn't hold back the sob that welled up inside her. She took hold of his hand and pressed a kiss to it. "Hold on, dinna leave me." Tears streamed down her face.

"Aww *gràdh*," he whispered once more, "Yer tears break my heart." Slowly, he reached up and wiped away a tear holding it upon the end of his finger to look at it. Carefully, he pressed a kiss to it. "Kiss me, love." He spoke softly.

With tears falling she leaned down and whispered in Manx that she loved him, against his lips. "*Ta graih aym ort.*" She pressed her lips softly to his lips. She felt his magick connect with hers then fade. A cry broke from her lips.

"Nay Relia," Toslar scolded her. "Ye must get him into the sea now, there is nay a moment to lose." He looked at the men around him, "Come lads."

The men lifted the litter again and walked into the sea with Duncan between them. Once they were deep enough that he was floating in the water, they helped Raven remove him from the litter.

Toslar, Rhiannon, Crìsdean, Seòrsa, Deocan, and the rest of the *Irish Sea Water Guardians* dropped to their knees in the edge of the water and began to chant. Rhiannon looked up as Ferran MacKinnon knelt next to her with Bryanna and Kandra in tow. Though Ferran was not comfortable with the magick, she wanted to help her nephew.

What surprised everyone even more was when the entire MacKinnon clan knelt all over the beach. Ian looked at Toslar and Rhiannon, "Tell us what to say, how to help."

"Believe," Rhiannon spoke to them, "Believe deep within yer hearts, that he will live."

Toslar spoke the words in Gaelic to them, "*Manannan Lord of the Sea, Tamesis Lady of the Water, Miach God of Natural Healing, Aine Goddess of Healing, hear our call. We beseech ye to help us save one of our own. Bless him and make him hail and whole. Lend us yer might to so that we may heal him.*"

On the beach, a chorus went up as voice joined voice to recite the ancient words of healing. Over and over they beseeched the Gods and Goddesses to intervene and save Duncan's life.

Raven was in the water with him reciting the words of the ancients. "Do ye hear that love, do ye hear them all?" She asked as tears streamed down her face. "Please, I beg ye, *Manannan*, save his life. I'll trade my own if needs be." She begged the God of the Sea.

Waves began to roll, the sea rocked and bounced them. Raven had a hard time holding onto Duncan. As a large wave came through and ripped them under, Raven had no choice, but to wrap her arms around him and hold on for dear life as they tumbled through the sea. Water filled her mouth and nose as the sea swirled them around and around and head over heels. 'I'll nay let ye take him without me.' Raven thought furiously wrapping herself around him tightly.

Twenty-Nine

The water was gone, and Raven fought to push the water she had swallowed from her lungs. Lying there she coughed the water out and choked. They were in some sort of throne room, she thought with a frown looking about. Rolling onto her stomach she looked around and spied Duncan laying a few feet from her on his side. Crawling to him, she checked to see if he was breathing and let out a sob as she discovered he wasn't. Rolling him onto his back, she began to use her magick to try to start his heart and lungs once more.

"Dinna bother." The voice behind her boomed. Raven sat up looking over her shoulder at the man standing there. He was tall and muscular, with long brown hair. He had the look of a highland warrior, but it was his shifting golden eyes that made him stand apart. "Who are ye?" She spoke quietly.

"Ye dinna ken me?" He held his arms wide for her to inspect him.

"Manannan," she whispered in awe. When he smiled she quickly bowed, "Forgive me, my lord."

"Up, Princess Relia," he waved her up to her original sitting position. "Ye have many a people callin' upon me to help ye."

Raven closed her eyes as he allowed her to hear the people upon the beach and those upon the Isle of Mann praying for him to help her. She opened her eyes to see a beautiful woman in flowing blue and green robes appear.

Manannan and the woman spoke in an ancient language for a few moments. Finally, the woman turned to her, "So yer the woman we are being summonsed to help." She looked Raven over in her wet and bedraggled state. "Tell me immortal why should we help ye?"

Raven bowed her head, "So that I may save my husband's life." She placed a hand upon him and looked up, "Because he is a good and honorable man."

"He is mortal." She spoke harshly.

"And deserves to live out the rest of his days." Raven countered heatedly. "Ye sound like my father."

"Ahh Toslar, he is a good man, a smart man." She waved her hand, "His wife is a good woman too."

"She saved your life, aye?" Raven spoke quietly.

"Aye, the little mortal did." She frowned, "She was cunning for a mortal."

"Ye would think ye'd like mortals." *Manannan* rolled his eyes at *Tamesis*, the *Goddess of Water*. He turned his attention back to Raven. "What is it yer askin' us for?"

"To save his life." Raven spoke quickly.

"And tell me Princess Relia, what do I get in exchange?" *Manannan* spoke harshly.

"My life if ye wish it," she spoke without hesitation.

"Yer life?" When she nodded slowly he raised a brow, "And what of the life of yer child?"

"I have nay child." She spoke firmly. "I lost my child." The last came out in a whisper.

Manannan looked her over, "Ye dinna lose yer child." He grinned at her, "Yer husband saved the bairn quite nicely. He has exceptional powers as a healer."

Raven placed her hands over her stomach and frowned. Would she not have known she was still with child? A smile slipped into place as she realized her hands were splayed over their child. Slowly, the smile slipped from her face, as it dawned on her.

She raised her head, "Is there nay way for ye to forfeit my life, but spare that of my child and my husband?"

"Ye ask higher favors?" The room shook around them as his voice boomed and echoed off the walls.

"I am sorry." She bowed her head, "Ye may have whichever life ye choose. I offer ye mine, or mine and my child's if ye'll but spare my husband's." The words came out as a sob, but she couldn't help herself.

"Pull the arrow from his chest." *Manannan* spoke simply. "What?" Her gaze snapped to his in shock.

"I can nay." She placed a hand to her throat.

"Ye must." *Manannan* inclined his head. Raven moved to the far side of Duncan and placed a shaky hand upon the arrow. She looked up at *Manannan* and he merely inclined his head. Tears pooled in her eyes. She leaned down and brushed a kiss across Duncan's lips as her tears fell. "I will always love ye, Duncan MacKinnon, yer my life, my breath," she sobbed, "My heart and my soul." With that she pulled the arrow out. Blood coursed from his chest.

"Use the tip of the arrow to cut open yer finger and bring forth yer own blood." When she did as he told

384

her, he smiled, "Good now, exchange blood with him." When she pressed on the end of her finger and several drops of her blood fell into the wound along with her tears that streamed down her cheeks. She thought nothing would happen.

Blue pulsing light swirled around him, and Raven felt it drain from her. She leaned back as weakness over took her. She smiled as Duncan took a breath. Her eyelids grew heavy, even as his fluttered open.

She watched him sit up as the blue aura swirled around him bringing him back to life and healing him. He looked at her and she smiled weakly, "I love ye, Duncan." She whispered even as he took her into his arms.

"What did ye do, Raven?" He pressed a kiss to her mouth, "Tell me what ye did, love?"

She reached up and placed her fingers over his lips, "Just tell me ye love me," she whispered softly, weakly.

"Aye, I love ye Raven Relia MacKinnon." He spoke against her lips as he kissed her and tears filled his eyes. "I love ye." He whispered as she collapsed against him. He let out a roar of rage and hurt. "Why?" He asked her even as he hugged her to him.

"Because she loves ye, foolish mortal." A woman spoke from behind him.

Duncan looked at her then to the man standing next to her. "Undo it." He scooped Raven into his arms and stood holding her to him. "Undo it!" He commanded them.

"Dare ye command me?" Manannan boomed, but Duncan didn't so much as flinch. "I could kill ye like that." He snapped his fingers.

"Then do so," Duncan snarled, "For I have nay life without her. She is my heart, my breath, my soul. Without her there is aught for me to live for."

"Touching," The Goddess spoke sarcastically.

Duncan strode forward. "Give her back to me, or take my life as well." He looked eye to eye with the sea God. "I can nay live without her."

"And what will ye give me?" *Manannan* frowned down at Duncan.

"I have aught, but my own life." He sighed, "What 'tis it ye wish."

"Yer child."

"I have nay child." Duncan shook his head. "Ah, but ye do, for when ye healed yer wife, ye saved yer child." *Manannan* smiled swiftly, "'Twould appear yer a powerful healer."

Duncan was staggered under the news of his child. "Yer certain?" He whispered.

"I am a God, aren't I?" *Manannan* boomed once more. "Ye wish the life of my child?" When the God inclined his head, Duncan looked down at Raven then at her stomach. They could have more children, he thought as much as it hurt him, but he would never be able to have Raven once more.

"Hurry Scotsman, make up yer mind." *Manannan* commanded. "What will it be?"

Duncan blew out a breath. "I ken she gave up her life for me, but I can nay allow it. I dinna wish to lose our child either, but I want her life back." He shifted Raven's still form in his arms and pressed a kiss to her still lips. "I am sorry, my love." He laid her down at the Gods feet then stood. "I choose to take my own life, because ye give me an unfair choice."

"'Tis nay unfair." *Manannan* growled disappointed in the man.

The Goddess put out a restraining hand to stop the God. "Yer game is over Manannan." She looked at Duncan, "Another clever mortal." She walked over to Duncan and ran a finger over his chest. "Ye would make a stunning God."

Duncan blushed slightly. "Thank ye, Goddess." She laughed softly, "Yer wife gave up nay only her life, but yer child's life as well for yers."

"I want them both back." Duncan growled as power snapped in his eyes.

"Testy are we nay?" She frowned down at Raven, "Why do ye wish to have such a weak immortal back, when ye could have a Goddess."

Duncan reached up and brushed his fingers over her cheek, "Because, she owns my heart and is a part of my soul." He traced her lips, "Do ye understand love, Goddess?" When the Goddess shook her head negatively, Duncan frowned, "Then I am sorry for ye, because it is the most wonderful and precious gift in the world."

The Goddess met his mouth in a searing kiss that made him tingle all the way to his toes. When Duncan broke the kiss, she stepped back from him, "Ye fascinate me with this deep love of yers." She shook her head, "Mayhaps, I shall keep my eyes upon ye and learn of it."

She walked away from him, "Take yer woman and child, return home with them and live happy, Duncan MacKinnon." When he scooped Raven into his arms and cradled her to him the Goddess sighed. "Ye shall both have eternity to enjoy this love ye share."

Duncan looked at her with tears in his eyes, "I thank ye, Goddess." He would have walked away, but stopped to turn back, "Do ye mean I am immortal? What of our children?"

"Dense immortal." She laughed and shook her head.

Duncan flashed a quick smile, "Yer welcome to visit us at *Dun Akin*, or wherever we are, to learn 'bout love any time ye wish it. We would be honored to receive ye, Goddess." With that he bowed courtly and turned to leave.

"Walk through the portal and it shall return ye home." She called after him and smiled as he hesitated at the watery portal.

Duncan walked out of the sea with Raven cradled in his arms. Spread out before him on the beach and the edge of the water were the MacKinnons and Raven's family. Rhiannon gave a cry of joy as he walked to the edge of the water and laid Raven down.

As everyone crowed around, Raven's eyes fluttered open. She looked up at Duncan and a sob broke from her lips, "Tell me, I'm nay dreamin'." Her arms went around his neck as she held him tightly to her.

"Nay *gràdh*, yer nay dreamin'." He brushed a kiss over her lips as he pulled her away from him. "We're all safe and alive, together." He laid a hand over her stomach and smiled.

"All of us?" She squeaked then looked up at him with hopeful eyes. When he inclined his head, she hugged him hard, "Oh Duncan, I love ye, so verra, verra much."

He hugged her back and rained kisses over her face, "I love ye as well, both of ye." "Both of ye?" Rhiannon beamed, "Does that mean what I think it means?"

Raven and Duncan looked at her beaming, "Aye." They both spoke in unison then laughed and let her hug them. Ferran MacKinnon joined in and wiped away tears of joy as Raven proclaimed she was going to have to take the place of Gram to their baby as well.

"Gram?" Toslar exclaimed loudly. "Gram? What does that mean?"

Seòrsa threw an arm around his father's shoulders, "It means yer goin' to be a grandpapa, old man." When Toslar gave him a horrified look everyone laughed, "That's the right of it Da, yer baby girl is pregnant."

He laughed hysterically at his father's bellows of rage. Toslar growled at Duncan, "How dare ye do such a thing to my daughter? First she marries a mortal..."

Duncan cut him off, "She's nay married to a mortal, but an immortal."

Everyone stopped and stared. So, Duncan continued, "'Twould seem the Goddess *Tamesis*, has a thin' for love and decided it would take her a few centuries, or more to study our love and hopefully figure it out."

Rhiannon laughed heartily, "She's such a softy." "She's the Goddess who gave ye yer immortality." Duncan smiled brightly.

"Aye that she is." Rhiannon smiled at her daughter as Duncan stood and helped both women to their feet. "We will have to make haste and have a real wedding."

Duncan turned to Toslar and held out his hand, "I ask that ye stay and attend the weddin', majesty?"

Toslar took Duncan's hand and shook it with narrowed eyes. "I'll be keepin' an eye on ye with my daughter and grandbairns."

"I promise yer majesty, I shall do aught to make them unhappy." Duncan promised sincerely.

"I'll be keepin' ye to that MacKinnon." Toslar inclined his head.

"Oh my," Kandra said as she placed a hand over her stomach.

Lachlan took her elbow. "What 'tis it, *gràdh*?" He looked at her with concern.

"I think the babe is coming." She hissed through her teeth then groaned. Before she could finish groaning he swept her into his arms.

"Raven." Kandra held out her hand, "'Tis too early."

Raven and Rhiannon flanked her as they made their way to the castle. Rhiannon ran a calming hand over Kandra's stomach, "He's ready to face the world. A strong one this one." She raised a brow at Kandra, "He'll be a handful for certain."

After only a couple of hours, Lachlan MacKinnon appeared in the great hall with his babe swaddled in his arms and a huge smile upon his face. "'Tis a son." He pulled back the blanket to show off his rosy colored baby boy to all in the room who gathered around him. Congratulations were given all around as Lachlan beamed. "We've named him Ciaran MacKinnon."

"A fitting name," a voice from the back of the room drifted forward. When people parted, a smile beamed upon Lachlan's face as Kandra's brother Jonas stepped forward, "Tell me Laird, how fares my sister?"

"She's the bonniest woman in the world." Lachlan chimed then held out the babe for Jonas to take. "'Tis good to see ye, English."

"I have a knack for making it in the nick of time." Jonas laughed and cooed over the baby then handed him off to Aidan for his turn as uncle. When at last

Lachlan left the great hall, Aidan looked over to see Bryanna moping.

Striding across the room he scooped her up, "Why the long face, dumplin'?" He settled her upon his hip.

"I wanted a baby sister nay another brother." She frowned, "I dinna need another brother, I dinna even like Braydon all that much."

"Why dumplin' ye'll get a sister, and I ken 'tis so." Aidan whispered to her.

"How do ye ken?" Bry perked up.

"I heard Raven's Mam speakin' of it to Raven and yer Mam as they were walkin' toward the castle." He raised a brow, "Ye ken she is a Manx witch, aye?"

Bry beamed, "Then it must be true." She hugged Aidan, "Aunt Raven told me so, but I thought maybe she was wrong."

"Aww always listen to yer Aunt Raven, she's a smart woman." Aidan smiled brightly then set Bryanna down and shooed her along, "Go see yer new brother." He watched her run off and frowned after her. One day he prayed to be as lucky as his brother and his cousin and find a woman who would love him, not for his looks, but for himself.

"Why the long face cousin?" Duncan frowned at him with worry.

"Yer a lucky man, Duncan." Aidan clapped him on the shoulder.

"Aye, that I am. That I am." He smiled as Raven came walking into the room and he caught her eye. Excusing himself from his cousin, Duncan strode across the room and swept Raven up in a hug, then caught her mouth in a soul-searing kiss.

When at last they broke apart Duncan looked at her, "I'm the luckiest man in the world 'acause, I love ye, Raven MacKinnon."

She smiled brightly, "Then I must be the luckiest woman in the world, 'acause ye love me." She laughed then brushed her lips over his whispering, "*Ta graih aym ort*, with my heart and soul."

Epologue

The sun was bright and sparkled across the sound like a million diamonds, as Raven walked down the beach on her father's arm toward Duncan where he stood at the edge of the water. He looked so handsome in his blue dress tartan and bare sun bronzed chest, the golden armbands encircling his muscular biceps. A multitude of small braids with tiny gold beads pressed to the ends, shone throughout his hair as the sun reflected off them making him glow like a God. His deep greyish-blue gaze locked with hers.

Duncan watched her walk toward him, and his gut clenched with longing and desire. Raven in an off-white gown that looked as if sea foam had created it with all its laciness. Tiny sparkles that looked like drops of dew rained over her gown and headpiece. Her hair flowed behind her blowing in the breeze. Her face was full of color as excitement filled her. The swirling mystical bluish green eyes that held his were filled with love for him and it humbled him.

Alongside his lovely bride walked their shy new daughter, Sarila MacKinnon. She had been orphaned while Raven had lived with Clan Brodie and had taken a liking to Raven. When Ewin had fled in fear, he had left her behind, that was just as well to Duncan's thinking. He and Raven had decided to adopt her and make her their daughter. Sarila was still shy around newcomers and men, even her adopted father, but he figured in time she would be a healthy child, if given lots of love. Duncan smiled at his daughter and was rewarded with a soft shy smile in return.

Raven's cousin Lucas stood at the water's edge waiting to unite the couple while the guests along with Duncan and Raven faced him and the beautiful sunset reflected on the brilliant sea. Lucas smiled as Toslar stopped in front of Duncan, "Take care of her, she is precious."

"I give my word." Duncan replied and nearly laughed at Toslar's next words.

He turned to Raven and spoke softly, "Yer sure this is what ye want?" When she inclined her head, Toslar kissed her cheek. "I just want ye happy."

"I am, Da." Raven assured him.

Toslar handed his daughter over into Duncan's keeping and the ceremony began. They mixed the Celtic handfasting, with the traditional Celtic marriage ceremony. The words were spoken in a mix of Scottish and Manx Gaelic for both parties. After their hands were wrapped Toslar and Rhiannon, Ian and Ferran gave blessings to the couple. Ferran had made and embroidered the tie that was wrapped around Raven and Duncan's hands to symbolize their unity, everyone had raved over the beauty of it and Raven knew it would become a precious heirloom.

As the end of the ceremony finally came and Lucas blessed them, Duncan was smiling like a fool. "Ye may kiss yer bride, Lord MacKinnon."

Duncan looked from Raven to Lucas once more then back at Raven. Pulling her into him, he cupped the back of her neck and kissed her long and lovingly, until Raven was sure her toes would never come uncurled. At last after Lucas had cleared his throat several times and everyone was laughing, Duncan released her. Raven swayed on her feet, "Easy *grádh*." He grabbed her and smiled.

Everyone came forward and offered congratulations and hugs. Then the happy couple was whisked off to the feast. No one saw the small beautiful blonde Fae woman at the back of the crowd, as she smiled and wiped away tears of joy and pride. Only Ferran met her gaze and frowned slightly, she had not seen Senna MacKinnon in many years, not since the death of her husband Magnus.

As everyone celebrated and cheer after cheer was given, speech after speech was made, Duncan danced with his wife to the music and laughed. "Well, Lady MacKinnon where would ye like to go after all of the festivities are over?"

Raven looked up at him in surprise, "What do ye mean?" "We can go anywhere in this world ye wish. What would ye like to see?" Duncan smiled, "We can even go to the English court if yer wishin' it."

"I'm nay sure, I'll have to think upon it." She smiled, "I'm happy to just be with ye, Duncan."

"I'm glad *gràdh*, for I intend to make ye happy all the rest of our days." Duncan brushed a kiss over her lips then frowned as the sight of his brother leaving the great hall caught his attention.

"I worry 'bout him." Duncan inclined his head toward his brother then looked from where his brother disappeared back down to his wife.

Raven watched her mother slip out of the hall as well. "Dinna worry, he'll be fine." Raven sighed, "In fact, he will find a wonderful woman of his own and be as happy as we are."

"Yer sure?" He raised a brow.

"I've seen it." She smiled, "And now I believe my Mama is settin' him on that course." She laughed as Duncan looked around for Rhiannon.

When Sarila came over and tugged on Raven's skirt, Duncan slowly reached down and opened his arms. He was surprised when the little girl threw her arms around his neck and hugged him, "I love ye, Da." Duncan felt this heart nearly burst with love. As he picked her up he saw the same stunning woman from the beach standing across the room smiling at the three of them. She smiled and inclined her head knowingly, but he had no clue who she was. He took Raven back into his arms and danced with his wife and daughter, happily forgetting about the strange but familiar woman.

Ian sat upon the boulder and frowned. How he wanted what his cousin Lachlan and his brother Duncan had found. But he still wasn't sure the Gods had such a fate planned for him. Ian knew what Raven had said, but he had his doubts. He sighed heavily.

"'Twas a bonnie ceremony was it nay?" Rhiannon's voice floated to him out of the darkness.

"Aye that 'twas." Ian smiled over at her, "Raven looked verra bonnie."

"Aye she did," Rhiannon inclined her head, "Yer brother makes her verra happy."

"I shall see to it he continues. Raven deserves nay less." He inclined his head as he made the promise to her.

"Yer an honorable man, Ian MacKinnon." She sat next to him on the boulder and took his hand in her own. She was quiet for a long moment then spoke, "She awaits ye ken, upon the shores of Eire. Ye'll go through much to be with her, but dinna lose faith, for she is literally yer heart, yer soul, yer life. Dinna let anyone stand in yer way, have faith that yer meant to be, the Gods have declared it so." Rhiannon opened her eyes. "She is nay the one ye'll expect." She smiled softly at him then cupped his cheek. "I see many hardships, but much love in yer future."

"I'm nay sure I should leave here at this moment." Ian frowned, "Duncan will want to take Raven away for a while."

Rhiannon inclined her head, "Then ye've some time to prepare for yer journey."

Ian looked at her and frowned, "I'm afraid I will nay be a very good husband, my father was a hard man, and died when I was verra young."

"Yer father was who he had to be, and ye shall be who ye have to be." She laughed at his furrowed brows, "Ye'll be a good father and husband, Ian, just let it come naturally." With that she pushed off the rock and headed back inside toward the wedding party.

Ian sat there a little while longer and thought over her words. Perhaps, it was time he paid his Irish cousin a visit. With a smile, he pushed off the boulder and walked back toward the castle, as he thought, 'aye that was exactly what he would do, he would send word that he would be visiting Erie verra soon.'

Raven and Duncan lay in bed both naked and sated from hours of lovemaking. Raven lay sprawled across Duncan's massive chest listening to his heartbeat. She sighed, "Do ye want a son, or a daughter?"

He shrugged his shoulders. "I dinna care either way, so long as we have this bairn."

"What shall we name our bairn if we have a son?" Raven frowned in thought.

Duncan was quiet a moment, "If 'tis a boy I would like my brother's permission to name him Alistair."

"And if 'tis a girl?"

"I'm unsure, but we shall think of something." He stroked a hand down her back.

"What of Sarila?" Raven frowned, "Can we take her with us when we leave here?"

Duncan opened his eyes and gave her a hard look, "I would nay leave our daughter behind." He frowned at her, "We shall engage a nursemaid to travel with us, but I shall nay abandon our daughter. After all she needs us."

"Yer a good man, Duncan MacKinnon," Raven smiled at him then stretched up to brush a kiss across his lips. "I love ye."

"And I love ye, lass." Duncan rolled her under him and looked down at her, "Ye've given me the greatest of gifts, love." He whispered then caught her mouth in a soul touching kiss, as their magick combined making their hearts one.

Coming February
2018

The MacKinnon's
Aryana

Prologue

Long, long ago two powerful Fae sisters, Aoibheal and Mabh, jointly ruled over the Fae people. Their kingdom was still within the human realm. One day the eldest sister Aoibheal, met a human man who was a mighty king, and she fell in love with him. Their love was the kind that bards would later sing about. Aoibheal was so in love with her human male, she gave him the gift of magick.

She had planned to marry him, and make him immortal, as well as king of the Fae. To rule by her side forever. The man left on a Herculean journey to save his own kingdom.

When the human king returned, Aoibheal was over joyed and rushed to greet him in the courtyard of her palace. When she ran into the garden, she stopped short at the sight of her human male and her younger sister Mabh locked in an intimate embrace.

Aoibheal was stunned, then anger ripped through her. She confronted the two and found out that her human male and her sister were in love, and had been for some time. Placing a hand over her heart that was shattering, anguish poured through her.

In a fit of rage and jealousy, Aoibheal cursed her sister with coldness, and damned her to become the dark Unseelie Queen. To exact revenge even further, Aoibheal took the child that her sister and the human male had conceived from her sister's womb and placed the child in her own womb.

Furious she banished her sister and the human male to the shadow lands. Hurt, sad, and enraged, she moved the entire Fae kingdom to Faery, and forbid all contact with humans. That dark day Aoibheal's long beautiful golden hair was stained black, due to her pain and anger. Mabh on the other hand, now had hair as white as snow and an icy heart that barely beat in her chest.

From that day forward Mabh swore vengeance upon her sister, for cursing her. For centuries, she plotted her revenge. With the help of her consort, she finally began the Seelie wars as she tried to overthrow her sister and extract her revenge. Due to the interference of the human world, she was unsuccessful and driven back into the darkness to wait for her chance once more...

Senna stopped writing and set her quill aside as she sighed. She knew if Aoibheal ever found this she would likely kill her, but history needed to be preserved. Pushing up from her desk, she closed the ancient tome and hid it away, then flashed from Faery to the human realm, she did not want to be late for the wedding of her grandson, she thought with a sad smile.

Ian looked around the hall at all the revelry and smiled. He watched his younger brother Duncan and his new bride Raven, leave the hall followed by well wishes and shouts of lurid advice for their wedding night. He met his brother's eyes as Duncan paused in the doorway. Ian lifted his hand in salute and smiled. Duncan returned the gesture then strode out of the hall.

He was happy for Duncan and Raven, they were deeply in love. Ian himself wanted to find a woman who was as wonderful as Raven, a woman he could spend his life with. More than anything he wanted a family of his own, he wanted children to cuddle as babes and to watch them grow and teach them to be true highlanders. A few weeks ago, Raven had predicted that he would have three sons and a beautiful wife.

Every night since he had dreamed of this future family and imagined what they would look like. Tonight, when Raven's mother had confirmed her daughter's vision, Ian had felt a longing to begin packing his belongings. Then board the first ship he could find to visit his cousin on the shores of Erie. However, being the MacKinnon and Chieftain of his clan prevented him from simply following his dreams. He had immense responsibilities to consider first. Ian knew that his brother Duncan and his wife Raven, would want to leave and visit her family, not long after their baby was born. He had considered asking his cousin to stay longer, but he knew that both Lachlan and his wife Kandra were anxious to take their new son Ciaran home.

That just left his younger cousin Aidan to mind Ian's home. Ian considered the thought of just saying the hell with it and walking away. From the moment, he had taken his first breath, his father and mother had trained him to understand that he was responsible for every single member of his clan. His father had told him over and over that he would after all, one day be the MacKinnon.

So here he was held in place by the yoke of responsibility. Ian knew he had to do what needed to be done since the death of their father when he and Duncan were merely young lads. Ian would put his own needs aside and put his people and responsibilities first. He would wait until later to go look for the woman he was meant to take to wife and have wee bairns with.

About the Author

As a graduate of Western Michigan University, Treasa holds degrees in Communication, History and Cultural Studies. Along with a minor in English, as well German. She has worked as a newspaper reporter and columnist for several years, but found she has a passion for not only reading, but writing novels. She strives to write in multiple genres, including Historic, Historic Paranormal, contemporary and contemporary paranormal. She enjoys going to Renaissance festivals and anything to do with hands on history. Writing is her passion in life. She is currently working on multiple series including the Immortal MacKinnons Saga as well as the Texas Heat Series. Next spring, she will be introducing another passion of hers Viking with her newest series The Harrow. Treasa is a true believer in love as she married her high school sweet heart and they have raised three children together.

She enjoys hearing for her readers, you can follow her and leave her comments/reviews on her website at: www.TreasaKloth.com or find her on Instagram, twitter, amazon or Facebook. Feel free to leave her a review and/ or let her know that you enjoyed her book and that you want to see more of her different series or check out other great novels by her.

Made in the USA
Middletown, DE
13 October 2018